ABOUT THE AUTHOR

Guy Hale lives in rural Worcestershire with his wife and son. He spent his early life avoiding serious employment as a professional golfer. He then spent several years trying to end it by racing motorcycles. Having failed, he then concentrated on business, which proved to be a safer and more suitable destination for his talents. He sold up and retired in 2018, and then started a record label in Texas. This led him to becoming a songwriter, and writing novels was a natural progression. He confesses to having a low boredom threshold.

KILLING ME SOFTLY

GUY HALE

Produced in United Kingdom.

For permission requests, please contact:
guyhale@hillside-global.com

Project management by whitefox

Typeset by seagulls.net

Cover design by Peter Adlington

Scan the QR code to hear Jimmy Wayne's record.

Find the author on Twitter, Facebook, Instagram
or Linktree under @HaleWrites

To Lou and Fraser,
thanks for putting up with me!

MIKE ZITO

This book came out of a conversation Mike and I had in a restaurant in LA. The character of Jimmy Wayne is based on Mike ... without the murdering ... I think. As an aspiring musician, Mike had played venues like the Riviera and he told me that he had an idea about a down-on-his-luck singer who accidently kills someone and then discovers the ability to write a song whenever he kills. The idea blew my mind, and I asked him if I could turn it into a novel. The soundtrack that I wrote to go with the novel is performed by Mike and he arranged all the music. Mike is like a brother to me ... his talent and generosity seem to have no bounds and I am forever grateful that we have got to work on so many great records and now the Jimmy Wayne saga together.

CONTENTS

CHAPTER 1
VACANT STARE

Jimmy Wayne rolled over. His eyes squeezed shut against the morning light with the throbbing pain of yet another hangover. The sheets felt damp beneath him, and the thrumming of the ancient air conditioner hummed like a constant reminder of the fact that this was a dump. Failure washed over him like a polluted wave. Welcome to another day in Blackjack, just the same as any other day in this third-rate casino town, but it wasn't just another day!

He opened his eyes and winced. The light seeping past the blinds certainly didn't help his hangover, but he couldn't close them because hanging by the neck from the door of his wardrobe was Wendy. Naked and clearly dead. Very dead.

He sat up as if struck by lightning and stared at the gruesome vision hanging at the foot of his bed, struggling to comprehend what it meant. Panic had not hit him yet, or revulsion at the blue distended tongue and bulging eyes of his late lover. For now, he just stared, trying to work out what it meant.

Wendy's hands were tied behind her by what appeared to be his belt – *not suicide, then*, he thought. He tried to remember what had happened the previous night. There had been drink –

there was always drink – lots of drink. Sex … yes, he remembered that. Wendy was good at that – 'was' being the operative word.

Slowly, his memory cleared and he remembered how she wanted him to tie her up and choke her a little, take her to the edge. Wendy had been a shock to Jimmy. He thought he was a man of the world, but Wendy … wow! She was into some weird stuff.

And now he remembered her saying, 'Tie me up, Jimmy.' Her eyes had challenged him, daring him to do it. He did, and tied her hands behind her. He had turned her around and kissed her hard. Like a fist into his face, Jimmy suddenly saw it all and the full horror of what he had done swept over him.

The sheet he had looped around her neck at her instruction and tied to the rail inside the wardrobe and pulled over the door. The way he had slipped the knot tighter as she gasped for breath. How she had pushed back against him as he took her … and then … *Oh God!* He saw it all as if playing back on a video.

He fell away from her, spent, drunk onto the bed. The last thing he saw as he passed out was Wendy struggling to get free, her eyes pleading with him.

Jimmy was numb. The realisation that he had killed some-one, someone he cared for, was too much to take in. He sat there for some time trying to process it, eyes transfixed on the deadly sculpture he had created. For now, he couldn't bring himself to touch her. Guilt, remorse, anger at his own drunken incompetence.

Wendy was dead; he had killed her.

It was an accident of course, but that would be a tough one to explain, yet explain it he must.

He reached towards the phone at the side of his bed and then he saw it; scrawled on a piece of hotel notepad was a song, a song he hadn't seen before. Hell! He hadn't written a song in years – part of the reason he was sleeping in this crappy hotel and singing in this casino where losers came to lose.

He should have made that call, but he needed to know what it said … who wrote it. It was titled at the top in capitals 'VACANT STARE'. *Strange title for a song*, he thought, and then he looked at the first line: '*You look at me with your vacant stare, I see you but there's no one there*'. As he read on, the sickening realisation that he had written the song and his muse was hanging from the wardrobe hit him.

Had he accidently killed his lover, passed out, then come round and written a song about her? The answer was in his hand. So, what kind of monster did this make him? Again, the answer was in his hand. A damn talented one – this song was the best thing he had ever written. It was actually the only thing he had ever written that was good enough to perform. It was really, really good.

God, he had prayed for material like this for years, and now here it was, written by him. His dad had been a singer, not a very good one, but he had written some good songs. 'Write about what you know, son,' was the only decent bit of advice he had ever proffered.

Jimmy looked at Wendy, then back at the song. Well, this one certainly came out of personal experience. He really wanted to sing this song, get those losers in the casino to stop gambling, to stop watching the strippers and to turn around and listen, just once.

He looked at the phone … he wasn't calling the cops. This song needed to be sung. For once in his crappy career, he was going to get something right; he just needed to bury a body to do it!

Jimmy looked at the clock. 9:30 a.m. His first show wasn't until 6 p.m. This gave him time to take Wendy out for a little drive into the desert. He started to think about what he needed. A sheet, obviously – he couldn't just drape Wendy over his shoulder, fireman style. But even if he could, how was he going to get her out to the car without raising suspicion?

When the other staff realised Wendy was missing, the receptionist was bound to mention the fact that Wendy had been in Jimmy's room the night before. Their relationship was an open secret among their colleagues, some of whom had also been involved with Jimmy over the years. Jimmy Wayne, like his father, tended to operate a revolving door policy with his relationships. All welcome for a while at least. The Wendy-shaped shroud on his shoulder was bound to raise a question: 'Who was on your shoulder, Jimmy … the one you put in the back of your van?'

It had taken Jimmy about an hour to figure it out. He drove his van to the back of the hotel by the loading bay. In the loading bay there were a couple of linen holders on castors. He had looked inside and saw that one was empty. He grabbed it and headed for the service lift. He was on the sixth floor; there were only six floors. He prayed that no other staff would see him. Hard to explain that the hotel cabaret was pushing dirty linen around. His luck held, and he got back to his room.

After pulling the under sheet off and spreading it out over the bed, Jimmy turned towards Wendy. He had to lift her onto the bed, but he couldn't touch her. Her eyes just stared blankly through him. Where once the flames of desire had flickered, now there was just a void, endless and deep.

He flopped back onto the bed and sobbed. *Oh, Wendy, I am so, so sorry.* His words were unspoken, there was no saliva in his throat, no words would come. Just a numbness. How'd it get to this?

Jimmy closed his eyes and began to sob, and then he heard it. Quiet and calm, maybe a little sarcastic.

'You gonna cut me down or what?' Wendy's voice!

Startled, he opened his eyes and there was Wendy, still dead, hanging from the wardrobe like a badly pressed dress.

'Come on, Jimmy, you gotta get moving or else you're gonna be dead, too.'

He turned and there standing by the bathroom door was Wendy. She was wearing his bathrobe. He looked back to the wardrobe and Wendy was there ... still dead. Very dead.

A laugh came from behind him. 'Pretty weird, huh, Jimmy? First person you kill, and they come back to haunt you.'

Jimmy jumped to his feet. He felt shock, not horror or fear. 'Wendy ...! What the ...?' His words trailed off as Wendy put her finger to her lips. She pointed towards her corpse.

'Come on, Jimmy, you gotta get me out of here. No one's gonna believe you. Focus, you damn fool.'

———◆———

As Jimmy cleared the town limits he took a deep breath. He had done what Wendy's ghost, or whatever she was, had told him. He'd lowered her from the noose and wrapped her in the sheet on the bed. She had been hard to get into the basket – rigor had started to set in and her once so supple limbs had stiffened. With a lot of effort and a bit of cracking, he had managed to get her into the basket and close the lid.

He'd then opened the door of his room – nobody was there. He'd turned to grab the handle of the basket when that voice spoke again.

'Forgetting something, Jimmy?' Wendy stood by the bed.

After shaking his head, he'd muttered, 'Don't think so.'

'My clothes, my handbag, my shoes. Come on, Jimmy, you gotta wise up. They got the death penalty in this state. I should know.'

There, spread like washing blown off a line, was the evidence that would get him convicted. He'd raced around the bed gathering everything up before throwing them into the basket, slamming down the lid. He'd looked once more at Wendy, the one who could talk. She was leaning against the bathroom door still wearing his bathrobe, just watching him.

'You coming?' he'd asked.

She'd laughed. What kind of a dumb question was that? 'What do you think, Jimmy?' And then she was gone.

Jimmy was standing alone in his room with a laundry basket containing his dead lover and her worldly possessions. He was having a very strange day.

The trip down to the loading bay had gone without a hitch. He'd then pulled the basket up to the back of his van, opened the rear doors and simply rolled Wendy in. That was one of the few good things about being a musician – the van. Drums and amps, guitars and keyboards all fit real easy. As for a dead body, no problem. Made for it.

CHAPTER 2
THE SONG CEMETERY

As he turned off the highway and headed down the gravelled track, Jimmy felt himself relax. He knew this track. He had discovered it a couple of years back when he was looking for somewhere to hide away from the crushing sense of failure that he'd felt at the casino. It was an old, gravelled road that used to lead to a long-gone farmstead; he had been here many times.

If you followed the track for ten miles you came to a fork in the road. If you took the road less travelled – not travelled at all would be a better description – it led up to a dead end, a horseshoe-shaped canyon. About half a mile before the end of the valley was an outcrop of rocks nearly forty feet high. Jimmy had found this place that day and scrambled to the top. It was bigger than it looked from below and ran back some forty yards. He could remember standing there and staring into the natural amphitheatre formed by the end of the canyon. It was as if he was on stage looking out at this huge natural auditorium. Finally, a theatre worthy of his talent! He had sung a couple of lines of 'Strange Fruit'.

'Southern trees
Bear strange fruit
Blood on the leaves
And blood at the root.'

The haunting lyrics had echoed around the valley and sounded like a beautiful but painful memory-given voice. The acoustics were simply amazing. He had decided there and then that this is where he would come to find himself and write the songs that he knew were inside him. A place of inspiration.

He had come every week on his day off, sat down with his guitar and … nothing. He ate his sandwiches, drank his coffee, and then picked up his guitar again. *This time*, he'd thought. And this time, nothing happened again. There were no songs in him. Like the desert around him, he was dry. He had become a desert. His talent, his inspiration, both were withered. Bleached to desiccation and devoid of new life. He was caught in a drought, and rain seemed a long, long way off.

'Oh my, how appropriate. You brought me to the "song graveyard".'

Jimmy awoke from his reverie. Wendy was sitting next to him. 'What the hell?' For a moment he had forgotten why he was there.

'Is this where you're gonna bury me, Jimmy Wayne's song graveyard, where lyrics come to die? Well, at least it'll be quiet.'

He looked at her. She was smiling, amused by her own joke. 'Wendy, what the fuck are you doing here?' He was more surprised than frightened.

'Duh, I'm in the back of the van, dummy – remember?'

He did remember, and once again guilt washed over him, drowning him with emotions he just could not verbalise.

Wendy looked at him; she almost seemed sorry for him. 'Get over it, Jimmy. With my lifestyle choices, it was only a matter of time – and besides, this being dead shit is better than I expected.' Wendy looked down at the van some forty feet below them. 'So, what's the plan, Jimmy? You gonna bury me up here? Hope you've been working out because that's a tough climb with a dead body on your shoulder.' She was laughing at him.

'Wendy, that's just not funny. You're dead. It's your body, and I killed you!'

'Accidently, Jimmy. No court would convict you – manslaughter, worse case.' She paused before looking sidelong at him. 'Manslaughter, right up until the moment you brought me up here and buried me like a guilty secret. You wanna let me in on the reason?'

Jimmy looked into Wendy's eyes. How could he tell her? There was no way he could make it sound reasonable – but hey, this whole situation was crazy. He was talking to the ghost of his dead lover who he had accidently killed. Was she even there? Could he be imagining it?

'Well?' Wendy stood there with her hands on her hips waiting for his reply.

He let out a slow sigh. 'This ain't easy, Wendy.'

'You're telling me.' Again, she was mocking him. She just stood there looking at him, waiting.

He slumped down on a nearby rock. 'Sit down. I guess I owe you a proper explanation.'

'I'll stand if it's OK with you. Hell, I may even hover. I wonder if I can?' She scrunched up her face in concentration and slowly rose from the ground. Her face burst into a huge grin. 'Hey, get me! Guess I'm gonna save a fortune on shoes!' Wendy proceeded to waft back and forth testing out the boundaries of her new-found skills.

Jimmy just sat there watching. For so long he had been bored with his everyday life, hating the routine of getting up and singing songs to total strangers who never listened. His voice was just musical wallpaper that nobody ever heard, and now this. Death, murder? New song, ghosts. It was too much to comprehend; how he wished for his old, boring failure of a life.

'Do you remember when I first brought you here – must've been about a year ago?'

Wendy slowly descended and sat down on a rock facing him and nodded. 'Course I do. Our first date.' She smiled and looked at him, waiting for him to continue.

'This place is special to me. You're the only person I have ever brought here. I thought it would help me find something deep inside me that I couldn't reach. I've always been able to sing and play, but I just can't complete the circle. I have all these words floating round in my head. I just can't get them out.' He shook his head. 'It's like a river, I'm standing by a river and all these songs are floating by but the current is too fast. I just can't reach out and grab them. I see them, but they're always just out of reach. I'm like a dairy cow that has no milk!' He sat there looking down at the dry earth beneath him.

'Well, that's a beautiful image, Jimmy … dry udders! Just don't understand for the life of me why you've never won a Grammy!' They both laughed, and it broke the tension.

Jimmy looked up at her. She still seemed the same happy-go-lucky, slightly crazy Wendy that he had fallen in love with over the last year. Did he just say fallen in love? This was new territory for him. Slowly, it was dawning on him that he actually loved this girl. He didn't know what to say. What could he say? As bad dates go, this was right up there!

'Can I ask you something, Wendy?'

She nodded. 'Go right ahead, I've got nothing else on today, or ever, by the look of it.'

Again the guilt hit him, but what could he do? What was done was done. 'Are you … dead?' He hesitated awkwardly trying to formulate his thoughts. 'I know you're dead, dead … but what are you?' He looked at her. 'Are you a ghost … or … or am I just imagining you? Could this be a dream?'

She picked up a stone and threw it at his knee. It caught him just below the kneecap and stung like hell.

'*Ow*!'

'Did you dream that?' She was laughing at him again. 'Jimmy, this is what you're seeing. If it's a dream or a hallucination. Maybe I am a ghost, whatever. It's your dream – your hallucination. I'm new to this. If you can't work it out, how the hell am I going to? I only just discovered I could hover a couple of minutes back, remember?' As if to bang the point home, she slowly rose from the rock where she was sitting. 'Think I'm getting the hang of this.' She hovered for a moment, and then saw the look on his face and slowly descended. 'Sorry … you were saying, Jimmy?'

What was he saying? They were just a couple of life's losers, underachievers if you wanted to be more generous, rubbing along near the bottom of the line, waiting. Waiting for what, neither of them had worked out. Jimmy thought it was fame for him. He could sing and he could play – and boy, the ladies had loved him. Even now in his forties he was still beating them off, but now they weren't what he would call young and innocent. Now they were older, not too old, but they were more predatory. Sometimes when he played, he could see one of them watching him, licking her lips. He felt like a plate of prawns at a barbeque. Where once he had been the hunter, now he was the hunted. Jimmy was a pretty liberated guy, but the change in this dynamic, as he'd got older and fame had not come his way, was getting harder to take.

Wendy was a different matter. She was hard to define. Slim, attractive in an understated way. She would never enter a room and have all the boys following her every move, but she was a grower. She was the racehorse that had ended up pulling a milk cart but still looked like she could win the Derby, but you had to look hard to see it. Jimmy had seen it. It had taken him a few months but he had seen it, and when he did, he fell hard. He fell in love. This made the fact that he had accidently killed Wendy a real shame, as well as a real crime. How had he managed to fuck it up so completely?

It had been a struggle carrying Wendy's body on his shoulder up the steep, slippery incline. The midday sun beat down hard, and Jimmy was sweating profusely. He would have heard the blood pounding in his ears if it hadn't been drowned out by Wendy's singing.

'She ain't heavy, she's my lover. When I'm laden with sadness, when—'

'Will you shut the fuck up! And stop hovering right by my ear!'

Wendy pretended to be hurt by his outburst. 'Don't you like The Hollies?'

Jimmy stopped and peered at her over her dead bottom, balanced on his shoulder. 'Yes, Wendy, I do like The Hollies, but not sung in my ear by the floating ghost of my dead lover, who I killed!'

Wendy continued to hover by his ear. 'That, if you don't mind me saying, is the most specific reason I have ever heard for not wanting to hear a Hollies song. This murdering is having a weird effect on you, Jimmy Wayne. Next you're gonna tell me that you don't like Johnny Cash or B.B. King!' Jimmy glared at her, and Wendy hovered another ten feet further away because Jimmy looked like he was about to throw her body at her. A thought occurred to her, *can I be hit by my own body if I'm not actually in it at the time it's being thrown?* She considered it for a moment before wishing that she had tried harder in physics class. 'I suppose it's like when a tree falls in a forest and nobody is there to hear it.'

Jimmy stopped and leaned her body up against a rock. This was made easier by the rigor giving Wendy the same handling characteristics as a plank. 'What the hell are you jabbering on about now?'

Although Jimmy seemed to be a bit stressed, Wendy continued, 'I just thought you were gonna throw my body at me for a moment back there.'

He nodded. 'I was!'

'Well, that's my point!'

Looking confused, he asked, 'What point?'

'Could I be hit by my own body? It's an interesting philosophical point, don't you think? Technically, I'm not in it at the moment. But it begs the question, could I be thrown at myself? Is it a philosophical point or a physics conundrum? This naturally made me think about a tree falling in a forest or Schrödinger's cat even?'

'Trust me, Wendy, if I had a cat I would definitely throw it at you right now! Who is this Schrödinger anyway, and what's his cat gotta do with this?' Jimmy stood there sweating and breathing very heavily and looking extremely confused.

Wendy tried to explain. 'Schrödinger was a physicist who put this theory forward that if he put his cat in a box with radium and poison and sealed it would—'

'For fuck's sake! What kind of a monster puts a cat in a box filled with radiation and poison? Was he a Nazi or something? And what's a dead cat gotta do with a tree falling in a forest?' Jimmy was more annoyed than confused now.

It was at this moment that Wendy realised maybe Jimmy hadn't gone to college. 'Not far now. Do you want to un-lean me from that rock? I might start going soft in the sun, and that will make your job a lot harder.'

Jimmy nodded. 'No more cats or trees until we reach the top,' he muttered.

She nodded in agreement, and then floated off up the hill just to piss him off.

Jimmy finally got to the top of the hill and wandered over towards the sandy area near a large rock formation on the left-hand side of the outcrop. He tenderly laid down Wendy's body and turned to look at her. She was hovering about twenty feet above him.

'Could you come down please, Wendy?' he asked gently.

She descended to his side. 'You called.'

'Two things. First, you're not wearing any knickers, so hovering that high might not be a good idea. And—'

Her laughter cut him short. 'Oh yeah, no knickers. That's such an important consideration right now. As if being dead wasn't bad enough, you want me to be a lady. Jeez, Jimmy, you're a very picky murderer!'

'I ain't a murderer. I'm a man slaughterer … woman slaughterer. HELL! You know what I mean—' Jimmy's words tailed off as he realised that he'd run himself up a verbal dead end with no reverse gear.

'Jimmy, Jimmy, Jimmy. How is it that you never wrote a great song with such a command of the English language?'

He looked at her for a few moments, and then a smile cracked at the corners of his mouth. 'You always could make me laugh.' He paused for a second as if not knowing what to say next, but he knew he had to ask. 'Is it OK if I bury you here? It's a nice spot with a lovely view.'

Wendy shrugged. 'What are the neighbours like?'

CHAPTER 3

IT'S THE SINGER AND THE SONG

As he stood under the hot shower in his bathroom, Jimmy knew there was no amount of water that could wash away his actions. He had taken a life, accidently, drunkenly, but he had cost poor Wendy her life.

The only person who didn't seem terribly bothered was Wendy. When he'd finished burying her body she was still hovering around singing with an upbeat attitude that seemed totally out of keeping with her burial. Jimmy was annoyed about it. Maybe he was old-fashioned, but he thought that this kind of situation deserved a bit of solemnity.

'Wendy, you wanna come down while I say a few words?' he'd asked.

She'd landed with a thump next to him. 'You are kidding me, right? This aint a church service, Jimmy. You're burying a body that you snuck out of your room in a laundry basket.' She'd looked at him as though he was mad. 'Well, if you must … say something!'

Jimmy looked down at the freshly dug grave he had levelled off and raked over with the back of the shovel. In a couple of days no one would ever know the ground had been disturbed. 'Our Father—'

'Please NO!' Wendy interrupted. 'You can't be saying a prayer. You are quite literally the most ungodly person I have ever met. You put the "A" into Atheist. Just say it in your head or let me do it.'

He'd shook his head. 'You do it … I just can't.'

Wendy turned breezily and looked at her grave. 'Here lies the body of Wendy Walmart. She was a classy girl, but nobody ever noticed it. She kinda drifted through life and had a bit of fun but never really took it too seriously. Now I'm dead, it doesn't seem so bad … least I can fly. I just can't wait to see what else I can do. I always wanted to travel, and now I don't need a plane! Amen!'

There was a moment's silence before Jimmy had remarked, 'Wendy Walmart! You gotta be kidding me? Walmart! You never mentioned that before.' He was almost laughing.

Wendy seemed offended. 'Yeah, well, I wasn't related to the shop dynasty, so I didn't see the point. Wasn't it bad enough that my dad named me after his favourite breakfast destination?'

Now Jimmy had laughed out loud. 'Ha! He named you after *that* Wendy's. Jeez … thank God he didn't go to the Cheesecake Factory.' He chuckled.

Wendy just looked at him as if he was an idiot. 'Factory is a boy's name!' With that, she took off like Superman shouting over her shoulder as she soared away, 'See you around, Jimmy,' and in a moment she was gone.

Jimmy was still standing in the shower, his skin starting to wrinkle, before turning it off and reaching for his towel. This had been a strange day. How was he going to explain Wendy's absence if asked? No one had seen them go to his room last night; maybe it would be best if he just said he hadn't seen her. Just act surprised and concerned when she wasn't found around town … and he knew she wouldn't be.

He had a feeling he would be seeing Wendy again before long, and he just prayed that he remembered not to acknowledge her unless anyone else did, otherwise he was going to look pretty crazy talking to someone who wasn't there.

As he dried himself off, he noticed the piece of notepaper with the song he had found still lying on the bedside table. He picked it up.

'VACANT STARE
You look at me with your vacant stare
I see you but there's no one there
I try to reach you
Let you feel my touch
But the moments past
And it hurts so much.'

Jimmy couldn't believe that he had written it, but it was in his handwriting. Wendy had had a vacant stare when hanging from the wardrobe. Looking into her eyes, he could see that there was no one there. This song was about her. It was about them, and he had written it after she'd died.

What kind of a monster did that make him? He had no memory of writing it. Did he do it in his sleep? He tried to remember but couldn't remember a thing. All he knew was that it was the best song he had ever written, and he could hear the melody in his head.

He reached for his guitar and began to play. Tonight there was going to be a new song in his set, and those bastards were going to listen. He owed it to Wendy to try and make something good out of this tragedy. He wondered for a moment where Wendy was. She was headed for California as she'd disappeared over the horizon – at least he thought she was.

Thinking over the events of the last few hours, he didn't know what was real anymore. He knew Wendy was dead, he knew he had buried her, but had he really seen her ghost or whatever that was? Had he really written this song?

So much had happened; most of it he could not explain. But he knew for sure that this was a great song and he was going to sing it tonight.

———◆———

As Jimmy walked through the slot machines, he could hear the rattling of coins as gamers poured their hopes into the void. No one looked up as he passed by, eyes fixed intently on the strange fruits that rolled before them, fruits they could see but would never pick. Jimmy hated the gaming floor, especially the slots. The poor creatures that sat with glasses full of coins just tipping them down the thirsty throat of mammon until there was nothing left. Everybody lost … eventually. He hated them, but on the bright side it did help to pay his wages, so best not to be too judgemental.

As he hurried through the slots floor, he could see the Desert Bar. He always liked to grab a drink before a show, sometimes two. It didn't really matter if he was a little worse for wear because nobody ever listened. What with the dancers and the slots, he stood no chance.

The stage was in the corner of the bar. It was a nice little stage and it was a nice bar, if only it didn't have two raised platforms situated at the far end where the pole dancers gyrated. They only stopped when he started, and all the middle-aged men would turn and look at him accusingly as if he had stolen their girl. The girls would smile and wave to Jimmy as they came down off their poles, their G-strings stuffed with dollar bills. Jimmy paid more attention to the money than the girls. Maybe he should wear a G-string.

'Good evening, James.'

Jimmy turned in the direction of the greeting, but he knew who it was. Only one person in Blackjack called him James. 'Good evening to you, David,' he replied in a truly awful attempt at an English accent. 'How the hell are you, old boy?' he continued, still in the same exaggerated Queen's English.

'Well, old son, I was a lot better before you went all Austin Powers on me.' David Parker was in his early fifties, slim and debonair, and to Jimmy's eyes the quintessential English gentleman. 'Drink?' he enquired.

Jimmy thought for a moment. 'Well, I don't usually like to drink before I sing, but tonight I'm celebrating.'

David smiled at Jimmy's blatant lie. 'Oh, do tell, James. It must be something very special to inspire you to a pre-show libation.' Jimmy chuckled. He loved the way David took the piss while appearing to be oh-so polite. The English were so good at irony. Most of Jimmy's fellow countrymen thought irony was something that made your clothes look nice.

'Well, if you're buying, I think a nice gin and tonic will hit the spot.'

David nodded to the barman who had been listening in; the drinks were soon underway. 'So … ' David leaned closer to Jimmy. 'What are we celebrating? Have you found the missing rhinestones?'

Jimmy shook his head. 'No, they're still in your wife's bed where I left them.'

David laughed. 'If only I did have a wife, James, I wouldn't have to waste my time talking to you.'

Jimmy enjoyed his nightly chats with David. David was totally out of place in Nevada. He was totally out of place in the Riviera Casino. To call it third rate would be a compliment, but David gave it an air of class, and his way with clients and his excellent management skills had certainly improved the place over the last five years.

The Riviera actually made good profits, and that was down to David's astute management. He could have been running a major hotel anywhere in the world but he liked the casino element to the business which had brought him to Vegas in the 1980s.

David kept his cards close to his chest regarding his past, but when he and Jimmy had got to know each other better, he did reveal late one night, after a lot of gin, that he'd once been in senior management at the Golden Flamingo.

As one of the oldest hotels along the Vegas strip, it was a prestigious place. It had a chequered history when it was opened by the Mob in 1946. Bugsy Cohen, the owner, had allegedly named it after his girlfriend, who apparently went by the nickname of the 'Golden Flamingo' because of her golden hair and very long legs.

'Is that true or just a bit of Vegas folklore?' Jimmy had asked David.

David had thought for a moment before replying, 'Well, it was a long time before I was there, but I have seen the photos and she did have very long legs. She also had a long neck, but "The Emu" wouldn't have had the same ring now, would it?'

Jimmy couldn't help but agree. He couldn't understand why someone as capable as David would leave the Golden Flamingo for the Riviera. He had asked the question and, as usual, David was slow at revealing anything about his past, but he did give Jimmy a bit of a clue.

He'd leaned towards Jimmy conspiratorially. 'All I could possibly say is that it was a boardroom incident.'

Jimmy was surprised. 'I knew you were pretty high up in management at the Golden Flamingo, but I didn't realise you were on the board.'

David shook his head. 'I wasn't. When I say "boardroom incident", I am being somewhat economical with the truth. The circumstance of my demise was boardroom related.' He looked at Jimmy as if that was enough of an explanation. It wasn't.

'And … ?' Jimmy had pressed. 'Give me the full story. I've told you mine.'

David had winced in mock horror. 'Yes, you did, and what a tawdry little tale *that* was. I still feel unclean every time I think about it, but still … I suppose it's only fair.' David then sighed and took a deep breath, which he let out with his first word. '*Weeell*, let me explain. The incident occurred in the boardroom but was unrelated to any board meeting. The head of finance had a much younger and very attractive wife. She was naturally drawn to my suave English sophistication and my devastating good looks. You think I look good now, James – wow, I was stunning back then.'

'And so modest.'

David promptly ignored him. 'Well, the natural order being what it is, the alpha male attracted the alpha female, and the mating occurred in the boardroom … on the table!' David had paused and sighed with a regret that seemed genuine. 'It was all going really well until in walked said finance director with three top clients. I tried to explain that I was trying to help his wife with her breathing difficulties—'

'No doubt caused by you lying on top of her.'

David frowned at him. 'Shame on you, James, a gentleman always takes his weight on his elbows. Did they teach you nothing at school? Suffice to say my explanations fell on stony ground and, after our somewhat awkward uncoupling, I was invited to the owner's office where I expected an instant dismissal.'

'You were lucky the Mob didn't still own it or you would've been swimming with the fishes!' Jimmy's observation brought a nod of agreement from David.

'Quite. I really wasn't sure what was going to happen when I got in there. Sam, the owner, and I had always got on very well, and he'd been watching me over the years as I rose swiftly through into management. He pointed me to a chair. I tried to explain, but he shut me up. Sam was a big man and you wouldn't mess with him, so I sat down, shut up and waited to hear my fate. He said, 'OK, Davy boy, you have screwed up … literally screwed up!' I went to say something, but he gave me this look and I knew to keep quiet. 'Now, I know why you screwed Frank's wife. She's a good-looking woman and as hungry as a hyena, but I gotta ask you … this hotel has hundreds of rooms. You're a senior manager. Why the fuck didn't you take her into one of those?' I attempted to answer, but Sam held up his hand. 'That was a rhetorical question, David. Fact is, I know why you did her on the boardroom table. You were sticking two fingers up to the board who you know are a bunch of underachieving idiots. Especially that moron husband of hers.' I hadn't expected this, so I just sat there waiting for whatever came next. Sam walked around his desk, sat on the front of it and smiled at me. 'Look, I know you could run rings round any of those fools, David, but I tolerate them because we make big profits here. They earn good money and none of them are smart enough to take anything from me, but they are smart enough to know it. We have a nice, settled status quo here and I can't afford to change it. Frank caught you in the act with his wife; he was with three of our biggest clients. Word is going to get out.' Sam shook his head sadly. 'I gotta sack you, Davy, I have no choice.' I then nodded and stood up. 'I understand, sir,' I replied. 'I apologise for the difficult position I have put you in.' Sam smiled. 'Not as difficult as the position you put Frank's wife in from what I heard!' We both couldn't help but laugh. Sam then gestured for me to sit back down. He walked back around his desk and slumped into his chair. 'I have a proposal for you, Davy.' I hadn't been expecting this; I said nothing and listened. 'You know and I know that Frank is an idiot, but he is a director. You on the other hand are a senior manager, so you have to go but ... and it's a big but, you are the best manager I've ever seen. The way you deal with people, clients and staff is fantastic. They all love you. You don't miss a thing on the floor, and the restaurants and cabaret are always spot on, so I don't want to lose you. Problem is, you're too well known on the strip, so you have to go, but here's the deal.' *Here it comes*, I thought, without a clue what "it" actually was. 'I have another casino; it's called the Riviera. It's a shithole and it's in Nevada in a town called Blackjack. It's a blue-collar version of this place. Has potential, though, and it makes money, but I want you to go there and run it for me. You keep the same wages as you're on here with all the benefits. You get a ten per cent cut of the profits, and I give you a full membership at the golf club, and you can have one of the best suites decorated to your taste. It's that or I just sack you, and Frank will probably get someone to break your legs!' I nodded and said, 'Could I have some time to think about it?' Sam then smiled. 'You're funny, Davy, very funny. You know the answer to that one. Listen, I am offering you a partnership in a new venture. Sure, it's in butt-fuck Blackjack, but you're dead in Vegas for now. It's a nice little place, and you're gonna make some serious money if you get it right. So, what do you say?' David looked at Jimmy when he had finished, a wry grin on his face. 'And now you know all there is to know, James. Happy now?'

Jimmy had nodded. 'Very happy. I now know you're a true music lover.'

Looking at him quizzically, David had asked, 'Explain?'

'You're a partner here, so you get to hire and fire, yet you keep bringing me back every year ... you gotta love me.'

A pained expression then crossed David's face. 'Love – that's not quite how I would put it. Watching you is like watching an excellent driver run into the back of a stationary bus. You're a great driver, but you just don't seem able to get around the bus.'

'What does that actually mean in English?' Jimmy had asked with a shrug.

David, after slowly shaking his head, had replied, 'That, dear James, is what we call a metaphor. The point I'm attempting to illustrate is that you can sing and you can play, but it just doesn't come across and move the audience. You sing other people's songs as if they don't belong to you. There is no emotion, no feeling. If I were your manager, I would say write your own songs or get a good writer to write something you believe in, something that is real to you, and then go out there on stage and bare your emotions. Stop phoning it in!'

That conversation had taken place over two years ago and until tonight, Jimmy hadn't come up with a new song that was worth singing. Tonight was different.

The gin and tonics arrived. David raised his glass to Jimmy. 'Bottoms up, old chap. Got anything new for us.' David asked Jimmy the same question every night, to which Jimmy would tell him about a new song he had incorporated into the act, and then David would shake his head. 'I meant one you had written yourself.' Tonight, however, Jimmy was going to surprise him.

'As it happens, I have. I wrote it last night, and I think you're gonna like it.'

David nodded. 'What's it called?'

'Vacant Stare,' Jimmy replied.

'Autobiographical, then?' he said with a smirk.

'Piss off.' Jimmy drained his glass. 'Just make sure you're listening to the third song of the set and get ready to eat humble pie.'

'Ah, dear Steve Marriott. Hope you have written a song worthy of him!'

Jimmy looked quizzically at David. 'Steve who?'

David sighed. 'Dear God, have you ever looked at anything except a mirror? Steve Marriott … Humble Pie … Small Faces?' The penny dropped.

'Oh yeah. That Steve Marriott. Did he write his own songs?'

With that, David downed his drink and departed in a show of mock disgust. 'Be back in twenty minutes, James. Hope it's worth coming back for.'

So did Jimmy; it had cost Wendy her life.

He finished his drink and walked over towards the stage where his guitars stood waiting for him to tune. When Jimmy stood up to the microphone, he was alone on the stage. He only had a full band on Friday and Saturday nights.

'Good evening, folks, my name's Jimmy Wayne and I'm here to play you some music.'

The girls took this as their cue to stop gyrating on their poles and gather up the dollar bills from the stage. As their music stopped, Jimmy heard the audible sigh of the delusional male of the species as their personal dancers proved they were only for hire and not being held in place by their magnetic personalities. They turned towards Jimmy and groaned. It wasn't an overly loud groan, but Jimmy could see it on their faces. As he strummed the opening chords of his first number, they slowly turned away from him and the barman got busy. Outside the bar, the rhythm section of the slots played on and Jimmy became invisible. He didn't mind. He just had to get to the third song – then they would see.

———◆———

David had been doing his rounds of the floors but as he walked through the slots towards the Desert Bar, there was something strange going on. He couldn't put his finger on it at first. Then, as he looked around trying to gauge what was different, he realised that all the people playing slots nearest the bar had stopped and were listening to Jimmy.

He hurried to the entrance and had to squeeze his way through the crowd. The barman looked at David and shrugged. Nobody was buying drinks; they were all listening to Jimmy.

For a moment, he struggled to compute what was going on, then he started to listen. This wasn't the usual Jimmy. His eyes were open, but he was looking into a huge void that nobody else in the room could see, singing directly to someone. And his voice – there was an emotional depth of feeling that he had never heard from Jimmy. He listened to the words.

'I had no words to hold you close
Never said the ones you wanted most
But the tide came in
And you were gone
To a far horizon
Can't hear my song.'

David looked around the room; everyone was hanging on Jimmy's every word. He caught the barman's eye, who just shook his head in bewilderment. There was a hushed silence when Jimmy finished the song, and then the room erupted into applause.

Jimmy seemed taken aback by the warmth of the reception he was receiving. He stood there acknowledging the applause while David made his way over to speak to his barman.

'What happened?' he asked.

The barman shrugged. 'Never seen anything like it. He played his first two numbers and there was a bit of polite applause, same as usual, but nobody was really paying him much attention, and then he started playing this song, and by the end of the first verse everyone had stopped talking, even some of the slots had come in to listen. It was incredible. Though, to be fair, Mr Parker, it was a really good song. Never heard him do it before.'

David nodded. 'That, Steven, is because he only wrote it last night!'

Steven looked surprised. 'Jimmy wrote that? I didn't even think he could read! Wow, it was really good.'

David smiled his agreement. 'It certainly was, but it looks like normal service is about to be resumed.'

———◆———

Jimmy had waited for the applause to stop and then said, 'Thanks very much. Glad you all seemed to like that one. I wrote it last night. My next song is by the Reverend Gary Davis called "Death Don't Have No Mercy in This Land".'

As Jimmy started to play the song, the crowd slowly drifted away, politely at first, but by the second verse they were back at the slots and the barman was busy again. Jimmy overheard one man say to his wife, 'Oh man, death would be a mercy if you had to listen to him sing this again. Pity he don't do more of his own stuff.' Even though he was singing, Jimmy agreed.

He couldn't put himself in the shoes of Reverend Gary. They had no shared experience, and the emotions that were in the song were not his. As he sang, he saw his audience shrink away like an ebb tide, but he was happy. The reception his song had received was unbelievable. He thought it was a great song, and now he knew it. He would sing it again in his second set. He craved that feeling, and knew he had to find a way to write more songs.

After the show, David had reappeared and called him over to the bar. He passed him a large G&T. 'There you go, James, this one's for the new song. That was quite some reaction you got there.'

Jimmy couldn't help but agree with him. 'Yeah, seems like I'm on to something.'

'You certainly are,' agreed David. 'Never seen you just lose yourself in a song before. There was no phoning that in; you sang it like you meant it. Who were you singing to?'

Jimmy didn't know how to answer that one. 'I don't really know. I just kinda went for it like you suggested. I just imagined I was singing to the girl in the song.'

David took a sip from his drink, and then pressed Jimmy further. 'But who is the mystery woman, James? Anyone we know?'

Before Jimmy could reply, Wendy appeared behind David – hovering. 'You gonna tell him?'

Jimmy spat his drink all over David's suit.

David jumped back but couldn't escape the spray. 'What the hell, James!' cried David as he reached for a bar mat to wipe his jacket.

'Man, I'm so sorry. It just went down the wrong hole.'

David shook his head. 'No problem. You were probably choking on the name of the girl you didn't want to tell me.' He winked at Jimmy. 'Got to go, need to do a sweep of the blackjack and roulette tables. See you after your last set, and it will give you a chance to think up a cover story for the girl in the song.' With that, he spun on his elegant heels and departed.

Jimmy looked at Wendy. She was still by the bar but no longer airborne. It was obvious nobody else in the room could see her, so he gestured with his eyes to head for the door that led to the hotel bedrooms.

Wendy nodded with a mock conspiratorial candour, which she really didn't possess, and strode out of the bar and through the doors to the corridor – literally straight through them despite the fact that they were closed.

It was not what Jimmy had been expecting, nor was the fact that Wendy reappeared almost immediately through the wall at the side of the doors.

'Hey, Jimmy, Jimmy, Jimmy! You know what this means?' she cried with excitement.

Jimmy managed to stop himself replying in this roomful of people and made it through the doors into the empty corridor before acknowledging Wendy. He was shocked and surprised. He hadn't expected to see her here. He assumed that her ghost, or whatever this was, would be confined to somewhere near her body. He should have realised when she shot off into the canyon that she was going to travel.

Wendy was not in the corridor, but before he could open the door he had just walked through to see where she was, she rose from the floor in front of him. It made him jump.

'Jesus, Wendy! Any chance you could just stick to using the doors and staying on the ground – not above or below it? You're gonna make me look crazy.'

Wendy shrugged. 'You're the one talking to a dead person that nobody else can see. Seems to me that *you* just might be the crazy one.'

She does have a point, thought Jimmy. 'Where've you been? I've been worried.'

Wendy looked at Jimmy. 'I'm dead. What have you got to worry about?'

He was struggling to put together the words that would adequately respond to her question. 'Yeah, if you put it like that, I suppose you're right, but … but I just … I dunno. It's been a strange day.' Jimmy paused for a moment to gather his thoughts, such as they were. He looked at her. 'Where *have* you been?'

Wendy looked as if she was going to burst. 'Oh, Jimmy, it's amazing. I've been meeting my neighbours.'

Jimmy was shocked. 'In the canyon?'

Wendy shook her head and looked at him as though he was losing the plot, which to be fair he probably was. 'My neighbours in the afterlife. Wow, Jimmy, there's a lot of them. Most of them are lovely, but some of them are really pissed. Jimmy, Hoffa ain't happy … He's still looking to get even!' Wendy let that one sink in. She saw the flicker of understanding in Jimmy's eyes and then continued, 'Yeah, he is dead, hold the front page.'

Jimmy held up his hand. 'Wendy, Wendy. Please just hang on a second. You're going at a hundred miles an hour; I just can't keep up. Tell me about your dead friends later. What is it you were going on about this *meaning something*?' Jimmy had registered her excitement but couldn't pick up what she had been going on about. Was she talking about the meaning of life or something to do with the song?

Wendy thought for a moment trying to remember what Jimmy was talking about before realisation spread across her face. 'Oh that! Well, it seems that we have an open link between the living world and the dead. Must be because you killed me in a consensual manner. Maybe if you had battered me to death with a hammer, this link wouldn't be open.' Jimmy was still struggling to understand the concept of consensual manslaughter as Wendy ploughed on with her explanation. 'Because we can communicate, we have an edge.'

Jimmy pulled a face that made it clear he still didn't have a clue what she meant.

Wendy spoke slowly, as if to a child, to try and explain what was on her mind. 'Most of the dead don't have a living person they can communicate with. It's a big advantage!'

Jimmy sighed. 'How is it an advantage? I don't understand.'

Wendy paused, thought for a moment and then smiled angelically. 'Say you wanna rob a bank.' Wendy ignored Jimmy as he put his head in his hands and continued, 'I can just float through the walls and get the money from the vault and then float back with it. We know I can move stuff because I threw that stone at you. So, I could just fill up a holdall and float out of there straight through the wall of the vault. We could be rich, Jimmy. Well, you could, and then you could buy a really nice place for me to haunt, or just hang around if you prefer.' Wendy waited for Jimmy to respond.

Slowly, he pulled his hands away from his head. He looked tired. When he spoke, it was almost in a whisper, calm and slow, as though he was speaking to a very old person with a thin grasp on reality. 'That's very nice, but are the money and holdall ghosts? I don't want to be a party pooper, but if they aren't dead – or shall we say inanimate – I can't really see how they're going to pass through a wall.' He let it hang there, watching Wendy's face as she worked it out for herself. If he expected realisation to take the smile off her face, he would be disappointed.

'No problem! I'll just grab it when they're delivering it to the banks. They'll have to open the doors of the security wagons. I can get it then.'

Jimmy really didn't quite know what to say next. It had been a long and strange day, and he still had two more sets to do. 'Can we pick this up later, Wendy? I have another show in ten minutes.'

'No problem. I got plenty to be getting on with.' She turned to go, but then paused and looked at him. 'How'd the song go?'

He nodded and smiled gently. 'It went great. Really great.'

Her eyes sparkled in triumph. 'I knew it would, Jimmy.' She blew him a kiss, and then just vanished through the wall to who knew where.

At that moment, the doors from the bar flew open and a large man in a suit designed for someone much smaller appeared. He stared at Jimmy. 'You OK, buddy? You look like you've just seen a ghost!'

CHAPTER 4
NEWTON'S THIRD LAW

Two weeks had passed since that terrible morning. Jimmy lay on his bed considering the strange turn his life had taken. He was lonely without Wendy; he hadn't seen her since she left the casino after his first show with the new song. Had she gone forever? He doubted it. Wendy, dead or alive, was a force of nature. She would be back just when he least expected it.

He smiled at the thought and had to admit to himself that he missed her. He regretted killing her, even if it was an accident, but Wendy seemed happier than ever as a spirit. That's how he thought of her – not a ghost. There was still so much life and vitality in her. No, she was a spirit and her spirit shone very bright.

Jimmy, however, wasn't for the first couple of nights after the event – that's what he was calling it, 'the event'. Sounded so much better than 'the night I accidently hung Wendy'. Which, to be fair, sounded like a country and western song. Maybe if he'd mixed a dead dog killed by the last train out of town with a cowboy dying of TB, he could turn it into something. Two and a half deaths were about average for a country song, so it was hitting all the metrics for success. He reached for his notepad and started to scribble '*The Night I Hung Young Wendy*'.

He settled on that title, as he knew rhyming something with 'accidently' was going to be too much of a stretch … unless she was rich and had a Bentley. *No*, he thought, *don't be too fanciful – she was just a small-town girl.*

'Well, she's hanging from the ceiling
And it's giving me this feeling
That I've gotta catch the next train outta town
But the dog he is a howling
And I can see that cowboy frowning
Cause that TB thang it's really got him down.'

Jimmy read the first verse he'd just written – there wasn't going to be a second. He really wasn't very good at this writing malarkey. No matter how hard he had tried, and he had tried, all he could come up with was rubbish like this. He flipped over the pages of his pad to see a song he had written yesterday.

'Love's a Bitch'

Jimmy didn't want to, but he read on.

'Well, love's a bitch
Gonna give you the stitch
Drive you in a ditch
Cus loves a bitch
Gonna spit on your potatoes
Gonna poison your tomatoes
And that girl of yours
She never will get hitched.'

'My God.' Jimmy sighed, finally realising how bad things were. If a seven-year-old brought him a song like that, he would have sent them to bed with no supper. He didn't understand how he could be so bad yet still write a song like 'Vacant Stare'.

Those were his words from his imagination. Despite the fact he had no memory of writing them, he knew they were his. The handwriting was his and so were the emotions.

Jimmy knew those emotions. He felt them every time he remembered Wendy, but how was he going to conjure those feelings onto the page? How was he ever going to write the songs he needed to escape this place and get back to Nashville or Vegas? To do something good, to try and make up for what had happened.

The reception he received every time he sang 'Vacant Stare' was like nothing else in his career. Customers in the casino would stop him as he walked towards the Desert Bar for his set and ask him, 'When you going to play that good song?' Jimmy would feign surprise. 'Which one? They're all good.' He would get this sidelong look every time and just give in. 'Number three in about twelve minutes.' He would get a nod of thanks before, 'well, that's just great, Mr Wayne. I only want the good stuff!' Jimmy would force a smile and move on. He wasn't offended. How could he be? They were right!

The rest of his act could generously be described as lacklustre and uninspiring. As a quote on a billboard it was a little down-beat. 'Jimmy Wayne, lacklustre and uninspiring'. In his defence, Jimmy thought they could add, 'but he is technically proficient'. He tried to imagine his name up in lights on the strip in Vegas. 'Jimmy Wayne … technically proficient'. It made him sound like a plumber. He needed more great songs. *This*, he thought, i*s my only problem*.

Jimmy was wrong.

His big problem had just driven into town. Two of them. Jack Lantern's boys had just arrived from Vegas, and the bad debt he owed Jack was way overdue for collection.

———◆———

Carmine Mallotides and Vinny Zito climbed out of their pickup truck. It had been a long drive from Vegas – 440 miles to be precise. It had taken them nearly seven hours including a half an hour stop for coffee and some food. They were booked into the Hoover Inn just down the street from the Riviera.

They were big men – not fat, but definitely past their athletic prime, like two old athletes who had been trapped in a huge mountain made of burgers and had to eat their way out.

Vinny's neck bulged, the veins pulsing like a mating toad. The man was a bull in a jacket. He went to the trunk of the car and pulled out his huge case as if it were a handbag. Carmine, on the other hand, was more laid back. He was clearly strong, but he displayed power by his posture. Upright but relaxed, confident and commanding. He was in charge and they were on a mission for Jack Lantern, their boss.

It wasn't complicated. 'Kill Jimmy Wayne. Kill him slow and kill him painful and film it. I wanna hear that punk beg for mercy.'

Vinny had laughed. 'Better than hearing him sing, boss!' he'd ventured.

Jack had silenced him with a withering stare. You never wanted to see that stare. Vinny had seen it that day three years ago when one of the new guys had got overfamiliar with Jack.

'You Irish, boss?' he'd asked.

Jack looked irritated but answered, 'No, I'm half Italian. The other half is English. Why you wanna know?' he'd demanded.

'Because—' he'd sniggered, barely able to contain a laugh '—if you were Irish, you'd be Jack O'Lantern ... d'ya get it?'

Jack did. 'Very funny. D'ya like baseball, kid?' This wasn't really a question.

Feeling confident, the new guy had nodded. 'Yeah, boss. Who doesn't like a bit of baseball?'

Jack then reached under his desk. 'Glad you feel like that, son, because I'm about to hit a home run!' Jack had moved with a speed that belied his age. The baseball bat he'd grabbed came up from beneath his desk and he'd swung it in one sweeping deadly arc across the desk and straight into the head of the open-mouthed new guy. It hit with a sickening *crack*. Blood spurted from the wound where four inches of his skull had been just a second before. Jack then walked slowly around his desk and looked down at the corpse he had just created. He raised the bloody bat above his head. 'It's outta here. Home run, Lantern!'

The new guy just lay there motionless, with eyes still open and a look of surprise on his face.

Jack smiled. 'Guess he never saw it coming.' He'd laughed a humourless laugh. 'Get rid of him, and make sure the next one knows how to be respectful.'

Vinny still shuddered when he thought about it. Even after three years it was still crystal-clear in his memory. The crack as the skull split, the spatter of blood, the look of surprise on the guy's face as he hit the deck and looked up at him with unseeing eyes. Just as quick as that, his life was over.

Jack was a ruthless bastard and what he said went. He had told him and Carmine to find Jimmy and kill him. No bargaining, not even if he had the money. Too many people knew that Jimmy owed Jack, so he had to be made an example of.

———◆———

Jimmy had grown tired of trying to write a new song; everything he started just turned to crap. He just couldn't figure out why he wasn't able to write another song like 'Vacant Stare'. It was in him, but how the hell was he supposed to get it out? He had been drunk the night he'd written it. In the spirit of research, he'd repeated the same dosage on two consecutive nights – but when he awoke in the morning ... nothing!

OK, he thought, *it's not being drunk that does it*. All these thoughts were running through his head as he showered. *Was it the sex?* No, it couldn't be just that. He'd had lots of sex, mostly meaningless, in his forty-four years and he'd never written a decent song. So not drink, not sex, and then like a key turning in a lock, it all clicked into place. *Death! Or to be more precise, the causing of a death.*

He turned off the shower and just stood there while he considered the implications of that thought. Could it be that simple? Had the act of killing Wendy, even though it was accidental, released some kind of artistic flow? Was there a metaphorical dam that could only be breached by the energy released when taking a life? If he'd said this out loud within his mother's earshot, he would have been told in no uncertain terms, 'hush up, Jimmy, you're talking gibberish. You sound like that man on *The Outer Limits*.'

Jimmy smiled. He could imagine Rod Serling introducing an episode: 'Jimmy Wayne was a singer without a song. He could sing and he could play, but he could never write the words that were going to justify his talent. Until the day he accidently killed his girlfriend and when he awoke the next morning, he had written a great song. Then he had realised, he could only write a song when he killed someone. Welcome to *The Outer Limits* and tonight's episode "The Song That Kills".' Jimmy shook his head. This made no sense.

His mother was right; he was jumping to a conclusion that wasn't there. Trouble was, Jimmy had thought the unthinkable, and now it was stuck in his head, and he just couldn't shake it.

Just like when he came home from a night out with a school friend and found his father dead on the kitchen table with his skull caved in. He was sitting in his chair, the glass of Scotch still clasped in his stiff fingers. Clearly, he had been hit from behind with a ferocious blow to the back of the head. Jimmy was in a state of shock, but strangely not surprised. His father had been living dangerously all his life. He had scraped a living as a song-and-dance man playing the small theatre circuit and clubs, but his real reward was the ladies.

Wayne Corvella was a good-looking man, not so much now with his head bashed in, but until then he was a real charmer. Jimmy had caught his father on more than one occasion on the downtown streets of Stroudsburg with a young lady. He had simply shrugged and said, 'it's only showbiz, Jimmy boy. Aint no need to tell your mother.'

He never did – he didn't have to, she knew! That's why they moved out of town to the country. Scotrun, they called it. Jimmy's dad called it Scrotum. It was a tiny rural community where his grandad had a small farm. When he died, he left it to Jimmy's mum.

She had moved them out there straight away to get his dad away from temptation. It hadn't worked; it just meant that his father had to commute to his infidelities. Jimmy never understood why his mother hadn't left him. He looked at his father's body, and then he realised that his mother had left him … permanently. It was so obvious in that moment that she had finally cracked, and so had his father's skull.

Jimmy ran from the room looking for his mother, but she was nowhere to be found. He had called the police and a manhunt or, maybe a better description, a 'mum hunt', had been started.

It took them two days to find her. She had taken herself down to the woods at the bottom of the meadow about half a mile from the house. She had sat on the bench her father had made many years before when she was a young girl. They used to sit there some days and eat their packed lunches together. The view of the rolling countryside and the Pocono Mountains on the horizon was truly beautiful. That was the last thing Lucy Corvella had ever seen.

The shotgun was still at the side of her body when they found her. Poor Lucy had sat there, placed the barrel beneath her chin and rested her head as she took in the view for the very last time.

Nobody would ever know how long his mother had sat there, waiting for the courage to reach down and depress that trigger. Remembering all the happy times with her father. Remembering also how he'd gently tried to warn her, when she had first brought Wayne home, that Wayne was not the reliable type.

Her father was a kind and gentle man, and he knew that to forbid Lucy from seeing Wayne would only force them closer together. His gentle warnings had fallen on deaf ears. Lucy had fallen for the illusion of perfection that Wayne Corvella had presented to her young and innocent eyes.

She married Wayne and soon gave birth to Jimmy and everything was wonderful. Wayne had been a doting father and husband at first. But like a child with a new toy, he had soon tired of domestic family bliss. The image he had created was melting away in the bright sun of life. Her father had been right.

Lucy tried very hard to be a good mother to Jimmy, and for the most part she had succeeded, but her unhappiness weighed her down. Some mornings, Jimmy would go down to breakfast before school and his mother would be sitting at the table staring out of the window but seeing nothing, a bottle of red wine open in front of her.

On mornings like this, there would be no breakfast for Jimmy. Lucy's descent had continued year on year as one affair after the other ground down her self-esteem. The neighbours would stop talking as she walked by, and she knew why. They were too embarrassed to say anything. Wayne did not hide his infidelities.

All these events had led to his mother sitting alone at the edge of the woods, a shotgun wedged beneath her chin, with only memories of what might have been if she had listened to her father. So sad that a life can hinge on a single moment. One wrong decision, and then a slow descent to disappointment and despair.

From that day on, Jimmy hated his father. He hated him for what he had done to his mother. The police wouldn't let him see his mother when they found her. He was angry at the time, but he was only fifteen; he hadn't considered the implications of a shotgun at point-blank range.

As he'd grown older, he looked back and was thankful: Jimmy wouldn't have wanted that as the last memory of his mother. He had gone back to the woods a few days after the funeral and sat on the same bench trying to feel her presence. He couldn't. He was just numb.

Both his mother and father were dead, and he was alone, two days short of his sixteenth birthday. He was an orphan.

It had already been decided that his uncle and aunt would take him in. His mother's brother, Frank, ran a lumber yard just a mile down the road. He was a good man, just like his father, and Jimmy liked him, but he knew he would be gone from there the day after he turned eighteen. A farm was no place for him. He could sing and he could play guitar, and he was headed as far from this place as he could get.

As he sat there, it gently started to rain. He watched the droplets fall to the ground at his feet and noticed the partial bloodstain that remained. The police had tidied up the scene, but they hadn't completely cleared everything. The raindrops slowly mingled with his mother's blood and gently washed away the evidence of her existence, erasing all memory of her from this place she had loved so much. Jimmy watched the last drops trickle into the soil through eyes misty with tears. 'Goodbye, Mum,' he had whispered.

Jimmy shivered. How long had he been standing in the shower since he'd turned it off? He hadn't thought about his mother for years – it was still too painful. He tried not to think about his father because he knew he was just like him. That's why he'd never had children: he couldn't do to another child what his father had done to him. He was glad his mother had killed him; she had probably saved him from doing it. That said, if he had done it, he could have got a song out of it.

———◆———

As Jimmy stood on stage for his first set that evening, he noticed two men at the bar, one of them seemed familiar to him. They looked like a couple of hitmen. He smiled inwardly. *I suppose even hitmen are entitled to an evening off*, he thought.

The show went well. How 'Vacant Stare' was being received had given him a huge boost in confidence, and the covers he sang in his set had all improved. He was starting to own them, but none of them came close to his song. Customers would come up and ask him to do more of his own stuff. He didn't have the heart to tell them that they were getting 'all' of his stuff.

After the last song of his set, Jimmy made his way to the bar. There was a gin and tonic waiting for him as always. He nodded his thanks to Steven the barman.

Jimmy then scanned the bar to see if David was around. They normally had a nightcap together after his final set of the day where David would drink one to Jimmy's four. David had commented, in his wry English way, that maybe it would be easier just to give him a bottle of each and let them mix on the inside of his less than athletic body. Those weren't the exact words he used, but even vulgarity sounded classy when David said it.

Jimmy never took offence; it amused him that David thought he had a problem. He'd been drinking since he was sixteen and he was forty-four now, so it clearly hadn't done him any harm, apart from the paunch he was developing ... and the accidental killing of Wendy.

When he thought about it, he had to concede that but for excessive alcohol intake on the night in question, Wendy would still be alive. So maybe David had a point. Alcohol was bad for you – well, it was for Wendy. He, on the other hand, was absolutely fine. He drained his glass, happy in the knowledge that he had resolved, for the moment, the question of his alleged drink problem.

'Excuse me, Mr Wayne,' said a voice from behind him.

As he turned, he was greeted by the huge neck and shoulders of Vinny Zito. Jimmy was five foot eleven, so not short by any means, but Vinny Zito was six-foot-five and two-hundred-and-forty pounds – only about twenty of which was fat. The rest was muscle. Unfortunately, that included the bit between his ears. Luckily for him, Jack Lantern was not employing him for the power of his thinking, just the power in his forearms.

As he introduced himself, Jimmy leaned back to take in the craggy good looks of his new friend. 'I really enjoyed your set, Mr Wayne. Could I buy you a drink?'

For Jimmy, this was not a question that ever needed to be asked. He nodded his acceptance of Vinny Zito's proposal. 'That's very kind of you. Gin and tonic, please ... Tanqueray ten. Teddy knows how I like it.'

Vinny nodded. 'No problem, Mr Wayne.' He pointed to a table in the far corner of the Desert Bar. 'My colleague,

Carmine, is over there. Why don't you join him, and I will bring the drinks over. We have a little proposal that might be of interest to you.'

Jimmy looked at him quizzically. 'Really? But you don't even know me.'

Vinny smiled. 'Oh, we know you, Mr Wayne. We've been keeping an eye on you.' That much was true. 'We like your new song and we represent a record label back in LA that is very interested in adding you to their roster.' That bit, however, was not. It didn't matter, though. From the moment Vinny had said 'record label', Jimmy had lost the power of thinking. To a forty-something musician doing cabaret in a third-rate casino it sounded like someone was throwing him a lifeline to resurrect his drowning career.

As Jimmy arrived at Carmine's table, he stood up to greet him. Like Vinny, he was six-foot plus and about two hundred and twenty pounds. Although still carrying the slight paunch, he had the look of an athlete. His competition days were long gone, but he still looked like he could shift if he needed to.

He held out his hand, and Jimmy eagerly took it. 'Carmine Mallotides. Pleased to meet you,' he said, the vice-like grip of his handshake making Jimmy squeal.

'Wow!' He tried to make light of it as Carmine released him. 'Sorry about that, Carmine, but these are my picking fingers, and you have a grip like the Boston Strangler.'

Carmine held up his hands. 'My apologies, Mr Wayne, sometimes I forget my own strength.' He ushered for Jimmy to sit down. 'Please, take a seat. Vinny and I would like to put a proposal to you.'

'You gonna make me an offer I can't refuse?' Jimmy quipped.

Carmine nodded and smiled knowingly. 'Yes, Jimmy, I guess we are.'

'Sounds exciting. What's the deal?' Jimmy was barely able to conceal his excitement.

Carmine held up his hands. 'All in good time, Mr Wayne. Let's just wait for Vinny to get back here with the drinks, then all will be revealed.'

And it was. During the course of the next hour, and several more drinks, the two 'A&R' men explained how they'd been following Jimmy for several years. They explained that it was common knowledge in the country/blues world that Jimmy Wayne had never yet realised his potential.

When he was in his early twenties, Jimmy had a minor hit, 'Last Train to Nowhere'. It got to number nineteen on the *Billboard* chart and was top ten in both the blues and country charts. Jimmy was hailed by a couple of magazines as the next big crossover artist; he got a lot of airplay too. But as the years had ticked by, the only thing that Jimmy had crossed over was opportunity. As each opportunity came up, he found a way to waste it. The song was still played regularly, but it had been written by his bass player, Desperate Doug Baker, who really wasn't desperate at all.

Doug had grown rich on the song writing royalties he had accrued over the years. He'd also written two massive hits for Kenny King. With regular 'fat' royalty cheques rolling in, Doug had retired to his ranch. Yes, he had bought a ranch on the proceeds. It made Jimmy sick. He'd been the one who sang that song, made it work, but old Desperate Doug just took the royalties and quit the band. He wasn't a great loss musically, he was a shit bass player, hence the 'Desperate', but he was the only one in the band who could write a decent song. Jimmy hated writers – probably because he couldn't do it.

Carmine's voice brought Jimmy back to the present. 'As I was saying, Jimmy … OK if I call you Jimmy?'

Jimmy nodded. 'You can call me anything you want if you have a record deal for me.'

They all laughed, and then Vinny took up the story. 'See, Jimmy, everybody knows that you're the full package. You can sing and you can play and you're a good-looking guy.' As he said this, his eyes glanced down at Jimmy's very noticeable paunch. 'You may have put on a couple of pounds, but the label will get you a fitness coach and help you get into shape before we release the record.'

Jimmy winced. 'Going to the gym? Will that really be necessary?' He had been avoiding physical effort all his life with a fair degree of success.

Vinny leaned back and held open his hands. 'Hey, Jimmy, no gain without pain, my friend.'

Carmine nodded. *Yes*, he thought, *there's certainly going to be pain, a lot of it!*

They talked for an hour or more, filling Jimmy's eager ears with tales of how they would put a team of writers around him. Jimmy had warmed to that idea. Given his newfound theory about his writing skills, he thought it best to let others write songs for him. Killing an album worth of people could be tricky, as well as wrong. What if they wanted a double album?

The conversation had continued with promises of playing at Carnegie Hall, the Hollywood Bowl, national tours, world tours. Jimmy had soaked in all this, never questioning for a moment that it could be a lie. He needed to believe there was a light at the end of the tunnel which wasn't a train coming the other way!

All the time they had talked, they kept Jimmy supplied with endless drinks, so much so that he never saw Vinny slip the mickey into his last G&T. It only took a few minutes to work; soon Jimmy became very sleepy.

Vinny and Carmine feigned mild concern as they helped Jimmy out of the casino, assuring several customers that he was 'fine' and that 'he'd just celebrated a bit too much'. They helped Jimmy celebrate all the way outside into the car park, and then bundled him onto the back seats of the twin cab.

Carmine got behind the wheel. 'Zip tie his hands and feet, Vinny, we don't want him making a run for it when he comes round.'

Vinny smiled and for the first time that evening, Jimmy, through eyes that could barely focus, saw Vinny clearly. There was evil in his smile. It was also in that moment he realised why Carmine had been so familiar when he'd first seen him. Suddenly, there was a sickening hollow in the pit of his stomach. Jack Lantern! He was Jack Lantern's general. Jimmy was awake now.

As the pickup rapidly pulled out of the casino car park, Jimmy asked, 'What's going on, boys? You don't have to kidnap me. I'm happy to sign any contract the label wants.' He tried to be funny, but he knew there was no contract waiting for him in LA.

Vinny got right in his face. 'The only contract we have is on you, Jimmy boy, and I gotta say this is gonna be an absolute pleasure.' His face was twisted in a way that can only be described as a snarl meeting a grin. It was very unattractive – as was Vinny.

Jimmy knew he was in for a beating, so he tried to mitigate it as best he could. 'Look, fellas, I'm guessing you work for Jack—' Before he could finish the sentence, Vinny's fist pounded into his solar plexus, folding Jimmy forwards like a deflating balloon.

It took a long time before Jimmy could get the air back into his lungs and when he did, Vinny was still in his face.

'That's Mr Lantern to you.'

Jimmy nodded as he tried to breathe through the pain in his stomach. 'S-s-sorry. I didn't mean no disrespect, but—' Jimmy stopped talking as Vinny held a finger up to his lips and shook his head.

Carmine looked at him in the rear-view mirror. 'You're gonna have a chance to speak to Mr Lantern in a moment, Jimmy, Soon as we get to the old quarry.'

Jimmy shook his head. 'The old quarry, What is this, an episode of *Scooby Doo*? I mean, come on, guys.'

Vinny put his hand firmly over Jimmy's mouth and whispered, 'Shut the fuck up. Carmine is trying to tell you something.'

Carmine turned off the road, and they were headed down an unmade gravel track. He looked at Jimmy in the rear-view mirror. 'This is the road to the old quarry. Apparently it's been disused for years, but tonight we intend to put it to good use. For the last Jimmy Wayne show.' Both he and Vinny burst into laughter.

Now Jimmy was terrified. This wasn't a beating – it was an execution. He flexed against the zip ties at his wrists and feet, but Vinny had done a good job.

As he sat there trying to figure out something that could save him, the pickup came to the edge of the old quarry. The old office building was still there at the bottom of the hill, which wasn't really a hill. They were on the edge of the quarry, which over the years had been dug down over a hundred feet and was probably half a mile across. Jimmy had been there once, many years ago, but it spooked him. The buildings were virtually as they were the day the quarry closed back in the 1950s. Now they just looked more derelict; gravity and nature were taking hold. The whole place was crumbling, held up only by the roots and branches of bushes and trees that were growing through the roofs and windows.

They slowly descended into the bottom of the manmade bowl. Carmine turned off the engine and turned around to face Jimmy. 'Now, before we conclude the evening's entertainment, Mr Lantern would like to say a few words.' He pulled out his phone, punched Jack's number and pressed. Nothing. 'Aw shit! No signal,' he snapped. He turned the key in the ignition.

Vinny looked confused – a look he often wore. 'Where you going, Carmine?'

'Back up the hill, you idiot. I need a signal.'

Vinny looked at the quarry buildings and then through the back window at the steep slope they were quickly reversing up. Realisation dawned. 'Oh, I get it.'

Jimmy, despite his terror, felt ashamed that he was going to be killed by someone so stupid.

They reached the top of the slope, and Carmine glanced at his phone. OK! We're good to go.' He keyed the phone and within seconds it was ringing. Then, as if by magic, Jimmy was looking at Jack Lantern. Jack did not look happy; when he spoke, his words confirmed his look.

'Jimmy Wayne, you sorry-assed piece of shit, where's my money?'

It wasn't really a question, but Jimmy tried to answer it anyway. 'Funny you should say that, Jack. Just so happens I have it back at the casino. In fact, I could pay you some interest.'

Jack exploded. 'INTEREST! Who do you think you're talking to, you little cocksucker? I tried to help you, Jimmy, gave you extra time to pay, but you just kept fobbing me off.' Jack was almost frothing at the mouth. 'Who the fuck do you think you're dealing with here?'

Jimmy tried to calm things. 'I'm sorry, Mr Lantern, I really—'

He never got the chance to finish the sentence. Jack had nodded, and Vinny had taken his cue and smacked Jimmy ferociously across the face. As Jack leaned forward into his camera, Carmine held it right up in front of Jimmy's face.

'Vinny and Carmine are gonna make me a little film because I wanna hear you sing one more time. Vinny's got some nice little bolt cutters, and he's gonna prune your fingers. One by one—' he paused a moment for dramatic effect '—after he's broken both your legs. We don't want you running off and missing all the fun now, do we?'

'But—' Jimmy tried to speak. Again, Vinny's huge hand delivered a stunning slap to his face. His ears rang and his face burned.

Jack shook his head. 'Now now, you should know better than to interrupt when I'm talking. You must let me explain the finale of this evening's entertainment. Two broken legs, ten chopped off fingers and then you get buried alive!' It didn't help that Jack sang Jimmy's death sentence to the tune of 'The Twelve Days of Christmas'.

Jimmy tried to sound cool, but his voice shook with terror. 'OK, Jack, you got me scared. Double the interest, I'm good for it.'

Jack slowly shook his head and when he spoke, it was with total malice. 'No, Jimmy, all you're good for is a warning video. You're gonna howl in agony when Vinny breaks your legs. You're gonna plead for death as Vinny snips your fingers off. And you'll scream like a baby as they bury you alive. This film will be a great deterrent to anyone who thinks they can get away with not paying Jack Lantern. Finally, you're gonna be a star, but in my public health and safety video.' He looked hard down the lens at Jimmy. 'Goodbye, Jimmy.'

Jimmy screamed back at Jack. 'Please, Jack. Please don't do this!' But his pleas fell on deaf ears as Carmine had already pushed the red button and ended the call.

Carmine slowly put the phone back in his pocket, and then looked Jimmy directly in the eye. 'Well now, Jimmy, you heard what Mr Lantern said.'

Jimmy shook his head. 'Please, fellas. If this is just to scare me, you've succeeded! I'm begging you, don't do this!' Jimmy was pleading for his life and he hated himself for it. He wanted to be the brave and stoic tough guy that he tried to portray both on and off stage, but he just couldn't do it. He was shaking with terror.

Carmine shook his head sadly. 'Sorry, you heard Mr Lantern. I can't even kill you quick because we gotta video it.'

Jimmy tried to get out of his zip ties but they were too tight. He was panicking now. Zito had climbed out and gone into the back of the pickup. Jimmy could hear him rummaging around, and then he appeared at the door with a big smile on his face holding bolt cutters and a hammer.

'Showtime, Jimmy Wayne.' Vinny Zito loved seeing the fear in his victim's eyes when they knew they were going to die. Working for Jack, he'd had several opportunities. Killing Jimmy real slow would make him happy for weeks.

It wasn't the same for Carmine – to him this was just a job, and the odd murder was in his job description. He never did the killing, though. He left that to Vinny. Vinny was a psycho, disturbed at the very least, and Carmine knew he would savour every broken bone and every clipped finger. If he let him, Vinny would take an hour torturing Jimmy, but he wasn't going to let him because he would have to spend the night editing the video down.

'Ten minutes from start to finish, Vinny. You got that?'

Vinny looked annoyed. 'Ten minutes? It's gonna take me longer than that. Say a couple of minutes for the legs. When I breaks the first one, he's gonna scream and squirm around, so you're gonna have to hold him down while I cracks the other one.' Carmine was watching Vinny working it out like a builder doing an estimate. 'Then there's the fingers. Sure, they clip off easy once you got the bolt cutters on them, but I gotta trap his hand under my foot and keep it there, and once the blood starts to flow it'll get real slippery under foot.'

Jimmy tried to say something, but the sheer horror of what was about to happen had just robbed him of his voice. All he had left was a murmur. 'Please, guys … please no–.' His voice trailed off and he started to sob.

Carmine had an idea. 'We got an axe in the back. Why don't you just chop off his hands. Two blows, job done!' Carmine looked pleased with himself. He felt like an engineer who had just found a quicker way to build a car, but Vinny was shaking his head in disagreement.

'We can't be doing that. One, he's gonna bleed out too quick and we won't get the screams when we bury him alive, and two,' he paused for dramatic effect. 'Jack was very clear about how he wanted it done.'

Carmine nodded. 'Yeah, suppose you're right. There is a third reason, though, ain't there, Vinny.'

It wasn't a question; Vinny looked confused.

Carmine continued, 'You're a sick bastard, Vinny, and you wanna take your time butchering old Jimmy here, don't you?'

A slow smile spread across Vinny's Stone Age features. 'You know, Carmine, I do! Look at this idiot. Black shiny suit and a black leather tie. What kind of a look is that? I'm gonna really enjoy making this ol' boy sing for his last supper!' He burst out laughing at his own joke, and then looked back at Jimmy. 'You make yourself real comfortable, Jimmy boy, while me and Carmine walk down the hill and dig you a grave. We won't be long; it's only gonna be shallow!'

Jimmy sat frozen in terror as he watched the two killers walk down the hill to the bottom of the quarry. They were about 140 yards away and although it was dark, Jimmy could see what they were doing. It was a full moon. In the silvery light, Jimmy could clearly see the shovels going back and forth as they dug his grave. His thoughts were spinning at a hundred miles an hour. Through his terrified haze, he tried to figure a way out.

There was no way out. Everything he'd done in his sorry excuse for a life had brought him to this moment.

He should never have borrowed money from Jack, and he really shouldn't have thought that he could fob off someone like Jack Lantern with promises. Jack had given him a chance, and he thought it was a sign that Jack liked him; maybe he did, but business is business, and he hadn't kept to the terms of their agreement. Jimmy had never been good at small print and despite the fact there was no written contract between them, failure to pay was always going to be painful. Jack was never going to let that happen, because if word got around it would make him look weak.

Jimmy started to cry. He had overplayed his hand again, but this time it was going to cost him his life – painfully and slowly.

'Jimmy, Jimmy! I leave you for a few days and look at the mess you've got yourself into.'

He looked up startled, and there beside him was Wendy. He felt a wave of relief wash through him; maybe there was a chance. 'How'd you know I was here?' he asked.

She shook her head. 'We aint got time for any chit-chat. Those boys are fast diggers.' Wendy looked around the cab and suddenly a smile crept across her face. She leaned down and grabbed something from the floor. 'These will do,' she said, holding up the bolt cutters triumphantly. Jimmy flinched at the sight of them. Wendy laughed. 'Relax, Jimmy, I'm just gonna set you free.'

It only took a couple of moments to snip through the zip ties. Jimmy rubbed his wrists and ankles trying to get the blood flowing back through them. He nodded at the dash. 'They left the keys. Let's get out of here.'

Wendy put her hand on his shoulder as he reached forward and pulled himself into the driver's seat. 'We can't run. You gotta kill them.' Her voice was calm and she looked deep into his eyes. 'These guys aint gonna stop until you're dead, and running away in their pickup is *really* gonna piss them off. The only chance you have is to kill them now.'

Jimmy pondered on what she'd said. Wendy was right – he couldn't run forever. Maybe if he could buy some time, he could do a deal with Jack. Jack wouldn't want word to get out that his enforcers had been taken out by Jimmy. 'Look at them. How am I gonna kill them?'

Wendy thought for a moment. 'Well, you're not gonna win a fight, are you? You're about one-eighty pounds and none of it's muscle. Those boys are about four-hundred-and-eighty between them and most of it's muscle.' She paused for a moment with a mischievous smile across her face. 'This truck, however, weighs about three tons.' She let her suggestion hang there for a moment, but Jimmy didn't fully understand. 'We can't fire up the engine because that will alert them and they have guns, so why don't you just let the handbrake off and prove old Newton's law about gravity.'

Jimmy looked confused. 'Wayne Newton?'

Wendy sighed deeply; Jimmy really hadn't been to college. 'Just let the handbrake off and by the time we get to where they are, we should be doing about fifty miles per hour. Nice silent approach – they won't even know what hit them.'

And they didn't. After Jimmy released the handbrake, the pickup swiftly gathered pace. As Carmine and Vinny dug Jimmy's grave, the pickup ploughed into them unseen and unheard in the moonlit desert night.

Wendy glanced at the speedo as the thugs flew through the air. Forty-eight miles per hour! *Close enough*, she thought.

'Wow!' exclaimed Jimmy as he watched the bodies fly high into the moonlit night sky. The impact was huge, but he hadn't expected the two hitmen to be flung so far into the air. He'd expected them to be splattered across the bonnet like raspberry jam. 'Look at them go!' he shouted with excitement.

Wendy turned to him as he brought the truck to a halt. 'Excellent example of Newton's third law.' She paused and waited for the inevitable question.

Jimmy turned to her, confusion across his features. 'Not Wayne Newton, then?'

Wendy reached out and took his hand. When she spoke, it was with love in her voice. 'Oh, Jimmy, you have so much to learn about … everything! The Newton in question was Sir Isaac Newton.'

'The one with the apple?' Jimmy interrupted.

Wendy nodded. 'That's the one. He discovered gravity, but he also had a third law, which stated that for every action there is an equal and opposite reaction.'

Jimmy seemed confused again. 'What does that actually mean?'

Wendy considered it for a moment. 'Well, I guess, if you put it in layman's terms, if you hit two thugs with a three-ton truck at forty-eight miles an hour, they're gonna fly a long fucking way!'

For the first time in his life, Jimmy understood something about physics.

It had taken Jimmy nearly forty minutes to find all the bits of the late Carmine Mallotides and Vinny Zito. It had come as something of a shock to him what a three-ton truck at nearly fifty miles an hour could do to a human body – two human bodies. He'd expected to find them a bit battered, but Vinny – when he finally found him, halfway up one of the few trees in the vicinity, was not the man he had been. He had a right leg but no left one. His ugly Neanderthal head was also conspicuous by its absence. Jimmy felt the nausea rise in his throat but fought it back. He realised he would have to drag Vinny by the arms despite having to look at the gaping wound where his head had been. After bending down and grabbing Vinny's arm by the wrist, he looked for the other arm but that too seemed to be absent without leave.

Wendy wandered over and looked down at Vinny. 'Those bull bars certainly did a number on him – that and the fact he was standing in a shallow grave. You tore him up pretty good.'

Jimmy looked at her in the pale moonlight. 'If I didn't know better, I would say you're enjoying this. Look what we did to these guys. We tore them limb from limb.'

Wendy shook her head. 'No, you tore them limb from limb. I'm dead, remember.'

Jimmy seemed indignant. 'Hold on a second, it was your idea to run them down. I just wanted to run.'

With a withering look, Wendy silenced him. She then spoke quietly and calmly. 'Jimmy, darlin', if I hadn't turned up, you would be lying in that grave with dirt in your lungs, broken legs and stumps for hands. Having to clear up a few body parts is a small price to pay. Besides, you have to look at the upside, Vinny and Carmine were big fellas. Now they're–' Wendy was searching for the right word. 'Dismantled, somewhat, they're gonna be easier to handle ... bit like Ikea.'

Jimmy looked at her with a mix of horror and astonishment. 'Did I ever mention you are one sick, crazy woman?'

Wendy smiled as if it were a compliment. 'You sure did, and you were right. Now, come on, we need to get a move on. We've got to find all the bits and get them up to the song cemetery. We can't afford for their bodies to be found; people saw you leaving with them.'

Jimmy hated the idea of having to get the bodies up that hill to the 'cemetery', but Wendy was right. Several people had seen them carry him out of the casino, and questions would be asked. 'Can't you help me lift them into the pickup?'

Wendy shook her head. 'Sorry, Jimmy, I tried to pick up one of Carmine's legs a minute ago, it's behind that old shed, by the way, but it seems dead people can't physically touch each other. Must be something to do with—'

'Isaac Newton,' Jimmy interrupted, somewhat sarcastically.

Wendy didn't rise to the bait. 'No, that one is probably Wayne Newton.' With that, she wandered off looking for parts; she didn't want Jimmy seeing the wide grin she couldn't suppress. Wendy hadn't tried to lift Carmine's leg. She was going to leave all the heavy lifting to Jimmy – he really did need the exercise!

It was nearly four in the morning when Jimmy had finished burying Carmine's and Vinny's battered bodies. The sun was just starting to come up and he was exhausted. It had been a horrible job, but better them than him. This now made three bodies that he'd buried here in the last two weeks; it was a habit he needed to break.

As he smoothed down the ground with his foot, Wendy appeared at his shoulder. She had been missing from the time he'd started digging, after first making sure the hitmen were planted well away from her grave.

'You get all of them?' she asked.

Jimmy wiped his brow; it was thick with sweat, blood and dirt. 'Yeah, I got them all. I may not have got them in the right order, but I got two heads, four arms, four legs and two torsos.'

Wendy winced. 'Messy. You reckon you got the right arms with the right heads?'

Jimmy shrugged; he was exhausted. 'I don't know and I don't care. There's the right number of bits in both graves, and that's gonna have to do. The archaeologists can sort it out in a couple of hundred years.'

'Hope you're right, Jimmy. They ain't gonna be happy having each other's limbs. Imagine if they come after you.'

Jimmy smiled. 'They won't catch me. Vinny had longer legs than Carmine. If I've mixed them up, those boys will be going round in circles for the rest of time!'

Wendy went up to Jimmy and hugged him. 'Don't worry, they won't be coming back. You only see those you want to see and those that want to see you after they pass.' She kissed him.

'Is that a fact?' he asked.

She shook her head. 'No, it's just a feeling, but I'm pretty sure I'm right.' She paused for a moment in thought. 'OK, Jimmy, we can drive the pickup back to the mine. There are some old caves up there. We can park it inside and set fire to it with all their identification inside.'

Jimmy pulled away from her. 'That's a three-mile walk back to the casino from there. I'm driving back.'

Wendy was annoyed and shouted, 'Jimmy! Sometimes you're so stupid I can't believe I allowed myself to get killed

by you! Frankly, it's embarrassing. I was a straight-A student.'
Jimmy went to speak, but she held up her hand. 'Do the math,
Jimmy. Two hitmen disappear from the casino with Jimmy
Wayne. Jimmy Wayne drives back to the casino in their pickup
– alone. Jimmy Wayne has their blood, hair, skin, maybe even
a tooth, in his clothes.' Wendy let that sink into Jimmy's
confused brain for a few moments and then continued, 'They
have to disappear completely, no traces. Lucky for you they'd
booked out of their hotel, so no bills to pay, no rooms to
empty. Do this right now and you're free and clear.' She was
right. She was always right, but Jimmy still wasn't happy.

'Goddammit, Wendy – I'm wearing cowboy boots. I can't
walk three miles in these,' he pleaded.

Wendy shrugged her shoulders and smiled angelically. 'You
know, Jimmy, you'd be amazed what you can do when you're
trying to avoid death row!'

CHAPTER 5

WELL, NOW YOU KNOW

Jimmy had finally got back to his room at 5 a.m. He had been accompanied on the long walk back by Wendy, who insisted on floating alongside him. His boots were killing him, and every step made him wince with a throbbing that told him a blister was forming.

For a person, albeit a dead person, who had just helped to commit a double murder, Wendy seemed very cheerful as she wafted along humming something. She was so far off-key that Jimmy couldn't work out what the song was, and he really didn't want to ask in case it encouraged her to sing more. Her singing seemed to make time slow down; perhaps time was a music lover.

As he walked, the image of Vinny's face kept coming to him in flashback. Just before he had mowed them down, Vinny must have sensed the pickup bearing down on them – he had turned a split second before the impact. It was almost comical. For a moment he was trying to work out how the pickup had got there, Jimmy saw the confusion in his eyes, and then *wham*! The pickup hit the two heavies full on, they both smashed onto the bonnet and then flew backwards through the night sky as if they had jumped onto a trampoline from fifty feet. The shovels went flying and stuff seemed to be going everywhere. It was only when he got out and looked for the bodies of his would-be killers that he realised some of the aforementioned 'stuff' was arms and legs which had been torn off by the impact and the shredding effect of the bull bars.

This had been no accident like Wendy; he had mowed them down. He wanted them dead. Now he was a killer. He knew it was self-defence, but any judge would say that he had the opportunity to flee the scene but chose to kill instead. First-degree murder. There were extenuating circumstances, like the fact that they were going to torture him and then bury him alive.

A good lawyer could maybe get it down to second degree and twenty years if he was lucky, but Jack Lantern would find him in prison. He had connections and killers on the payroll everywhere. No, Jimmy knew he was now officially a killer, so he had to think like one and cover his tracks. This was a whole new ball game and a new life where all the old rules just didn't apply.

As Jimmy unlocked his door, Wendy tapped him on the shoulder. He turned and she planted a kiss on his cheek. 'Get a shower and then try and get some sleep. You got twelve hours before you need to be up for your first show.' She turned to go, but Jimmy held her arm.

'You not coming in?' he asked. He wanted to talk; there were so many things going on in his mind.

Wendy shook her head. 'Nah. I got places to go and things to see.' She saw the disappointment in his eyes. 'Don't worry, Jimmy, I'll be back when you wake up.' She kissed him again on the cheek.

He held her close. 'How'd you know?' His voice was a whisper. Wendy looked confused. 'How did you know I was in trouble? How'd you know where I was? If you hadn't turned up, I'd be dead – horribly and slowly dead.'

Wendy pulled away from him gently but firmly. 'Well, you're not, are you!' She paused for a moment, almost as if she was trying to figure it out for herself. 'I dunno, Jimmy. It's just like a phone call – it just went off. I could see you in the car with those murdering bastards, and I just knew where you were. Only way I could describe it is Facebook Messenger meets Google Street View for ghosts and poltergeists.'

Jimmy just stood there as Wendy smiled and melted away through the wall. *This is fucked up*, he thought. *So very fucked up!* He went in and shut the door, but he never made the shower, he didn't even take off his boots. He just fell on the bed and was in a deep and dreamless sleep within seconds.

———◆———

When Jimmy awoke, his mouth tasted as though something had crawled inside there and died, and there was a nasty smell. He rolled onto his back and as he did so, he realised the aroma was him. He was still in the stage clothes he'd been kidnapped in. Was it only last night? It seemed like a lifetime ago.

There was blood on his shirt, jacket, and on closer inspection his trousers and … yeah, on his snakeskin boots, too. He had several black suits and ties, that was his look, so he didn't need to get them washed now. He knew he couldn't send them to be laundered like this – too many questions. He decided to just start his shower with everything on, wash the stains of last night away.

As he stood in the warm shower, he watched the dirt and sweat running off his clothes and down the drain. It mingled with Vinny's and Carmine's blood. He grabbed the soap and rubbed hard at the stains. Slowly they lifted and were gone. If only he could do that with his memory. There never was going to be enough soap to make him forget what he had done or unsee what he had seen.

While undoing his shirt, something fell onto the floor of the shower. He thought it was a button, but when he bent down to pick it up he saw that it was a tooth, a human tooth – unless it was one of Vinny's. He wasn't sure Vinny could be counted as human.

He picked it up and turned it around in his hand as he tried to imagine the force it had taken to send teeth, legs, heads and arms flying so far. That Newton's third law was a tough one. He made a mental note to get Wendy to explain it to him, but not today.

Jimmy left the clothes to drip-dry in the shower and was towelling himself down when he remembered the tooth. *Jeez*, he thought, *get rid of it. Gotta think like a killer – cover my tracks or I'm gonna get caught*. He picked it up off the soap dish and threw it down the toilet and flushed. 'Job done!'

As he walked into the bedroom, he glanced at the bedside table and there, just where the first song had been, were two pieces of paper. Both had songs written on them and both were in his handwriting. He just stood there looking at them from the bathroom door. *It can't be*, he thought, *it just can't be …*

Slowly, he moved around the bed and looked down without picking them up. He was afraid to touch. He could read the song titles at the top of each sheet. 'Safe'. *Nice title for a song*, he thought – and true … for now. He still had to try and find a way to get Jack off his back. He then looked at the other one, and it made his blood run cold, but it also made him smile. 'To Your Scattered Bodies Go'. *Someone's been watching*, he thought. For a moment, paranoia hit him. Had somebody seen? Was this a prelude to blackmail? It passed very quickly; the handwriting was his.

He sat down on the bed and read the songs. They were good, very good. Two songs. He had killed Vinny and Carmine last night, and now here the next morning were two new songs … two! No more theories, no more doubt, he knew.

CHAPTER 6

THE FEMALE OF THE SPECIES IS MORE DEADLY THAN THE MALE

Jimmy had worked on both songs for a couple of hours. He had managed to arrange them for his solo performances and the Friday and Saturday nights when he had a band to support him. It had been so easy; he just knew how to put those words to music. The time signatures and bridges were obvious to him. It was almost as if he had an innate understanding of how these songs wanted to be sung.

This was a new feeling for him. Although he could sing and play, he had always struggled with arrangement and song writing, but now – with these songs – it just came naturally. He couldn't wait to play them to the band tomorrow. He would play them solo first so they could hear them, but then he would get them to practise on Saturday morning so they could give the full band a go at them in the evening shows. The guys were just as bored of going through the motions every night as he was; they were all decent players. This was going to be fun.

It was about 4 p.m. when Jimmy got to the restaurant for what was theoretically his breakfast. Jimmy quite often slept late and ate his breakfast after most normal people have their lunch. He found it made the long days more bearable. He reckoned that most of the folks buried in the little cemetery at the back of the golf club had died of boredom – they'd just stopped living because there was nothing to live for. Death had been a blessed release.

Blackjack was a place where people ended up when everything else had failed. David was the one real exception, and maybe now Jimmy. Jimmy knew he was being unfair. Blackjack was built around the casino. It had no history and the only class it possessed was distinctly third rate, but the people were nice and the scenery was lovely – it's just that there was a lot of it. To someone who had spent so much time in LA and Vegas, Blackjack was just too damn quiet.

Jimmy sat down at his usual table. The restaurant was always quiet at this time of day. The breakfast people had come and gone and so had the lunchtime crowd. The floors and tables were now busy as the customers poured their hard-earned cash into the bottomless pit of Mammon.

Occasionally he would hear the clatter of a pay-out, but for the most part the drone of the machines digesting people's dreams clattered and tinkled in the background all day. Jimmy never gambled. He hated gambling. His father was a gambler, and he had seen where that led – nowhere. Bills that couldn't be paid, food that couldn't be bought, houses and apartments they had to run from before they were evicted. His childhood had been a mess until his mother had inherited her father's house. Finally, something his father couldn't gamble away.

Jimmy was immune to all the temptations the casino had to offer, apart from the drink and the sex, to which he was a committed participant of both.

Before Wendy, he had worked his way through dancers, waitresses and even a couple of croupiers, but he'd realised that this was not good for his everyday health. He had to work with these girls and dumping them on a weekly basis was giving him a pool of resentment that he had to swim through every day.

After an unfortunate incident in the steam room, he'd decided to mend his ways – not really mend them – it was more a case of changing strategy. For Jimmy it was a masterstroke. Every week there was a new intake of customers, so all he had to do was run what he called the 'Beauty Pageant' on a Sunday for the full-weekers or on a Friday for weekenders. He would check out the ones he fancied, find out who he thought 'would' and delete those who he thought 'wouldn't'. If he struck out on the shortlist, he could always go back to the long list.

This had worked very well. Short, sharp encounters, meaningless but nonetheless enjoyable sex, and then on to the next. He didn't upset the girls he worked with so he could move on with impunity.

David would often join him for the review, but his was only a voyeur's interest. He had learned the hard way that pleasuring female visitors could have serious consequences, especially when you were the boss.

The waitress arrived with his breakfast. There was no need to order as Jimmy always had the same breakfast every day: scrambled eggs, bacon and toast. Fruit and fibre were kept at arm's length in case they made him feel like going to take some exercise.

'Morning, Jimmy.' She placed the large plate in front of him. 'You look like shit. You been up all night up to no good again?'

Jimmy looked up at her. 'Morning, Valerie. You know what they say, a gentleman never comments.'

She smiled. 'But you ain't no gentleman, Jimmy, so spill the beans.'

Jimmy nodded; Valerie was right. 'If you must know, and I know you must, I got drunk with a couple of fans, and then we decided to go down to the Lazy for a bit of fun.' The Lazy was a whorehouse about five miles out of town. Everyone knew about it, and a lot of the male population of Blackjack had been known to frequent its less than salubrious environs.

Valerie didn't seem surprised by Jimmy's confession. 'So, what happened, they beat you up or something?' She was looking at the red mark on his cheekbone where Vinny had back-handed him in the back of the pickup.

Jimmy shrugged. 'Nothing so glamorous I'm afraid. I got car sick–' He paused for a second because Valerie was giving him that 'Who are you trying to kid?' look. 'OK, you got me. I was real drunk and I was about to ruin the leather on his back seat. He slammed on his brakes and the other guy just pushed me outta the door. I hit my head on the window on the way out, hence the graze. Then while I was heaving my guts up, the bastards just drove off and left me. Five-mile walk home.' Jimmy was pleased that he managed to sound so indignant. He was also pleased with the cover story he had just made up. No witnesses to dispute his story. If he'd said they dumped him at the Lazy the police could have checked that.

'Oh, Jimmy, you're a nice guy, but you really need to sort your life out. I thought you and Wendy were gonna be an item, so how'd you manage to trash that?'

He looked up at Valerie, his appetite suddenly gone. 'What makes you think I trashed it? Wendy just disappeared. She probably decided to get out of Blackjack for a bit – you know Wendy, she's a free spirit, she'll be back.' That was the story Jimmy had been sticking to since Wendy had disappeared, but now Valerie was suggesting she knew something. He leaned towards her. 'What you heard?'

She looked unsure about telling him; Jimmy feared the worse. There was a sad look crossing her features when she spoke. 'Sorry, you obviously aint heard yet. David got a letter from her yesterday. She's gone, Jimmy. Apparently, she had a fling with one of the guests – a wealthy one by the sound of it. She's done a runner. She married him in Vegas and they've moved to Florida.' Valerie placed her hand on Jimmy's shoulder, 'Sorry you had to hear it from me. I know you were keen on her.'

Jimmy sat there trying his best to look sad and shocked. Inside, he felt like bursting with laughter. *Wendy Walmart, you clever, clever girl*, he thought. *You even took the time to write a letter and give me a cover story.* Man, he loved that girl. He could sense that Valerie was waiting for some kind of response, so he decided to go for a slightly bitter one – in keeping with his character.

He sighed. 'Well, it's good to know she landed on her back – sorry, feet,' he corrected himself. 'Guess that'll teach me to get emotionally attached, won't it?'

Valerie nodded sympathetically and tried to comfort him the only way she knew how. 'I'll get you a couple of extra sausages.' He smiled. That girl knew the way to a man's heart!

While Jimmy was savouring his after-breakfast third coffee, David Parker came into the restaurant. Jimmy watched him;

he seemed to glide across the floor as though he were on castors. Elegant was the only word that Jimmy could think of to describe it.

As David reached the table, he nodded over to Valerie. Like Jimmy, he had a regular order, but unlike Jimmy, his involved some of his five-a-day requirement.

He sat down. 'Morning, James,' he said cheerfully.

Jimmy ignored the greeting. 'How'd you do that?'

'How do I do what?' David asked, frowning.

Jimmy gestured back along the route David had just taken to the table. 'Glide across the floor like a freaking ghost? It's like you're on rails.'

David smiled. 'Oh, that. Years of ballroom dancing and sneaking around in bedrooms that weren't mine, old chap.' He leaned forward and tapped his nose, 'I'm sure you follow my drift.'

Jimmy did, he had done the same himself, not the ballroom dancing, but sneaking around married ladies' bedrooms. He had done lots of that but never as elegantly as David, of that he was sure.

Before Jimmy could quiz him further, David's tea arrived in a nice little china teapot with a china mug bearing a picture of William Shakespeare. He poured the milk into the cup – always milk first. David was a real stickler about that. Let the tea stand for a couple of minutes to brew and then he would pour. It was a ritual that Jimmy had become familiar with over the last few years, but he still didn't understand it.

'What is it with you British and tea? It's just a drink, but you lot turn it into a religious experience,' he said, slowly shaking his head.

David looked disapprovingly at Jimmy. 'Well, James, if your fellow countrymen had not acted so impetuously in Boston a couple of hundred years ago, you would have been able to answer that question for yourself now, wouldn't you? Everything sort of went downhill for you after that, did it not?'

'You are such a pompous twat, David. Did anyone ever tell you that?' Jimmy leaned back and smiled.

David pretended to think for a moment before replying, 'I do seem to recall that you did, on several occasions.'

'Just me?' probed Jimmy.

Again, David pretended to think about the question. 'That's a hard one to answer. Most of the time I'm doing it, your fellow countrymen are too impressed by my dulcet English tones to notice me being pompous. Honestly, sometimes it feels like I'm speaking in tongues.' He winked at Jimmy and took a long sip of his tea. Afterwards, he exhaled with a deep, satisfied sigh. 'A touch of sanity in a crazy world. You really should try some proper tea, I'm sure it would do you good. That black sludge you're drinking will give you high blood pressure and bad dreams.'

Jimmy thought for a moment. He wasn't sure about the high blood pressure, but he did have bad dreams – that wasn't related to coffee, though.

David's breakfast arrived. Porridge, as he called it, with banana, apple, sultanas and walnuts mixed in, and some natural yogurt blobbed on the top.

'What the fuck is that?' asked Jimmy in mock disgust.

David loaded his spoon and took a mouthful. Once he had savoured and digested it, he looked at Jimmy triumphantly.

'That, my dear James, is life.' He glanced at the remnants on Jimmy's plate. 'Unlike that suicide pact you indulge in every morning. I swear if you left your body to medical research, they would contest the will!'

Jimmy shrugged. 'Don't matter, I'm gonna be cremated.'

David glanced at Jimmy's plate. 'Just like your bacon, then.'

Jimmy couldn't help but smile. David was one funny son of a bitch, but he was so dry with it you really had to pay attention or you wouldn't know he was sending you up.

'I hear you got into a spot of bother last night, old son. Someone give you a backhander?' David nodded to the red swelling by Jimmy's right eye.

The way he had just slipped the question into the conversation took Jimmy aback for a moment. Like the actor he was becoming, he quickly switched into character. 'Nah, just a drinking outing that got out of hand. Boys will play pranks.'

David nodded. 'You want to elaborate?'

He didn't. 'You want to eat your porridge!' Jimmy said with disdain. 'And keep your nose out of my drunken escapades with fans.'

'Fans? They must have been drunk!' David feigned surprise, and then took Jimmy's advice and concentrated on his breakfast. Being a man of some refinement, he took his time. After a sip of tea, he looked at Jimmy. He looked sad when he spoke. 'You heard about Sammy?'

Jimmy's heart sank. Sammy was one of his favourite people in the world. She had started at the casino when it first opened in the sixties. She was a dancer then, young and beautiful, and the Riviera was only going to be a stepping-stone on her way to

Hollywood. She acted as well and could sing. If not Hollywood, Broadway would do.

But the stepping-stone had turned into a millstone. The call never came and time had moved on. In her thirties, she was nearing the end of her dancing days, but being smart she trained as a croupier and did well. She was good and the punters loved her. She still went for auditions and applied to join theatre companies, but she never got the call back she so desired. She'd had chances to marry and settle down, but she didn't want a serious relationship because that would get in the way of her career.

When David arrived, he realised what a smart cookie Samantha was and promoted her to floor manager. It was only then, well into her late sixties, that she realised she was never going to be the star she'd wanted to be. She had put all her chips on the wrong number and now the wheel had stopped spinning.

When Jimmy arrived, she made friends with him straight away. As an entertainer she felt an affinity with Jimmy, and he with her. She would tell him stories about Vegas in the early sixties where she had first tried to get on the showbiz ladder before coming to Blackjack to climb the ladder, but the ladder had no rungs and she was left, stuck at first base. Jimmy would tell her about his early days and his first minor hit that had got him some attention and a tip for the top from several influential people. But like Samantha, after the first short bloom of promise, his star had gradually faded and he, too, had ended up at the Riviera. It could have been worse, but it wasn't what either of them had dreamed.

Jimmy sat back; this question worried him. 'What about Sammy? Is she OK?'

David sighed and slowly shook his head. 'Not really. I don't think she will be coming back to the Riviera. I spoke to her doctor.' He paused for a moment, knowing that what he was about to say would devastate Jimmy. 'Sorry, old son, it's stage four pancreatic. Nothing they can do. Just a matter of weeks.'

Jimmy just sat there. First Wendy, now Sammy. It felt like the bottom was falling out of his world. Why did everyone he loved die?

David said nothing; he just waited for Jimmy to gather himself.

'Is she in pain?' he asked.

David slowly shook his head. 'Thankfully no. Dr Donald has got her pain under control. He's going to monitor Sammy's medication carefully and make sure she doesn't suffer. He promised me.'

Jimmy didn't know what to say. They both just sat there thinking about a lady who was so full of life, so overflowing with fun, that it seemed impossible her flame was now just a flicker which would soon be extinguished. Sammy wasn't bitter about her plans never having worked out; she wasn't upset about not getting married and having kids. She had chased her dream but never quite caught it. She had given it her all, and that was all she could have done, so that was good enough for her.

Jimmy looked up at David with tears in his eyes. 'I love that lady. She's special.'

David leaned across the table and put his hand on Jimmy's shoulder. 'We all love her. She's the big sister we all need. Why don't you go and see her after your first set? I can push your second set back an hour. Get the girls to climb those poles a bit longer; they could do with the exercise. And, no offence, I don't think the punters will complain about an extra hour with our ladies depriving them of your singing, apart from that new song.' David paused and looked at Jimmy as if trying to work something out. 'Where the hell did that come from? I really like it, so did everyone else apparently. I reckon you have a hit or something very close there. Now, if you could write some more like that you could be dangerous.'

Jimmy wiped the tears from his eyes and smiled. 'Funny you should mention that, but I have.'

David looked pleasantly surprised. 'You have?'

Jimmy held up his fingers in a Winston Churchill salute, which he knew David would understand. 'Two to be precise.'

David looked impressed. 'Wow, and are they as good as the other one?'

'Better,' said Jimmy without hesitation.

'You have been a busy boy, James.'

Jimmy smiled. 'Busier than you'll ever know, David!'

By 6 p.m. Jimmy was all set up. He had arranged the song 'Safe', using his Telecaster and playing slide. He had set up some reverb and an echo on the mic. He had recorded a couple of loops to play behind the lead and set some drum loops. He had run through it a couple of times, and it sounded almost ethereal. It sounded like the song was haunted. It was just the effect he had hoped for, and he knew it would turn heads. He had rearranged 'Vacant Stare' in the same way to give them a kind of spooky similarity. He was developing a sound and it was different. He headed off to Sammy's house.

———◆———

At 9 p.m. Jimmy stood on the stage. *The girls look tired*, he thought. Good old David had kept them working for that extra hour. He could swear Diana's arms looked longer. He already had a bit of an audience. Word had got around that he was pretty good, and the confidence that 'Vacant Stare' had given him was now spreading through the covers he sang. He was starting to make them his own. Confidence is like a virus: once you have it, it spreads like a wildfire. You find a power and the timing to go with it, which he had forgotten all those years back.

As he gazed at the forty odd people looking at him, he knew he would soon have them in the palm of his hand. He started with just his acoustic plugged into his old Fender amp. The first two songs were covers but number three was 'Vacant Stare'.

He set some reverb up on the mic and then spoke to the sixty-plus people who were now listening to him in the Desert Bar. 'Thanks for all coming in to listen tonight. Unlike the rest of this place, I won't be taking any money off you guys. And please don't try and shove a dollar in my mouth. If you do, you better pray you don't win because if I pay out, you won't like where it comes from.'

There was laughter around the stage as the punters worked out his gag. As his confidence grew, he was starting to develop a patter between songs and pull people into the world he was creating. His father had called it 'stage craft'. Jimmy never had any time for it until recently. He always thought people would be bowled over in the first minute of his songs by the brilliant lyrics and tune, but time had taught him that he needed more. People needed to like you first and then they would give you a chance and listen to what you had to say – really listen.

His father didn't have much to say most of the time, but he really knew how to work a room. Perhaps that's why he hadn't done it but now, as his confidence grew, he wanted to form that bond, reach out to the audience, and make it a shared experience. Now he was singing his own songs, sharing his true feelings and telling his story. Not all of it – obviously. Just enough to make it real and keep him from being arrested. The days of going through the motions were long gone.

'You'll notice that tonight I have no band.' Jimmy looked either side of him and behind to make the point. 'I only get those guys on a Friday and Saturday night, usually after the manager has paid their bail.' He paused again for the laughter, and it came. He looked into the audience and saw David; he was laughing, too, but he was also looking around the room at the effect Jimmy was having on the punters.

More people had drifted in from the slots floor; there was now an audience of over a hundred people. Something had changed in Jimmy, and he liked it.

Jimmy continued, 'Until the boys are released, I took the trouble to record some backing tracks because I have some more new songs that I've just written, and I wanted you to hear them as nature intended ... electrified.'

A muted chuckling rippled around the room. It was a clever joke and a large percentage of the clientele were never going to get it, but over half did, and David laughed the loudest. Jimmy smiled. All that time spent talking to David was paying off.

He held up what looked like a CD. 'This is a DAT, and it has the bass, drums and keyboards that I recorded earlier. Yes, folks, I can play all those instruments, but I can't play them all at once. That's why we have to bail out the boys on the weekends.' Again, laughter broke out. Jimmy put the DAT into his amp. 'This one is called "Safe".'

He depressed the button on his pedal board to actuate the DAT, the drums and bass came slowly flowing from the speakers, and then Jimmy started to play his guitar. He played slide, and the sounds he was creating shimmered and soared in a ghostly dance with the backing rhythms creating a haunting and atmospheric sound that left everyone in the room totally absorbed in what he was playing. They were listening to every word of his song.

There was echo and reverb on his voice and as he sang the opening line, he listened to it. 'Safe … is just a state of mind'. Finally, he had found his voice, the one he'd been looking for all these years. It was just a pity that he had to kill three people to find it. He was comforted by the fact that Wendy was an accident, whereas Carmine and Vinny, they just had it coming.

At the end of his set, there must have been a hundred-and-fifty fans jammed into the room; and that's what they were now, fans. Jimmy couldn't get off the stage. Everyone wanted to shake his hand, even more asked him if he had a CD they could buy. When he told them no, they wanted to know who he was signed to. Jimmy was taken aback by the intensity of the reaction he was receiving. It felt strange to have another taste of stardom after so many years without a morsel. He liked it.

When he finally got clear some twenty minutes later, he saw David at the bar. He pointed towards the gin and tonics waiting. *Great*, he thought, *I feel like celebrating tonight.* He picked up his glass.

'Cheers, old man,' said David, clinking glasses before taking a long gulp. He put his glass down on the counter. 'Well, James, you are causing me a problem.'

Jimmy didn't know what to make of this comment. All he expected was a drink and a slap on the back for a job well done. He was an entertainer, and he had entertained.

'I don't understand. I went down an absolute bomb. You should be giving me a pay rise.'

David held up his hands. 'No criticism intended. Quite the opposite in fact. If you're going to sing and play like that, then this room just isn't big enough for you. I may have to move you to the Canyon!'

Jimmy put down his drink; for a moment, he was speechless. The Canyon Room was the concert hall for the Riviera. It wasn't a large room in Vegas, but it did hold three-hundred people seated. There was no bar or pole dancers. People would go there just to listen to him instead of his set being a distraction while customers did other things. He wasn't sure if David was winding him up.

'You serious? You only ever open that for conferences.' They also opened it for once famous comedians on their way down from TV careers but who could still pull in a decent crowd and command $2,000 a show plus room and board.

David nodded. 'I most certainly am serious. You've changed, you've raised your game, singing and playing, but those new songs– ' he trailed off as though looking for the right words. 'Those new songs, they are amazing. Moving. I don't know where you found them, but see if you can find some more because they are total hits. If you put a record out with those on, it would chart easy. Top twenty *Billboard*, no problem!'

Jimmy had never heard David talk like this before. Normally it was the caustic asides: '*Hey, James, if that song was rushed to hospital, it would be marked "Do Not Resuscitate".*' That was one of his kinder jokes – not anymore. David was animated, enthusiastic.

'We need to put a video together and get it out on the website. People need to hear what you are doing. You're– ' David frowned and scratched his head. 'I can't believe I'm actually saying this – an attraction. People may even decide to come to our casino because of you.'

Jimmy nodded. 'Do ya think?' he asked, but he already knew the answer.

'Oh, James, I think you are on the way back up that slippery pole called success.'

The second gin and tonic went down very nicely, and then David brought Jimmy's high back down to earth, as if it had been a balloon shot out of the sky.

'How was Sammy?' It was such a simple, innocent question, but by asking it David had taken all the joy from the evening.

Jimmy didn't really know how to answer him.

———◆———

Before the show, he had walked down the high street and into a quiet dead-end road filled with low-rise single-storey private houses. It was a nice little street. All the gardens were well tended and lawns were green thanks to the sprinklers that were kept going by the abundant waters of Clearwater Lake which sat in a small valley in the mountains to the west of Blackjack. Without Clearwater Lake, the town would not have existed; rainfall was limited to twelve days a year in this part of Nevada. This was where Sammy's dreams had come to retire. It was comfortable with lovely views of the mountains and, more importantly, it was paid for. Sammy had been careful with her money, knowing that one day she may need it because buying a place in Hollywood wouldn't be cheap.

Jimmy walked up the neat little path, which was lined with some beautiful flowering plants that Jimmy couldn't name. He wasn't strong on gardening, although he had done a lot of digging lately. Sadly, nothing he'd ever planted grew. He knocked on the door and waited.

From inside came a familiar voice. 'OK, OK, I'm coming. Just take a seat and I'll be there as quick as I can.'

That made him smile; there was no seat to take. Feeling mischievous, he decided to give the doorbell a long, unreasonable ring. It elicited the response he had hoped for.

'Goddamn motherfucker! Hold your horses! Make a sandwich or something till I get there.' That made him laugh.

Then the door swung open and there was Sammy. Smaller, thinner, clearly unwell, but she still had that sparkle in her eyes.

She beamed at Jimmy. 'Motherfucker! Aint you a sight for sore eyes. Get in here, you useless piece of shit.' She opened her arms, and Jimmy stepped into them. He wasn't offended by his welcome. Sammy, despite being one of the loveliest humans that ever walked the earth also had a mouth that could even make a sewer wince. That was one of the reasons he loved her. Even now, older and sick, it was clear she had been a beautiful woman. She still was, but not in a sexual way. No, now she had matured like a fine wine. She was elegant and thoughtful – but she still talked like a trucker.

As he hugged her, Jimmy could feel her ribs.

Sammy sensed this and leaned back from him. 'Goddamn, Jimmy. I aint a freaking steak.' She looked up at him. 'I'm OK for now, don't fret. Now come and sit down and we can have a coffee.'

He followed her down the hall and into the lounge. The French windows were open, and the view of the mountains filled them like a landscape painting. He stood there for a moment and just stared. He had been in here many times before, but that view still took his breath away.

'Reason I bought the place. Aint too shabby, is it?' Sammy looked up at him with a glint in her eye. 'You want me to leave it to you – I could.'

Jimmy knew she meant it. Sammy had no children or close family. Her friends were from the casino; those who had worked with her still kept in touch. She was that rarest of people who seemed to touch everyone she encountered. Love exuded from her, but it was edged with a shrewd mind and a wicked sense of humour.

'Don't answer that. I don't want you rooting around in my underwear drawer after I'm gone.'

He pulled a face and shrugged. 'Aww, Sammy, was a time you would've let me.'

Sammy nodded. 'True, but I wasn't wearing any then!' They both laughed and as she did, Sammy winced with pain.

Jimmy didn't comment; he knew she didn't want him making a fuss.

'Coffee?' Sammy enquired, as if nothing had happened.

'Please, Sammy– ' He hesitated for a moment, and then just plunged right in. 'How are you? David's been telling me about–'

Sammy held up her hand. 'OK, hold on right there. I thought David would tell you something, so just to make sure you got all the facts, here they are.' She passed him his coffee. 'Now drink that and shut up.' Jimmy did as he was told. Sammy took a sip of hers and then sat back in her chair. 'I got cancer, it's gonna kill me and it's gonna take about four months max. That's the downside.' She paused for a second awaiting a denial or interruption, but Jimmy knew better. 'On a more positive note, I'm already pretty old, so it's no big tragedy, and I don't have any pain. So, all in all, Jimmy, I can't complain.'

He nodded. 'Is it OK if I complain? I'm not ready to let you go.'

'Bless you, Jimmy,' Sammy replied with a smile, 'but we don't have a say in this and from what David's been telling me, you ain't gonna be around here much longer either.'

Jimmy pretended to be surprised. 'Did he tell you that he was gonna fire me?'

'No, he told me that you're killing it every night.'

Jimmy winced at the unfortunate but highly accurate assessment of his recent success. 'Well, it has been going really well.' He thought for moment wondering how best to put it. 'I just seem to have got my mojo back. I feel confident on stage and I can make people engage. It's been so long since I was able to do that.'

Sammy had been listening and watching him closely as he spoke. She nodded slowly. 'I can see it. You're different. I noticed it as soon as I opened the door. You're giving off that vibe. You're a star in the waiting, Jimmy.' Sammy seemed genuinely excited for him. 'Always thought you had it, but you'd just stopped believing. Me, I always thought I had it, but I didn't, and I never stopped believing.' Sammy thought for a moment. 'I dunno which one's worse.' She took another sip of coffee while she considered this. 'I suppose it's having it but not believing because then you're throwing something away. If you don't have it in the first place, you're not betraying a talent – you're just guilty of over-optimism.'

'You're probably right, but I wish I had what you have. Everyone loves you because you're a beautiful person,' Jimmy smiled.

She sighed. 'That's great, but sometimes it's just not enough. Now I'm old, I can see that everything worked out well for me. I've had a good life and it's been great, but it's just not the one I dreamed of. I didn't have that in me. You, Jimmy–' she put down her coffee and leaned towards him, there was a fierce conviction in her eyes. 'You have it. I knew it the first time I saw you. There's just something in your voice but up till now, you didn't believe. I don't know what you've done but keep doing it.'

Jimmy smiled weakly. *If you knew what I'd done*, he thought, *you wouldn't want me to keep doing it.* He leaned forward and placed his hand gently on hers. 'Thanks, Sammy, I'll try, but it's not that easy.'

Sammy let out a dismissive cuss. 'Jesus, Jimmy, course it is. It's not like you had to kill anybody.'

Jimmy sat there. There wasn't much he could say to that unless he wanted to make Sammy complicit in his crimes. He nodded slowly. 'I promise, this time I won't quit.'

They talked for another hour. When he was with Sammy, time just evaporated. She had so many wonderful stories of the old days.

Vegas when Sinatra and the Rat Pack were just getting started. He could listen to her all night; he had on many occasions.

As he smiled on the outside, he was crying on the inside. He couldn't bear the thought that this lovely lady would soon be gone from his life. He loved the time they spent together. He sometimes wondered if Sammy had become a surrogate mother, filling the role that his mum would have filled if she had lived. Somehow, he could never picture it. His poor mother was too damaged by the life she had endured with his father. Sammy hadn't quite achieved her dreams, but his mother hadn't even achieved happiness. She had hung on too long hoping his father would change. Then when realisation finally dawned that it was never going to happen, it was too late. She had rowed too far out on the sea of love and now, when the storm was raging, there was no way back to the harbour.

Even as Jimmy thought this, the words lit up like a neon sign: 'rowed out on the sea of love'. That could be a song lyric. He made a mental note to write it down as soon as he got back to the casino. Maybe he didn't have to kill anyone for the next song. He looked at his watch. Where had the time gone? He needed to be going, so he stood up.

'Well, this has been lovely, but I gotta get back for my set.'

Sammy smiled. 'No problem, but where's the joke?'

Jimmy checked his watch – he had time. It had become a tradition that every time he visited, he told her a joke before he left. He loved to make her laugh.

He sat back down. 'OK then, are you sitting comfortably?'

Sammy flicked him the finger. 'Fucker! You know I am! Now get on with it!'

'So, there's this country and western singer, and everything seems to have gone wrong for him, so he goes to see a psychiatrist. The psychiatrist listens to all his woes for about ten minutes and then says, "Mr Hoosier, I think you should learn to sing all your songs backwards." The singer looks at him like he's mad. "Just try it. Your wife will come back to you, your dog won't die and you'll get back your job on the railroad!"'

Sammy started chuckling. 'That's a good one. Did I ever tell you about the cowboy I used to go out with?'

Jimmy was shocked. 'You went out with a cowboy? I thought you only went out with showbiz people?'

Sammy shrugged. 'He wasn't a real cowboy. He was a showbiz pretend cowboy – think of a poor man's Roy Rodgers.'

'Do I have to?' He hated Westerns.

'I don't give a fuck! D'ya wanna hear this story or not?'

'Course I do! What was his name?'

Sammy gave him a mischievous look. 'His real name was Randy Bernstein.'

Jimmy looked at her waiting for the punchline, but Sammy just smiled back at him. 'For real?' he asked.

She nodded. 'Obviously he was Jewish; his dad was a stockbroker in New York. Randy came from a very privileged background, but he wanted to act. He was real good-looking, so he came to Hollywood. That's where he got lucky. This producer saw him in a bar and decided he was perfect for the part of Randy Randolph.'

'Oh, I remember him from *Randy Rides Again* when I was a kid,' said Jimmy.

'Well, that was him, Randy Randolph! The paperbacks were written back in the fifties and the studio had purchased the rights to make a TV series. Paul Raymond, the producer, was trying to cast the role when he just happened to see Randy in the bar ... lucky bastard!'

Jimmy was impressed. 'So, you knew Randy Randolph?'

Sammy burst out laughing. 'Knew him? I fucked him! And boy, Randy was the right name for him. Man, if it moved, he was on it!'

'Whatever happened to him? I remember he was pretty popular for a couple of years, and then he just disappeared.'

Sammy slowly shook her head. It's a very sad story, but it's also very funny. Are you sitting comfortably?' He nodded. 'Then I will begin. You may not remember, but in the first series Randy had a bargirl he was keen on; her name was Jenny. She worked at the Silver Dollar.'

Jimmy did remember. 'Yeah, she got run over by a wagon train halfway through the first series.'

Sammy sighed. 'Well, that was me. The fuckers wrote me out!'

Flabbergasted, he looked at Sammy in amazement and could see the similarity despite the passing of fifty-plus years. 'Why did they do that?'

Sammy shot him a sly look. 'I would like to call it artistic differences. Truth is, I was a pretty friendly girl in those days. I was also sleeping with Paul Raymond.'

'Did Randy get jealous?'

'Randy couldn't give two fucks!' Sammy smiled. 'He was nailing everything he could get his hands on and his johnson in. Stardom didn't go to his head; it went straight to his– ' Sammy pointed at an imaginary penis. 'No, it was Paul who got angry. He was married, but there's always been a double standard, especially in Hollywood. That's why the bastard had me run down by the wagon train – not just one wagon you understand, but a whole damn wagon train! Remember, I didn't even get to die in Randy's arms. They wrote me the fuck out without a good death scene.' Sammy sat and sulked.

'I remember. Didn't the wagons run over your head?'

Sammy nodded. 'Every one of the fuckers.'

'Randy came running over to your body, looked down and threw up!'

She shrugged. 'Yep, that Paul sure held a grudge – my nickname was "Flathead" for about a year after that.'

Jimmy tried to look sympathetic, but he was struggling not to laugh. Sammy was smiling, too.

'I got him back, though,' she added.

'How'd you do that?'

'Well, Randy had given me a dose of the clap, and luckily I had managed to pass it on to Raymond. Bet he had fun explaining that to his wife. Like I said, I was a very friendly girl back then, but I digress.'

Jimmy was losing the thread. 'You do?'

'Pay attention, Jimmy, this story is about the downfall of Randy.'

Jimmy took a deep breath. 'Man, I wish I'd known you when you were younger – you should write a book.'

'Aint got time for that now, so listen up if you wanna hear the story.'

'I'm listening!'

'So, Randy was doing well. His accent was a bit off. You don't get many Jewish cowboys from New York, but he looked good and he could ride a horse. That's pretty much all you needed to do back then. Well, after the first two series, Randy was getting hot and they decided to make a film. We shot it in Nevada.'

'I thought you'd been flattened by a wagon train.'

'I had, but I knew everyone, and they got me on as an extra because, apart from Raymond, everyone liked me.'

Jimmy was struggling to keep up. 'So, what happened next?'

'You ever been to Nevada?'

Jimmy looked through the window of Sammy's lounge. 'We're in it now.'

Sammy waved his comment away. 'I don't mean town Nevada; I'm talking about butt-fuck middle of nowhere Nevada with nothing either way for fifty miles. Sand in your crack Nevada.'

Jimmy shook his head. Sammy sure knew how to paint a picture.

'So, we're about six weeks into filming and things ain't going well. Half the cast and crew have had the shits from some dodgy catering and the less than satisfactory sanitation at the camp. Randy was like a caged bull. He had worked his way through all the willing females, and now he's chewing his arm off.'

Jimmy was beginning to fear this story wasn't going to have a happy ending.

'So, we get to this big set-piece scene where the corrupt sheriff–' Sammy winked at Jimmy. 'Sound familiar? – is holed up in jail with Randy's girl as hostage. She has witnessed him kill an innocent man and he was gonna bump her off, but our hero is on to him. Well, Randy was supposed to come charging into town behind a couple of wagons that he's stampeded down the main street to cover his entrance. Raymond shouts action, and Randy had to charge up behind the two wagons with the stunt drivers hidden in the wagons, fire his guns and stampede them down the street. Now Randy, being literally Randy, is chatting up some girls on the catering wagon. He hears Raymond shout action and realises that he should be in position to charge. He panics, runs around the back of the catering wagon and jumps on his horse, which he'd tethered to the back of the wagon, and pulls out his gun. Now, what he should've done was ride past the catering wagon, get behind the two stunt wagons a hundred yards away and then fire!'

Jimmy grimaced. 'He didn't–'

'Fuck, yes he did!' exclaimed Sammy triumphantly. 'That crazy son of a bitch unloaded his guns behind the catering wagon, so those horses took off like someone had stuffed a hot poker up their asses. Luckily, the girls managed to get clear, but boy, I reckon they invented the term "fast food" that day. So, the wagons are careering up behind the two stunt wagons, who are late starting because the two stunt drivers knew it was a false start. There's coffee and cups flying everywhere, cutlery is whistling around like sniper fire and the horses suddenly realise they're about to run into the back of the second stunt wagon. They can't go right because there are buildings, so they swerve hard left, and guess what was on the left?'

Jimmy shook his head. 'You're kidding.'

'No, fucking Paul Raymond, six feet up in his director's chair, megaphone in hand.'

'What happened?'

Sammy was chuckling as she remembered. 'I could see his eyes widen as he realised that the catering wagon was headed straight for him. Then he started shouting, "Cut! Cut! CUT!!"

Sadly, for him, those horses were crap at taking direction.' A big smile spread across Sammy's face. 'He got run over by a wagon – not a wagon train, but a catering wagon is close enough. Killed him stone dead.'

Jimmy was laughing now. 'That's tragic.'

Sammy sighed. 'It was – nobody got lunch that day!'

Once they had both stopped laughing, Jimmy realised that the death of Paul Raymond still didn't explain the sudden demise of Randy's career. 'I know that technically he caused the stampede that led to Raymond getting flattened, but that could be deemed an accident. He was a minor star. What happened?'

Sammy looked sad. 'Well, back in those days, folks weren't so enlightened. The actor playing the sheriff was a good-looking boy but not overly interested in the ladies, and Randy was very randy. He was supposed to storm the jail and shoot up the sheriff. He was caught doing exactly that a few days later in his trailer, by one of the studio bosses on a visit to the shoot. Poor old Randy was dead in Hollywood then – never got another job.'

'Poor guy,' said Jimmy sympathetically.

'Not really. Like I said, his dad was a New York stockbroker, left him about ten million dollars a couple of years later … lucky bastard!'

'Wow, that was some story. Is it true?'

'Every goddamn word.'

Jimmy marvelled at the spirit of Sammy and the way she had lived her life. He had come round to visit her with sorrow in his heart, yet she had lifted his spirits and left him feeling better than he had in weeks.

He stood up, 'I gotta get back for my next set.'

Sammy nodded. 'Get moving and knock 'em dead.'

He leaned forward and kissed her tenderly on the top of her head. 'I already did, Sammy, I already did!'

———◆———

'Well ... how was she?' David's voice brought Jimmy out of his reverie.

'Sorry, I was miles away.' He paused, struggling to find the words to express his feelings. 'It was a shock. I guess I hadn't noticed until you told me, but when she opened that door – man, it was still hard to see, but it was there. She's lost so much weight.'

David nodded sadly. 'She's a brave lady. We need to take care of her; she's family. I have drawn up a rota between you, me, Valerie and a couple of her old croupiers – we have her covered.' David handed him a freshly printed rota. Efficient as ever, he had made sure that Sammy would not be alone in the next few weeks even if she wanted to be. 'We should bring her when you open in the Canyon. She would love that.'

Jimmy felt a little knot of excitement tighten in his stomach. 'You mean it? I'm going into the Canyon?'

David nodded. 'First Friday of next month and do Fridays and Saturdays with the band. Eight o'clock and ten o'clock shows, one hour each. I have a videographer coming in on Saturday to film the set. That will give you and the band three shows on Friday – or, as I like to call it, tomorrow, to get the boys up to speed with the new songs.'

Jimmy was slightly shocked at how fast things were moving. David certainly didn't hang around. He had organised all this in less than a day.

'We can cut the video down to about ninety seconds, use samples from your three new songs and a couple of the strongest covers, and we can get Steve to voice it.' Steve was the casino maintenance man, but he had a voice like warm chocolate being melted and then poured over you as you sat in a giant chocolate fountain. Everybody always joked about Steve's voice, but David had recognised it for what it was straight away and utilised it to the casino's benefit. All the recorded messages on the hotel telephones were Steve's. When you got in the lift, Steve was telling you to 'mind the door'. Never had a closing door been so sexy and relaxing.

Jimmy grinned; he was impressed. 'You move fast, David, I gotta give you that, but don't you have to run this by somebody first?' He was finding it hard to accept that doors were suddenly being thrown open for him. Opportunity was once again knocking on his door, and all he had to do was open it.

David seemed slightly insulted by the question. 'You seem to be forgetting that I'm a partner here and I always make a good profit. As long as I make good profits, I pretty much have *carte blanche*.'

Jimmy didn't understand that last bit. 'Who's Blanche?' he asked.

'Oh, James, James, James.' David let out a long sigh. 'You never did go to college, did you?'

'Why does everyone always say that?' he asked, slightly indignant but without anger. 'I know it's Blanche from that *Streetcar Named Desire* by that Andy Williams, but what has she gotta do with this?'

David took a long sidelong look at Jimmy. *Can he really be that stupid? He is from Pennsylvania.* As he stared, he saw a small twitch at the side of Jimmy's mouth as he tried to suppress a laugh. Jimmy was winding him up. 'Touché, James. I deserved that.'

'Don't go speaking that Spanish stuff.'

'OK, I surrender, you got me. I'm a pompous ass, and you're a borderline genius,' David replied, holding up his hands.

Jimmy was happy to accept the somewhat fake apology. 'In answer to your question, no I didn't go to college, but I'm not stupid. I appreciate your faith in me, buddy, and I won't let you down.' He raised his glass and David raised his.

'I'll drink to that. Look out world, Jimmy Wayne is coming.'

I'll drink to that, thought Jimmy.

After David had departed to do his sweep of the gaming floors, which he did on a regular basis every night, Jimmy went back to the stage to pick up his guitar microphone and other bits and pieces that he didn't want to leave around the stage. Nothing had ever been taken because virtually all the people who saw him were residents in the casino hotel and not there for stolen guitars. They were too busy chasing a dream they would never catch. As he packed away his guitar, he was aware of somebody standing close behind him. He turned to see who it was.

'Hello, Jimmy.' The voice came from a lady who he recognised.

'Hello, Lena, long time no see.' Jimmy stood up and moved into the open arms of one of his biggest fans. Lena was in her late forties and she was a good-looking woman who had kept herself in shape. And judging by the two bowling balls pressing into his chest, she'd also had a little bit of help from a third party.

She gently pulled back from him. 'Let me look at you, Jimmy Wayne.' Her eyes devoured him as if he were a fillet steak, and

Lena was certainly no vegetarian. 'My, my, Jimmy, I swear you get better with age. You look good enough to eat.'

Jimmy looked pointedly at his slightly rotund waistline. 'You better have a big appetite.' He meant it as a joke, but Lena took it as though it was an order from a waiter.

'Oh, I do, Jimmy darling, I'm absolutely starving.'

He just stood there feeling slightly uncomfortable as Lena continued to gaze at him, her tongue playing across her lips like a snake trying to find the scent of its victim. Jimmy had been hunted down by Lena before; she was a true fan but also a bit of a groupie. The boys in his old band had christened her 'Lena Over', but somehow Jimmy had always avoided this oldest of clichés. 'Never get involved with your fan base,' his old manager had told him. 'You're bound to fall out one day, and when you do that's one less person who's gonna buy your record or come to your gigs ... and Jimmy, you need every one you can get.'

Jimmy smiled at Lena and took the opportunity to gaze upon the opulence of her curves. *Maybe tonight*, he thought. *A reward for all my hard work.* As that thought crossed his mind, an image of Wendy in the corner of the bedroom watching, commentating on his performance with Lena made him glance behind him. Wendy wasn't there. He looked back at Lena, whose vulpine eyes could not conceal her intent. She was a fox, and he was trapped in her henhouse.

'Fancy a drink?' he asked.

Lena smiled, and he heard the lock on the henhouse door click shut.

The next hour passed as Jimmy had imagined it would. He and Lena had gone to the bar and flirted over drinks.

'Jimmy,' she looked at him wistfully, 'what happened to you? Twenty years ago you were on the verge, and then – ' she trailed off, searching for the right words.

'Nothing,' Jimmy prompted. 'Nothing happened, Lena. I got it into my head that I was already a star and just stopped putting the hard work in. I didn't write any decent songs, and then just gently slid downhill until I reached here.' He looked pointedly around him. 'This place kept me from hitting rock bottom, but now – '

Lena finished his sentence for him. 'Now, Jimmy, you are on the way back up. I caught your set tonight, and you were amazing. Those new songs ... wow! So dark but so moving; I never expected that from you. Where the hell did that come from?'

Jimmy shrugged, embarrassed by the praise that Lena was heaping on him. 'I guess I just dug a little deeper.' *Six feet deep*, he thought. 'And when you go that bit deeper, you find the meanings that maybe you'd missed before. I think I always could do that, but I just couldn't get it on the page.'

Lena leaned into him, and he felt her hands grasp his bum. She pulled him into her. 'Never mind about getting words on a page, Jimmy Wayne, I want to get you onto my bed.'

For a moment, Jimmy thought about Wendy, but Wendy was dead. He had never been the faithful relationship kind of a guy, and it was kind of tricky to be unfaithful to a dead girlfriend. There just wasn't the same associated guilt attached. The only thing that gave him even a vague pang of guilt was the fact that technically, and in his mind it was a technicality, he had actually contributed to Wendy's death by hanging her. A warm hand around his genitals brought him swiftly back to the matter in hand. Lena's hand to be precise.

'Your room or mine?' He smiled. As Lena licked her lips, again he thought of a snake.

'Mine, darling. I have the key, so you can't escape,' she purred.

Jimmy wasn't sure he wanted to escape, and Lena sure as hell wasn't going to let him.

CHAPTER 7
AN OFFER YOU CAN'T REFUSE

The last two weeks had flown by. He and Lena had been an item for exactly two nights and one morning, and what a morning that had been. Jimmy smiled at the memory. *That Lena*, he thought, *didn't take any prisoners, but boy it was a good fight!* Lena had departed, back home to a husband probably, but that didn't concern Jimmy. She had promised to come back when Jimmy opened in the Canyon, and now it was about to happen.

Jimmy felt a nervous tingle in the pit of his stomach. He was excited; he felt like he was on the verge of something. The band had loved his songs and arrangements, and they had been really tight the last few nights they'd played together. Today they would be rehearsing on stage in the Canyon. They were like kids who had just joined their first band, but being seasoned old pros they tried to maintain a laidback demeanour.

Joe, the drummer, had even dyed his thinning grey hair a lovely chestnut brown. Sadly, he had not thought to do the same to his bushy grey eyebrows and porn star moustache. Given his slightly rotund figure, he now had the look of an ageing bull seal whose hair had been caught up in a trawler's net. The boys all tried to keep a straight face and nobody mentioned it at rehearsal, until the second number.

'Hey, Joe,' called Lewis from behind the keys. The moment he spoke, the guys in the band swung straight into the Hendrix song – Joe didn't join in. This shit had been going on for several years, and he did his best to ignore it. Lewis pressed on. 'Your hair is looking … interesting.' He paused to allow for the round of sniggering that was breaking out on the stage before pressing on. 'How is it that the hair on your head refuses to join the hair on your eyebrows and moustache in a colour-coordinated melange of loveliness?' It was a fair question and Lewis, with his slow Texan drawl, had teased it out to perfection.

Joe was not a raconteur, obviously, he was a drummer. He hit things for a living and sometimes he even did it at the right tempo. He thought for a moment before his witty reply came thundering out from behind his drum kit. 'Go fuck yourself, Lewis.'

Lewis nodded in acknowledgement of the rapier wit Joe had displayed. 'Why thank you, Joe. There was a time when I was supple enough, but then I was young and I didn't need to tend my own pasture so to speak.' He stopped as if fondly remembering those days of musical stardom with the Texas Trucking Company, aka TTC. It wasn't a great name but they were one hell of a band, and for ten years they had played all over the world to great acclaim. After a few moments, he looked up with a smile. 'Now I'm not supple enough, I find that most days I just don't want to, so things have worked out pretty well for me, unlike your hair.' Lewis delivered the punchline straight to the heart and everybody, including Joe, laughed.

He held up his hands. 'OK, you got me. Now, can we play some music?'

Lewis looked at him mystified. 'You're a drummer, Joe ... ' and once more everyone was laughing. Joe was laughing himself; Lewis was so dry.

The band had started to really get into the songs that Jimmy was writing; there was a bond growing that hadn't been there when they were just turning up and running through the covers. They all sensed that something was happening and they were fired up with an enthusiasm for the music they thought they had lost. Once more, it was a joy to play and it showed. They bounced off each other in rehearsals and were totally focused for the gig.

Jimmy looked fondly at this motley crew assembled around him. They could all play and, more importantly, they were available. He decided there and then that if this career thing developed, he would try to keep this group together whatever happened. He knew them, he trusted them and they had no agenda. They had been playing with him all the years he had been at the Riviera, apart from Kid, and they had never once criticised him or caused him a moment's trouble. They turned up, they played and they went home.

Lewis was the true star. He had been to the show, played the big stages and his band had sold a lot of records. He had done OK, no mansion in Bel Air, but he had a nice house on the golf course and it was paid for. He loved his golf and he loved to come and play with Jimmy two nights a week.

Joe was a different matter. He was from St Louis and reared on hard rock, but he could play anything pretty well. Solid and reliable, he lived on the edge of town with his wife, who was a realtor. You would never have put them together if you hadn't met them. He looked like an old rock drummer, scruffy jeans and T-shirt, with long uncombed hair and a moustache that looked like a gang of orangutans had used it as an adventure playground. His wife on the other hand looked like one of the Stepford wives, artificially beautiful!

The real wild card was his guitarist. Jimmy could play guitar but when it came to lead, he just couldn't do that and sing at the same time. It was OK with the acoustic, but he never had worked out how to deliver lead and vocal together – his brain just couldn't separate the two. He had realised this early on in his career, which had saved him a lot of mumbling as he struggled to remember lyrics and concentrate on chords. Good guitarists who would play out here in a small town like Blackjack were hard to find.

One day Lewis had told him that he knew this guy who could really play but he had paused for a moment, Jimmy wondered how big this 'but' was going to be, before he added, 'he aint your everyday person, but he's a good person and boy can he play.'

Jimmy was intrigued. 'So, what's different about him? He got two heads or something?'

Lewis thought about this for a moment before replying, 'Well, not physically, but he does seem to be on two planets at the same time ... most of the time.'

Jimmy knew what that meant. 'No, Lewis, I don't want any stoners in the band.'

Lewis shook his head. 'No, no, Jimmy, he's not a stoner. It's worse than that.' Lewis paused as if trying to work out how he was going to explain the guitarist's problem. 'He thinks about things.' He let the shock hit Jimmy; a guitarist who thinks was a new one. 'And,' Lewis continued, 'he reads books! Not just any books but philosophy and history. I even caught him with some Shakespeare once.' Lewis looked at Jimmy almost apologetically. 'He really can play, though.'

Jimmy knew that if Lewis was recommending someone, they had to be good. He wanted to meet this renaissance guitarist – a thinking, reading guitarist. *First time for everything*, he thought. 'What's his name?'

Lewis scribbled a name and number down on a page of his notebook, tore it out and handed it over.

Jimmy read it out loud, 'Kid Oscarson. What kind of a name is that?'

'He's from Chicago.' Lewis shrugged. 'One of them Scandinavian places I think, not sure which but they're all pretty much the same. Why don't you ask him?'

He did about a week later when Kid had rolled into town. Jimmy remembered the surprise when this giant of a man walked into the bar to meet him. He was six-foot-five with long shaggy blond hair and a dress sense that came straight from the sixties. Denim jeans and a tie-dye T-shirt topped with an Afghan jacket. Given Lewis's description of this philosophy-and Shakespeare-reading thinker, he was expecting a small jazz type, not someone who looked like they could grab an axe and pillage a whole town single-handedly.

When he spoke, his voice was deep and sonorous but also warm. 'Jimmy Wayne, I presume.'

Jimmy shook his outstretched hand. 'Then you must be Kid.' Jimmy knew he was going to like this guy straight away;

there was just something about him. He looked at Kid's hands, huge hands that were engulfing his. 'Man, you got fingers like a bunch of bananas. How the hell do you play the guitar?'

Kid scrunched his face as if considering the question. 'Carefully, and with feeling, but mostly carefully.' Jimmy laughed, and Kid was in the band.

Kid had turned out to be a real asset and a far better guitarist than Jimmy's lacklustre covers had required him to be. Looking back over the last couple of years he was surprised that Kid had hung around, but he seemed happy to make a few dollars and play with Jimmy two nights a week and do two or three shows a week elsewhere in a couple of bars in town. Now that Jimmy had something worthy of his talent, he watched as Kid grew into the songs and wove haunting melodies around his words.

They had stopped for a coffee and Jimmy sat down next to Kid who, as usual, was reading a book. 'What you reading?' he asked.

Kid leaned back. '*The Dice Man*.'

Jimmy nodded. 'What's it about?'

Kid put the book down and settled back in his chair. He took a sip of coffee while he considered how best to describe the book. 'I suppose you could say it's about a man who decides to live his life by chance – on the roll of a dice, literally.'

'He's a gambler?'

Kid thought for a moment about Jimmy's question. 'Depends how you define gambler. He's not a gambler in the sense you would consider one of the punters here. He gambles on the big decisions of his life. He struggles with choice, so he lets the dice decide. Say, on a very simple level, you couldn't decide between a tea or a coffee, he would say odd numbers mean tea and even mean coffee.'

'Sounds pretty boring.' Jimmy shrugged.

Kid shook his head. 'Quite the opposite. This guy takes it to another level and starts to incorporate darker and more sinister things. Like, roll a five, rape the woman in the apartment upstairs. Roll a six, rob a bank.'

'Wow, that took a dark turn from choice of beverages.' Jimmy was surprised.

Kid agreed. 'That's for sure, but is he really evil? He's just putting down a list of choices and letting the dice decide. He chooses the choices so he has to have some culpability in the outcome, but basically, it's down to fate. A roll of the dice decides.' He looked at Jimmy. 'You must've had moments in your life when something happened and the way you've reacted has had a dramatic effect. Like Frost says, you come to that old fork in the road and you choose the one less travelled or play it safe.'

Jimmy thought about Wendy, Carmine and Vinny. 'Nah. Can't say I have,' he lied.

'Somehow I doubt that.' Kid took another sip of coffee.

The rehearsal had gone well. Jimmy tapped his mic stand. 'OK, gents, that was good and you guys are sounding great. Big night tomorrow – it's gonna be a full house. David has pulled out all the stops, and that video has got us booked out this weekend and next weekend on both nights. If it goes well, we could start doing Thursdays as well. Now, my name is on the poster, but I gotta say that we've turned into a real band in the last few weeks. You guys stuck with me when I didn't give a shit and now that I've got something going, you really have stepped up your game, so I think we should have a band name. Jimmy Wayne and the – any suggestions?'

'Has-beens,' suggested Lewis.

Jimmy smiled. 'Actually, I quite like that.' He looked at Joe behind the drums. 'What d'ya think?'

Joe looked confused. 'Well, I was thinking something like Jimmy Wayne and the Devil's Seed.' Everyone just looked at him and said nothing. 'Too rock?' he ventured.

'Well,' said Lewis wistfully, 'if the Devil has seed as old as me, he sure as hell aint having no babies!' They all laughed.

As the laughter subsided, Kid spoke up. 'Jimmy Wayne and The Second Chance. Think that sorta sums it up for all of us.'

Everyone nodded and Jimmy pointed at Kid. 'That I like. All agreed?' Jimmy looked around at all three who were nodding. 'OK then, Jimmy Wayne and The Second Chance it is!' He thought for a moment. 'Technically it's probably about my forty-second chance, but who's counting.'

———◆———

Later that evening, Jimmy was in his room getting ready for the show. He kept looking over his shoulder half-expecting Wendy to show up. This was a big night for him and she was the catalyst for it happening, so he felt sure that she was going to be around. David had organised some press, and the video voiced by the velvet tones of Steve, the handyman, had certainly got some hits online. Everything was falling into place and he knew that his moment was finally about to arrive. If only he could just stop thinking about the elephant in the room – namely, how was he ever going to write more songs?

He'd established that he only wrote a great song when he was involved, no, he was being semantic, when he had *caused* a death. He wasn't a killer. Well, yes, he was, but only inadvertently; he couldn't go out and kill someone in cold blood. It just wasn't in his nature. So, how the hell, if this went well and things progressed, was he going to get more new songs? Songwriters!

Yes, he needed a top-flight songwriter to write songs just for him. The three songs he had written would give him enough credibility and success to attract a good songwriter to write for him. He knew he could put over other people's songs now, but would they be the same style as his songs? These new ones seemed to have a haunted quality that he liked; they gave him an aura which would separate him from other artists.

All these thoughts were flying around inside his head as he pulled on his jacket. He checked in the mirror. He wore a black suit made from a shimmering cloth that sparkled in a subdued manner as the stage lights hit it. There were blood-red buttons on the front and on the cuffs, and the button-holes were stitched around the edges with the same blood-red cotton. His shirt was white, again with the same buttons and stitching. His tie was jet black with what looked like drops of blood falling from a heart. It was quite dramatic, and he thought it suited the dark and brooding image he was looking to project. He was ready.

As he walked through the casino towards the Canyon Room, he was aware of people looking at him and saying hello. He smiled and answered, but his thoughts were entirely focused on the night ahead. He was in the zone.

He had a quick look into the hall half an hour before the start of the show, and it was already half full. This was happening. He was then startled by a tap on his shoulder. It was David.

'Shit, man, you made me jump.'

David seemed pleased. 'Never mind your nerves, James, come with me to the green room. I have something to show you.'

He charged off down the corridor with Jimmy following, not realising they even had a green room. It turned out that's where the band got changed.

David swung open the door. 'Ta da!' he exclaimed as he held out his arm in the direction of the band, and there they all were in black suits and white shirts. Surprisingly, they looked smart, nothing like a Goth at a wedding. 'Thought I would treat the boys to new stage clothes so you guys at least look good.'

Jimmy smiled. 'Cheeky fucker.' He grabbed hold of David and gave him a big hug. 'Thanks, mate, you didn't have to do that, but I really appreciate it.'

Lewis spoke up. 'Yeah, thanks, David. At my age, a new black suit is gonna be really handy for all the funerals I have to go to.'

David held up his index finger and shook it. 'Don't think so, Lewis, these stay on the premises – that is if you want us to get them dry-cleaned every week. Take them home, you pay for it yourself.'

Lewis acknowledged David's instruction. 'Seems fair.'

'Right then, boys, break a leg and I'll see you after the show.' With that, David gave them his most winning smile and disappeared.

'What does he mean by break a leg? Is that a threat or something?' Joe seemed confused, but as he was a drummer nobody bothered to explain.

The show went like a dream. As the boys walked on stage, a full house cheered and they felt like stars in their own little universe. It had been a long time since Jimmy had felt like that, and he was grateful for the second chance.

'Good evening, everybody. My name's Jimmy Wayne and this is my band, The Second Chance.' Then they launched into the first song.

Everything had gone down well and he had spread his three songs through the set finishing with 'Scattered Bodies', which had most of the fans up on their feet.

The second show went just as well, and the house was packed again. It was so different to playing in the Desert Bar where you were competing with dancers, drinkers and gamblers. People got really involved, and the boys all headed to the bar on a high. They didn't have to buy any drinks as David had taken care of that.

Lewis gave Jimmy a little hug. 'This reminds me of the good old days with the TTC. You got something going on here.' He squeezed Jimmy's arm hard and looked him in the eye. 'Let's not fuck it up.' He'd played with Jimmy for nearly eight years now and had seen him at his worst.

'No worries. This time I got it.'

———————◆———————

Jimmy barely had chance to stop signing copies of the A4 poster which David had had the foresight of getting printed of Jimmy in his stage clothes with the legend 'Jimmy Wayne & The Second Chance, Live from The Canyon'. The artwork was really good. David had priced them at $5 each, and a third of the audience had bought them.

'You finished signing posters?' he asked.

Jimmy nodded. 'Just! Fancy a drink?'

David smiled. 'Of course, but there is someone I would like you to meet first.' He waved for him to follow as he set off across the room.

Jimmy turned to the band. 'Just gotta schmooze one of David's clients. Be back in a minute.' But he wasn't. He didn't come back at all that night.

When he arrived at the table, David was already seated next to a guy Jimmy didn't recognise. He was a similar age, maybe a couple of years older, but you could see that he had kept himself in shape. Wearing an expensive shirt and jeans and an oh-so casual jacket that was clearly Italian and very expensive, Jimmy could have bought his whole wardrobe for what it cost.

He stood up and offered his hand to Jimmy. 'Michael Owens,' he said in a posh English accent that could have been David's. 'Very pleased to meet you, Mr Wayne.'

Mr Wayne, thought Jimmy, *last time somebody called me that was the judge at my drink-drive charge.* Jimmy shook his hand. 'Pleased to meet you, too, Mr Owens.'

Owens smiled. 'Call me Michael, please.'

Jimmy sat down. 'How can I help you?'

David and Michael exchanged a glance. Michael took a sip of his drink. 'Well, Jimmy, it's more a case of how I can help you.'

Jimmy looked at him. 'Really?'

'Yes, really. Perhaps I should give you a bit of background.'

Jimmy decided not to interrupt; he just sat back and waited. Judging by the broad grin on David's face, he was going to like whatever it was that this Rob Lowe lookalike was going to say.

'I'm from LA.'

Boom, thought Jimmy, *Rob Lowe lookalike indeed.*

Michael continued unaware of the internal dialogue in Jimmy's brain that was competing for his attention. 'I own Small Print Records.' That got Jimmy's attention. 'As you know, we're a pretty big label in the blues, rock, Americana market.' The guy was underselling himself. Small Print had a stable of twenty of the top artists in those genres in the USA and shifted an awful lot of product, probably in the top ten labels in the States and still on the way up. 'David and I go back a long way. In fact, we went to university at Cambridge together, and then both came to the States after our finals and basically never went home.'

Jimmy nodded. Now he was really listening. This guy owned a big label, he was a lifelong friend of David's and he was here at the Riviera in the middle of nowhere to see him.

David cut in, 'I told you I really liked the stuff you were coming up with, James, and once I was sure you were on to something, I gave Michael a call. I was sure this new dark spooky shit you're writing would be right up his street.'

Michael was nodding. 'Not exactly how I would have described it, but I do like it – a lot! I've been aware of you for fifteen years. I always thought you had potential, but somewhere you seemed to have lost your way.'

Can't argue with that, thought Jimmy.

'So, when David told me that you were suddenly coming up with great songs and performing like you meant them, I thought I'd better come and take a look for myself.' He took another sip from his drink. Coffee, Jimmy noted. This must be more serious than he thought. He decided not to reach for his gin and tonic. 'Jimmy, what you're doing here is nothing short of a miracle. It must have been a really tough job to come up with this quality of new songs.'

You're telling me … a really tough job.

Michael continued. 'They're amazing and this whole noir style just separates you from the bunch. David said there was a haunted quality to your work, and he wasn't wrong. There seems to be a depth, a sadness that you haven't touched on before, almost as though you have seen the other side. Have you had recent experience of death?' he asked.

Well, I've had recent experience of making people dead, he thought. Jimmy slowly shook his head and turned down his inner monologue. 'No, not really. I guess you reach an age when you just start to think about the bigger things, and that's when it really hits you. Love, life and death. I guess I've spent too many years feeling sorry for myself and blaming others, but I stood back and just took a good long look in the mirror.'

'Did you like what you saw?' asked Michael.

I bet he's in therapy asking questions like that, thought Jimmy, but he didn't let it show. He was in the character of Jimmy Wayne, artist and now superstar in waiting. 'Does anybody?' *Oh, that was good*, thought Jimmy, *answer an analytical question with an analytical question*. He let the silence sit there for a moment. Poor man's Rob Lowe was being the strong silent type, waiting for his answer. Jimmy pretended to be deep in thought; he wanted to give this guy the impression that he was a tortured genius coming to terms with a vast but dormant talent, as opposed to a serial-killing songsmith. 'Well, I didn't dislike who I saw in that mirror, Michael, I just didn't recognise him.

Where had the boy from the Poconos gone? All those hopes, all those dreams that had just been allowed to float away on a sea of drink and regret – ' He paused a moment for dramatic effect. He could see both David and Michael hanging on his every word. 'I guess I realised I was lost and it was only me that could find me.' He stared at them both as though he'd just revealed the darkest secret locked in his soul. They were both visibly moved. *God*, thought Jimmy, *if they think that's dark, they should come and take a look at the song cemetery.*

They all just sat there for a while. Jimmy was determined not to speak first, and Michael played the waiting game. David, being British, just sat there, far too polite to interrupt.

Finally, after what seemed like minutes but was only about ten seconds, Michael broke the silence. 'And how do you feel about that?'

Jimmy's silent monologue jumped to its feet. *Yes! How do I feel about it? Michael has definitely been in therapy.* He remained calm on the outside and delivered his next line to perfection. 'I think I'm ready for the next chapter, Michael. I'm ready to finish the story.' *Wow*, he thought, *that my, dear Jimmy, is world-class bullshit.*

David and Michael again exchanged knowing glances before Michael turned back to Jimmy. 'Well, I'm glad you said that because I feel the same way, too. So much so that I'm going to offer you a record deal right now and we are going to record it back in LA at my studio. What do you say?'

He didn't know what to say. Suddenly his internal dialogue had lost its voice. Michael was talking; Jimmy dragged himself back to reality. 'So, if we're aiming to start in four weeks' time, we can look at using those three new songs, and then if we can have eleven or twelve songs for the record, we should be good to go. All originals,' he added.

Suddenly, the whole evening had taken another turn. Jimmy was being offered everything he had ever dreamed of, but there was a huge problem. How the hell was he going to kill eight people in four weeks?

It must have shown on his face because David spoke up. 'You OK, James, you look shaken? I know it's a big shock, but it's your dream. Ah, I know what you're thinking.'

The internal monologue then rediscovered its voice. *Oh, you really don't, David. You REALLY, REALLY DON'T!* Jimmy was remaining calm on the outside, but he was like the screaming Edvard Munch painting on the inside. Jimmy desperately tried to think of something coherent to say. 'Eleven songs.' *Brilliant, any other gems where that one came from?* He thought harder. 'I can't just run off eight songs in four weeks, Michael.' *Unless you get a machine gun,* suggested the ever-helpful internal voice that he was now really growing to dislike.

Michael nodded. 'OK. I understand. This this is a lot to dump on you at short notice, but that has to be the deadline. I wasn't planning on doing this record until I heard you tonight. We're a busy label and I have a chance to record you in just over four weeks. David has agreed to release you, so it's this slot or nothing for maybe a year.'

'Can't we use a writer that the label likes to work with for me?' Jimmy thought he'd saved the day with that one, but Michael shook his head.

'I don't think we can. These new songs and the style are almost like a sub-genre I haven't heard before, and I don't have a writer I can think of who can write songs in this style.' Michael leaned forward, his hand outstretched. 'We got a deal, Jimmy?'

Jimmy just stared at his extended hand and then looked at David, who nodded to him and before he knew it, they had shaken hands on the deal. He then looked into the corner of the bar, and there pulling a face that literally said 'yikes' was Wendy.

Life was just about to get very complicated.

CHAPTER 8
DRAW UP A LIST OF SCUMBAGS

Jimmy sat on the edge of his bed just staring at himself in the mirror. He hadn't even taken off his jacket. This should have been one of the happiest nights of his life. Finally, the stars had aligned and he was going to get his shot. Maybe 'shot' wasn't the appropriate choice of word given the circumstances.

Eight more songs, in four weeks. There was no way he could do it. He wasn't a killer; Jimmy Wayne was a nice guy drifting through life and doing harm only to himself. He thought about all the famous serial killers he knew. Jeffrey Dahmer had killed seventeen people but he ate them! Jimmy felt sick; he couldn't eat eight people in four weeks. The Boston Strangler. That couldn't work for Jimmy; he couldn't risk his picking fingers with all that heavy-duty strangling. Ted Bundy. He stopped right there.

All these murderers were terrible human beings. They got off on hurting innocent people. He wasn't like them. His killing spree was one accidental hanging and a deliberate mowing down of two thugs who were digging his grave at the time. Nothing planned or calculating about that.

No, this was not going to work for him. It wasn't in his nature. He had to face the fact that this dream was over. That was all it ever had been, from the moment Michael Owens had said 'original material'. The four-week time frame didn't make any difference. There was no way this was ever going to happen. Best to make the most of playing the Canyon and enjoying the minor celebrity he had created for himself. There were worse ways of making a living. Also, who knows, he might knock down some hobo on a dark highway, purely by accident of course, and get another song to add to his repertoire.

Jimmy undressed and got into the shower. As the warm water ran over his head and down his back, he smiled. Tonight, he had been good – good enough to get the owner of a top label in LA to offer him a deal. That had been something. Confirmation of what he'd always thought. He really did have it.

Just then, his train of thought was interrupted by a face pressed up against the shower glass. He jumped. 'What the fuck!' It was Wendy.

'Relax, Jimmy, it's not Lena, it's your favourite dead girlfriend.'

Jimmy turned off the shower and took the towel that Wendy was so generously holding out for him. 'You know about Lena?' Jimmy felt bad. It had only been a few weeks since he had hanged Wendy, accidently, and it somehow didn't seem appropriate to have been unfaithful to her so soon. For a killer, Jimmy was a very moral man.

Wendy just shrugged. 'You're a man – and besides, you can't be unfaithful to a dead person … that's just your guilt talking.'

Jimmy buried his head in his towel. He just couldn't look at her for the moment, but Wendy kept going.

'I've been thinking about your little problem.' He pulled the towel down around his waist. Wendy just sighed. 'Not *that* little problem. I'm talking about the eight people you gotta knock off to get this record deal.'

He was still looking down at his groin. *It's not that little.*

'For fuck's sake, stop thinking about your knob for five seconds and pay attention.' Wendy wasn't shouting, but she had certainly got his attention.

'Keep your voice down. These walls aint that thick. People hear you talking about killing people, and my knob being small, you're gonna get me talked about.'

Wendy just stood there slowly shaking her head as though she was dealing with an idiot child. 'Jimmy, darling, I'm dead, no one's gonna hear me unless I want them to. I'm starting to get the hang of what I can and can't do over here, and if I don't want to be seen or heard I don't have to be. To be frank, you're the only living person that's seen me!'

Jimmy nodded. 'Like a Vulcan warship, invisibility cloak?'

Wendy just stood there. What could she say to that? She decided to use tact. When she spoke, it was gently and, again, the way you would address a young child who had chewed too many lead toys. 'Jimmy, Vulcan warships aren't real. *Star Trek* is not a historical document. Being dead, however, is very fucking real, and my version means I'm hanging around and not shooting off to the other place.'

Jimmy could see that Wendy was losing her patience. 'I was only using it as an example. I mean, I never believed that stuff. Who has ears like that?'

Wendy laughed; she couldn't help herself. Physicists had been working for years to perfect invisibility as a military weapon and failed, yet Jimmy only ruled out making a million-ton Vulcan warship disappear because he was suspicious of people with pointy ears. Had she really been in love with this man?

'Sit down. I need to give you some career advice.' Wendy sat on the end of Jimmy's bed and patted the space next to her. 'Sit right here and bring your notepad and pen.' Jimmy didn't argue. 'OK, we all sitting comfortably?' She received an affirmative grunt. 'We need to draw up a list of scumbags, but they all need to be within a fifty-mile radius of here.'

'Why would I wanna do that?' Jimmy sat looking at her.

'Because you're gonna kill eight of them!' She just came right out and said it. No preamble, no explanation. She didn't need to.

Jimmy threw down the pad. 'No, no, no! I can't do that. I'm not a killer!'

Wendy pulled a face and pointed at herself. 'Hello! You are a killer, Jimmy. You're just not a very good one. You mowed down Vinny and Carmine in cold blood, so you can do it when push comes to shove.'

Jimmy shook his head. 'But they were gonna chop my fingers off, break my legs and bury me alive.'

Wendy was having none of it. 'You could've run for it, but when I explained the situation there was only one rational choice to take, and you took it, Jimmy.'

He just sat there looking at Wendy, trying to fully comprehend what she was saying. She was right. He could have turned away and driven back to town, but when she had explained it to him, *he* made the choice to slip the handbrake and run down those killers. It was in him; he just didn't want to admit it. Jimmy picked up the pad and pen. 'What was the title again?'

Wendy touched his shoulder with her hand. 'A List of Scumbags.'

Jimmy scribbled it down and underlined it. That was all he did; he just sat there waiting for Wendy to tell him who to kill.

'What about Jackson Pollack, the drug dealer down at the Reservation Club?' The Reservation was a dive at the far end of town that certainly did not ever require one. As for 'club', it certainly wasn't overflowing with members.

'Good choice,' he agreed. 'I could petrol bomb it. If we get lucky, I could get all eight in one go. Do it on a Saturday night, and I might even get enough for a second album.' He nodded, warming to the task. 'Yeah, I like that, Wendy, one big hit. Do it next week, and that would give me over two weeks to get the arrangements sorted.' He beamed his most winning arsonist, serial killer smile, which failed to light up the room – or anything else, thankfully.

Again, Wendy adopted the 'talking to a child who had licked too many lead toys' voice. 'Look, I love your enthusiasm, and yes, there are scumbags that go to the Reservation, but aren't you forgetting they have a house band on Sundays and Tuesdays?' She waited for the penny to drop.

When it did, Jimmy let out a gentle, 'Fuck it!' He had forgotten about Half-Eaten Burger – probably the worst band name in history. When Jimmy had questioned them about it, No Relation said it represented the pleasure to come. This sounded like the worst kind of pretentious horseshit and he'd told No Relation so, but not before Kid, who was relatively new in town, had asked, 'Why do you call Joe "No Relation"?'

Jimmy had looked at Joe, and Joe just shrugged. 'You wanna tell him?'

Joe sighed and gave him a resigned smile. 'Go on, it was your idea. I don't wanna rob you of the pleasure.'

Jimmy then turned to Kid. 'He's a drummer, and his surname is Rich!' He slowly watched the realisation spread over Kid's face, and he dissolved into laughter.

Once he'd gathered himself, Kid managed to speak. 'Yeah, no offence, Joe, but you're definitely no relation.'

Joe did a mock bow. 'Some taken. Now go fuck yourself, you blonde-haired Viking bastard!'

In answer to the original question about the band's name, Kid had come up with something far deeper: 'Half-Eaten Burger is about lost opportunity. Life is so fast, you just never get chance to finish anything'.

Jimmy had seen Kid inhale food, and he somehow doubted that he'd ever failed to finish a meal. 'Really?' He was not convinced by Kid's reasoning.

Kid then thought for a moment. 'It's about the futility of life, the half-finished novel, the failed first marriage. Half-Eaten Burger is just a symbolic representation of all these things.'

Jimmy still wasn't convinced. 'Maybe you were halfway through a burger when you came up with the name.'

Kid had nodded. 'Yeah! That too!'

'Jimmy, pay attention, we need to get on,' said Wendy in a voice that was not to be disagreed with.

Jimmy snapped out of his daydream. 'Sorry, Wendy. You were saying about Jackson.'

Wendy nodded. 'He should be top of the list. He's a scumbag drug dealer and he's dealing to kids.'

'Yeah, I agree. He's a scumbag and has hooked a lot of people, but does that deserve the death sentence?' Jimmy wasn't convinced.

'He pushes to kids! He needs to go.' Wendy sat there simmering with anger. 'I really hate him. D'ya know he once had the nerve to tell me that one of my tits was bigger than the other.'

Jimmy didn't know what to say to that, mainly because it was. It wasn't like a deformity, but if you looked really close, you could tell. 'Yeah, guy's a scumbag. That alone is worth the death penalty.' He turned to Wendy. 'I just want to reassure you, your tits are perfect.'

Wendy blushed. 'Oh, Jimmy, you're so full of horseshit. The left one is bigger than the right. One's a thirty-three and the other is nearly thirty-four, but I do have a very slim back,' she added.

'I like 'em both. Nobody could accuse me of being sizeist!' Jimmy scribbled 'Jackson Pollack'.

'Why is he called Jackson Pollack? He's not an artist!'

Jimmy waggled his finger. 'Now that I do know. His surname really is Pollack, he does love to be paid in twenty-dollar bills and they have Andrew Jackson on. Somebody obviously put two and two together and decided to rechristen him. I think it's quite funny. That's why so many twenty-dollar bills have traces of cocaine on them.'

'OK, that's one, who's next?'

'What about the cross-eyed guy at the gas station? Never did like him. He once told me that country music sucks and the blues was for folks wanting to be dead.'

'Don't think being cross-eyed and hating country counts. Anyway, you're an Americana blues singer, so it was nothing personal.'

Jimmy seemed disappointed. 'Suppose. What about Sleazy? He's a real piece of shit.'

'Good choice.' Wendy nodded enthusiastically. 'He reminds me of a hyena in a suit. Just seeing him used to make me feel dirty.'

Sleazy Peterson owned the Big Easy, the whorehouse a few miles out of town. All the locals called it the 'Lazy' because Sleazy never made enough effort to merit 'Easy'. He had been arrested many times, accused of bringing in illegals and under-age girls, and everyone in town hated him, but someone in high places must have liked him or been on the payroll because they could never make it stick.

Some of the local menfolk would describe in detail what they would like to do to him – usually about an hour before they drove up there to avail themselves of his establishment's services. Jimmy used to drink there, but he was banned now. One night, Sleazy was slapping one of his girls around, and Jimmy had gone down the corridor because he couldn't stand the fear he'd heard in the girl's voice. He burst into the room where the commotion was coming from just in time to see Sleazy slap the girl to the floor.

Sleazy turned to Jimmy with a big smile on his face. 'Howdy, Jimmy. Just doing some staff training.'

Before he could start the next sentence, Jimmy had stepped forward and knocked him out cold. He had turned to the girl who was still terrified and tried to talk to her, but she cowered away. 'I'm not going to hurt you,' he'd offered.

'You already have.'

Jimmy recognised the voice. He turned around and there was Valerie. She was the manager who tried to look after the girls, keeping them clear of Sleazy's worst excesses, but, like tonight, she wasn't always successful.

'She's an illegal. She can't go to the police. Besides, you know and I know that Sheriff Pence and Sleazy are big buddies. Let me sort this out. She'll be OK.'

Jimmy didn't move; his fists were still clenched. He wanted Sleazy to get up so he could knock him down again.

Valerie continued in a slow, world-weary voice. 'Best you're not here when Sleazy comes around. He's got guns, and you have just humiliated him in front of his girls. This girl will be fine. I'll make sure she gets her tips and she already has some saved. Three years of this and she's away to a new life with some money behind her and a new identity. You know Sleazy likes to keep things fresh.'

Jimmy looked around at the tatty drapes and carpet that your shoes stuck to. 'Yeah, real classy.' He pointed to the girl. 'You make sure that she's OK, Val. The poor kid's a slave.'

Valerie shrugged. 'We're all slaves – it's just that some of us have worse bosses.'

He had left and never gone back. Not that he could because Sheriff Pence had come by the next day. He had walked into the Desert Bar at the Riviera and sat down next to Jimmy.

'Afternoon, Jimmy, guess you know why I'm here.' He had gone to reply, but Sheriff Pence stopped him. 'Best if you just shut up and listen, son, and we can get this done real quick. Now, what you did to Sleazy last night was unacceptable and unlawful. Sleazy is a respected business member of this community.'

Jimmy snorted. 'A real pillar!'

Sheriff Pence ignored his derisive comment. 'Now, son, I know you like cocaine and even if you don't, it would be real easy to find some in your room, and then you're looking at ten years for dealing because it's gonna be a lot. Do I make myself clear?'

Jimmy looked hard into Pence's eyes. 'Just like that, plant drugs on an innocent man?'

Sheriff Pence gave him a smile of contempt. 'Oh, you're guilty all right. I just haven't decided of what yet. You're banned from the Big Easy for life and step out of line again, you'll be seeing the inside of a prison cell for a long, long time.' He then just got off the barstool and left.

The memory still filled Jimmy with anger. 'Let's put Sheriff Pence on the list too!'

'Too risky,' said Wendy. 'He's the sheriff – that would bring down too much heat. Let's just put down Sleazy and go from there.'

Jimmy thought about it for a moment. He really would like to sort out that corrupt bastard, but Wendy was right, the town would go crazy. Sleazy was a much better option. He scribbled down his name.

Wendy looked at the list. 'Well, that's a good start. Let's both sleep on it and see who else we can come up with.'

He looked at her. 'Do you sleep, y'know, when you're dead?'

Wendy pulled a face. 'Good question, Jimmy. Let's hope you don't find out too soon.' And with that, she was gone. That girl sure knew how to make an exit!

CHAPTER 9

JUST LIKE BUSES

Jimmy loved Mondays; he was pretty keen on Tuesdays and Wednesdays too. Those were the days he had no gigs. Normally he would have just lay around wasting his life away, but not anymore. He had a purpose, places to go and people to kill.

It was strange how the idea no longer filled him with revulsion. Wendy's idea to just go after scumbags had made it seem acceptable. It could almost be viewed as a public service. Jimmy was pretty sure a judge wouldn't see it that way, but maybe the jurors would.

He didn't have to buy a gun because hidden under the rear seat of Vinny and Carmine's pickup had been a small arsenal of weapons. Four assorted handguns and a couple of semi-automatics. There was also enough ammunition to invade a small country. Those boys were obviously expecting trouble. Their road trip hadn't been just to see him, not tooled up like that, which is probably why he hadn't heard from Jack Lantern yet. There is no way Jack would have expected Jimmy to kill his two hitmen and if Jimmy had been the only target for the trip, Jack would have known that he was still alive by now. No, Jack must be in his office in Vegas wondering what the hell had happened to his boys. It was only a matter of time before Jack Lantern would be calling.

Jimmy had buried the weapons at the song cemetery in a shallow grave in a watertight box, which he had also found in the back of the hitmen's pickup. Those guys had saved him a lot of shopping.

The drive to the canyon was quiet, as always. Not many cars on these Nevada backroads and none on the long track to the canyon. He had the window wound down and the warm air was blowing in off the mountains, not too hot, not too cold, and he had Glen Campbell blasting out of his CD player. Today, life was good.

When he reached the hill at the foot of the song cemetery, he paused and took a long look around. Nobody following him and no strangers on the horizon walking around the top of the canyon. He had never seen anyone walking out there in all the time he had been coming here, but you never could be too careful – not with what he was planning.

Once he was happy that the coast was clear, Jimmy jumped out of the cab and grabbed his shovel from the back of the pickup. He had digging to do – again. This time it wasn't six feet. The guns were only buried a couple of feet down, so it wasn't long before Jimmy felt the shovel scrape across the top of the gun box.

He bent down and pulled it out. The box was heavy; there was a lot of ammo and six weapons. He looked at his options. He knew how to shoot a gun, but there was some pretty fancy stuff he had never seen before. There was a military-grade fully automatic machine gun of some sort, but that would literally be overkill! There was a sniper rifle – nice if you wanted to assassinate a world leader, but not really what he was looking for. Then he saw it in among the pistols. It was a Glock. He had used one once at a range. He checked the clip, and it held thirteen rounds. *Unlucky for someone*, he thought. But the real clincher for Jimmy was that this gun had been adapted and it had a silencer. He picked it up. It felt good in his hand – not too heavy but solid enough.

He looked in the weapons box and there beneath a Beretta 9mm and a Browning Hi-Power was another full clip of thirteen rounds and four boxes of ammunition. He took one box, figuring he had two full clips, which was twenty-six rounds, and he only needed to kill eight scumbags. Jimmy wasn't the greatest shot in the world, but he reckoned that he would be very disappointed in himself if he needed to resort to the full box.

An unpleasant thought struck him. What if he got caught up in a shoot-out with Jack Lantern and his boys? Or what if the scumbags rumbled him and fought back? He hadn't considered that.

After grabbing a Heckler & Koch MP5 compact sub-machine gun and ten clips, he now felt ready for any eventuality. He buried the rest of the weapons again and headed down to his pickup armed and dangerous.

He stowed the MP5 underneath the rear passenger bench in a secret little compartment he'd had made to hide his guitar when he was touring. It made a great concealed weapons lock-up. The handgun went in his glove compartment so he could get to it quickly if needed. Jimmy climbed into the driver's seat, took a deep breath and sank bank into its deep leather contours. He was glad to have got that out of the way. *Right*, he thought, *let's go and kill someone.*

The someone he was thinking about was Jackson Pollack. He headed back into town with a gun in his glovebox and death in his veins. Jimmy never drank during the day so heading into the Reservation before noon was an unexpected pleasure – they served a really fine breakfast, who knew? He had only been there in the evening before, when the clientele was definitely from the wrong side of town.

Although that statement wasn't strictly true because when you looked at it on a map, Blackjack was almost round. From the main street, it had sort of organically expanded, like a boil. It wasn't unpleasant, but what it lacked in charm it made up for in … Jimmy thought for a moment. *What are Blackjack's redeeming features?* It was in a beautiful location, if you liked your beauty dry and mountainous with a bit of desert thrown in for good measure. It was pretty quiet, a place where you could find some space to breath. *Yeah*, thought Jimmy. *Forget the casino, forget the seedy bars and the Big Easy brothel. This would be a good place to bring up a dysfunctional family. Hell, it would be a great place to become a dysfunctional family.* It even had a golf club.

Jimmy's breakfast arrived: scrambled eggs, bacon and hash browns. He was just about to tuck in when a familiar figure filled the doorway. Kid Oscarson. Jimmy waved him over.

'You wanna join me, Kid?' He motioned for Kid to sit down. It was fascinating watching Kid manoeuvre his six-foot-five frame into the fixed seats on the other side of the table. A sea captain docking a huge liner at a small harbour would have had similar problems. Kid wasn't fat; he was just a giant of a man.

After several moments of twisting and shuffling, Kid docked opposite Jimmy.

The waitress had witnessed the whole procedure and at the appropriate moment said the immortal line, 'The usual, Kid?'

Kid looked directly into her eyes and smiled. 'Why, Sally, that would be most acceptable, thank you.' He paused for a moment before continuing, 'And what, pray tell, are the specials today?'

Sally looked at him as though he had just suffered a stroke. 'Specials … ah, honey, no specials on this menu. It's set.'

Kid smiled amiably. 'Then I shall stick with the usual.'

Sally nodded, pulled a face and walked away.

Jimmy smiled; he had enjoyed the brief theatre of Kid ordering breakfast. 'You come here often for breakfast?'

'Every day,' Kid replied with a nod.

Jimmy was puzzled. 'So, you must know there's a set menu with no specials. Why ask?'

Kid smiled. 'One day, who knows, there could be.' He leaned towards Jimmy before adding, 'I always like to travel more in hope than expectation. I find it opens me up to the universe.'

Jimmy loved Kid but the guy really was deeply eccentric, funny too. 'And did hope bring you to Blackjack and a place in my band?' Jimmy's question was meant to be ironic, but Kid wasn't fazed.

He raised the index finger of his left hand and waggled it thoughtfully, as if he were denying something. 'Now, here's the interesting thing, Jimmy.' Kid leaned towards him again. 'When I joined you, we were going nowhere, and that was fine by me. Nowhere has been on my bucket list for years. It was just a bit sad to see this man, with so much talent, driving the bus that took us there.' Kid let his words sink in.

Jimmy didn't try to deny it. How could he? It was the truth, but Kid hadn't finished.

'But suddenly, out of a clear blue sky, the old Jimmy Wayne is back! Better than ever and writing great songs, and I'm now in a band that's going somewhere and the driver's switched the satnav on. I don't know what you had to do, what sacrifices you had to make, but I'm damn glad you did.' Kid leaned back in his chair and just stared into Jimmy's eyes.

Jimmy felt as though Kid was looking into his soul but said nothing because he knew Kid still hadn't finished.

Kid stroked his chin thoughtfully, considering his words. When he spoke, it was quietly and without malice but it was intense. 'Sometimes when we want something too much, we can lose sight of the journey. It's never been about the final destination for me, it's about the journey. What's the value of being at the top of the mountain if you have to throw people off to get there?' Kid slowly nodded his head deep in thought.

Jimmy couldn't stay quiet any longer. 'So, what exactly are you trying to say?'

'That's a very good question, to which I don't have an answer.' Kid smiled. 'But what I will say is this, if you —' he pointed at Jimmy '— are comfortable that what you're doing is right, then all will be well. Just don't lose sight of the reason for the journey.'

Jimmy nodded. 'Well, if I had the slightest idea what you're on about, I'm sure I would have found that very profound.'

Kid laughed. 'Man, if I had the slightest idea what I was on about, I'd probably start drinking again.'

They sat there looking at each other. Jimmy felt sure that Kid must know something. Kid just felt sure that he was ready for his breakfast.

After they had finished eating, Jimmy and Kid talked about the gig and Jimmy revealed that he had been offered a record deal. He also made it clear to Kid that he would take the band with him.

'That's great news, Jimmy, but eight songs in four weeks, wow! That's a stretch. You got any ideas?'

Just as Kid asked, Jimmy saw an idea pull up in the car park. Jackson Pollack. He nodded towards him. 'That scumbag is up early.'

Kid turned to see where Jimmy was nodding and there looking like a man whose razor and washing machine had been stolen several days ago – around the same time they took his shower and ironing board – was Jackson. The man was a dirty mess. 'Pablo Escobar in da house!' exclaimed Kid. 'Man, I hate that fucker.'

'Not like you. I thought you were peace and love to all men.' Jimmy was surprised.

Kid shook his head. 'Not all men. That skunk sells drugs to kids. Now, if you're on the way to the top of the mountain and you meet him, well, please throw him off. No one's gonna miss him!'

Jimmy was taken aback by the anger in Kid's voice. It was also a bit unsettling that he seemed to be implying that he should kill Jackson metaphorically while he was actually planning on doing it physically. 'Must be someone who loves him.'

Kid shook his head. 'No way. He probably hates himself, and with good cause. When the time comes for him to have a good hard look in the mirror, he won't like what he sees.' Kid pushed his empty plate to one side. 'Remember what I told you about the journey.' Jimmy nodded. 'Well, he ain't going anywhere. He just stays where he is and spreads misery. He's a user himself, and he's climbing so far down the pit that he won't ever get out. I always try to travel with hope in my heart, but him … just look at him.'

They both looked out of the window to the car park where Jackson was leaning on his bonnet. His face was pale and gaunt, a skeleton in waiting. His eyes shifted around like a fox in a henhouse. It was just after noon – an early start for him. He yawned, revealing the fact that the tooth fairy had made several visits over the years.

'Excellent set of tooth,' observed Kid.

Jimmy laughed. 'Yeah, I don't think the ivory poachers are gonna be bothering him anytime soon.'

'Well, much as I'm enjoying this character assassination of our local drug dealer, I have to go. I was gonna have a few hours' practice this afternoon.'

Jimmy was genuinely surprised. Kid was one of the greatest guitarists he had ever heard, definitely the best he had played with. 'You don't need to practise, Kid, you're a natural.'

'Thank you, that means a lot coming from you, but we all have to practise. I find the more I practise the more effortless it gets. Now, can I get the bill?'

Jimmy shook his head. 'No, this one's on me, Kid. Maybe catch you later.'

Kid then started the whole process of pulling out of the table harbour. Shuffling along the bench seat, his legs jamming to the underside of the table as he wriggled towards the open sea of the aisle. Jimmy watched fascinated; in his head, he could hear an imaginary foghorn sounding HMS *Kid*'s departure from port. He really was a big, big man.

After Kid had gone, Jimmy paid the bill and sat there sipping his coffee, all the time watching Jackson in the car park.

Jackson just leaned against the side of his pickup soaking up the sun's rays. He had a coffee in one hand and a cigarette in the other. He didn't seem in a rush to be anywhere, and Jimmy just sat watching and waiting for him to make a move. He'd decided that he was going to follow him until he could get him alone and then ... well, he didn't know exactly, but he was sure he would kill him!

Before Jimmy had finished his coffee, Jackson answered his phone. He seemed to be very animated. Somebody was giving Jackson some bad news. He finished the call, and Jimmy could see him cursing. He watched Jackson open the trunk of his car. He then rummaged around for a few moments, after which Jimmy clearly saw him tuck a handgun into his trousers and pull his baggy T-shirt down over it. *Ho-hum*, thought Jimmy, *I may be needing the machine gun*. He watched carefully as Jackson pulled off the car park and headed east on the road towards the desert.

Jimmy ran to his pickup and headed down the road after him. He stayed about a mile back. There were only a couple of dirt roads for the next ten miles, so it wouldn't be hard to see where he went. The ground was so dry that he could track him for miles.

Jackson was doing over seventy. *Something has really fired up his ass*, thought Jimmy. Obviously, he was headed for an emotional meeting and with drug dealers, which often meant violence. Jimmy reached down and pulled out the Glock from the glovebox. The fresh clip was in it and the spare lay alongside, also full. *Twenty-six bullets, that should be enough*, he thought.

Up ahead, he saw Jackson turn off the highway and head down the dirt road that went towards Twin Springs. He had been there once before expecting a beautiful little river where the Twin Springs met. The reality didn't live up to the description. There were two springs, but for most of the year they were just a damp stain in the soil. A mud bath for a rat. Only when it rained up in the mountains did the springs become streams and form a little river where they joined.

According to Steve, the velvet-voiced handyman back at the Riviera, when that happened the river would run for about three miles before it receded back into the aquifers of the desert and it became just a dry riverbed once again. Steve had lived around Blackjack all his life and had photographic proof from the late eighties. He had showed it to Jimmy. It did look lovely, so he took a little picnic and headed out there on a day off only to find two muddy stains. That was three years back, and he hadn't returned since. He tried to remember what was down the track. He remembered that it wound through some low hillocks and became quite a twisty track but apart from that, he couldn't recall a thing.

As he reached the turn for the track to Twin Springs, Jimmy slowed and came to a stop about twenty yards onto the track. He could see Jackson about three-quarters of a mile further along, or, more precisely, he could see the dust cloud being thrown up behind Jackson's car. That was good news on two fronts:

Jackson wouldn't be able to see him because his mirrors would be full of his own dust cloud, and he could stay well back and just track the cloud from a distance.

Slowly, Jimmy started to feel very nervous. This was his first planned murder – he didn't like how that sounded. *Let's call it … an assassination*, he thought. *Much better. This is like killing an evil bug.* He was about to perform a public service and make Blackjack a better place. His confidence was ebbing. *Maybe take the machine gun as well, just to be on the safe side.*

He turned and knelt on his seat and pulled up the bench seat in the rear of his twin cab and lifted the lid on his secret compartment. The Heckler & Koch lay there looking menacing, waiting to deal death indiscriminately. He picked it up, checked that the magazine was full and then grabbed a couple more clips, just to be sure. He laid it down next to the Glock on the passenger seat. Overkill? It was, but Jimmy was working on the assumption that if Jackson had a weapon, so had whoever he was going to meet. Then an unpleasant thought occurred to him. *What if there's more than one person meeting Jackson?* He could be seriously outgunned here.

Looking over to where Jackson was headed, the cloud of dust was now disappearing behind the cover of the hillocks that marked the foothills leading to Spring Mountain. The cartographers around here sure hadn't put themselves out when naming these places.

Jimmy took a deep breath; he had made his choice. Putting the pickup into drive, he followed the dust cloud. He slowed while rounding the first bend which led into a low valley between the hillocks; he didn't want to run straight into a drug deal unannounced. He decided to pull over and climb the hill-ock on the left to see what was around the next bend. It was only about eighty feet high, and he was really glad he'd made the effort when he got there.

As he edged towards the top of the ridge, he saw the two vehicles parked by the ruin of an old barn which had been abandoned way back in the thirties. It had been slowly collaps-ing ever since. Jackson was out of his car and having a heated argument with another man who Jimmy didn't recognise, but his black leather jacket and shirt with a crisp pair of chinos hinted that he wasn't a farmer come to check on the viability of rebuilding his barn. Their voices carried up the hill to where he was observing, and it was clear that all was not well in drug dealer world.

'Pollack, you owe Mr Lantern for two deliveries.' Jimmy was momentarily stunned. Jack Lantern! Was there any illegal pie this man didn't have his finger in? He listened closely; this whole thing was getting closer to home every minute.

'Fuck you, Baker. Those last two deliveries were cut with so much flour I could've opened a fucking bakery. I'm not paying for that shit, and you can tell your boss that he needs to get the quality of his product sorted or he won't have any distribution.'

Baker slowly nodded his head. 'Is that your final word, because I have to tell you that Mr Lantern didn't send me here to negotiate?'

Even from a hundred yards away Jimmy could hear the menacing tone in Baker's voice. Obviously his hearing was better than Jackson's because he got right in Baker's face. This was clearly an error, Baker looked like an ex-boxer, but one who hadn't taken too many blows to the head. Jackson, on the other hand, had clearly been using too much of his own stock and was now working up a head of steam.

'And just what are you gonna do about it!' he screamed.

Baker proceeded to show him by headbutting him brutally on the bridge of his nose. Even at this distance Jimmy could hear the crack as Baker's forehead flattened Jackson's nose. He let out a cry and fell to the ground moaning. His nose was now pumping blood and bent so far towards his right ear that he could probably sniff it.

Jackson rolled around in agony. 'Shit, Shit, Shit! You broke my fucking nose!'

It all happened so quickly that Jimmy didn't have time to do anything. Jackson reached into his trouser belt and pulled out his gun, but Baker was too quick for him. Before Jackson had time to take aim, Baker stepped forward and kicked the gun from his hand. Clearly Jackson already had his finger on the trigger because the gun went off, missing Baker but breaking Jackson's finger between the trigger and the guard. Again, Jackson howled with pain.

Baker stood menacingly over Jackson as he moaned in agony. 'Where's the money, douchebag!' This clearly wasn't a question; it was a demand.

Things were escalating so quickly that Jimmy didn't know what to do.

'Go fuck yourself, Baker. I didn't bring any because I'm not paying for the shit you sold me.'

Baker straightened up and pulled a 45mm from a shoulder holster beneath his jacket. He smiled at Jackson. 'That's a real pity, because now I have to kill you. Mr Lantern was real clear about it. If Pollack don't pay, kill him!'

Suddenly, Jackson realised that he had overplayed his hand but he'd gone too far to pull back. He held up his hands. 'Don't shoot! I'll get you your money!' His voice sounded like he had a heavy cold, but when a nose has been folded flat it does tend to sound blocked.

Baker shook his head. 'Sorry, Pollack, you can't go back to town looking like that. Too many questions.' Then, without any hesitation, he shot Jackson in both kneecaps. Jackson immediately screamed like a wild animal.

It jerked Jimmy out of the trance from which he'd been watching the drama play out below, and a sickening thought occurred to him. *If I don't move fast, Baker will kill Jackson and I'll lose the song.* For a split second, the morality of the thought made Jimmy pause, but only for a split second. He needed that song, and Jackson was as good as dead; he certainly wished he was, when Baker put another round into both ankles. Jackson's screams were now pitched so high that only dogs could hear them.

Luckily for Jimmy, Baker was something of a sadist and had decided to kill Jackson slowly. Jimmy pulled himself up onto the edge of the ridge and took aim at Baker with his machine gun. The Heckler & Koch felt solid and deadly in his hands. He took aim and squeezed the trigger. But nothing happened. *Shit!* He realised that he hadn't released the safety. *Where the fuck is the safety?*

As he was desperately searching the gun for the safety, two more shots went off. Jimmy thought his chance had gone, but thankfully Jackson was still screaming. The two additional bullet holes where his elbows used to be probably had something to do with this.

Finally, after what seemed like minutes, Jimmy found the safety. He eased it off and took aim. When he pulled the trigger, the whole world seemed to explode. The first few rounds smashed into the ground in front of Baker and as Jimmy raised his aim, the arc followed up Baker's body and the first three rounds landed in the part of his anatomy that no man would ever want a bullet, let alone three.

Baker's gun flew through the air as his hands moved to grab what was left of his balls. As he fell backwards, his screams climbed to a crescendo where he and Pollack were performing an a cappella of agony.

Jimmy got to his feet and looked up and down the track to see if the shooting had reached the ears of any passers-by. There was no one to be seen. He looked back to the road about a mile and a half away, but there were no vehicles in sight. He headed down the hill towards the screaming. As he did, he put the Heckler on to single shot. These boys weren't going anywhere.

When he reached them, he expected to be revolted by the scene, but he could feel no sympathy for either of the screaming criminals. They were not worthy of his sympathy. He stood between them and even through their agony they saw him.

'Who are you?' Baker spat out the words fiercely through his pain, defiant to the end.

Jimmy frowned at him. 'Well, I'm a better damn singer than you boys. You're the worst barber shop duo I've ever heard.' He moved towards Baker. 'Sorry, Baker, but you gotta go.' Before Baker could utter a word of protest, he put a bullet through his brain. The barber shop choir was now down to one very out-of-tune singer.

He walked over to Jackson. Through his agony, Jimmy saw the light of recognition in his eyes. 'You're the singer from the Riviera. Man, I'm so glad you turned up.' He let out another cry of pain. 'You gotta get me to the clinic in the town.'

Jimmy shook his head. 'Sorry, Jackson, I can't do that.'

Jackson looked confused. 'Why not? You just saved my life.'

Jimmy nodded slowly. 'I can see why you might think that, Jackson, sadly, you would be wrong. I killed Baker but not to save you.' He paused as he saw the confusion on Jackson battered features. He knelt down by his side, 'I killed Baker so I could kill you.'

The confusion on Jackson's face deepened. 'Why would you do that? What have I done to you?' Jackson wasn't begging, he was in too much agony to do that, but the confusion had pushed the pain back a little.

'Jackson, you're a piece of shit drug dealer. You push to schoolkids for fuck's sake, but today –' Jimmy trailed off; he didn't know what to say. Slowly, he raised his gun and pointed it at Jackson's head.

Jackson tried to crawl back from him, but with arms and legs full of shattered joints and lead that just wasn't going to happen.

Jimmy rested the barrel on Jackson's forehead. 'I just got one question for you. Do you know who Jackson Pollock is?'

Jackson's eyes were darting around looking for a means of escape, but there were none.

'Well?' prompted Jimmy.

'It's me. I'm Jackson Pollack, that's what everyone calls me. It's a nickname for Christ's sake.'

'No, Jackson, who is the real Jackson Pollock? I'll give you a clue: he's not a drug dealer.'

Jackson thought desperately. He was in so much pain that he wasn't sure if this was a quiz and he would be free to go if he got the right answer. 'I think he's a sculptor.'

Jimmy smiled and stood up. 'Close enough.' He took two steps back and shot Jackson through the head with a single shot; he didn't want blood all over his clothes. He looked down at Jackson's battered body. His blood was splashed across the dry sandy ground as though it were abstract paint scattered on the floor, except the only colour available was red. Jimmy sighed. 'He was an abstract painter, Jackson, and it was Pollock … not Pollack.'

———◆———

From the top of the hillock where Jimmy had shot Baker, Wendy stood watching. *Wow*, she thought, *Jimmy has changed!* She waited for him to load the bodies into the back of his twin cab. Before he did this, he put on a boiler suit he'd brought with him. *Jimmy is getting organised*, she thought.

She watched him tidy up the scene and then drive the two vehicles around the corner into a blind gully where he put rags into both fuel tanks and lit them. He jogged out of the gully and waited for the bangs as they exploded. The flames reared above the rocks for a few moments and then died back as the smoke from the burning plastics and leather seats took over.

Jimmy turned and did a full recon of the scene to make sure he hadn't missed anything. He wasn't just organised – he was professional.

Wendy appeared by his pickup as he walked towards it watching the smoke rise. 'Well, Jimmy Wayne, I do declare, you're a stone-cold killer,' she said in her best Blanche DuBois accent.

Jimmy looked up and smiled; he looked tired. 'Well, if these boys had depended on the kindness of strangers, it hasn't worked out too well for them.' He nodded in the direction of the back of his twin cab.

For a moment Wendy was shocked. Jimmy knew the work of Tennessee Williams; this man was full of surprises. 'Guess not, but they really didn't deserve any kindness. Full-on pair of scumbags if you ask me. I have to say, Jimmy, you seem to have lost your squeamishness about killing.' Wendy walked around the back of his truck and peeked under the corner of the tarp. 'And another two for the price of one. You planning a double album?'

Jimmy laughed, he couldn't help himself, Wendy had always been able to make him laugh. 'Well, you know, sometimes scumbags are just like buses – you wait for hours for one to come along, then two come together!'

CHAPTER 10

EXIT STAGE LEFT
(LAUGHING)

It was Tuesday morning and the clock on Jimmy's bedside table had just clicked past 11 a.m. Jimmy was awake. He lay on his back staring at the ceiling and replaying the events of the day before. He had executed two men in cold blood, and hadn't found it hard. He thought that the very fact he had found it so easy should disturb him, but it didn't.

His victims would both have been a real disappointment to their parents if they knew how sordid their sons' lives had become. If you had a rabid dog that bit people, you'd put it down: it would almost be a kindness. Men that live that kind of lifestyle usually ended up in a police morgue or a shallow grave. All Jimmy had done was get them there a bit sooner. Hell, he may have saved a few innocent lives in the process.

Baker had clearly killed before, and Jackson would have surely gone on to hook more kids and adults on drugs. Jimmy smiled – he was becoming a benevolent social reformer, taking on the responsibility of removing human cancers from the body of nice society. He would need a very creative lawyer to use that argument in his defence, if he ever got caught. He could call it the 'Robin Hood' defence. Killing the criminals to give everyone else a better chance.

He looked towards the bedside table where two new songs lay next to the endlessly ticking clock. There was no doubt about it now; every death was a song. Two sheets of paper in his handwriting, which he had no knowledge of writing, lay on the bedside table. They weren't there when he went to bed. The one called 'Rage' was clearly about drugs, but the other called 'Too Much' was a gentler more introspective song. He picked it up and read the chorus.

'Nobody told me
That dreams don't all come true
And wanting it too much
Will make a fool of you.'

And then everything was clear to him. Dreams don't all come true – his certainly hadn't up until now. Wanting it too much will make a fool of you. Well, now he was killing people to get songs. There was obviously a case to be made that maybe he did want it a bit too much. Jimmy shrugged; too bad for the scumbags. He was on a mission to fulfil his destiny, and they were the collateral damage.

He had taken the bodies to the song cemetery and buried them, without military honours or even a few words, on the far side of the hillock away from Wendy in an area he described as Scumbag Alley. He felt bad about Wendy being there with them, but as she seemed to be a wandering spirit, she didn't spend much time around them. There were moments when he wanted to dig up Wendy's body just to see if she was really there but he could never bring himself to do it because he knew that whatever he thought, her body would be there. Wendy was dead. Whenever she turned up out of the blue and spoke to him or, indeed, saved him from Vinny and Carmine, it wasn't the real Wendy. She was gone.

Thankfully, none of the scumbags had made an after-death appearance, which was just as well, because now he would be seriously outnumbered.

He had arrived at the song cemetery around two thirty. It had been tough going carrying the bodies of both Baker and Jackson up the steep, rocky hillock to their final resting place, especially Jackson. All the bullets that Baker had fired into his joints had made Jackson extremely floppy, and he swung around like an oversized ventriloquist's dummy, making him very hard to handle. Baker, on the other hand, had developed a very nasty case of rigor mortis. He was like the most ungainly surfboard known to man. It had taken Jimmy a while to get him in just the right position on his shoulder to balance him.

When he had shot Baker, he'd initially grabbed his balls – or at least the place where they had been. The Heckler & Koch rapid fire had removed Baker's cock and balls. Even so, as Jimmy had moved towards him to finish him off, he had reached behind his head to try and grab his gun, which he'd dropped behind him as he fell. When Jimmy had pulled him off the back of the twin cab, his body was stiff and his right arm was stretched out above his head, still groping for the gun he never found. Jimmy had tried to bring it down but the rigor was too set in.

As Jimmy carried Baker up the slope to his final resting place, he appeared to be carrying Superman in full flight. He saw his shadow on the rocks as he climbed. If only Baker was Superman; he could have flown up. When he dug the graves, Jimmy didn't have the heart to break Baker's arm to get him to fit in a six-foot-long hole. Baker was buried in a seven-foot-ten grave. The guy had arms like an albatross. Jackson, however, made up for it. Because Baker had shot all his joints to pieces, he, like a ventriloquist's dummy, would have folded into a suitcase. Six-foot deep by three-foot-six, Jimmy didn't lower Jackson in – he poured him.

Once he had filled in the holes and smoothed over the surface, he leaned on his shovel and just stared at the ground where his victims lay.

'You gonna say a few words?' It was Wendy once again, scaring the crap out of Jimmy.

'For fuck's sake! You gotta stop doing this. You're gonna give me a heart attack.'

Wendy smirked. 'That would be ironic, don't you think?' Her eyes sparkled, and Jimmy smiled.

'Well, just for you.' He paused and thought for a moment before clearing his throat. 'Here lie the bodies of Superman and Pinocchio. Superman wasn't that super and Pinocchio had his strings cut. Good riddance to the pair of them.'

Wendy sighed. 'That was beautiful,' she lied, 'but Pinocchio wasn't a dummy.'

Jimmy shrugged. 'He was made of wood, wasn't he?'

Wendy had to agree. She nodded. 'Yeah, suppose so.'

Jimmy put the shovel over his shoulder and started to walk away. 'Close enough, then!'

It was 10:30 a.m. when Jimmy rolled into the restaurant for his breakfast. There were still a couple of guests finishing off, something Jimmy hadn't witnessed before, mainly because he didn't arrive until 11:30 a.m. at the earliest most mornings.

Valerie gave him a look of mocked shock. 'Some husband chased you out of his wife's bed early this morning?'

'That's a bit unkind, Valerie. I normally take them to a separate room!' Jimmy replied with a smile.

It was Valerie's turn to smile. 'Sorry, Jimmy, I forgot how much of a modern man you are. Very noble of you, especially as you get the keys to an empty suite for nothing.'

Jimmy rolled open the palms of his hands in a gesture of innocence. 'I would happily pay but David won't have it, says I deserve a few perks.' He winked at Valerie and sat down at his usual table. 'You seen David?'

'He popped in ten minutes ago and said he would meet you here at 10:45.'

Jimmy looked at his watch. 'How'd he know I'd be here? I don't normally get up until eleven thirty.'

'You know Mr Parker; he knows everything about everybody.' She paused for a moment as she wiped down the table that Jimmy was sitting at. 'Usual?'

Jimmy nodded distractedly; he was hoping that David really didn't know everything about everybody who worked for him.

Jimmy had asked Valerie to get David his usual breakfast and serve them together. He knew David would be bang on time, and it would give them chance to talk. Sure enough, seconds after the breakfasts arrived, David Parker breezed into the restaurant like a swan floating across a lake. Jimmy listened for his footfall, but there was barely a sound and then David glided into the seat opposite him.

He smiled broadly. 'Morning, James, how are we this fine morning?'

Jimmy looked around. 'We? I'm alone, David, but if you mean me, I'm fine.'

'Got out of bed too early this morning, did you?'

'How'd you know I was up early this morning?' Jimmy said, leaning back in his chair. 'Valerie told me you would meet me here at a quarter to eleven.' David smiled.

'The Lord moves in mysterious ways, that plus the fact that I saw you draw your curtains and you were already dressed. Got to be on the ball when you are running a place like this.'

'Not spying on me then, that's a relief.'

David grimaced. 'My God, with your lifestyle I don't even want to see you when you know you're being watched! I try not to imagine the debauchery you get up to behind closed doors.'

'And in boardrooms,' Jimmy interjected.

David held up his hands. 'You have me there. Shall we eat or just sit here insulting each other's morals?'

'We could do both,' Jimmy suggested.

A pained look spread across David's handsome features. 'We could, but we have more important things to discuss. Michael Owens phoned me this morning.' Now he had Jimmy's attention. 'He suggested that we make a single of "Vacant Stare". I sent him all of the film from the video we shot, and he said that we could use it for the single. All he has to do is change it to black and white. He thinks that will add to the darkness of the material.'

Jimmy sat for a moment taking it in. The boss of the record label wanted to put out the first single already. 'What if I don't manage to get the songs written for next month, will he still want to do it, we haven't even signed a contract yet?'

David laughed. 'Michael's an English gentleman. You shook hands and he gave his word.'

Jimmy grunted dismissively. 'A verbal contract ain't worth the paper it's written on.'

'Well, it's just as well that I have the contract for you to sign in my office. It arrived this morning by courier. I took the trouble to read it for you, and it's absolutely fair – more than generous, in fact. To be honest, Michael has done you a huge favour.' David paused expecting Jimmy to ask something, but Jimmy was too busy thinking. His mind was racing.

This is really happening!

David grew impatient; it was clear he couldn't wait to tell him the good news. 'He wants to do "Safe" as the second single as well. He realised that eight songs is asking a lot in four weeks. How's that going by the way?'

'Pretty good, did two yesterday.'

David looked surprised. 'Wow! You're killing it, James! What's the secret?'

Jimmy smiled. 'I just got focused. I drew up a list, and I just started working through it.' David was nodding like an encouraging university professor with a keen student.

'Excellent idea. Draw up a list of topics and just knock them off one by one.'

'That's exactly what I'm doing – just knocking them off one by one!' replied Jimmy.

David explained that Michael thought he could release one single at the end of the month and then the next song three months later. He was sure they were both going to hit the charts.

'So is he saying I have three months, then?'

David shook his head. 'No, he's going to say they're coming from the new album, but he's not going to put a date on it. If you miss the deadline next month, you're going to be waiting for nearly a year.' David looked at Jimmy. 'No matter how well these singles do, if you take too long to follow them up you will lose momentum. You *have* to get them done, James.'

He could see the passion in David's eyes. David was a good man; he had always looked out for Jimmy, and Jimmy wanted to repay his loyalty. He leaned across the table and put his hand on David's. 'You can count on it ... I only need another six after yesterday.'

David took a sip of his tea and then became very serious. 'Imagine if these singles go big ... say top ten in the Americana or blues charts and maybe top thirty on *Billboard*. Let's also imagine that you get the songs done and record the album and it does really well. We need to have a plan for what happens then.'

Jimmy just laughed. 'We get rich and famous! I'm assuming you wanna be my manager.' David seemed a little irritated by Jimmy's interruption.

'Listen, Jimmy, this is serious.' There was a something in his tone that made Jimmy listen closely to what David was saying. Also, he had called him Jimmy; he only did that when there was something serious to discuss. 'We have to prepare. You know and I know that these songs and the way you're performing them have transformed your career prospects. Look at those shows in the Canyon. The crowd went wild. We sold all the signed posters and everyone wanted a CD or a vinyl signed by you. Hell, even the boys in the band were signing autographs. They've raised their level, too. This is a game changer. Michael knows his stuff and he says you're going to go big. He has links in Vegas and he's already told me that he can get you a residency at one of the big casinos. Michael has great relations with the Golden Flamingo, and if he gets your show on there, you will pull in an audience of seven hundred and eighty every night. This is going to be serious stuff and big money!'

All this sounded great, but Jimmy didn't understand why David was getting so intense about it. It could take months to happen. 'What's the rush? Say we do the record next month, that's gonna take a couple of weeks to record, plus the four weeks before we get there. Then we've gotta get it mixed and mastered – that's gonna be another couple of weeks. Artwork, promotion ... then you've gotta get the radio play.' Jimmy was counting the weeks off on his fingers. 'Say we get a big hit and everything that you're talking about comes off, it's gonna be sixteen weeks before we could be in a position to do a show in Vegas, and that's assuming there's a slot for me.'

David slowly shook his head. 'Jimmy, sixteen weeks is nothing. You will have to leave the Riviera. I will need to negotiate your leaving with Sam Estrin the owner.'

'But he owns both places, so if I do end up there it's just a transfer – win, win.' Jimmy smiled.

David took a deep breath and continued, 'It's not that easy. For this place you have turned into a big pulling act, but that's only just happened. At the Golden Flamingo or any other big

Vegas casino, they have top-line stars on offer all the time. You're going to be a gamble over there but here, with what we pay you, you're a safe bet. Especially now you have raised your game. There are a lot of variables at play.'

Jimmy sat there trying to digest what David was saying. Leave the Riviera – he had dreamed of doing that for years, but now it was being proposed as a possibility, he wasn't sure he wanted to go. He had grown to like it here. He liked the people and he liked the place, and now everything was going well with the music he really enjoyed playing in the Canyon to three hundred people every Friday and Saturday evening. There was even talk of a Sunday show. Then he thought about the song graveyard and all the graves slowly being added. Maybe it was time to move on.

'So, what's the plan, David, seems like you have this all figured out?' Jimmy leaned back knowing there would be a plan; David always had a plan.

David pulled a small notebook from his jacket pocket. 'I've made a few notes.'

Jimmy smiled. 'Thought you might.'

———◆———

As Jimmy walked down the footpath that wound along the edge of the golf course, he could smell the fresh cut grass. Out here in this part of Nevada, you didn't smell grass often unless it was in a public space or a resident's garden. Without regular watering, it just couldn't survive in the arid climate. The birds were singing and a gentle breeze accompanied the water sprinklers as they fought the endless battle with the hot, dry desert breeze. How did Joni Mitchell put it? 'The Hissing of Summer Lawns'. What a perfect description. She had always been one of his favourite artists and he had hoped to get a chance to sing with her someday, but twenty years ago when his star was rising he had lost focus and now that it was rising again, Joni had retired. Another box on his bucket list that wasn't going to get ticked. Still, things were certainly looking up.

David didn't come right out and say it, but it was pretty obvious that a tentative deal had been struck with Sam Estrin at the Golden Flamingo. Now that would be something. Great audience every night, terrific exposure for him and great money. He had been there once to see Donny and Marie Osmond, and the show they had put on was incredible, the venue was incredible. It ran for more than ten years. Now they had retired from the show, the place had been opened up to several acts. Opportunity was knocking, and he just had to knock off another six victims to grasp it. Sleazy Peterson was on borrowed time – now all he needed to do was find another five scumbags to go with him. Sometimes the creative process was very hard.

After about an hour he reached the little road where Sammy lived. He had meant to see her regularly since she retired, and especially since she became ill. It hadn't quite worked out that way. As he walked down the front path through the neatly tended garden, he wondered how much longer he would be coming to visit Sammy. She was getting noticeably thinner and weaker since he saw her last, but her spirit was as bright and strong as ever. He knocked on the door even though he knew it was open and waited for the swearing to begin. He didn't have to wait long.

'For fuck's sake, Jimmy. I know it's you, come the fuck in.' If you were looking for a sweet old lady, Sammy would not have been your first port of call. She was still a young dancer trapped in an old lady's body. Jimmy walked into the lounge. Sammy was in her chair. Her eyes shone brightly as if she was using the force of her personality to hide the fact that her body was fading away around her. She smiled at him.

'Sit down, Jimmy, pour the coffee, it's in the pot in front of you.' If he'd closed his eyes, he could have imagined the young dancer talking to him. Sammy still sounded young. That voice belonged to someone bursting with energy, standing on the edge of her future, anticipating the things to come. Even now, Sammy was still shooting for the stars she was never going to reach. Her eyes shone and her personality glowed like the glittering of a dying star sending its final pulses before it disappeared from the galaxy, imploding into oblivion.

Sammy saw Jimmy's expression. 'Jesus, you look like you've seen a fucking ghost. Give it a couple of weeks and you probably will!' Sammy burst out laughing at the darkness of her own joke.

Jimmy tried to smile but couldn't. He loved this crazy old lady so much.

Sammy wasn't going to let it lie. 'What's wrong, Jimmy? Too soon for ya?!' Again, Sammy burst out laughing. She caught her breath. 'Oh Lord. I'm gonna have to cut back on this laughing, it's killing me!' She cracked up again and started cackling like one of the three witches in *Macbeth*. 'Say something, Jimmy. I can't do all the fucking talking!' Once more, she was chuckling away.

Jimmy poured the coffee. 'Would Madam care for a finger?' he said in his best English butler accent.

Sammy stopped laughing and looked at him. 'Is it chocolate?'

'It can be any kind of finger you want, Madam … Chocolate or –' he raised an eyebrow '– sponge!' They burst into laughter.

As she recovered her breath, Sammy smiled at Jimmy. 'You're a funny fucker, Jimmy Wayne, and I'm gonna miss you –' She never finished the sentence, but they both knew what she was saying.

Jimmy finished pouring the coffee and placed a chocolate and a sponge finger on a small plate beside her drink. Sammy was about to say something disgusting, but Jimmy held up his hand to silence her. 'Not while we're eating, you know the rules.'

Sammy snorted. 'Jimmy Wayne, you are such a pussy!'

After talking for over an hour, Sammy was starting to get tired. 'I'm gonna need my afternoon nap soon, Jimmy … pisses me off!'

He looked at Sammy a little surprised. 'Why's that? I wouldn't mind a little nap myself.'

Sammy frowned. 'This fucking cancer, makes me so tired, but who wants to waste the time you got left sleeping. Terminal illness needs to have a treatment that acts like speed. Takes the pain away and lets you live at a hundred miles an hour. Man, if I could get me some cocaine, I could pack three years into three weeks.'

Jimmy thought about this for a moment. 'If we went to Yellow Creek, I'm pretty sure the doc there would let you have some on prescription.'

'Doctor Donald will let me have what I what, as long as I explain it to him, and spell it.'

They both nodded at that. Doctor Donald was the only doctor in Blackjack, but no one believed he was a real doctor. The certificate on the wall of his home surgery came from a college that nobody recognised. Strumpf College of Doctoring was all that could be made out from beneath the faded golden symbol of two golden towers. The certificate signature at the base of the framed document looked very similar to Doctor Donald's.

'Do you reckon he really went to medical school?'

Sammy thought for a moment. 'Well, he's got a certificate and warm hands, so in my book he's better than nothing, provided you know what's wrong with you before you go and can tell him what to prescribe. If you don't do that, he will probably shoot you up with disinfectant!'

Jimmy nodded in agreement. 'I always go to Red Rock; they have a proper little hospital there.'

'And a clap clinic,' Sammy said with a wink, before starting to yawn. 'Come on, Jimmy, time for you to go. I need my beauty sleep. One thing before you go –' Sammy held his hand '– David tells me you're gonna make it this time. Says he's done a deal that will get you on the big stage at the Golden Flamingo.'

This was news to Jimmy; he thought it might be true but if David was telling Sammy, he must have been doing some work behind the scenes. 'Yes, it's looking like it could happen.'

Sammy gazed up into Jimmy's eyes. She was still a beautiful woman, despite the years and the pain etched around her eyes. The young dancer and actress who had made so many men fall in love with her was still there, trapped inside an old and dying body, but still so full of a passion for life. 'When you're up on that stage, will you do a song for me and dedicate it to me? I would just love for the people to hear my name on that big stage.'

Jimmy could feel tears welling up in the corner of his eyes. He knew Sammy would never live to hear him sing it. He knelt down next to her and kissed her forehead tenderly. 'Every night on every stage I play till the day I die, Sammy, I promise!'

She nodded. 'Thanks, Jimmy. Now, where's my fucking joke?!' That was Sammy for you. Just as things were getting sad, she turned the tables.

Jimmy got up awkwardly. Sammy wanted her joke; she always wanted her joke. He sat down. 'Are you sitting comfortably?'

Sammy waved him away. 'Course not, I've got cancer, just tell me the joke.'

'So, there is this guy and he's out for a long ride on his motorbike. It's a beautiful morning and he's up on the mountain roads but still going through the wooded part of the slopes. Suddenly, a deer runs out in front of him, and he swerves and crashes into a deep ditch at the side of the road. About ten minutes later, he's crawling out of the ditch; he's got a big gash on his arm and a cut on his forehead. As he reaches the kerbside, a sportscar pulls up alongside and a very attractive young woman is looking down at him. "You OK?" she asks. The man says nothing for a moment. The girl has a low-cut top on and a very nice set of jugs.'

'Dirty fucker,' said Sammy.

Jimmy smiled but carried on with the story. 'Anyway, the man says, "Not really, I feel a bit groggy." The girl gets out of the car and takes a look at his head and arm. "Those need cleaning up and some butterfly stitches. Hop into my car, and I'll take you back to my place and I can patch you up." The man pulls away. "Oh, I can't, my wife wouldn't like that." She says,

"Nonsense. I'm a nurse and only live ten minutes down the road. Get in the car and we can get you sorted in no time." The man hesitates. "Sorry, I just can't, my wife really wouldn't like it." The young lady won't take no for an answer. "Get in the car. I'm sure your wife would want me to treat your wounds." The man gives in. The young lady does indeed only live a couple of miles away and before he knows it, he's cleaned and butterfly-stitched up. "There," she says, "good as new. Would you like a coffee before I take you back?" The man replies, "No, I'd better get back. My wife really won't be very happy about this." The young woman ignores him and makes the coffee. As they sit on her patio drinking, she looks up at the man. "Where is your wife by the way?" The man hesitates before replying, "Still in the ditch!"'

Sammy looked at Jimmy for a moment as the full realisation dawned that the man had left his wife in the ditch. 'No wonder the bitch wasn't gonna be happy. For fuck's sake, Jimmy –' Sammy couldn't finish the sentence because she was laughing so hard.

Jimmy was laughing with her. He knew she would like that one.

Sammy slowly subsided into a snigger; she was breathless with laughter. 'Still … in … the fucking … ditch,' and then she was off again. Suddenly, she stopped, her body stiffened. She looked into Jimmy's eyes and her hands clamped onto his arm. 'Oh fuck!' Those were Sammy's last words. In her weakened state, her heart had just given out.

Jimmy lay Sammy on the floor and started to massage her heart, but after a few seconds he stopped. Sammy wouldn't want to come back. She knew her days were short. What would be the point of bringing her back to suffer? He put a cushion under her head, closed her eyelids, and then he cried. Cried like a baby. He had loved this old lady and she had loved him. A true friendship untainted by anything but a love of each other. When he had stopped crying, he phoned David. David would know what to do.

As he sat there waiting for David to arrive, he knew that he would keep his promise to Sammy. Her name would be spoken on every stage that he ever played from this day until the end of his career. She had exited stage left (laughing). This lady really knew how to make an exit.

CHAPTER 11

WHO'S KILLING MY KILLERS?

Jack Lantern sat brooding at his desk in Vegas. May was turning into a very bad month. Four weeks ago, he had sent two of his best operatives, which was a nice way of saying enforcers, which is also a nice way of saying cold-blooded killers, on a road trip.

Vinny Zito and Carmine Mallotides were supposed to sort out a couple of dealers at two casinos who seemed to be struggling with skimming off the agreed amount. Failing to do this on a regular basis usually meant that your kneecaps would be parting company with your legs.

On this occasion, the boys were just issuing a warning. The two dealers concerned had been good earners for several years and were both struggling under the watchful eye of new managers. He would soon find a way to get to the managers – everyone has a secret – and then all would be well.

They also had some drug money to pick up, Jack had a very diverse portfolio, and that was with an old customer, so again he wasn't expecting trouble. Lastly, they had been told to kill the singer Jimmy Wayne. That little turd had been defaulting on a loan for nearly two years, and he was to be made an example of. Nice little video for recalcitrant customers of legs being broken and fingers being snipped off. The whole performance was to be rounded off with a nice live burial. Jimmy's screams as he was being buried alive would really focus his debtors on settling their accounts.

The boys should have returned two weeks ago but nothing. They had visited both dealers, because he had checked and the money from the drug deals had been deposited into his account from a branch in Red Rock. That was over two and a half weeks ago. He knew they had made it to the Riviera at Blackjack, and he had seen with his own eyes that they had captured Jimmy and were about to kill him. What he needed to do was get down to the Riviera and see for himself if Jimmy Wayne was alive. If he was, then he knew where the trail had stopped for Carmine and Vinny. Fate, however, was about to intervene and save him the trouble.

There was a knock on his door but before he could grunt enter, Lena Lantern swept into his office. She was wearing a pair of figure-hugging jeans and a blouse that certainly displayed her assets in their best light. She was a good-looking woman, his wife, yet it didn't stop him being unfaithful with the girls from several of the clubs he owned. But the lovely Lena was someone you could take anywhere and she would look good on his arm.

Lena was holding a sheet of paper she had just printed; she held it up to Jack. 'Fancy a couple of days at the Riviera in Blackjack? Jimmy Wayne is playing some of his new songs and he sounds amazing.' Jack let this information sink in for a moment. Lena took his hesitation as reluctance. 'I've spoken to David Parker, and he has promised us one of the presidential suites, just been refurbed. They have their own sundeck with hot tub. He's also booked you a tee time at the golf club.' Lena waited for Jack to consider.

'Well, the Riviera is a bit third rate, but those presidential suites sound OK and I like the golf course, but Jimmy Wayne ...?' He let the question hang for a moment. 'You still wanna see Jimmy Wayne? Last time I saw him he was well past his sell-by date.'

Lena seemed excited. 'Oh, Jack, you won't believe how he's changed. He has new songs and a new image and he's on the verge of signing a big record deal. I think he's going to be a star.'

'OK, get it booked.'

Lena rushed over to him and kissed his forehead. 'Thanks, Jack, you won't regret it.'

Jack smiled as she turned and rushed from the room like an excited schoolgirl. He knew that Jimmy Wayne had been sleeping with his wife and now, thanks to Lena, he knew that Jimmy had survived his encounter with Vinny and Carmine. So, what had happened to Vinny and Carmine? Surely that washed-up lounge singer couldn't have bested his boys. He was terrified and tied up when he'd spoken to him on the phone. It just didn't add up.

Ted Baker had also gone missing, but he was just doing the rounds of some of the dealers. His real name was Edward, but for obvious reasons everybody called him Ted. Ted was a stone-cold killer and one of his best men. Now he thought about it, he had told him to sort out the dealer, what was his name? Jackson? Jackson Pollack, just like the painter. The punk was refusing to pay, and Ted had been told to get the money or kill him. That was in Blackjack, too. This was all becoming too much of a coincidence. This trip to Blackjack needed to answer a lot of questions.

———◆———

Jimmy, 448 miles away, was sitting on his rocky outcrop looking up at the mountain ridge that curved around him and formed the horseshoe canyon. He was alone, except for Vinny, Carmine, Jackson, the Baker man and Wendy. The song cemetery was filling up. Thankfully, Sammy wouldn't be coming here. They were going to lay her to rest in the little cemetery outside Blackjack with the view of the mountains she had loved so much. She once told him it was the view from her patio that had sold the little house to her. After a lifetime of chasing a dream, she had found her piece of paradise, surrounded by people who loved her and in a place where she belonged and had become truly happy.

Jimmy felt terrible that it was his joke that had killed her; he consoled himself with the knowledge that she hadn't suffered and had been laughing up until the moment she died. He also consoled himself with the fact that when he woke up, the morning after Sammy died, there was another song on his bedside table. Apparently, he didn't actually have to kill someone to get a song. Just being the cause of death, even if indirectly, seemed to do the trick. It was Sammy's parting gift to him. He pulled the sheet of paper from his pocket and read the lyrics.

'Lonely old lady ... '

That wasn't Sammy; everyone loved her. Still, each murder or death didn't have to reflect the reality of the situation. He read on.

> *'She waited for a day*
> *That never did come.'*

That was true. For so many years she had dreamed and worked at becoming a star, but it just didn't happen for her.

> *'Invested in shade*
> *But never saw sun*
> *All the time hoping*
> *When hopes let her down*
> *The lonely old lady*
> *In the lonely old town.'*

It was the first time since Sammy had died that he'd actually read the words properly. Sammy wasn't that lonely old lady; her spirit was too strong to let an unfulfilled dream hold her down, but it could have been. He had seen so many in this business see their dreams of fame and fortune come to nothing, and for many it defined them. Jimmy scanned to the last verse.

> *'Time left her stranded*
> *By its incoming tide'*

Wow, that was the truth. Sammy just ran out of time. The dream ran faster than she could, and she never caught it up. This was all starting to make sense. He scanned down to the final chorus.

> *'Lonely old lady*
> *In a lonely old town*

Your future has faded
The past let you down.'

As he finished reading the last lines, his eyes were filled with tears. The past did let poor Sammy down. She had it all, she could sing and dance, but somehow she just never got her chance. He wished he could have taken her with him on this next stage of his journey, but he would honour her memory. He would sing this song at every show and explain that although Sammy never made it, she found happiness in Blackjack with an extended family who loved her. He would make it a tribute to a woman he had loved and respected.

'That's beautiful.'

Jimmy spun around. It was Wendy – who else? 'Oh, hi, Wendy. You know about Sammy?'

'Yeah, I've seen her, she's happy. She was still laughing at that joke you killed her with.'

Jimmy sat there for a moment trying to process what Wendy had just told him. 'You saw Sammy?'

Wendy raised her eyes and sighed. 'I'm dead, she's dead. We kinda mix in the same circles now!'

Jimmy felt as though his mind was exploding. 'Are you in heaven?'

She shrugged. 'Fucked if I know. I haven't seen any of the losers you buried up here, so it's got my vote. If you want my theory, we only see the ones we wanna see. Seen my grandma and a couple of friends who died young. I haven't seen Uncle Trevor who used to try and fiddle with me. Maybe all the scumbags go somewhere else.'

'Probably hell,' was all Jimmy could think to say.

Wendy didn't seem convinced. 'I'm not really into that heaven and hell stuff. I always thought when you're dead, you're dead.'

'Well, you are dead. I killed you, kinda.' Jimmy trailed off his interruption, partly because he felt guilty and partly because of the way Wendy was looking at him.

'As I was saying, I always assumed that when you're dead, you're dead, but now I'm not so sure. Could you still be alive if people who knew you still talk about you and smile when they remember you?' Wendy was asking this as a hypothetical question, but Jimmy looked at her as if she was talking another language. Wendy warmed to her subject. 'Suppose two of your best friends leave you after a party. One flies off to Alabama and the other goes skydiving in the Andes but his chute doesn't open. A week later, you think about both of them and the fun you had at the party together. One is alive in Alabama and the other is dead but you don't know it. To you they're both still equally alive and part of your memory. So even though one is dead, he is kinda still alive. It's a philosophical point I grant ya, but it's relevant. You're never really dead until you're forgotten and everyone you knew is also dead. D'ya get where I'm coming from?'

Jimmy just stared at Wendy. 'If your chute doesn't open, you're gonna be dead. If you fly to Alabama, you might as well be dead!'

Wendy shrugged. 'OK, you have a point about Alabama, but who are you talking to now?'

Jimmy thought for a moment. 'You?'

'Yes, obviously, but what am I? Do I exist or am I just a figment of your imagination? Socrates said that the soul must be immortal because the living come from the dead.'

'I thought Socrates played for Brazil.'

Wendy threw herself off the cliff in frustration. Jimmy then jumped to his feet but before he could look over the edge to see what had happened, Wendy floated back into view. She held open her arms.

'So how do we explain this?' she asked. 'My theory is that the spirit, if it is strong and positive, can go on, but negative energy is just spent after the earthly life is over. That's why I saw Sammy; that's why you see me. Good, positive energy. That, or you're just tripping on a guilty imagination.'

Jimmy thought about what Wendy had just said. 'Did you do philosophy and physics at college, cos since you died that seems to be all you wanna talk about? You never went on about this stuff when you were alive.'

Wendy landed next to him. 'That's because I was alive, too busy living to really think, but now I'm not, well, it makes you think about stuff. Doesn't all this make you think?'

Jimmy shook his head. 'I'm too busy trying to keep all these balls in the air. I got five dead people buried up here. I am kinda responsible for Sammy, and I have to kill another five scum-bags in three weeks before I go into the recording studio. This murdering ain't easy, especially when you're a nice person!'

'When you put it like that, it's hard to disagree.' She paused for a moment. She could see that Jimmy was still upset by Sammy's death and she knew he was feeling the pressure of his deadline. Wendy still cared for Jimmy, and she was desperate for him not to miss his opportunity. She also had her own agenda; now was the time to bring it up. 'Who's up next, Jimmy? Sleazy Peterson?'

Jimmy nodded reluctantly. 'Yeah, I reckon he's looking my favourite. That's gonna be tricky, though, getting him on his own. That place never stops doing business, and Sleazy is always in his bar or in one of his girls.'

Wendy pulled a face. 'Ugh, a naked Sleazy don't bear thinking about. You're just gonna have to stake him out and wait for an opportunity.'

Jimmy kicked at the ground in frustration. 'But that could take days, maybe weeks, and I don't have that kind of time. Sleazy is on the list, but I need some softer targets.'

Wendy saw her chance. 'Well, I have a suggestion for you.'

'I'm listening,' Jimmy replied, looking at her.

Wendy sat down on a rock. 'I was raped two years ago by three bikers who are part of that gang that run out of Little River.' She was staring at the ground not wanting to look at Jimmy. 'I never went to the police because Sheriff Pence is on the take from the gang. He turns a blind eye to their bootlegging for a nice backhander. I was trying to be clever and taking the piss out of one of them. I made him look stupid in front of his friends one night in the Reservation Club. Two nights later when I was walking back to the casino from the Reservation, they grabbed me. Three of them in a white panel van. They drove me out of town and took off down the old track to the mine. I thought they were gonna kill me but they raped me instead, all of them. Then they kicked me out and told me to keep my mouth shut in future.'

Jimmy could feel a rage rising within him. 'Why didn't you tell me? I would've—'

'What?' Wendy interrupted him. 'There was nothing you could do, Jimmy. You couldn't beat three of them up. Besides, we weren't going out then; it wasn't your fight. Sheriff Pence wasn't gonna do anything – my word against theirs.' As she looked up at Jimmy, a slow wicked smile spread across her face. 'But now, Jimmy, now you have a reason to kill. You have the means to kill, and I want my revenge. The three of them tend to ride together, so from where I'm standing this is a winner. What d'ya say?'

Jimmy didn't hesitate. 'I'm in.'

———◆———

Jimmy wasn't the only person planning a murder. Back in Las Vegas, Jack Lantern was sat in his office. He was sure Jimmy had something to do with the murders of his men. They had been missing for too long for them still to be alive; people didn't tend to take hostages in this game. No, Vinny, Carmine and Ted were all dead, and the answer to their deaths lay in Blackjack. Jimmy Wayne had questions to answer.

Jack had lost three of his best men but, luckily, murdering scumbags were not hard to find in Vegas – if you paid them well. They were loyal too, mainly because they knew Jack would have them killed if they overstepped the mark.

The relationship required no contract and opportunities for advancement frequently occurred. Jack now had three senior positions to fill in his customer relations department. That's what he called it. His customers didn't usually complain – if they did, it was never for long. That said, Jack wasn't big on kill-ing too many people. Once you were dead, you couldn't make Jack money, couldn't pay his loans or buy his drugs, and you certainly wouldn't be able to make those illegal bets.

No, Jack relied on ruling by fear, but he applied it in a prag-matic fashion. Criminal Economics 101 was how he liked to regard it. Suck you in first and then, once you were trapped in his web, there was no escape. He had done that with Jimmy years ago. Jimmy was struggling. He had got near to making it but had just missed his chance and he was on the slide, but he still had money and he liked to drink so Jack took his orders and never stopped filling his glass. He actually thought that Jimmy was going to make it because he was pretty good – he was wrong.

Jimmy was on a one-way ride and falling. He was even ignor-ing Jack's demands for payment, thinking Jack would never hurt him because of their special relationship, but that relationship was over. Jack had realised that Jimmy was never going to turn it around, and that was why he'd decided to make an example of him, but somehow something had gone wrong.

What made it even more complicated was that Jimmy seemed to be on the way back up. Jack had decided he would hold off killing him until he knew what the comeback was going to be. A successful Jimmy would be perfect for exploiting. You don't kill the goose that lays the golden egg, and Jimmy looked like he was just about to lay a bunch of them.

Jack's intercom buzzed. 'The boys are here to see you.' It was Margo, Jack's PA, a heart of stone and a face even harder.

'Let them in.'

'OK.' She hung up and a couple of seconds later the door swung open and two more of Jack's customer relations men entered.

Tony C was a giant of a man and had worked for a New York mobster before moving to Vegas and transferring his skills to Jack. Jack never found out what the 'C' stood for because Tony clearly did not want to say. He was good at his job, collected the money owed, broke a leg or two when required and was very efficient at hiding the bodies when the public relations process had become deadlocked. With him was his partner-in-crime Terry Moist. Terry was a strange man who also had a strange surname. Jack had once joked about Terry always being moist. Terry had said nothing; he'd just stared at Jack as though he was considering how best to dismember and eat him. Jack actually liked that about Terry. If he could disturb Jack, his boss, imagine what he would do to the non-paying customers.

Jack indicated that they sit down on the large sofa opposite his desk. They looked a bit incongruous next to each other. Tony was six-foot-five and Terry was five-foot-nine, but they both gave off an air of violent menace. This pleased Jack very much; in public relations, it was so important to send the right message.

'I expect you're wondering why I brought you in here.'

They both just looked at Jack. 'Someone need killing.' It was Terry. He spoke in a slow Texan drawl. 'Or just a light maiming.'

Tony smiled. 'That's funny, Terry.'

Terry didn't look away from Jack. 'I wasn't joking. Mr Lantern didn't call us back from Chicago to issue threats.' He looked questioningly at Jack. 'Did you!' It wasn't a question.

Jack thought for a moment before answering. 'To be fair, Terry, I'm not sure. I have a very delicate situation going on in

Nevada. Vinny, Carmine and Ted have all gone missing there. They're over a week late now, so I'm guessing they're all dead. The person I sent Vinny and Carmine to kill is still alive. They sent me live pictures on their phone showing the guy they were about to kill. He was tied up and begging for his life but now they're missing and he's still alive.'

Terry was nodding. 'He must have an accomplice, then.'

'You're probably right, but we need to tread carefully. This guy is Jimmy Wayne. You heard of him?'

'The singer,' interrupted Tony. 'He was good. My wife and I went to see him once about twelve years ago.'

'That's the guy. He has a new record coming out, and it looks like he's gonna make it big this time, so—'

'We don't wanna kill him. You want us to find out if he did the murders and if he did, we can blackmail him for a lot of the money he's about to make.' Jack let Terry finish. He always seemed to spot the angle straight away and, as usual, he was right.

'Spot on – Criminal Economics 101! You and Tony go to Blackjack, pretend to be gamblers, try not to look too menacing.' Terry just stared back at Jack. His face was expressionless, cold. Jack then looked away and smiled at Tony C. Six-foot-five and two-hundred-and-sixty pounds. How were these guys ever going to blend in? They looked exactly what they were: mobsters.

Terry tried to smile. 'I could use my happy face, Mr Lantern.'

Jack shivered. Terry's happy face looked like he'd just eaten a baby ... live. A Rottweiler with indigestion. 'Maybe just pretend to be two married guys having a break from their wives on a road trip with a bit of gambling and golf thrown in for good measure. You do know how to play golf, don't you?'

Terry nodded and a wry smiled cracked the corners of his mouth. 'If it involves hitting things, I find I'm pretty good at it, Mr Lantern.'

Jack returned his grin. 'I'm sure you are, Terry.' He pushed two large Manila folders over the desk to each of the men. 'In there are all your booking details for the Riviera, false identities, credit cards and cash. Margo has also taken the trouble to give you a full outline on Jimmy Wayne and about the final contact we had with Vinny, Carmine and Ted. There's a vehicle in the car park downstairs with a weapons case concealed in the trunk as usual.'

'Mind if we take my car, Jack? I think it will blend in better with our cover story. I can swap everything over in the car park,' said Terry.

Jack thought about it for a moment. 'The one with the cow horns on the front?' Terry nodded. Jack shrugged and replied, 'Fine with me – as long as it can't be traced back to me and it has a weapons case in it.'

'It does.'

'OK, just don't do anything until we speak. I'm gonna be there at the weekend with my wife, we can talk then. Just act natural and try to blend in.'

Terry grimaced from a face that looked like an image from a Stephen King novel. 'Act natural, I can do that.'

From six foot five above the floor Tony towered over the others. 'Blend in. Got it!'

Jack watched as they left his office. The only place those guys would blend in is a line-up. He sat at his desk pondering the events of the past two weeks. It had to have something to do with Jimmy Wayne, but how had Jimmy pulled it off. He was a middle-aged, out of condition lounge singer, and his guys were hardened killers. None of it added up.

Jack had been in this game a long time, and you only stayed on top if you knew exactly what was going on – all the time. There was a slight fear tugging away in his gut that maybe there was more to this.

Maybe someone else was using Jimmy as bait to draw him out. Could someone be trying to move in on him? It was a question he'd been asking himself ever since the boys disappeared. Did someone want his empire? Jack decided he was going to be tooled up when he went to Blackjack. Always best to be prepared.

CHAPTER 12
IMMORAL GUIDANCE

Jimmy sat on the stage in the Canyon Room. He was picking a tune out on his guitar while waiting for the band to roll in for rehearsal. They had three new songs to learn. 'Hanging Around' and 'Rage' were already fully arranged, but it was a different story with 'Lonely Old Lady' – he just couldn't seem to get it to work. The lyrics were so sad, and that wasn't how Sammy was.

He hummed it as he tried to figure it out. He was concentrating and didn't notice Kid Oscarson stroll into the room. Kid hung back by the edge of the stage and listened intently to what Jimmy was trying to do. After a couple of minutes, Jimmy hit another dead end and slapped the strings in frustration. As he looked up, he saw Kid watching at him.

'Oh, hi, Kid.' He looked down at his fretboard. 'Just can't seem to get this song right.'

'That much is clear. Mind if I offer some advice?'

Jimmy respected Kid as a musician and was more than happy to hear whatever he had to suggest. 'Please do, I'm kinda stuck.'

'This is the song you wrote after Sammy died?' Jimmy nodded. 'You're trying to fill it with too much emotion. You loved her and you want the music to portray this swelling emotion that carries the listener off, but it's not that kind of song. It's not about Sammy; it's about a lonely old lady. Sammy was everything this lady wasn't. Don't give it too much love and emotion or you will choke it to death.'

Jimmy listened and started to understand the point that Kid was making. 'So how would you play it?'

Kid smiled. 'To me this song has to be wistful, melancholic. You're reflecting on what might have been as an observer. Don't make yourself emotionally involved with the central character or you kill the song. Wistful detachment, and then you can reflect all the nuances of the lyrics. I could write you a lovely soaring soundscape as a backdrop to it if you like.'

Jimmy did like – he liked very much. 'Man, I don't know how you do that. Now I think about it like that, I can hear it already. I've been going down the wrong road for days.'

Kid smiled a slow warm smile. 'Well, Jimmy, they do say it's all about the journey.'

While they had been talking, Lewis and Joe had shown up. They were all happy and joking around, but Lewis seemed to be reserved. As the leader of the band, Jimmy knew how to recognise problems.

They rehearsed 'Hanging Around' first. As it seeped from the speakers, it sounded dark and moody, and the boys knew they were on to something. Bands can play for years and never really find their groove, but not this band. They had found their sound, and they were putting some grease on it.

They took a break after they had finished 'Hanging Around'. Joe and Kid disappeared outside to smoke whatever it was they were smoking while Lewis fetched a couple of coffees and brought them over to where Jimmy was sitting.

'Thanks, what d'ya think of the new song?' asked Jimmy.

Lewis sat down in the chair next to him and leaned back as he thought about the question for a moment. 'Well, you know it's good, very good. Unfortunately, it's too good!' It wasn't just what Lewis had said but the way he'd said it. He sounded so full of regret.

Jimmy turned and looked at Lewis looking sad. 'Strange thing to say. Never heard anybody complain that a song was too good before. What's going on?'

Lewis took a sip of his coffee as if bracing himself. 'Jimmy, the stuff you're coming up with now is off the scale. I've been there with the Texas Trucking Company. Top of your game and everything is flying. You're filling venues and selling records by the lorry load. I've seen it before, and I can tell you it's gonna happen to you.' Lewis was speaking as though he was a preacher delivering a prophesy, so certain did he seem. 'Jimmy, take it from me, you're going all the way this time. Name up in lights in Vegas and in LA and New York.'

Jimmy had never heard Lewis talk like this before; usually he would just poke fun at him for phoning it in. 'So, what's the problem, then? If we're gonna be big stars, I'm struggling to see a downside.'

Lewis just sat there. It was obvious he wanted to say something, but he just didn't know how to start.

Jimmy reached across and placed his hand on Lewis's shoulder. 'Whatever it is, Lewis, just say it. You've been with me through thick and thin these last few years, mostly thin. You're entitled to say what you think.'

Lewis let Jimmy's words sink in and he seemed to relax. He took a deep breath and turned to look him straight in the eye. 'Jimmy, I love you like a brother. Even when you were a drunken fool I still loved you. You're a decent man and you're a damn fine singer and musician. It's always been fun to be around and play a couple of nights a week with you, but that Jimmy left about six weeks back. Since you wrote that first song, you've changed, and it's all good. The new songs are amazing; the old covers are beautifully reimagined and performed.' Lewis shook his head as if in disbelief. 'Jimmy, you have just become a star while I watched from the keyboards. You're on a journey and much as I want to, I just can't go with you.' They sat there looking at each other, Lewis waiting for Jimmy to say something and Jimmy trying to work out what Lewis was trying to tell him.

Jimmy leaned back in his chair. His brow was furrowed as he tried to put everything together.

Lewis said nothing. He was just waiting for the penny to drop.

Finally, Jimmy worked it out. 'Are you trying to tell me you're leaving the band?' There was a degree of incredulity in his voice.

'Took your time getting there, but that's the top and bottom of it.'

Jimmy sat there shaking his head. 'Why would you do that when we're just about to go to LA to cut a record and then on to Vegas for a massive residency which will make us a fortune.'

Lewis sighed; this was as hard as he'd expected it to be. When he spoke, it was quietly, gently. 'I'm sixty-seven years old. I'm married to the love of my life. We have a house on the edge of town looking out over the golf course to the mountains. We have friends and family nearby. This –' he gestured towards the back of the hall where the large windows showed the mountains bathed in sunlight '– is where I live. I've been to the big time when I was young with the Truckers; I'm too old to go again. This is your time, grab it with both your hands and I will be watching you, cheering you, but I just can't come with you.'

Jimmy just sat there trying to take in Lewis' news. Lewis was like an older brother to him, offering guidance and support. He had also never been afraid to tell him when he was being a fool. He was one of the rocks his precarious life was built on, and all these rocks seemed to be crumbling. First Wendy, then David, because David wasn't going to be coming to LA or Vegas, and now Lewis.

'I'm not sure I can do it without you, Lewis.' The words were heartfelt, but Lewis just chuckled.

'Course you can, Jimmy. You don't need any of us now. With these songs and your voice, any band could back you up.' Lewis took another sip from his coffee. 'Jimmy, you cannot imagine what fame is like. It's like trying to hold back the incoming tide. It's gonna wash over you and drown you in feelings and emotions that you just can't comprehend. It will eat you up if you're not careful, but, man –' Lewis looked up into the distant mountains and when he spoke there was wonder in his voice. 'What a ride, Jimmy, what a ride! I wish I was twenty years younger, and I would be with you every step of the way, but I'm not.'

Jimmy couldn't look at Lewis. He nodded slowly. 'I guess I understand when you put it like that. I really wanted to take you with me. A thank you for all the times you had to bail me out.'

Lewis laughed out loud. 'There aint enough thanks in the world for that.'

When Kid and Joe returned from their smoke break, Jimmy and Lewis were almost crying with laughter. 'What's so funny?' asked Joe.

When Jimmy finally stopped laughing, he turned to Joe. 'Lewis is quitting the band.'

Joe looked shocked, and Jimmy and Lewis burst out laughing once again.

When the rehearsal had finished, they had all three new songs arranged just the way Jimmy had hoped. The set now comprised six new songs – all of them the best that Jimmy had ever written and the only songs he'd ever written that had been worthy of publishing.

Jimmy was the last one to leave. Kid and Joe were giving Half-Eaten Burger an outing as a Steppenwolf tribute tonight. Jimmy wasn't sure how many motors it would set running, but he quite fancied getting down there to watch and have a couple of beers. Those boys could play, so it was bound to be pretty damn good.

David came hurrying into the room. 'James, so glad I caught you.' For once in his elegant, sophisticated life, David Parker actually looked slightly flustered. Jimmy found this amusing.

'You OK, David? You look like you've just been in the boardroom.'

David didn't miss the reference to his dalliance with a previous employer's wife, but he chose to ignore it. 'I have some news about one of your dalliances that may just wipe that smirk off your face.'

'My dalliance? I haven't had so much as a cuddle since Wendy left.'

David raised an eyebrow. 'You sure about that, James?'

'Ah,' said Jimmy. 'I was forgetting the lovely Lena.'

David nodded enthusiastically. 'Well remembered. I come bearing news of the lovely Lena.'

'Great, can't wait to see her again.' He winked at David. 'If you know what I mean.'

David did know what he meant. 'Well, I have good and bad news. First the good.'

Jimmy smiled. 'Always like good news, especially where Lena's concerned.'

'Well, the good news is that Lena will be here for your shows at the weekend.'

This cheered Jimmy up. 'That's great.'

David held up a cautionary finger. 'The bad news, she's bringing her husband.'

Jimmy frowned. This was bad news. Having sex with Lena was going to be tricky with her husband around.

David had known Jimmy long enough to have worked out exactly what he was thinking. 'Perhaps you would like to know who her husband is.'

Jimmy looked at David and just shrugged. 'Not really. I don't wanna sleep with him!'

David slowly shook his head. 'James, if you're going to sleep with a man's wife, you really should check out who she is married to.'

Jimmy shrugged again. 'Go on then, I can see you're dying to tell me.'

David became solemn. 'The lovely Lena has informed me that she will be arriving with her husband … Mr Jack Lantern.'

Jimmy stood motionless. David had just said that Lena was married to Jack Lantern. This couldn't be true, it wasn't true. But then he looked at David's face – it was true. Jimmy couldn't move; he couldn't speak. He felt as if his whole world was falling around him. Everything he had started to build was about to crumble to nothing. The man who just a couple of weeks earlier had laughed at him through a phone screen as he'd told him how he was going to die was married to Lena. When he arrived and saw Jimmy, he would know he had killed his men. He had to run – to stay would mean certain death. But running, he would be running away from the record deal, the Vegas residency, the fame and fortune – everything. He looked at David and could see that he understood his dilemma but only with regards to sleeping with Jack Lantern's wife.

'You're going to have to brazen it out. Maybe he doesn't know you're sleeping with her,' said David, trying to sound supportive. Jimmy laughed.

'Jack Lantern knows everything.' He had to get away and think. Wendy would know what to do; he had to find her. He grabbed his guitar and shoved it into the case. 'Look, David, thanks for the heads up, but I gotta go.' He started to hurry from the hall. 'Speak to you tonight,' he called back over his shoulder.

David stood there watching the panic-stricken Jimmy run out of the room. *Poor Jimmy*, he thought. *He'd got so close this time.* He didn't think Jimmy's comeback would survive the wrath of Jack Lantern, at the very least he could make sure he didn't work in Vegas or LA. David didn't want to consider what

Jack Lantern would do if he found out that Jimmy had been sleeping with Lena.

———◆———

Jimmy rushed back into his room and threw his guitar case on the floor. He felt sick to the pit of his stomach; the memory of that night in the pickup with Vinny and Carmine swept over him like a nightmare he could not forget. He sat on the bed; he was shivering. It wasn't cold in the room – it was pure terror. He couldn't think straight. Since the moment David had spoken Jack Lantern's name, all the lights in his world had been extinguished. He wrapped his arms around himself and rocked back and forth. *Jack Lantern, married to Lena … fuck, fuck!* His thoughts were like clothes in a tumble dryer. Everything was moving. He just couldn't focus. He needed Wendy.

'Now THAT, dear Jimmy, is what you call karma!'

In Jimmy's terrified state, he nearly jumped off the bed. Wendy was sitting next to him. 'Jesus!'

Wendy raised an eyebrow. 'Now, I thought you'd be pleased to see me.' She stood up. 'I can go if you like?'

Jimmy grabbed her arm. 'Please don't. I'm in trouble.' Jimmy sounded desperate – he was.

Wendy was slowly shaking her head, but there was also an amused twinkle dancing in her eyes. 'Jack Lantern's wife?' It was a rhetorical question, and Wendy just let it hang there between them. 'Are you fucking mad, Jimmy? Can you imagine what he would do to you if he found out? If he was gonna cut your fingers off for a gambling debt, imagine what he's gonna cut off for doing his wife.'

Jimmy put his head in his hands. 'I know, Wendy, I resisted for years but she caught me at a weak moment.' He looked up quickly. 'It stopped before we went out, though.'

Wendy put her hand on the back of his head. 'I know, and started again about four weeks after you killed me.'

'That's not fair, it wasn't like that,' said Jimmy, springing to his feet.

Wendy pulled him back down beside her on the bed. 'Jimmy,' her voice was soft now, 'I'm only winding you up because –' She paused for a moment, uncertain of how to frame what she wanted to say.

Jimmy said it for her. 'Because I'm a fucking idiot who can't keep it in his trousers. Because I'm the fool who always blows every chance he gets. Because –'

Wendy put a finger to his lips to silence him. 'Well, I wasn't gonna put it exactly like that, but you're close enough. Now, Jimmy, do you wanna sit here feeling sorry for yourself or do you wanna know how we're gonna get you out of this?' Wendy's words sounded good, but he knew there was no way he could make this right. This time he had gone too far. Wendy then slapped him hard across the face.

Jimmy yelped in pain. 'Aww! That hurt!'

Wendy ignored him. When she spoke, she was serious and her tone implied that Jimmy really shouldn't interrupt her unless he wanted another firm smack. For a ghost, she had one hell of a right hand.

'Here's what you need to understand. Jack Lantern knows you're alive. He would've checked that out the second Lena told him they were coming here, to see you. He thinks you killed Vinny and Carmine, but he can't prove it. He suspects that you had something to do with the death of the Baker man but, again, he can't prove it. My guess is he knows you've been having an affair with Lena for years ... but he's not bothered. Jack sleeps with all the girls in his clubs and strip joints. Lena is just an ornament that he wears to big functions. He may like her, but he doesn't love her.' Wendy was walking up and down the side of the bed as though delivering a tactical talk to a football team before a big match. Jimmy listened. 'If Jack wanted you dead, you'd already be in the ground. Jack's coming because he's curious; he wants to know what happened to his boys. He also wants to know what's going on with you.'

'Me? Up till last week he thought I was dead.'

Wendy opened her arms. 'Doh! And how'd he find out you weren't dead. His wife told him you were headlining the Canyon Room, that's how! Jack Lantern would've checked that out. Why was Jimmy Wayne now filling a three hundred-seater every time he plays at the Riviera? Then he would've seen the Rivera advertising your show. Jimmy Wayne's got new songs. He's having a comeback. He has a big record deal in LA. These are all things he could've found out on the grapevine very quickly. Your Jimmy Wayne fan club seems to have risen from the grave as well.' Wendy paused and looked mildly nauseous. 'Unfortunately, the Waynettes seem to have also done a Lazarus.'

The Waynettes were Jimmy's hardcore female fans from the nineties, when he was breaking through for the first time. They dressed like high-school cheerleaders from the 1950s. Had it been the Dallas Cowboys circa 1970 onwards, Jimmy wouldn't have complained, but by the start of the new millennium he felt like he was being stalked by the female cast members from *Happy Days.*

Wendy continued, 'we have to assume that Jack knows all this. So, why aren't you dead?' Wendy waited for Jimmy to fill in the blanks.

He shook his head. 'Fucked if I know.'

Wendy gave him a knowing look. 'Then let me tell you. Jack Lantern is coming here to see just how good you are. If you're really good, which you are, it wouldn't make any sense to kill you because you'll be able to repay him. That's the good bit; the bad bit is that whatever you owe him is just about to treble.'

Jimmy was interested now. Ever since Wendy had said it made no sense for Jack to kill him. He liked the sound of that. 'Why has the debt gone up, out of interest?'

Like a high-school teacher encouraging an enthusiastic pupil, Wendy congratulated him. 'Good point, Jimmy. There are gonna be reparations involved.'

Jimmy was confused. 'Repair whats?'

'Re-pa-ra-tions.' Wendy said it slowly pronouncing every syllable. 'Atonement, damages. Mostly for screwing his wife, but also for late payment on your loan. Jack will come to a deal with you as long as he can see that you're gonna be able to repay him. Men like Jack worship money and power – nothing else matters.'

'I get what you're saying, but how do we make good killing his men?'

Wendy shrugged. 'We don't. We just say that you tried to escape after the phone call to Jack. Vinny punched you and knocked you out. When you came round, you were lying at the end of the mine track and you were alone but someone had untied your hands. Mention just after the phone call that Jack's boys had spotted a car turning off the road but the lights had been turned off as soon as it hit the track. Stick to that story and Jack is gonna think that someone else is silently moving in on his action. He's never gonna think that a middle-aged, out of shape lounge singer took down three of his men, is he?'

'Easy, Wendy, you're hurting my feelings. I don't sing in a lounge anymore.'

'That bit's correct, but as for the rest of it –' Wendy smiled.

'Hey,' Jimmy interrupted her, 'I got feelings.' There was one thing still bugging Jimmy. 'You said three?'

'That Baker guy with Jackson was one of Jack's boys, but he has nothing to link you to him in any way, and the story we're spinning about Vinny knocking you out and then someone else knocking them off makes sense – more sense than you killing them. If we get Jack Lantern worried about a turf war, he won't be thinking about you.' Wendy looked at Jimmy triumphantly. 'Can you sell that to Jack?'

Jimmy nodded. 'Sure can. What do I do about Lena?'

Wendy gave him a withering look. 'Do what you always do, deny everything! Lena sure as hell will!'

———◆———

Jimmy sat alone in the restaurant that evening. He was looking at the menu, but he didn't know why. It was Wednesday. He would have rib-eye steak, fries and mushrooms with a peppercorn sauce – that's what he always had on a Wednesday. It's at times like this you realise that you've been somewhere too long. He could tell the days by the food he was going to eat. Jimmy needed more variety in his life and, judging by his waistline, his diet.

That said, Jimmy liked rib-eye steak and fries. Why did life have to have so many conundrums? Today had been a strange day. The high of playing the new songs with the band had been spoilt by the news of Lena being Jack Lantern's wife. That was a real killer – potentially.

As always, Wendy had provided a rational plan, which actually had him believing it could work. *Damn! For a dead girl she's really smart.* While Jimmy was playing back the events of the day in his mind, Kid walked into the restaurant. He saw Jimmy and made his way over.

'Mind if I join you?' he asked.

Jimmy nodded and pointed at the opposite chair. 'Be my guest. I thought you were playing the Reservation with Joe tonight.'

Kid looked rueful. 'So did we. Been practising our Steppenwolf routine with Freddie and Matt.' They were the bass player and rhythm guitarist who made up the other half of Half-Eaten Burger. 'We were getting pretty good. Freddie had the vocal down.'

Jimmy looked disappointed, and he was. He had been looking forward to a night just chilling and listening to some Steppenwolf. Hearing Kid play, when he didn't have to sing in front of him, was a real treat. Kid was such a lyrical and inventive guitarist; he was always interesting.

'What happened?' asked Jimmy.

Kid looked angry. 'Turned out that the guy who'd booked us was that piece of shit drug dealer Jackson Pollack – apparently he's gone missing.' That got Jimmy's attention. 'He was supposed to pay upfront yesterday for the band and hire of the stage, but he seems to have just disappeared. If I'd known it was that piece of shit who was hiring us, I wouldn't have taken the gig.'

Jimmy looked non-committal. 'No harm done, then.' He then pretended to think for a moment as if trying to remember some of the characters in the Reservation Bar. 'You sure it was Jackson?'

'Yep, Gary told me it was Jackson who booked it.'

Jimmy smiled sympathetically. 'It's hardly a surprise that it's all gone wrong if that idiot's involved.'

Kid scowled and looked as though he was ready to break something.

'You don't like him, do you?'

After thinking for a moment, a smile slowly spread across Kid's features. When he spoke, all the anger he had shown just a few moments before had disappeared. 'No, I didn't.'

Jimmy caught the use of past tense by Kid. 'Didn't? Do you know something the rest of us don't?'

Kid didn't reply straight away. He then picked up a menu and looked at it. 'What you having?'

Jimmy pointed at the picture of the juicy T-bone cooked to perfection with perfect fries and an immaculate peppercorn sauce dribbling down its beefy flanks. 'It never looks like that when it arrives, but it aint bad.'

'Artistic licence.' Kid smirked as he said it.

The waitress came over and took their order. They both ordered a small beer. Neither were in recovery but both had managed to virtually stop drinking; but with a nice steak, it would be a crime not to have a little beer with it.

Kid leaned towards Jimmy. 'Could I offer you some advice without prejudice, my friend?'

It seemed a strange way of phrasing the sentence, but Jimmy didn't have a problem with answering any questions Kid had to ask.

'Listen, Jimmy, I know you're a good man, but– '

That, thought Jimmy, *is not a good start.*

'It's obvious to me that this sudden burst of creativity you seem to have found coincides with Wendy's departure.'

Jimmy said nothing; he couldn't work out where Kid was going.

'Sammy has also died and Jackson Pollack has disappeared. Those two thugs you went off with after the show a couple of weeks back have disappeared as well.'

Jimmy tried to appear calm; he was anything but. 'What makes you think that?' He tried to sound cool, but the tension was clear in his voice.

Kid continued, 'There was a guy called Baker came looking for Jackson at the Reservation a few days back. While he was asking about him, he also showed me a picture of those two guys you went off with after the show. He said they'd disappeared.' When Kid had finished talking, he looked straight at Jimmy. 'Kinda makes you think, don't it?'

Jimmy sat there trying to work out what Kid knew. 'You seem to be inventing a fantasy world all of your own here. I don't have the first clue what you're on about. Wendy ran off with another man, Sammy died of natural causes and as for the other four, well, they were all scumbags if you ask me, so who cares where they went.'

Kid watched Jimmy as he spoke and nodded in agreement when he had finished. 'Undoubtedly those men were all scumbags – we know that Jackson was.'

'Why do you keep saying *were*? Do you think they're dead?'

A knowing smile broke across Kid's features. 'Oh, I am certain they're dead, Jimmy. I just don't know how, or why.'

Jimmy had lost his appetite, but he sat perfectly still and listened to Kid. He didn't want to do or say anything that gave his secrets away.

Kid was playing with the salt cellar, and then he picked up the pepper grinder in his other massive hand. 'Let's say that the salt represents good and the pepper represents evil. There are times in the universe when these things can come up directly against each other.' He butted the two condiments up against each other. 'Sometimes for good to triumph over evil it has to do bad things. The end justifies the means sorta scenario. There are those –' Kid looked intently at Jimmy as he spoke '– and I'm not among their number, that think good should never cross that line. Evil, wherever we find it, must be defeated, Jimmy. The ends really do justify the means ... sometimes! Do you understand what I'm trying to say?'

'Kid, I haven't understood a damn word you've said since you asked if you could join me.'

Kid chuckled gently at the strength of Jimmy's denial. 'Course you have. You have understood every word.' They both sat there looking at each other saying nothing. Kid then reached across the table and placed a huge hand on Jimmy's arm. 'There is a balance to the world. There is an energy that is released when a life is born and when a life departs. I think you've managed to harness the energy from deaths and channel that into your creative process.' Jimmy tried to deny it but the grip on his arm tightened like a vice being turned. 'All I'm saying is that this is fine as long as you're on the side of right. The death of evil is never bad. If you need help identifying that evil, I can help. Immoral guidance if you will, but only in the service of our art. I shall say no more unless you want to discuss it, but be assured I'm on your side.'

Jimmy slowly shook his head. Kid knew what he had done, he didn't know how but he was sure he knew, but he also appeared to understand. At this moment, Jimmy just couldn't admit it. 'Kid, anyone ever told you that you're batshit crazy?'

'Several people, and a couple of times they were right, but not this time, Jimmy.'

Just then, the waitress arrived with their steaks. They took them and thanked her. As she walked away, Kid winked at Jimmy. 'Immoral guidance. Bon appétit!'

Jimmy picked up his cutlery and slowly began to slice his beef. Man, if this day got anymore fucked up, he was staying in bed tomorrow.

CHAPTER 13
FANCY A THREESOME?

Jimmy hadn't slept well. His evening meal with Kid was still running through his brain like a broken record. Kid knew. He knew, but he seemed on board with what he was doing. If he had understood Kid correctly, he was offering his services as a kind of 'scumbag selector'. He would line up potential victims for Jimmy to knock off. Jimmy just couldn't decide if this was a good or a bad thing. He had always been reasonably private about his private life, mainly because he was usually having sex with other men's wives, but also because he preferred people not to know his business.

Now Jack Lantern knew he was having an affair with Lena, and Kid seemed to understand that he was busy killing the local criminals and the occasional accidental girlfriend. Oh, and an elderly lady friend – that one really wasn't his fault, though.

Normally, this would be a disastrous turn of events, leading to a shallow grave in the desert with no fingers, or the electric chair – apparently this wasn't a problem anymore. Jack Lantern would welcome the additional repayment, Jimmy also assumed, when he made it big, and that favours were going to be asked. As for Kid, he just seemed keen to help ensure that Jack only killed the most deserving cases. *Right now*, he thought, *my life just couldn't get any weirder ... then it did!*

'OK, Jimmy, you need to get up and dressed.' Wendy had just entered his bedroom – through the ceiling right above his bed. He was staring at the ceiling at the time. It's impossible to convey the surprise that the appearance of a deceased girlfriend through your bedroom ceiling brings. Let's just say that Jimmy rose, almost vertically from his bed.

'WENDY! What the fuck! You're gonna kill me with a heart attack if you keep doing this!'

Wendy smiled. 'That would be ironic, killing you in bed, accidently.' She gave Jimmy a mischievous look. 'D'ya think that kinda thing really happens?'

Jimmy thought about it for a moment. 'Go boil your head, Wendy.'

Wendy switched on Jimmy's coffee machine. 'Let's just boil some water and see if we can get you in a better mood. You've got a busy day ahead of you.'

Jimmy was puzzled; he wasn't doing anything until tonight's show in the Canyon Room. He had been hoping to be doing something to Lena, but now he knew her surname was Lantern that probably wasn't going to happen again, ever!

'Show doesn't start until eight, sound check at seven.' Jimmy looked at his watch. 'It's only nine thirty in the morning, Wendy, way too early.' Wendy was now poking around in Jimmy's wardrobe. 'What you looking for?'

Wendy leaned out from behind the door. 'Well, if it's style I'm obviously gonna be disappointed.'

Jimmy walked over to the wardrobe to see what Wendy was rooting around in – his porn stash was hidden in there and he didn't want her finding it. 'Can I help you find what you're looking for? It is my wardrobe after all.'

Wendy appeared from behind the door. She had a white polo shirt in one hand and a pair of red slacks in the other. She thrust them into his chest. 'Have a shower and put these on.'

Jimmy, looking aghast at the deep ruby red of the trousers, replied, 'I can't wear these.' He held them up to the light. 'Just look at them!'

Wendy ignored him. 'Why are they in your wardrobe, then? Look, Jimmy, you're only playing golf, and everyone knows you're supposed to look like an idiot when you play golf. It's part of the etiquette!' Wendy looked at the trousers as Jimmy held them up. 'You'll look an idiot in those, so you'll blend in perfectly with the soon-to-be dead that pass for members at Blackjack Golf Club.' Wendy started to make Jimmy's coffee. 'Come on, get showered and dressed. Jack Lantern has booked you a tee time for ten thirty.'

This new information stopped Jimmy dead in his tracks. 'Say that again.'

Wendy didn't even turn around when she spoke. 'You heard, Jimmy, Jack Lantern is inviting you for a game of golf and you can't say no. One of his boys is gonna be here in a few minutes. I was eavesdropping on his phone calls.' Wendy poured Jimmy's coffee. 'There you go.' She held out the steaming mug, and Jimmy put down the polo shirt to take it. 'What's your golf like?'

Jimmy sipped his coffee and shook his head. 'Well, it's not gonna be good enough to beat Jack Lantern. I heard he was pretty good, and he cheats!'

Wendy laughed. 'Don't matter how much he cheats, he won't be beating you today. Just remember to stick to the story we discussed.' She reached out and ruffled Jimmy's hair while saying, 'Don't look so worried – everything's gonna be fine.'

Just then, there was a knock on the door.

Wendy mouthed the words, 'That's him!'

Jimmy went over to the door and opened it. Standing there was Terry Moist, two-hundred-and-ten pounds of simmering resentment and a product of a home devoid of love.

'Mr Lantern requests your presence on the first tee in forty-five minutes.' The invite was delivered with the gravitas of a judge handing out a death penalty.

'I don't think Mr Lantern mentioned it,' said Jimmy.

Terry Moist's features did not move. In his slow Texas drawl, he continued unfazed. 'Well he did now. I recommend you get those clothes on.' Terry looked at the red trousers still hanging from Jimmy's left arm with a degree of disdain. 'Those are very red.' He seemed somewhat perturbed by the scarlet of Jimmy's trousers. 'What colour are your shoes?'

The question took Jimmy a little off guard. 'Green, I think. It's been a while since I played.'

Terry Moist's face always displayed a look of contempt for most things, including human life, but green shoes and red trousers seemed to have pushed his disdain to a point where he had to verbalise his true feelings of revulsion.

'Green shoes and bright red pants, that's disgusting!' He turned and began to walk away. 'I'm parked outside. You got ten minutes. Don't make me come and get you.' It was a clear ultimatum; Terry Moist never asked twice. As he disappeared down the corridor, he was heard muttering, 'Green shoes and red pants?'

Jimmy closed the door and turned to Wendy, coffee in one hand and red pants draped over the other arm. He looked lost, and stupid. 'How's this being dead thing working out for you, because right now this being alive thing is turning batshit crazy?'

Wendy shrugged. 'Jury's out at the moment. I need to spend more time being dead to make a fair comparison. One big plus point, though, nobody's trying to kill me!' She smiled and then swung an imaginary golf club. 'Fore!' Her follow-through took her through the wall and out of Jimmy's life once again.

Jimmy looked at himself in the mirror. Coffee in one hand, red pants in the other. He really hoped fame was going to be worth it.

———◆———

When Jimmy reached the car park, it wasn't hard to spot Terry's car – mounted on the front bars were a set of cow horns. Jimmy opened the passenger door and climbed in. 'Nice horns.'

Terry nodded. 'They were a gift from my granddaddy.'

'What did he give your daddy?'

Terry scowled. 'Never did know my daddy.'

'Oh, sorry. When did your daddy die?'

As Terry Moist pulled out onto the road, he turned to look at Jimmy. With no expression on his face, he replied, 'he ain't dead ... yet.'

Jimmy decided that was enough small talk for this trip.

When they reached the golf club, Terry told Jimmy to fetch his clubs, put on his shoes and meet Mr Lantern on the first tee.

As Jimmy opened his locker, he saw that his golf shoes were as he remembered: green. Only he hadn't remembered that they were an almost fluorescent green. He held one up against his pants. It was like something out of an Andy Warhol dystopian nightmare. Jimmy smiled. Back in the Poconos, he would be considered pretty fly wearing this get-up. It's amazing the effect that years of marrying your cousins has on your dress sense. He pulled on his shoes, grabbed his bag and headed for the first tee and a date with destiny.

When he got there, destiny looked very prosperous. Jack Lantern was looking like a pro on the Seniors Tour. Everything neat and colour coordinated. He had a big fat cigar stuck in the corner of his mouth.

Watching Jimmy approach, the cigar's red glow seemed to burn white-hot as he sucked hard and drew a sharp inward breath. He gasped and pulled the cigar from his mouth. 'Jimmy, if I'd known you'd been at a clowns' convention, I would've given you more time to change.'

Terry Moist broke the habit of a lifetime and laughed out loud at his boss's joke.

Jimmy smiled weakly. 'I don't play much golf, especially with someone who tried to kill me!' He didn't know why he said it, but it just felt like the right thing to do. He was sick of reacting to events. His words made an impact.

Terry looked visibly surprised at the way Jimmy had spoken to his boss, and Jack Lantern's smile faded like a light being extinguished. For a couple of moments, they all stood silently. Jimmy feared he had overplayed his hand.

Jack took another drag on his cigar and then fixed Jimmy with a smile without warmth. 'Fancy a threesome?' Jimmy looked around; Terry didn't have any clubs. 'Lena plays. We could have a threesome with Lena. You know my wife, don't you, Jimmy?' The pretence was over; the real Jack Lantern was now in plain view. He fixed Jimmy with a look that promised a slow and painful death was still on the cards.

'Yes, we've met several times at my concerts. She's a very nice lady.'

Jack wagged his finger. 'Come now, Jimmy, she's a lot more than nice, wouldn't you say? She is a very sexy lady!'

What was he supposed to say to that? He decided on nothing and waited.

Jack Lantern looked long and hard at Jimmy, almost as though he was sizing him up for a coffin. A look of disdain mixed with pity crossed his features. 'What shade of green is that?'

Jimmy just shrugged; it was uncategorisable.

'What's your handicap? I play off eight.'

Jimmy tried to remember. 'About fourteen I think.'

Jack did not look impressed. 'Well, it's fourteen or it's not fourteen. Which is it?'

He could see that Jack didn't like being messed about. He was like a ticking time bomb, and Jimmy didn't want to be the one to make him explode. 'Fourteen.'

Jack pulled the driver from his bag and took a new ball and tee peg from his pocket. 'So, I gotta give you six shots, but you have to give me three back for making me look at those pants and then another three for the shoes.' Jack feigned the arithmetic and then smiled like a crocodile in a kindergarten. 'That makes us even, Jimmy, that OK with you.'

It wasn't a question, but Jimmy decided to agree. This particular crocodile looked hungry.

'So, what we gonna play for? Who sleeps with my wife tonight?'

Jimmy remembered what Wendy had told him: deny everything. So, he did. 'Look, Jack, I don't know where you got this idea that Mrs Lantern and I have been involved – I have far too much respect for her to do that.' *Yeah, respect for that ass,* thought Jimmy.

Jack teed up his ball. 'Have it your way. What we playing for?'

'Fun,' Jimmy replied with a shrug of his shoulders.

Both Jack and Terry burst into laughter. 'Fun,' said Jack when he had recovered, 'is for the weak of mind. Let's play fifty dollars front nine, fifty dollars back nine, and if you lose I kill you.'

Jimmy was just about to agree to the somewhat hefty wager when he grasped the last part of that sentence. He tried to act calm, as if he were a man with nothing to hide. This was going to take some acting. 'Fifty dollars front and back is fine by me, but I think the killing bit is over the top. Why not fifty dollars the match and ten dollars the birdies.'

'Yeah, that's fine by me. You like your birdies, don't you, Jimmy? Seems that you like my birdie too.' Jack inserted the accusation into the conversation like a warm knife sliding through butter.

Jimmy ignored it again. 'I prefer an eagle – much rarer and sought after.'

Jack stepped up to his ball. As he was addressing it, he let one more sentence escape from his reptilian lips: 'As opposed to the albatross you have around your neck.' He swung smoothly, and the ball arced away into the distance bisecting the fairway and came to rest some 250 yards from the tee.

'Nice shot,' said Jimmy.

Jack pushed his driver back into his bag. 'No pressure then, Jimmy. You take your drive and we can chat about what happened to Vinny and Carmine on the way to wherever it goes.'

Jimmy didn't bother to argue the point. It was best just to concentrate on hitting the ball; Jack would decide when it was time for answers. Jimmy teed up, took out his driver and had a couple of looseners. The swing felt good. He breathed out slowly – less is more, as his old teacher used to say. He swung smoothly and hit the ball while he was still breathing out, which stopped him tensing up. The contact was surprisingly good. The ball sailed off into the distance for nearly 270 yards, 200 of which were straight, the other seventy more a slow slicing arc into the rough.

Jack couldn't keep the pleasure from his voice. 'Bad luck, Jimmy. Good strike, but now you're behind those rocks you got no chance of the green in two.'

Jimmy was about to agree when his ball, which appeared to have come to rest, suddenly leaped up and flew laterally back to the middle of the fairway thirty yards ahead of Jack Lantern's ball.

Jack nearly swallowed his cigar. 'Did you see that, Terry?! Luckiest bounce I ever did see!'

Jimmy just smiled to himself. Now he knew where Wendy was.

By the time they reached the fifth tee, Jack's mood had grown worse. 'I can understand why you're still alive now. You must be the luckiest man in the world.'

Jimmy had received several very kind bounces, and Jack had been the recipient of balls that seemed to have a mind of their own. Jimmy had just birdied the fourth after his putt had missed on the low side and then proceeded to run up the slope and double back into the hole. For a change, Jack Lantern was speechless.

After picking his ball out of the hole, Jimmy winked at Jack. 'Some interesting borrows on these greens. Takes a while to get to know them.'

Jack shrugged as he threw his putter into his bag. 'You some kind of voodoo priest?'

Jimmy shook his head. 'No, but I do like chicken.'

When they reached the bar at the back of the ninth hole, Jimmy was two up and two birdies clear.

Jack grabbed three beers and passed one to Jimmy. 'Well, your luck seems to be going pretty good today, so why don't you see if you can use it to convince me that you didn't kill Vinny and Carmine.'

Jimmy took a deep swig from his bottle. 'Easy, I didn't. You saw the screen. Your boys had me bound up like a turkey. I was getting pretty hysterical when you told me what was gonna happen. When you rang off, I just lost it. Vinny was wrestling with me, and I remember hearing Carmine say that another car had just turned off the road onto the track that leads to the mine. Then he said that the driver had turned their lights off. I started to cry out for help.'

Jack snorted. 'They must've been over half a mile away – you'd have to shout pretty damn loud.'

'I was terrified. I thought this was a chance. I was just about to really let rip when I saw Vinny pull back his fist and then it was … lights out until I woke up at the side of the road with the zip ties gone and no sign of Vinny or Carmine.'

Both Terry and Jack had been listening carefully to every word that Jimmy had said. They exchanged knowing looks. 'And you never saw anyone else?'

'No, took me hours to walk back to town, and all the time I was looking over my shoulder waiting for your boys to come and finish the job.'

Jack had listened closely to every word. He was weighing up Jimmy's words against what he thought he knew. His eyes interrogated Jimmy's face for any signs of a lie, but Jimmy had years of performing on stage and hiding his nerves to fall back on.

'So, why didn't you reach out to me?' asked Jack.

It was Jimmy's turn to laugh out loud now. 'Ha! Reach out to the man who told me he was gonna have my legs broken, fingers chopped off and bury me alive. Why do you think, Jack?'

Terry Moist leaned forward. 'He has a point, boss.'

Jack nodded slowly. 'He does indeed. It all sounds very plausible, maybe too plausible.'

Jimmy didn't take the bait to dive in with a desperate justification. He just sat there letting the facts, or his version of the facts, offer Jack Lantern a plausible reason to believe him.

Jack and Terry were conferring, but Jimmy couldn't hear what they were saying other than the odd word, one of which was 'Delta' and the other two were 'Three Rivers'. Not a lot to go on, but it all made perfect sense to Jimmy. There was a biker gang called the Delta Riders that ran out of Three Rivers, the very gang who had three members responsible for raping Wendy. He could sense opportunity beginning to knock and knew he needed to work the conversation around to implicating the Deltas in Vinny's and Carmine's murders. He had to do this carefully, because in an ideal world he wanted to kill all three himself. He tried to catch some more details but Terry and his boss seemed to have concluded their secret conversation. Jack was the first to speak.

'OK, let's assume for now that we believe you, where do you think they are?'

Jimmy took a swig of his beer while he thought. Now was the time for him to sow some seeds of doubt. 'Early on in the evening, when we were drinking at the Riviera after my show, I had just been to the toilet and when I came back they were talking about some gang called the Deltas. I asked them about it because there's a biker gang called the Deltas that run out of Three Rivers. They're into drugs and anything else you care to mention. I said to keep away from them – that was before I knew they were your killers.' He could see this new information being absorbed by both men. Hopefully they were putting two and two together and coming up with five – not Jimmy's favourite number, but it would do for now.

Jack said something to Terry, who then drained his beer and disappeared towards the clubhouse at a steady jog. Jack turned to Jimmy. 'Terry has to leave us – bit of business he needs to attend to.' Jack was smiling, but Jimmy could see that he was worried. His little lie had hit the mark, and Jack Lantern was now thinking that the Delta bikers were trying to move into his patch. 'Looks like you might be in the clear for Vinny's and Carmine's murders. What you just said could explain the situation … I said *could*.' Jack was wagging his index finger at Jimmy. 'Not in the clear yet, Jimmy boy. There's also the little matter of sleeping with my wife.'

Jimmy slammed down his bottle. 'Never happened. God knows I would've loved it to happen but it just never did!' Jimmy hadn't raised his voice to a murdering gang boss before, but he thought he had done a pretty good job – just the right amount of anger and indignation.

'Well, at least you admitted that you fancied her. Let's face it, if you were denying that, there's no way you'd be telling the truth!' Jack seemed pretty convinced. He finished his beer, and then put his hand on Jimmy's shoulder. 'Look, things may have gotten a bit tense between us, but if all this blows over let's try and be friends.'

Wow, thought Jimmy, *Jack's definition of 'tense' is the equivalent of saying the Titanic hit an ice cube.* That said, Jimmy was happy to move on with all his digits and limbs intact and mercifully still be above ground. 'Jack, things are looking up for me, and you know I'll be able to pay you all your money back very soon.'

Jack smiled. 'That you will, Jimmy, and the circles you're gonna be moving in could be very advantageous to both of us.' It was clear that Jack Lantern had decided Jimmy was part of the Lantern empire, even if there would never be a contract to prove it. For now, Jimmy would go along with it, mainly because he liked breathing, but a day would come when Jack Lantern was going to get what was coming to him.

The thirteenth was a dog-leg par four. This suited Jimmy's power fade, which is a nicer way of saying slice. He stood up to the ball and swung through with his driver. The ball shot off the middle of the club and soared into the distance before slowly starting to turn to the right like a planet being sucked into the gravitational pull of a black hole. As the ball disappeared over the tall trees, he waited to hear the tell-tale clunk of ball against tree. Neither he nor Jack heard a sound.

Jimmy picked up his tee. 'Do you think it made it?'

'Like I give a fuck. Knowing your luck, it's probably on the green.' Jack had lost the last three holes. If he lost this one, it was game over, six and five.

He wasn't used to losing and he didn't do it often, but this was starting to look like a hopeless cause. Jimmy was displaying the abandon of a golfer who didn't have a care in the world. This was another reason that he thought Jimmy was indeed innocent. So, if Jimmy was telling the truth, he had bigger problems to resolve. The biker gang in Three Rivers needed to be sorted – that's why he had sent Terry to organise the troops. Six of his best men would be arriving in Blackjack tomorrow before heading off to Three Rivers to end the problem with the Deltas forever!

He hit his drive. Once more, it flew straight and true down the middle of the fairway to the point where the hole dog-legs off to the right. When he reached his ball, he was delighted with where it had come to rest. Nice tight lie so he could punch in a nine iron and give himself a chance for a birdie, but when he looked up his good mood vanished. There on the green, some hundred-thirty yards away, was Jimmy's ball, two feet from the hole. He looked back to the high trees that should have gathered in Jimmy's ball as it tried to cut the corner. It should never have made it, but somehow it had. Not only that, it had bounced over or between the three bunkers that guarded the green.

It was the last straw for Jack. He punched his nine iron onto the green, conceded Jimmy's tap in for an eagle and then proceeded to miss his birdie putt. He held out his hand. 'Congratulations, Jimmy, I concede. Let's get back to the bar. You can buy the drinks with the two hundred dollars you just took off me.'

As Jimmy entered the golf club bar, a familiar figure was waiting for him. David Parker was leaning against the bar with a big smile on his face. 'Good day to you, James. I hear you have been robbing gangsters on the fairways.' His crisp English accent seemed out of place in this little golf club bar.

Jimmy smiled. 'I wasn't on the fairway for most of it, but I seemed to have one of those days when every bounce went my way.'

'Well, I'm glad you've had a good morning because I am going to have to ask you a favour.' David smiled a little weakly. He never asked Jimmy for favours – quite the reverse, he had been doing Jimmy favours for years.

'Anything.'

'Perhaps you'd better hear the favour first.' He paused and waited for Jimmy to ask, but Jimmy was happy to do anything that David wanted – he owed this man so much. David understood what Jimmy's silence meant. 'Thanks, I appreciate your help. The hotel is fully booked and we have so many people wanting to come to tonight's show I could fill the Canyon twice over.' This was music to Jimmy's ears. 'So, could you do a seven-thirty show and a nine-thirty show?'

'No problem. I've got three new songs too.'

David looked relived. 'You sure, Jimmy? It really would be a lifesaver. It was sold out last week, but so many of our guests want to come who hadn't booked, plus a whole group of your fan club have block-booked the Hoover Inn, and they thought they would be able to get in.'

Jimmy felt sorry for them. 'Man, if they're stopping at the Hoover, they've already suffered enough.' He was amazed at how his life was turning around. Just a few weeks back nobody listened to a word he sang, and now, amazing what a difference a few weeks makes – and a few killings.

David grabbed Jimmy's shoulder and gave it a squeeze. 'Thanks. You're going to knock them dead.'

'I may just do that.' As David disappeared through the door leading to the car park, Jack Lantern appeared from the changing rooms.

'You've just missed David Parker,' said Jimmy.

Jack shrugged. 'No problem, he's having a pre-show drink with me and Lena tonight.' Jack looked at Jimmy mischievously. 'Perhaps you'd like to join us.'

Jimmy thought about accepting for a moment, but then he remembered how much he loved his kneecaps. 'No, but thank you. I have sound checks to do before the shows.'

This seemed to amuse Jack. 'Sound check? Does this mean you're gonna be in tune?'

Jimmy smiled. 'Real funny, Jack.'

'You said shows.' Jack never missed a thing.

'Had to put on an extra show because we've sold out the Canyon twice over.'

'Man, pity you haven't made that record already, you could sell a lot of CDs after these shows.' Jack looked genuinely impressed.

'Yeah, that would've been nice,' Jimmy said with a sigh.

Jack patted Jimmy on the back. 'Never mind, you'll soon be packing them in at the Golden Flamingo and making the label and yourself a lot of money. What label are you on by the way?'

For a moment Jimmy didn't answer, he was still trying to work out how Jack knew about the Golden Flamingo and, for that matter, the label. 'Well, it's not official yet, but I've been offered a deal by Small Print Records, and they have influence with the Golden Flamingo.'

Jack seemed to find this very amusing – too amusing.

Jimmy felt a horrible feeling creeping up his spine. 'Am I missing something?'

Jack was still chortling with laughter but managed to get himself under control. 'You know, Jimmy, when you're in business sometime, you gotta be lucky – just being smart ain't enough. Now, when Vinny and Carmine didn't kill you, most people would say you got lucky, but I got lucky as well.'

'Why, because you didn't kill an innocent man?' Jimmy gave Jack a puzzled look.

Jack waved his comment away. 'You weren't innocent; you owed me money and you were taking liberties. But I am so glad they didn't kill you because I didn't know you'd turned your career around and got this deal with Small Print Records. That's perfect!'

Jimmy was more confused than ever. 'Why?'

'Because, Jimmy, I own fifty-one percent of Small Print Records!'

That creeping feeling of dread ran straight up Jimmy's spine, around his waist and rested in the pit of his stomach.

'We're gonna be partners!'

CHAPTER 14
THE LONG ARM OF THE LAW

Jimmy should have been in a great mood. Both concerts had been fantastic and the crowd had gone wild. The boys in the band had played up a storm and the new songs received an amazing reception. At the end of the second gig, Lena had rushed up to him after the show and covered him in praise and a couple of kisses. Normally, he would have enjoyed this but standing behind Lena was her husband. Jimmy wasn't afraid of Jack seeing her kiss him, but he was afraid of that smug look on Jack's face. Jack was enjoying seeing just how good his latest signing was, and his greedy little eyes were already counting the sales. Somehow, Jimmy was going to make enough money to get out of debt to this monster but still be working for him. The anger threatened to eat him up; he just had to get out of there.

Once he had cleared the last fan's embraces, he made for the back of the stage. Kid was packing up his guitar. 'Could you pack my stuff up? I gotta get out of this place.'

Kid could sense there was something wrong. 'You OK, Jimmy?'

'No. I need to write a song.' He turned to leave, but Kid grabbed his arm. His huge hand closed like a vice to the point where it was almost painful.

'Jimmy, don't do anything rash. You seem to be upset, that's not a good time to –' he looked for the right words '– write a song.'

Jimmy understood the metaphor, but he was so full of anger he didn't want to listen. 'You don't know the full story,' he hissed.

Kid shrugged. 'Then tell me.'

He stared at Kid's passive face and felt all the anger drain from him. 'I just found out that Jack Scumbag Lantern owns fifty-one percent of Small Print Records, the label we're signed to.'

'And your problem is?'

Jimmy hadn't expected that reaction. 'Isn't it obvious?'

'Not to me,' Kid replied with a shrug. 'You have the goods on Jack should you ever need to use them. You're also a very proficient killer, so if he does get heavy just look on him as a song that's waiting to be written, if you get my meaning.'

When Kid put it like that, what did he have to fear? If he was going to fall out with a label boss, it might as well be someone he was happy to kill. It would make contract renegotiation so much easier.

Kid pulled Jimmy to the very back of the stage. 'Lantern has arranged for a squad to come into town tomorrow. They're gonna sort out the biker gang from Three Rivers. Some major shit will be going down, and this will give us an opportunity to exploit the chaos. You want me to try and kidnap the three that raped Wendy?'

Kid's question stopped Jimmy in his tracks. *How does Kid know about Wendy?* Kid must have read the confusion on Jimmy's face.

'You're not the only one Wendy used to confide in, Jimmy. My counsel has been sought by many, but to you, I offer it regardless of the fact that you may not want it.' He paused for a moment and let go of Jimmy's arm. 'Let go of that anger – it will make you careless.'

Jimmy knew Kid was right. He nodded his agreement. 'OK, let's meet at nine for breakfast.'

'A.M.?' Kid asked in shock.

'Yes, early bird kills the bikers.'

Kid rubbed his chin ruefully. 'I can stomach helping you kill scumbags, but breakfast at nine seems a bit extreme.'

Jimmy started to walk away. 'I'm going up to the Lazy for a drink and a – ' Jimmy didn't finish the sentence. If he was going to the Big Easy, he didn't need to. 'You coming?'

Kid shook his head. 'Not if I'm having breakfast at nine!'

It was a ten-minute drive out of town to the Lazy, and there were only six cars there when he pulled up into the car park. The name had changed since he was last there. The 'G' on the 'BIG' no longer shone, and now proclaimed 'Bi Easy'. That too was probably true if you paid enough money. Typical of Sleazy Peterson not to repair his own neon sign – guess it wasn't just the nickname that was 'Lazy'.

When he entered the bar area, it was exactly as it always was: seedy. Sleazy was leering over one of his new bargirls. He looked up when Jimmy entered. His face went from bored to rage in about half a second.

'What the fuck are you doing in here? You're banned for life!'

Jimmy hadn't forgotten, but he hoped that Sleazy would have. 'I came to apologise,' he lied. 'Things were going bad for me back then and I took it out on you. I'm really sorry.'

Sleazy had drawn himself up to his full six-foot-two, which would have been impressive if he hadn't measured the same around his stomach. 'Sorry aint gonna cut it. You made me look bad in front of my girls.'

You look bad in front of a mirror, thought Jimmy. Pulling out a large roll of twenty-dollar bills, he asked, 'Why don't you and me have a drink of the best champagne you have, on me?' Jimmy knew that the real value of one of Sleazy's best bottles would have been more than covered by just one of his twenty-dollar bills, but the roll of notes had done the trick.

Sleazy's greedy little eyes were counting them already. 'You think just coming in here and flashing some cash is gonna make everything OK?'

'Pretty much.'

Sleazy stood there looking at him and the roll of money – but mostly the money. 'What you drinking?' he scowled, but Jimmy knew the hook had been swallowed.

'Like I said, hit me up for your best champagne.'

Sleazy nodded to the barmaid. 'That's gonna cost you one hundred and forty dollars.'

Jimmy walked over to the bar and offered his hand to Sleazy. 'Let it be the down payment on my apology.'

Begrudgingly, Sleazy took it. His hand was fat and sweaty, which made Jimmy's flesh crawl, but he didn't show it – only wiping it surreptitiously on his trousers when Sleazy turned his back to fetch two champagne flutes.

'You gonna join me?' asked Jimmy.

'No, this is for the girl you're picking tonight. This is a whorehouse, not a bar.'

'I don't usually go for that; I just wanted a late-night drink in a quiet bar away from town.'

Sleazy's unpleasant features creased into an approximation of a smile. 'I ain't telling you to fuck her, just pay as if you did. Three hundred and fifty dollars will cover it, and then you and me are square.'

Jimmy counted off the notes and gave the barmaid a twenty-dollar tip. 'Sounds fair to me.'

Sleazy stood by the door to the corridor that led to the bedrooms. 'Got any preferences?'

'Valerie, please.'

'She's my manager, she don't do customers,' retorted Sleazy.

'That's OK then because I just wanna have a drink with her.'

Sleazy shrugged. 'Suit yourself, but if I'm paying for it I wouldn't just be talking to it.'

'Us showbiz folks are funny like that,' Jimmy replied with a smile.

Sleazy disappeared down the corridor. 'Valerie, got a faggot here wants a drink with you!'

When Valerie walked into the bar and saw Jimmy, she smiled. 'Hello, stranger. I wondered when you'd be showing your face in here again.'

Jimmy pulled back a barstool for her. 'I was banned for life, remember?'

'Life's a long time around here, but cash is still king,' Valerie said with a sigh.

Jimmy slid a glass of champagne over to Valerie. 'That it is.' They clinked glasses and both took a swig.

'So, I hear you're the next big thing – whole valley's talking about it.'

He nodded modestly. 'I'm an overnight sensation that took twenty years to get to the next day. My mum always said patience was a virtue.'

'And was she patient?'

'Well, she shot herself in the head with a shotgun, so I reckon any patience she did have expired.'

Valerie put down her glass; she looked a little shocked. 'Hell, Jimmy, I'm so sorry. I didn't know.'

'It was a long time ago and a lifetime away. She had just killed my father, so she couldn't really see a way out. I was sixteen at the time.'

Valerie squeezed his arm. 'So, you were an orphan, that's so sad.'

Jimmy shook his head slowly. 'No, what I was, was free. My dad was a womanising piece of shit. If my mum hadn't done it, I probably would've within a couple of years. I would never have left her with him, but once they were both gone, there was nothing to keep me. Day after my eighteenth birthday, I left Scrotum and the Poconos forever.'

Valerie gave him a sidelong look. 'Scrotum?'

'Scotrun. All us kids called it Scrotum. We all wanted the bright lights and the big city, but when I think back it was a really beautiful place.' Jimmy sipped his champagne wistfully. 'Do you ever look back and wish you'd taken a different path?'

'What, and miss winding up here working for Sleazy?'

'I'll take that as a yes, then,' Jimmy said with a smile.

Sleazy had come back into the bar area and was chatting to a customer who was in a cubicle with one of his girls. It wasn't until he got up that Jimmy realised the customer was Sheriff Pence – good old happily married, God-fearing Sheriff Pence.

Jimmy raised his glass. 'Evening, Sheriff Pence. You decided to come to the place where the crimes are hatched because a hundred-and-forty dollars for this shit is daylight robbery.'

Sleazy gave Jimmy a filthy look. 'You can be banned again, Jimmy Wayne. You can also be chucked out with a good beating thrown in.'

Jimmy didn't want a scene, so he raised his glass to Sleazy. 'Just kidding, this champagne is beyond compare, way beyond.'

Thankfully, Sleazy was too thick to be sure that Jimmy was taking the piss. He turned back to Sheriff Pence, but he was already on his way over.

The sheriff pulled up a stool across from Jimmy and nodded to Valerie. 'I seem to recall that you're banned from here for life.'

'Sleazy decided to let bygones be bygones.'

Pence leaned into him. 'Well, I didn't, so get your shit together and get out of here now.' He was angry but trying to keep it hidden from the fellow customers.

Jimmy didn't move. 'If the owner has let me in and I aint breaking any law, I don't think there's anything you can do, so why don't you slink back under whichever whore you crawled out from under.'

Valerie put down her drink and quietly slipped out of her chair and away from the impending fight. She could see that Jimmy was spoiling for trouble, but surprisingly so was Sheriff Pence.

Pence had steam coming out of his ears. Any moment now he was going to blow. This was what Jimmy wanted, but Pence saw other guests looking over so decided to play it down.

He was still in Jimmy's face. 'You've gone too far now, Wayne. I'm gonna finish you once and for all.'

Jimmy leaned right back in his face. He spoke slowly and quietly but did not attempt to mask the contempt in his voice. 'So, how's a fat butterball like you, who hasn't got the first clue about proper detective work, gonna do that?' Jimmy leaned back and took a sip from his glass. 'Let me think, Sheriff Pence. I'm either gonna find a commercial quantity of coke hidden somewhere in my house. Or maybe I'm gonna get shot while being arrested by you. You know the drill: "I was trying to arrest him, but he went for his gun – self-defence again!"'

A slow evil smile spread across Pence's face. 'Yes, one of those two will do. You're never gonna make it to Vegas.'

Jimmy nodded sceptically and slowly pulled his phone out of his pocket. 'No, Sheriff Pence, it's you that's not gonna make it to captain.' Jimmy clicked play on his recorder, and Sheriff Pence's threats came ringing in his ears. 'Now, I wonder what your bosses will make of this. A frame-up and a murder threat, and all to an upstanding member of the community.'

Pence was looking like a cornered animal. 'Nobody's gonna believe you. You're just a loser, a good-for-nothing washed-up singer.'

'You believe what you wanna believe. I'm the one with the record deal and a residency at the Golden Flamingo coming up.' He held up the phone. 'And, of course, I have this. In the words of the great detective Sherlock Holmes, "You, dear boy, are fucked!"' For a moment Jimmy thought Pence was going to go for him, his eyes flashed with pure rage, but somehow he held it in check.

He slowly stood up and brushed his shirt. After feigning a very forced smile, he said, 'Well, we'll have to see about that now, won't we, Mr Wayne? Good luck getting home. These roads can be dangerous.' He turned and walked to the door. 'Night, Sleazy. Catch you later in the week.' His voice was calm and he smiled, but Jimmy knew he had got to him.

Sleazy looked up from the paper he was now reading. 'You going already, Pete?'

Pence nodded. 'Got a drug dealer in town and I need to catch him.' He turned and looked at Jimmy as he said it before turning and leaving, slamming the door behind him.

Hook, line and sinker, thought Jimmy.

Valerie slid back onto the stool next to him. 'Looking for trouble?'

'Not really, but sometimes it just seems to follow me!' he said after taking another sip of champagne.

Just then, the door opened and Sheriff Pence re-entered. He walked over to Jimmy. 'That your Ford Thunderbird on the car park, Wayne?'

'Yes, it is, Sheriff. I got it out of the lock-up. Figured I would sell it before I move to Vegas. Just gonna have a run around in it for a couple of weeks for old times' sake.'

'That right, Wayne. Well, in that cherry red convertible you aint gonna be hard to spot.' It was more a threat than a statement.

Jimmy swivelled round on his seat to face Pence directly. 'Thought I would make it nice and easy for you to come and find me, you being such a shit detective an' all.'

Pence's eyes blazed with anger and his hands balled into fists, but he just stood there glaring at Jimmy. Slowly, a fake smile spread across his face. 'Real thoughtful of you, Wayne. I'll be sure to take advantage of it real soon.'

Jimmy turned back towards the bar, throwing one last insult at Pence as he did, 'You drive careful now, Sheriff, that valley road gets a bit narrow for fatties.'

Pence stormed out without returning the insult.

'Wow, Jimmy, you do wanna get busted, don't you?' Valerie said before a deep sigh.

Jimmy took a swig of his drink. 'Not really, Val, but that crooked son of a bitch has been riding me for about six months. Just thought I'd give him some back before I leave.'

Valerie smiled appreciatively. 'Well, you certainly did that.'

Sleazy, as Jimmy hoped, had been paying attention to Jimmy's disagreement with Pence and sidled up to where he and Valerie were chatting. 'You in the Thunderbird?'

Jimmy nodded. He had driven it here before, and Sleazy had fallen in love with the bright red classic. With the soft-top down, even a big fatso like Sleazy could slide in behind the wheel and imagine the wind blowing through his hair – both of them!

So far, everything was going just how Jimmy had planned it. He held up the keys. 'In the spirit of our renewed friendship, Sleazy, how'd you like to take it for a spin?' He let the keys swing in his fingers as though trying to hypnotise Sleazy.

'You mean it, Jimmy?' Sleazy sounded surprised.

'Course I do. Take the road back to Blackjack – those bends by the canyon are great, just don't go too fast, I don't want my baby taking that hundred-foot drop.'

Sleazy moved with a speed that belied his girth and whisked the keys from Jimmy's fingers. 'Thanks, Jimmy.' There was a big cheesy smile on Sleazy's face. He looked like a walrus who had caught a tuna. He hurried out of the door, and within moments the engine of Jimmy's Thunderbird burst into life and squealed away from the car park.

Valerie stared at Jimmy. 'What the hell are you up to?'

Jimmy gave her a sly smile. 'I'm just lighting the blue touch-paper and retiring to a safe distance.'

'Go on, don't keep a girl hanging.'

Jimmy tried to look nonchalant, but inside his heart was beating like a jackhammer. 'Well, I know that Sleazy loves my car and I know that Pence hates my guts. Now, if Pence is riled up, which he is, with me, and Sleazy is in my car headed to town on the route that Pence knows I'll be taking, it seems a logical conclusion that they're gonna be meeting at some point.'

Now Valerie was smiling. 'Jimmy Wayne, you are a cunning bastard.'

Jimmy nodded in acknowledgement. 'Thank you, Valerie. I reckon you're right.' Should be really funny when Sheriff Pence pulls me over to find Sleazy driving, don't you think?' Valerie thought that was funny, too. What Jimmy hadn't accounted for was just how mad he had made Sheriff Pence.

Sherriff Pence had driven away from the Lazy with only one thought: to get Jimmy Wayne. Seething as he drove down the valley on the way back to town, he went through the bends by the canyon too fast and his tyres squealed. As he got back onto the straight, he saw the track off on the right-hand side and pulled in.

After a rapid three-point turn, he drove to the crown of the last bend, pulled over and turned off the ignition and lights. He was going to wait here for Wayne, and then he would pull him over. He had some cocaine in the back, which was going to become part of Jimmy Wayne's property just as soon as he came by. He didn't have long to wait – he could already hear the roar of the Thunderbird's big V8. The anger was still boiling inside him; it was time to teach that slimy singer a lesson.

He fired up his engine and moved slowly and silently to the crown of the last bend. He still hadn't put his lights on. He checked his mirror. The road back to town was dark, no witnesses, just how he liked it!

Sleazy was enjoying the ride, gunning that Ford towards the canyon curves. He grabbed a cigarette from the packet he had placed on the passenger seat, stuffed it into his big fat mouth and reached for the cigarette lighter, but he couldn't find it. He looked along the dashboard but couldn't see it. He felt around by the ashtray, found the tell-tale stub of the lighter handle and pushed it down. Only then did he look up and see that he was almost at the first bend.

'Shit!' he hissed as fear filled his gut. He pulled hard to the left, but the tail end of the large coupe began to drift. Sleazy was dumb but he knew how to drive. He kept the power on and counter steered into the drift. All four tyres squealed under the slide, but the car slowly swung back into line, and Sleazy smiled as he lined up the next bend. *That was close*, he thought. But now he was fully focused, so he wouldn't be making that mistake again.

As he entered the next bend, Sheriff Pence hit his full beam. Sleazy was totally blinded by the light. All he could do for a moment was shout, 'what the fuck!' and then he realised that he had to stop the car because he couldn't see a thing.

Just as he went for the brakes, there was a loud crack at the front of the Thunderbird as it splintered the low fence that ran along the edge of the drop into the canyon. Sleazy pumped the brakes – nothing. Only then as the nose of the car started to point down did he realise that he was flying.

He was clear of the blinding beam now; the illuminated Thunderbird headlights were the last thing Sleazy Peterson would ever see. The rocky bed of Blackwater River ran up to meet him with its cold embrace.

Sheriff Pence sat there for several moments. That hadn't gone according to plan; he had just meant to scare Wayne a bit and maybe try and plant the cocaine in his car. He checked his mirrors, still nothing, and then he listened hard down the road beyond the bends back towards the Big Easy. Silence.

Slowly, he turned his car around and then walked back to the edge of the road where Jimmy Wayne's car had plunged through. He could see the mangled wreckage over a hundred feet below. The water was only just deep enough to submerge it, but it was badly damaged and upside down. Somehow, the lights were still on.

As the surprise wore off, Sheriff Pence's face broke into a smile. He looked down at the headlights of the Thunderbird twinkling in the ripples of the river as it flowed downstream.

'Let's see if you can swim your way to Vegas from there, Jimmy Wayne.'

He walked slowly back to his car, fired up the motor and headed back to town happy in the knowledge that Jimmy Wayne had not escaped the long arm of the law!

CHAPTER 15

REVENGE AIN'T ALWAYS SWEET

Jimmy and Valerie had sat drinking in the Big Easy for nearly two hours but Sleazy still hadn't returned. One by one the last few punters had come and gone – literally, in most cases.

As the clock ticked towards midnight, Jimmy decided it was time to call a cab. As he pulled out his phone, he heard a vehicle screech up to the Lazy. Within moments the door burst open and there, almost entirely filling the opening, was Kid.

He looked distressed until he saw Jimmy sitting at the bar. A beaming smile broke out across his hairy features, revealing a boyish face Jimmy had never noticed before. Kid ran across and gave him a huge bear hug.

'Man, you're alive, you're alive!'

Jimmy tried to struggle free, figuring that if he didn't, Kid was going to crush him. 'Easy, what's the problem? Why wouldn't I be alive?'

Kid looked at the barmaid. 'Could I have a beer, please?' She nodded, and Kid turned back to Jimmy and Valerie. 'I decided to come up and join you for a drink. If I gotta be up for breakfast at nine, I didn't think there was much point in going to bed.'

Jimmy thought about it for a moment. 'Yeah, eight hours' sleep is hardly worth getting undressed for.'

'Exactly. Anyway, I was on the way up here and as I was coming round the canyon bends, I noticed the fence had a hole in it.'

Jimmy and Valerie exchanged glances.

'I went to have a look; I had my big torch with me.' Kid shook his head as he thought about what he had seen. 'Your Thunderbird is at the bottom of the cliff, Jimmy. Upside down and smashed to pieces. Nobody could have survived that crash. Man, I thought it was you. I raced here to raise the alarm.' Kid pointed at Jimmy. 'If you're here and your car is at the bottom of the canyon, who was driving?'

Jimmy and Valerie answered him together, 'Sleazy!'

Kid looked at Jimmy. He didn't say anything, but Jimmy could see the questions in his eyes.

Valerie slipped off her stool. 'I'd better call the police and the emergency services.'

'You aint gonna need an ambulance.'

'No, but I'm gonna need a job!'

———◆———

It was three in the morning when they finally pulled Sleazy's body from Jimmy's car. Jimmy and Kid stood on the road and watched as the rescue guys jacked up the totalled Thunderbird and dragged out the bundle of rags and blubber that had once been Sleazy Peterson.

'I feel kinda bad,' said Jimmy to Kid.

Kid placed his hand on Jimmy's shoulder. 'I know, that was a nice car!'

Jimmy pulled away. 'I meant about Sleazy.'

'But I thought he was on your hit list,' Kid said with surprise.

Jimmy nodded ruefully. 'He was, but we kinda made it up and I was just using him to get to Sheriff Pence.'

Kid didn't say anything; he just inclined his head to one side and looked at Jimmy waiting for an explanation.

'I deliberately wound up Pence in Sleazy's last night. He was making threats about framing me with drugs and shooting me – same old things he's been doing to anyone he doesn't like or who don't get on his payroll. Well, I wound him up pretty good, and I was sure he would be waiting to pull me over on the way home. Sleazy's always loved my T-bird, so I told him he could take it for a drive.'

Kid was nodding slowly now as he began to understand.

'I thought it would be really funny for Pence to pull over my car and come across all high and mighty only to find Sleazy behind the wheel. I guess Sleazy went for it a bit too much.'

'I doubt that, Jimmy. I heard stories that Sleazy used to run moonshine when he was a kid and no police could catch him. He knew how to handle a car.'

'What you suggesting?'

Kid rubbed his fingers through his beard. 'I think you wound up Pence more than you know. See that track over there after the last bend.' Kid pointed to where Pence had turned his car around. 'If you pulled in there and waited for a car to approach and then just lined up your car with the exit from that bend –' Jimmy was following Kid's explanation. 'All you'd have to do is hit full beam outta nowhere, and whoever was driving would be totally blinded. If they were moving quick, they wouldn't have time to react before they missed the next bend and go straight through the fence.' Kid pointed to the T-bird-sized hole. 'Pence probably didn't expect that to happen, but then he didn't expect Sleazy Peterson driving down the road like he was running moonshine.'

It all made perfect sense. 'So, if you're right, Pence thinks I'm dead.'

'I would almost guarantee it. Funny that he hasn't come out, aint it?'

It was unusual. Sheriff Pence was all over everything that happened in his county. Unless he was trying to keep his distance.

Kid looked at his watch. '3:30 a.m.' A warm smile broke out over his features, 'only five and a half hours to breakfast.'

You had to admire the commitment that Kid was giving to his 9 a.m. breakfast.

'You can think about food at a time like this?'

Kid nodded. 'Naturally, if you're alive, unlike Sleazy, you need to eat. This having breakfast actually at breakfast time is something of a novelty for me. I intend to embrace it, as it may never happen again.'

Jimmy stared at Kid as an amused smile played on his lips. If there was a God and God was an electrician, he had definitely wired Kid up differently. He marched to a different drummer. Actually, he ambled, and it wasn't a drummer but more a jazz percussionist as he freestyled through life.

Suddenly feeling very tired, Jimmy said, 'Come on, I need to get some sleep before breakfast.'

Kid nodded eagerly and glanced at his watch. 'Five hours and twenty-nine minutes to go. Man, I hope I'm not building this up too much!'

Jimmy chuckled and started walking to Kid's van.

'Can't wait to see what song you come up with in the morning,' Kid said as he caught up with him.

Jimmy turned to Kid. 'Why would I write a song? I didn't have anything to do with Sleazy's death directly.'

Kid looked at him dubiously. 'I wouldn't be so sure. You wound up Pence, and then you sent Sleazy out into the trap you'd set. Sure, you couldn't have foreseen the outcome, but you put both of them in a position to collide. I would say you caused the death of the late and mostly unlamented Sleazy Peterson.'

Jimmy carried on walking to the car. When Kid put it like that, it was hard to disagree.

When they got back to the hotel, Jimmy and Kid headed for their separate rooms. Jimmy was exhausted and just wanted to sleep. He fell on his bed without removing his clothes and within moments was fast asleep. A dream came rapidly.

He was sitting on the fence next to the hole where Sleazy had plunged to his death. It was night but moonlight illuminated the waters below as they flowed over the rocks like black ink. Wendy was sitting on the fence next to him.

'Gotta hand it to you, Jimmy, that was very clever. Very Machiavellian. Almost Shakespearean, in fact.'

Jimmy looked wearily at Wendy. 'Who's Mack Vellian?'

For a moment Wendy considered throwing herself off the cliff, but then she remembered she was already dead. 'The way you wound up Sheriff Pence and then sent Sleazy out in your car.

A work of genius.' She put a hand on his thigh. 'I'm so proud of you, Jimmy. You finally managed to kill someone with your brain instead of a blunt instrument. To be fair, most of your life has been a blunt instrument just banging up against a wall, but you're starting to grow.' This was effusive praise indeed.

'Thanks, but it wasn't intended. I was just hanging around waiting for him to bring my car back.'

Wendy pulled a sardonic smile. 'You don't say.'

The image of Wendy hanging from his wardrobe flashed back into his mind. 'Sorry, Wendy, unfortunate turn of phrase.'

Waving his apology away, she said, 'Doesn't matter. That's number seven – only four to go!' Wendy seemed very excited. 'So, how you gonna kill the bikers tomorrow? Painfully, I hope.'

He tried to ignore her. 'Go away, Wendy, I need to sleep.' In the dream, they sat there side by side. Below in the inky black waters of the river, the headlights on Jimmy's T-bird still flickered, like a dying beast breathing its last before the final darkness descended. He loved that car but he knew there were major problems coming. Rust like a cancer had begun to spread through the subframe. The kind of rust that has a mechanic rubbing his chin and taking a long, drawn-out breath and, if it's really bad, releasing it with a whistle. Jimmy had heard three of these performances and come to realise that if his T-bird were a dog, he would have to send it to the retirement farm in the country. His insurance, on the other hand, covered him for a car in pristine condition, so he was actually going to benefit from his policy for the first time in his life. The accident report was going to make interesting reading: Fat man borrows car. Fat man drives too fast. Fat man is blinded by crooked cop who was waiting to frame somebody else. Fat man drives over the cliff.

'What do you think Sleazy's last thoughts were as he went over the edge? My guess is he was thinking about that steak sandwich he was never gonna finish.'

Jimmy thought about it for a moment. 'Maybe he was thinking is this why they call it a T-bird.'

Wendy laughed. 'That's very good, but the glide angle of a '66 Thunderbird is basically vertical. Newton cannot be refuted on that one.' Jimmy looked questioningly at Wendy. 'Gravity, Jimmy. Remember the apple?'

He sat there for a moment and the lights finally flickered out. The Thunderbird was dead and its mighty heart beat no more. The water danced in the moonlight through the torn panels of the bodywork. 'D'ya think it will buff out?'

The alarm went off and Jimmy woke with a start. His hand came down on the clock and silenced the intrusion to his dreams. There on top of the table was another song. Sleazy's death *had* been his fault, then.

He picked up the paper. Sure enough, it was his handwriting again. The title at the top read 'Too Much'. He put it down without reading it; this was all getting too much. Did he really want fame this badly? Was it worth killing all these people for?

He thought about the ones he had deliberately killed: Vinny, Carmine, Ted Baker and Jackson. He probably had to include Sleazy Peterson as well. Everyone of them was scum!

He picked up the song again and started to read. By the end of the first verse, he concluded that it was definitely worth it and Sleazy Peterson had not died in vain. The road to hell is paved with good intentions and if he was going to hell, he intended to take as many scumbags with him as he went. A few Grammys would be nice as well!

By the time Jimmy had showered and dressed, he was in exceptionally high spirits. As he brushed his hair, he saw reflected in the mirror the legs and feet of Wendy coming down through his ceiling. He really had to try and get her to come through the walls. This vertical entry she was so fond of was most unnerving, especially if you were lying in bed looking at the ceiling when she arrived.

'Song's on the table, Wendy. Put the coffee on, would ya?'

Wendy saluted. 'Captain, my Captain.' She then sat on the bed and picked up the song. '"Too Much" – snappy title. I reckon Sleazy was about one-hundred-and-forty pounds too much!'

Jimmy walked over to the coffee machine and put it on himself. He sat down next to Wendy. 'It's not about him, it's about me.' He took the song from her and began to read.

'Fame, I wanted it too much
Put an image in my head
Of a dream I could not touch
Never tried to turn
From this road that I am on
Trapped here forever
A singer with no song.'

Jimmy turned to look at Wendy. 'What d'ya think?'

Wendy pulled a face as if she had just smelled something that had been left in the bottom of the fridge for far too long. 'Makes Leonard Cohen seem upbeat. Does it get any better?'

Jimmy began to read again.

'Nobody told me
That dreams don't all come true
And wanting it too much
Will make a fool of you.'

'That's the chorus?' Wendy let out a long sigh. 'Wow! That'll have them tapping their toes, in the mortuary.'

Jimmy held her face gently in his hands. 'Wendy, this is exactly how I felt. Every night I would go out there and no one would listen. They drank and gambled, watched the strippers while I sang my heart out. It was as if the words I was singing were dissolving as they left the stage. Do you understand how soul-destroying that is?'

'Is that why you stopped believing and started phoning it in?' Wendy gently pulled his hands from her face. 'I understand, Jimmy, I really do, but this is some dark shit. Do you think the fans will like it?'

Jimmy couldn't help but chuckle. 'Haven't you listened to the other six songs? They're not exactly happy, smiley people territory, but people love to be moved.' Jimmy was becoming passionate as he spoke. 'A great song needs to move you – doesn't matter if it's happy or sad as long as it gets to you and pushes the emotional trigger. Sad songs are just as successful as happy ones – probably more so.'

Wendy understood what Jimmy was saying, but she didn't seem completely convinced. 'I hear you, but some of these songs are really dark. They're the kinda songs you wouldn't want to bump into in a dark alley. Frankly they're a bit scary.'

Jimmy nodded enthusiastically. 'Exactly. They were born in blood, they come from a dark place, from a corner of my soul that I've sold for fame. It's the price I have to pay to write good songs but they're still good songs and people seem to love them.'

Wendy couldn't argue with that. Jimmy and The Second Chance were selling out the Canyon Room every time they played, and most nights that was two shows. 'I suppose it's like horror films – sometimes people enjoy something that makes them scared or forces them to look at the darker side of life.' She looked at Jimmy. 'You could be the Stephen King of blues Americana. Let's face it, you've got your own *Pet Sematary.*'

Jimmy ignored that comment; although Wendy did have a point. The song cemetery was now filling up with his own pets. At least Sleazy wouldn't have to be buried there; he really couldn't have faced trying to drag that lump up the rocky path. He looked to the last verse. The words described exactly how he felt.

'I cry out my emotions
They just turn away
I have no words to reach them
No songs to make them stay
The room it is silent
My hopes all are crushed
Just another night I wanted it too much.'

Jimmy put down the song. 'Maybe I did want it too much, but they're listening now. If this is a curse, it's one I can bear because those people I actually killed, present company accepted, deserved it.'

Wendy nodded slowly. 'Despite being part of the collateral damage, I do kinda agree with you. Me? I prefer show tunes, but these songs do certainly make you think – dramatic shit. Bit like Johnny Cash. What was that song?'

'"Hurt" as in I hurt myself today?' suggested Jimmy.

'That's it! Really dark shit, but people liked it.' Wendy thought for a moment. 'You could do really well with the depressed and recently bereaved market. Undertakers could sell your records with a coffin just to get mourners in the right frame of mind for the funeral.' Wendy seemed delighted with her marketing train of thought. 'Pity I can't do your advertising campaign.'

Jimmy gave her a forced smile. 'Is it, though? Maybe we should leave that to David and the label.'

'Please yourself, it's your record,' she replied with a shrug.

Jimmy had decided he would. He folded the song and put it in his pocket. 'Right, I gotta meet Kid for some breakfast. He has a plan to kill these bikers of yours.'

Wendy clapped her hands. 'Yippee. Try to make it painful!'

CHAPTER 16
STAIRWAY TO HELL

Sheriff Pence sat alone in his office mulling over the implications of the previous night's events. Jimmy Wayne had pushed him too far, but why? Did he really believe he could get away with that shit in his town? Jimmy knew not to mess with him; he had seen him crush anyone who stepped out of line and some who didn't. Why now did he seem to have no fear? Did he have something on him?

Like a rat in a trap, Sheriff Pence was trying to figure out his escape, only he didn't know what he was escaping from. All he knew was that he had a horrible feeling that the walls were closing in; he just didn't know why. That's the only problem of living such a big lie for so long. There comes a point when the truth is so obscure that it's almost impossible to see.

On the drive home, he had been happy: Jimmy Wayne was at the bottom of the canyon and he wasn't coming back. Turned out it was the perfect murder – or it would have been if Wayne hadn't loaned his car to Sleazy. Now Sleazy was dead, and with him went the two hundred dollars a week for him to turn a blind eye. Plus the percentage on the girls he helped Sleazy to import from Mexico. This was going to leave him twenty-five thousand down on cash income.

All this on top of Jackson Pollack disappearing was getting worryingly expensive. He had turned a blind eye to Jackson's dealing around town, mainly in the Reservation Bar, but also at Sleazy's. He'd also had a nice line in selling Jackson confiscated drugs. Sheriff Pence was big on recycling. He had a sickening feeling in his gut that all this was somehow linked. He could link Jimmy Wayne to Sleazy and he could link Sleazy to Jackson, but he just couldn't link Wayne to Jackson. And now Jack Lantern was coming to see him.

He had been on Jack's payroll for many years. Turning a blind eye here, arresting a rival there, but when Jack had called and told him that he would be in his office at nine, it was out of the blue, and it wasn't a request.

Jack's boys had been in town a couple of weeks back; he had seen them. Why hadn't Jack told him they were going to be there? Usually he let him know when and why they were coming. Were they checking up on him?

Paranoia was not something that Sheriff Pence had ever worried about. Normally he would be the cause of it in others, but events were moving so fast and he had no control over them. Worse still, he had no clue as to the cause of them. Like a drowning man trying to reach the surface, he was thrashing around but couldn't work out which way was up.

There was a knock on Sheriff Pence's door. 'Enter.'

His secretary, Dolly, entered. 'Mr Lantern is here to see you, Sheriff.'

'Show him in, Dolly.'

Before she could get out of the door to fetch him, Jack Lantern breezed past her as though he owned the place. He owned Pence, had done for years, but this was the first time he had been so upfront about it.

He turned to Dolly. 'Black coffee, no sugar.' There was no please or thank you; there seldom is when you are issuing an order.

Pence nodded at Jack as he sat down in the chair opposite. 'This is a pleasant surprise, Jack.'

Jack Lantern snorted with derision. 'No it ain't, Pence, you're shitting your pants. And if you're not, you should be.' This conversation was going downhill rapidly. Pence tried to bring it onto level ground.

'Suppose you tell me what I can do to help you, Jack; you seem a little angry.' It was a huge understatement. Jack Lantern was like an unexploded bomb. The clock was ticking and the eruption was getting nearer as each second passed.

Jack put his feet up on Pence's desk. It was a show of contempt but also a display of dominance.

When Dolly arrived with the coffee, she was visibly surprised by the way Jack Lantern had made himself at home. Sheriff Pence would never stand for this kind of behaviour. Self-consciously, she placed the coffees either side of Jack's feet.

'Thank you, Dolly, please close the door as you leave.'

She could hear the stress in her boss's voice. She backed out of the office and shut the door.

'Nice ass. You tapping it?'

Pence just stared at Lantern. 'No, I'm a happily married man and a churchgoer.'

'That you are, Sheriff. You're also a grade-A hypocrite who steals, frames innocent people and is banging at least three of the girls in Sleazy's joint. I have a file on you that would put you inside for the rest of your life, so don't waste your breath with anymore lies, you pious bastard.'

Pence had always feared this day. He'd always worried that Lantern was keeping a file on all their shady deals, and this confirmed it. The fact that he knew about the girls was even more concerning. Lantern had done his homework; he was in deep trouble.

He tried to play it cool. 'Well, that file must be nearly as big as the one I have on you, so I would say they cancel each other out. Mutually assured destruction, if you will.'

A large grin slowly formed on Jack Lantern's craggy features. 'That's very good, Pence, glad to see that we understand each other. If I go down, you're definitely coming along for the ride. Now we've established that we need to work together, I'd better tell you why I'm here today and what I need you to do.'

And there it was, in a matter of seconds and a few words, the whole power dynamic was set. He now worked for Jack Lantern.

'So, what is it you want from me?'

Jack slowly took his feet down from the desk and reached over to take a sip of coffee. 'Glad you asked that. I've lost three men around your town in three weeks. Vinny and Carmine were supposed to be taking care of Jimmy Wayne, but they disappeared. Ted Baker was supposed to either resolve a supply issue with Jackson Pollack or kill him. Both of them have disappeared as well. Seems you have a thief in your town who's stealing my men.'

Despite the fact that Jack had him over a barrel, Sheriff Pence could not hide his anger. 'You can't just send your men into my town to kill people. This is MY town!'

Jack slowly shook his head. 'You're wrong. This is MY town, and you just run it for me.'

Pence felt disoriented. The ground seemed to be moving beneath him and everything he had built his power on was crumbling to dust. 'I need to know about this shit so I can control it. You can't just kill who you like when you like – there are consequences.'

Jack didn't seem impressed by Pence's assertions. 'Squawk all you want, Sheriff, but I'm the boss in this town and you are my deputy. Are you gonna listen or are we gonna keep playing games?'

Pence knew that he had been outmanoeuvred; he also knew that for now he had no choice but to comply with anything Jack Lantern requested. 'OK, what is it you want?' He spoke the words but the reluctance was clear in his voice.

Jack smiled. Sheriff Pence knew he was beaten. Now he could be made to do whatever Lantern wanted him to do. 'There's a biker gang called the Deltas that run out of Three Rivers. Is that town within your jurisdiction?' asked Jack.

Pence nodded. 'Yeah, but you don't wanna be messing with them. They can be real trouble.'

'Not when they're dead.' As he said the words, a cold smile formed on Jack Lantern's lips. 'We're gonna wipe them out today, so that will be one less thing for you to worry about.'

Sheriff Pence was struggling to take in this new information. This was a big gang. When he spoke, he could not hide his disbelief at what was being proposed. 'Are you mad, Jack? There are never less than twenty of them in town. This would be a major shoot-out. How'd I explain it?'

Jack Lantern just shrugged. 'Well that, dear Sheriff, is what I pay you to figure out. These guys have been trying to move into my territory and steal my business. They have killed my men. I have to stop them and send a message to anyone else who thinks Jack Lantern is weak. I'M NOT!' Lantern's rage was clear, but he just about kept it in check. 'We're gonna send a message.'

Pence sat there shaking his head. 'And how'd you propose to send this message, Pony Express?!'

Jack permitted himself a humourless smile. 'No, I don't think that's gonna do it, Sheriff. I was thinking that you and a few of your men, acting on a tip-off, head up to the Deltas' clubhouse looking for drugs and illegal weapons.' Pence started to complain, but Jack shot him a look that made him bite his tongue. 'Regrettably, this raid will go horribly wrong for the Deltas. When you pull up outside, they'll panic and open fire on you.'

'They won't do that; they know what I'm like.'

Jack took another sip of coffee. 'Why don't you just listen and let me do the talking, then you'll know exactly how this is gonna go down.' Jack paused for a moment, waiting for Pence to come to terms with the fact that this had ceased to be a negotiation from the moment he had entered his office. 'You see, Sheriff, I've six guns coming in this morning, and they're gonna do most of the killing for you. I suggest you get some of your men together and head over there. My boys will assemble behind the clubhouse and when you guys turn up, get out of your cars and move in behind them with your guns drawn and call the Deltas to come out with their hands up.' Jack glanced at his watch. 'I think 11 a.m. would be a nice time to start the festivities. The second you call them to surrender on your mega-phone – you do have a megaphone, don't you?' Pence nodded grimly; Jack smiled. 'Excellent! Well, as soon as we hear your dulcet tones, we're gonna let all hell break loose from the back of the building. You pretend you're under attack and fire back. The Deltas will get cut to pieces and realise it's a trap and prob-ably return fire. We should be able to pick them off in a minute or two. My boys will go in and mop up. You keep your boys out of the place until I message you that mine are clear, and then you can go in and claim the glory.'

Pence just sat there, his mouth open. He was angry when he finally spoke. 'Are you fucking crazy? We can't just massacre twenty bikers because you think they may be moving in on your patch. There will be investigations. I can't justify a massacre on my patch without good cause.'

Jack had this covered. 'We have two hundred thousand dollars' worth of heroin to plant on the property and an arsenal of stolen guns – several which can be connected to murders. That's gonna give you plenty of "good cause".'

Sheriff Pence felt as though he was falling; Lantern's voice became just a distant hum. This couldn't be happening, but it was. A firm squeeze of his arm brought him back to the present.

'This is no time for daydreams, Sheriff, we have bikers to kill.'

Pence made one final attempt to dissuade Jack. 'Why don't you let me go up there and arrest them under suspicion of dealing? We can plant some gear and get them all locked up. Problem solved with no bloodshed.'

Jack shook his head. 'No good. Some of them will be out in two years; all of them will be out in five if they keep their noses clean inside. And they ain't gonna be happy at being framed, so we'll have some serious shit coming at us. They're like a cancer; we just gotta cut them out.'

———◆———

As Jimmy walked into the restaurant, he saw that Kid was already there with a coffee but no food. 'Morning!'

Kid looked up. 'I'm glad you didn't say good morning. This early rising has made me see things my eyes should never have seen.'

'What, at 9 a.m.?' Jimmy was intrigued.

Kid shook his head. 'I've been here since seven forty-eight.'

Jimmy gave him a 'WTF' look. 'Why?'

'Well, I tried to go to sleep but with all that excitement over Sleazy, I just couldn't stop thinking about breakfast, especially having it at the right time. This is new territory for me,' Kid replied with a foolish look on his face.

Despite what lay ahead that day, Jimmy couldn't help but feel amused. 'So, what did you have?'

Kid looked mildly surprised at the question. 'Nothing, I've been waiting for you.'

'For an hour and twelve minutes, are you serious?'

Kid was. 'We said nine, so nine it is. Besides, I got a coffee, or two, and it's given me time to think.'

'About breakfast? Decided what you're gonna have yet?' Jimmy couldn't help himself.

Not rising to the bait, Kid replied, 'Well, there are gonna be some tense moments later this morning, so fruit with a high acid content is out – don't wanna be shitting my pants literally as well as figuratively. We also have to consider that with the adrenaline running high, we're gonna be burning calories at an increased rate, so we don't wanna run out of gas. A loss of blood sugar will reduce our ability to think clearly under pressure.'

Jimmy just stood there. Was this guy for real? He was working out the right carb load for a killing spree. Lateral thinking on steroids. 'I was just planning to shoot the fuckers and then go and get some lunch.' Kid looked at Jimmy the way you would at a six-year-old who did not understand his maths homework.

'Sit down, Jimmy, there are situations in play here that you do not fully understand. This needs planning and, to be fair, a shit load of luck.'

Reluctantly, Jimmy took a seat. 'So, are we still planning to kill those three bikers from Three Rivers that raped Wendy?'

Kid thought about it for a moment. 'Planning yes, that's my department. Delivering them to you for despatch, also my department, but the actual killing is down to you. I'm a pacifist.'

This amused Jimmy; he could clearly remember at least four occasions when he'd seen Kid knock out rowdy drinkers who had crossed the line. He reminded him of the facts, after which Kid held up his hands.

'You have me there. Perhaps a better way of putting it would be in football terms. My pacifism only applies to offence, I never go out to hurt, but if you attack me, my defence goes into action.'

Jimmy had seen Kid's defence and it could be very offensive. 'So, you're gonna strap them into the electric chair, but it's me who has to throw the switch.'

Kid nodded enthusiastically. 'Obviously.'

'Why obviously?' Jimmy asked.

'You need the songs. Three scumbags equal three songs. That's an album.'

Jimmy thought for a moment as he looked at the broad smile on Kid's face, and then he realised that Kid had miscounted. 'Sleazy was number seven. If we get the three bikers, that will give us ten, but the label wants eleven. We're still gonna have to find another scumbag.'

'This is America, that won't be a problem.' Kid had a point.

He wanted these bastards dead for what they had done to Wendy; he also wanted the songs. If he got them today, he would still have a couple of weeks to find another scumbag and he would still be on the label's deadline. 'OK, what's the plan?'

Kid leaned forward conspiratorially. 'Well, here's what's going down.' Before he could continue, they were interrupted by Valerie.

'Usual, gents?'

All the thoughts about getting the right carb loading for a massacre disappeared as they both said, 'the usual, please.'

Valerie shrugged as another Groundhog Day in Blackjack began. As she walked away, she realised that some of her life choices weren't panning out the way she had hoped.

Kid waited for Valerie to move out of earshot and then continued, 'Jack Lantern has six guns going to Three Rivers before eleven this morning. They're going to the Deltas' clubhouse.'

'How'd you know that?' Jimmy was surprised by this news.

Kid waved him quiet. 'I just do. Lantern has got Sheriff Pence in his pocket and he's roped him into the raid, against his will, but he has no choice. Lantern has plenty of dirt on Sheriff Pence, and he will use it.'

Jimmy was struggling to take in all this information. 'Pence couldn't be involved in a shoot-out without good cause – he'll get crucified in the press and by his bosses.'

'You're right, that's why Jack has drugs and guns that have been used in murders to plant at the Deltas' clubhouse. This ain't a raid, it's a massacre, and Pence is in it whether he wants to be or not.' It sounded like Kid's plan to catch the rapists was doomed.

'We can't get caught up in this. We could die.'

Kid sat there and waited for Jimmy to shut up, which he did when he saw the look on Kid's face. 'I've identified the three. I know them and they know me. I have a plan, but it's not written in stone because this is gonna be a moveable feast.'

'Look, Kid, I appreciate your help, but we could get ourselves killed here. Let's just sit back and see what happens.' Jimmy wasn't convinced.

Anger crossed Kid's features and then subsided. Slowly, he began to recite the names and crimes of the three bikers. 'Rat Face, rape, murder, drug dealing. Vincent, rape, murder and pimping. Hoffa, rape, murder, GBH.' As he said their names, he pointed out each of them on a photo he'd taken.

It was clear that Kid had been doing his homework. The photo showed the three bikers on the balcony outside the Deltas' clubhouse. It was obvious why Rat Face was called Rat Face; all he needed was a bin to stick his head out of and a fleshy tail.

'Which one's Vincent?' asked Jimmy.

Kid pointed at the guy in the middle without sunglasses. 'He's Vincent because he only has one ear.'

Jimmy looked closely and could now see that the less than handsome face was indeed missing an ear. 'Well, guess that explains the lack of sunglasses.'

'And the name,' added Kid.

Jimmy pointed to the last biker. 'So, this must be Hoffa.'

Kid nodded.

'Dare I ask why?'

'Apparently he's always disappearing.'

'I take it these aren't their christened names.' Despite himself, Jimmy smiled.

Kid frowned. 'I very much doubt these scumbags were ever christened. They just climbed out from under a rock in some primordial swamp in Alabama and evolved – but not very far.'

David Parker had a horrible uneasy feeling; he had woken up with it and just couldn't shake it off. The air was full of menace. Jack Lantern being in his casino was something he didn't want. The guy brought nothing but trouble. He was an old-style mobster who hadn't evolved, still stuck in a world where a base-ball bat and a gun could solve most of his problems. He had seen him marching over to the police station where he'd remained for over twenty minutes. David was no fool; he knew that Sheriff Pence was on the take from Lantern. He knew that he had also been on the take from the late Sleazy Peterson.

He'd been keeping an eye on the main street and saw Jack emerge from the police station looking very happy with himself. After crossing the street, Jack had walked up to a black jeep with blacked-out windows. As he approached, the driver's window came down and David could see that there were several men inside. They all looked like thugs. Jack had stood at the open window for no more than forty seconds, but all the time he was giving instructions.

Jack then turned on his heel and headed towards the casino. The window slid up on the jeep, and the men inside the blacked-out interior remained a mystery as the jeep sped off. They were headed out of town on the road to Three Rivers.

David ducked back inside the confines of the entrance hall before Jack saw him watching. There was something going on, he knew it. The air felt heavy; it was like an approaching thunderstorm and he was in the eye of it.

As he walked back through the hotel, he was just in time to catch Jimmy and Kid leaving the restaurant. 'Morning, gents, where are you off to this fine morning?' He managed to sound cheerier and more optimistic than he felt.

Jimmy and Kid exchanged furtive glances, and David Parker's feelings of foreboding multiplied.

Kid spoke first. 'Just gonna take a little drive. Got a friend up near Three Rivers who has a couple of guitars to sell, so I figured me and Jimmy would go take a look. One's a vintage Gibson 335.'

The guitar type meant nothing to David, but the fact that they were also headed for Three Rivers seemed too much of a coincidence. He had to speak up. 'What's really going on in Three Rivers today, boys? You know Jack Lantern's boys are going up there?'

As he spoke, Sheriff Pence came out of his office with six of his officers and they climbed into four squad cars. They drove out of town on the Three Rivers Road. The same road that Jack Lantern's boys had just taken.

'Well, we don't really mix with those kinda people, David, mainly on account that I've been shagging their boss's wife!' They all smiled.

'That makes sense, about the only thing today that has!' David moved closer so he could whisper. 'Listen, I don't know what's going on. I don't want to know what's going on, but I don't want you boys getting caught up in something you can't handle. Jack Lantern is borderline evil and Sheriff Pence is as corrupt as they come.'

Kid held up a hand. 'We're just gonna look at a couple of guitars. Hell, I might even buy them.'

David pursed his lips. There was so much that he wanted to say but couldn't. Jimmy was on the verge of something big and he would take Kid along with him. He cared about these men. 'Whatever you say, Kid. All I'm saying is that there is something going down in Three Rivers and I think it has something to do with the bikers.'

Jimmy and Kid exchanged glances. They were like naughty schoolboys, and David could read their secrets as if they were written on their foreheads.

'Boys, you've got great things coming your way, please don't fuck it up.'

Jimmy smiled. 'I love it when you say "fuck" in that English accent!' Then they just turned and hurried away.

David watched them go, wondering if they would ever come back – and if not, who he could put on in the Canyon Room tonight.

———◆———

'Keep your speed down, Cooper, we don't wanna get there too soon.' Sheriff Pence's deputy obliged and eased back on the throttle. 'We need the drug deal to go down first – once the drugs are in the Deltas' clubhouse, we can move.'

'Good thinking, boss,' said Cooper, who had never had a good thought in his life. Obviously, this made him perfect to be Pence's deputy.

Sheriff Pence's mind was running at a hundred miles an hour. He was on a runaway train that he couldn't slow down. For a man so used to shaping events to his own ends it was an uncomfortable and unfamiliar feeling. He had to find a way to gain control of the situation. The Deltas gave him kickbacks for looking the other way, and in return they also stayed out of Blackjack, apart from the Reservation. He didn't want them dead because that meant even more of his dirty money disappearing forever, but Jack Lantern did – and he had enough information to send him to prison for life, or worse!

The only way out was to kill Jack Lantern. Easier said than done. Jack would not be in Three Rivers; he would be back in the safety of the Riviera and seen by many guests. His alibi would be bulletproof. Just a shame that he appeared to be bulletproof for the moment. His time would come.

———◆———

As they rolled along the highway heading for Three Rivers in Kid's van, Jimmy asked the question he had wanted to ask all morning. 'How are we gonna get them into the back of your van?'

Kid looked very pleased with himself. 'I'm glad you asked. I'm a bit like the Child Catcher from *Chitty Chitty Bang Bang*.'

'*Titty Titty* what?'

Kid smiled. 'It's an English film from the sixties. In it there was a sinister character called the Child Catcher, and he would come around in his van and tempt the children into the back and kidnap them.'

Jimmy looked appalled. 'This was a children's film?'

'Yeah, but those Brits were doing a lot of drugs in the sixties. It was a little dark, but the basic premise is the same as we're gonna use. I have some stuff in the back that will tempt them in. The Child Catcher used lollipops.'

Jimmy was intrigued. 'And what are we using?'

'An assortment of Hecklers & Kochs and a couple of Uzi 9mm machine guns,' replied Kid, jerking his head towards the back of the van.

Jimmy whipped back the curtain, and sure enough there was an assortment of automatic weapons. He turned to Kid. 'Are you fucking crazy? We can't arm three bikers and then try and kill them, this is a suicide mission!'

Kid gave Jimmy a playful slap to the side of his head that damn near knocked him out of the van. 'Calm yourself, Jimmy, the guns have all been decommissioned. You would have to fire them to discover it, but it fooled you so there's no reason why it won't fool them.'

Jimmy's ear was ringing, but Kid had actually made sense. 'That hurt you know,' said Jimmy, rubbing his ear.

'It was meant to. You're acting like a girl, and we need to be calm and focused.' Kid was grinning at him.

'OK, but that's a bit unfair on girls – I know some tough motherfuckers.'

'True,' agreed Kid. 'I know many girls tougher than you, Jimmy Wayne, but none of them can sing for shit, or write decent songs.'

Jimmy took a deep breath. He had another question to ask, but he knew he was going to regret it. 'So, we get them in the van, we maybe persuade them to drive somewhere quiet to look at the weapons, but how the hell do we get them to squat in the back to get them to the canyon?'

Kid flipped open the glove compartment and produced two gas masks. 'Ta da!' he announced, holding them up.

'You gonna fart them to sleep?' Jimmy just looked at them without comprehension.

'Although I do believe, given the right diet, I could be capable of it, sadly it would take too long and probably leave a nasty aftertaste! No, I've rigged up the back of the van with nitrous oxide.'

Jimmy had heard of that. 'Laughing gas?'

'Exactly, but when you deliver it in the quantities I have planned, it renders you unconscious in a matter of seconds. We then simply drive to the canyon and you can do your thing.'

Jimmy just sat there. Kid had really thought this through. It could work. 'What if they overdose on the gas? You will have killed them and I don't get the songs.'

Again, Kid gave him the look of a college professor mildly offended at the stupidity of the question his pupil has just asked. 'That, Jimmy, is why the button is next to you. Gassed or shot, the kill is yours!'

Jimmy was now beginning to wonder if Kid had done this kind of thing before. 'So are you gonna help me kill them?'

'Regretfully no. As I said before, I'm a pacifist. These scumbags deserve to die but it has to be by your hand, Jimmy, because we need the songs. This is about justice, and art!'

Jimmy sighed. 'I'm sure that Rat Face, Vincent and Hoffa are gonna be delighted with their posthumous Grammys!'

———————◆———————

As Sheriff Pence's convoy of police cars cruised up the quiet highway towards Three Rivers, they were overtaken by a black Dodge Ram.

Cooper turned to Sheriff Pence. 'He's over the limit, boss, shall I pull him?'

Pence sighed with disgust. 'Just how stupid are you, Cooper? We're on the way to a big drug bust which could end up with a violent confrontation, and you wanna stop and give someone a speeding ticket for doing five miles an hour over the limit. Swear to God if you weren't my sister's nephew I'd be arresting you instead of employing you.' Sheriff Pence then glanced across at the Dodge and there in the passenger seat was Jimmy Wayne! *What the hell is he doing?* It was a coincidence, it had to be, but that didn't make him feel any better.

Jack Lantern's plan was very risky. Before he arrived with his men, one of Lantern's men disguised as a biker had infiltrated the gang and planted the drugs and guns. He was supposed to pull up outside, form a firing line behind his vehicles and call out the Deltas. Jack Lantern's men would move in undercover of the confusion and then just start killing the bikers. It was not a good plan. It left Pence and his men exposed, and it was going to be really hard for Pence to cover it up. Who fired first? Which bullet came from which gun? If it was ever properly investigated, there was no way they could explain the events. His only hope was that he ran this county and the governor and local judiciary were as corrupt as he was.

Events were spiralling out of control and he, for a change, was just a pawn in the game. For a man used to being in control of the game, this was not a comfortable place to be.

———◆———

Back at the Riviera, Jack Lantern was sitting on the patio enjoying a quiet coffee and the morning sunshine, safe in the knowledge that in the course of the next couple of hours the Deltas would be destroyed and any threat to his empire that they posed would be gone along with them.

The fact that he had forced Sheriff Pence to take part in this massacre was an added bonus. Pence had thought himself to be immune from Jack's influence, despite being on his payroll for years, but after this, he would be so deeply implicated in mass murder that he would now forever be Jack's puppet. This made Jack very happy.

'Morning, Jack, mind if I join you?' It was David Parker.

Jack liked Parker. He knew him when he worked in Vegas and he admired the way he managed the casino. He had hinted that he should work with Jack – not on the books, but in a subcontract sort of a way. He had wasted his breath; David Parker was not for sale at any price. Jack liked that – just like you always fancy the girls who ignore you.

'What can I do for you, David?'

David sat down. 'Jack, it's none of my business, but could you shed some light on what the hell is going on at Three Rivers.'

'Well, I could if I knew where Three Rivers was.'

David had expected a denial, so went on the attack. 'We all know that's not true. We played golf there two years back in that charity event. You seemed to know a lot of the local characters as well.' When David said 'characters' what he really meant was criminals. Three Rivers had a casino as well, but it wasn't managed to the same scrupulous standards that David applied to the Riviera. He pressed Jack further, 'I seem to remember that you had an interest in the casino there. What was it called? The Jackpot. Not much of a place, but always full of the wrong sort of people.'

Jack didn't respond; he just sat there looking at David.

'I saw you going into Sheriff Pence's station this morning and not long after you came out, he took off with three squad cars. They followed your van full of goons towards Three Rivers. Does that help jog your memory, Jack?'

David was treading on dangerous ground and although he hid it well, he could tell that Jack was not happy with his line of questioning. When he did reply it was slow and measured, but he left no doubt in David's mind that to push any further would be bad for his health.

'I like you, David, and because of that I'm gonna pretend you never asked those questions. What you're doing is imagining something that aint really there – bit like aliens. People think they've seen them, out on these lonely desert roads at night. Some even think they've been kidnapped by them and used for some kinda experiment. Look at some of these folks, you wouldn't even kidnap them to make dog food! However, folks that start poking into business that is none of their business, well, they can end up as dog food!'

The two men just sat there looking at each other. Jack had basically threatened to have David killed if he didn't back off. This was fine with David, because at least now he knew that something big was going down in Three Rivers and Jack Lantern was definitely involved.

David stood up and nodded. 'Thanks, Jack, that was very informative. I think I will take your advice as I'm not keen on dog food and I don't own a dog.'

Jack smiled. 'Be a lot safer, David. Those trousers of yours look so much better with knees intact.'

David flashed him a fleeting smile, and then turned and headed for his office.

Jack Lantern put on a show of civility but David could see that just below the surface was the cold, hard killer who had built an empire on criminality and would destroy anything that threatened his wealth and position in the community. Whatever was about to happen in Three Rivers, there was nothing David could do to prevent it.

He thought about phoning Jimmy and Kid to warn them, but they obviously knew that something was going down and they were party to it. He didn't know how or why, but somehow they were caught up in this spider's web. All he could do was return to his office, get on with his work and hope that when the show began this evening, he would still have a band.

———◆———

Jimmy was now very concerned for his safety. He had seen Sheriff Pence's convoy when they overtook it; they looked deadly serious. They were headed for a fight, but he didn't want any part of it. He turned to Kid. 'You saw that, didn't you?'

'Course I did.' Kid smiled. 'Just like I saw the blacked-out van full of Jack Lantern's goons head out of Blackjack ten minutes ahead of Pence and his boys. We're headed for a shitfest, the like of which Three Rivers has never seen, and that place is a shithole.' He actually seemed to be enjoying himself. 'Cheer up, Jimmy, you're never so alive as when you're near to death.'

'Yeah, and you're never so dead as when you've been killed.'

Kid waved his comment away. 'Cheer up, I have a plan!' He winked at Jimmy. 'It's almost, very probably, fool-proof. All I need now are some fools to make it work.' Holding the steering wheel with one hand, he pulled out his phone with the other and made a call. 'Now, let's see if we can find us some!'

The phone rang out via the Bluetooth in the van. Kid held his finger to his lips warning Jimmy to keep quiet.

A slow southern accent answered the phone. 'Low – is that you, Keed?'

Kid put his hand over the microphone. 'Praise the Lord, we have us a fool!' He uncovered the speaker. 'Hi, Leroy. Got that package you boys wanted to look at.'

Jimmy mouthed silently, 'Leroy!'

Kid covered the speaker again and glanced at Jimmy unable to hide the amusement on his face. 'Kinda ironic for a white supremacist.' He uncovered the speaker.

'Brung it on to the clubhouse.'

'Too dangerous. Meet me out back with Vincent and Hoffa in two minutes. We just passed Sheriff Pence coming toward town with three squad cars, so it could be about time for your quarterly inspection. We don't wanna get caught with a van full of sub-machine guns now, do we?'

There was a pause at the other end of the line; you could almost hear the clockwork ticking of Leroy's brain. 'Guess not. Meet you out th' back.'

Kid gave Jimmy the thumbs up. 'Be there in two minutes. Just climb in the back, and we'll shoot down the canyon road and get away from prying eyes.'

For a moment there was silence, and then a slow wary voice came back on the line. 'How'd I know it's your van?'

For a moment, Kid took both hands off the wheel and held his head. 'Well, Leroy, if you look at the pointy bit, I'll be driving.'

Again, there was silence as the information was absorbed. 'You yanking my chain?'

'Yes. See you in ninety seconds,' and rung off. He sighed. 'Swear to God, if his brains were dynamite he couldn't blow his hat off.'

Jimmy nodded and started giggling. 'Fucking Leroy!'

Kid started to laugh, too. 'Yeah, he should just stick with Rat Face.'

———◆———

Terry Moist looked around. They had pulled up on some waste ground behind the Deltas' clubhouse. All they could do now was wait for Sheriff Pence to arrive and hope that a load of Deltas didn't come out the back and find them – that would be a tricky conversation.

Suddenly, the rear door of the club, the one they had planned to enter by, swung open. Luckily the engine was already off. Three of the Deltas appeared.

Terry slipped the safety off his gun. 'Nobody moves unless I tell you.' His men said nothing, but all slipped off the safeties on their guns.

The three bikers stared at the van. One, who looked for all the world like a rat with a human body, moved towards them.

'Shit,' said Terry as he got ready to open the door and send Rat Boy to rat heaven. He got within about ten paces and suddenly another van pulled onto the far side of the waste ground. He watched.

As the other van pipped its horn, the bikers stopped and looked over to it. The window came down on the driver's side and a man called out something he couldn't catch. There seemed to be a short discussion, and then the back door of a van slid open and the three bikers climbed in. The door slid shut and the van moved rapidly off the waste ground.

Terry Moist let out a sigh. 'What the fuck was that all about!'

'Shouldn't we have stopped them, Terry?'

'What, and let the other twenty bikers inside know something's going down before Pence gets here? No, we stick to the plan. We can mop up those guys anytime. Besides, when we've finished there won't be a club to be a member of!'

There was some nervous laughter from the back of the SUV. The boys were always a bit highly strung before a mass murder.

'You lot keep quiet – I need to speak to Mr Lantern.' Terry punched in Jack's number. It rang twice and then Jack answered.

'Well?' There was no preamble or small talk, but Terry was used to this.

'We just pulled up. We're waiting for Pence to arrive. The drugs and guns have been planted – Marco texted me about ten minutes ago.'

Jack nodded as he listened. If you were sitting on the sundeck at the Riviera watching Jack on his phone, you would have thought he was talking to a friend, not ordering a mass killing. But this was Jack's world, and death was as inevitable as taxes – not that he paid many taxes.

'You got those guns from Pence's office?' he asked.

'Yes, boss, picked them up last night. All the wounds will be from police issue weapons from Pence's arsenal, should anyone decide to look into it.'

Jack smiled; this was good. His boys would be killing the bikers with legitimate police weapons that were issued to Pence's station. As long as nobody tried to work out why six officers had used twelve weapons, they would be fine.

'Don't shoot them all in the back, Terry. We wanna make it look like a fight,' Jack said before briefly pausing. 'And don't kill any cops – that would make things very awkward.'

Terry nodded despite the fact that Jack couldn't see him. 'No problem, boss. By the time we've finished, there'll be no bikers left in the Deltas.' He stopped for a moment, not wanting to tell Jack about the three bikers they wouldn't be killing, but he knew there would be hell to pay if Jack found out later. 'Just one thing, boss, three of them left the clubhouse as we arrived. We couldn't take them out because that would've blown the plan.' Terry waited for the explosion from Jack, but it never came.

Jack figured that he didn't need to kill all of them, just most of them. Whatever was left of the Deltas after this morning's operation would just thank their lucky stars that they had escaped. If most of your gang had been massacred, would you go back to the scene of the crime? Jack didn't think so. Besides, a few frightened survivors to spread the word among the criminal underworld in which Jack moved would just strengthen the message. This was all good news for Jack.

'You reckon you can do it without the cops realising you're out the back?'

Again, Terry's head was nodding. 'Easy, boss. Kill most of them while the cops are out front of the building. Cops are gonna think that they're coming under fire because they're about to find something. Pin down a couple of survivors and let them think we're all cops on Pence's payroll here to kill them, and they should go down fighting. After they're dead, we can fire a few shots using their weapons over the heads of Pence's boys just to keep them firing, and then we beat a retreat out the back. As long as your boy only comes from the front, it won't be a problem.' It sounded as if Terry had it all worked out.

'That's good, Terry, very good, happy hunting.' Jack hung up safe in the knowledge that the twenty or so bikers he had just ordered to be killed would be dead in a matter of minutes and his drug dealers would have unfettered access to the noses and veins of the good citizens of Three Rivers and all surrounding towns.

He leaned back in his chair and let the sun warm his face. Some days, life was really good!

———◆———

As Kid sped off down the road, he looked at Jimmy. 'That was a bit too close for comfort, don't you think?'

Jimmy, looking very pale, just nodded. Leroy was not looking at the guns; something didn't feel right to him. 'Who was in that blacked-out SUV and what's your hurry?'

Kid looked at Leroy in the mirror. 'I think it was the drugs squad. Pence hasn't got any vehicles like that.'

'I thought you were winding me up. We gotta go back and warn the boys.' Leroy looked angry.

Kid shook his head. 'Have you not seen what's in this van? And you want me to go back? There's a police drugs raid about to take place, you crazy?'

Jimmy watched the confusion playing across Leroy's rodent-like features. For several moments, things could have gone either way and then Vincent spoke. Jimmy guessed it was Vincent because he clearly only had one ear.

'Kid's right, Leroy. We get caught with these it's five years minimum. Pence is on our payroll and we only got grass in the clubhouse – personal use, gonna be a fine worst-case scenario,' he said with a shrug.

Leroy considered this for a moment, but then Hoffa stepped forward with a sub-machine gun. 'Look at this beauty.'

Leroy wasn't capable of deep rational thinking and his attention span was already approaching its limit. He looked at the gun and his eyes lit up. 'Hey, that's nice.' He reached over and took the gun from Hoffa. 'Taca! Taca! Taca!' he screamed while pretending to be Rambo.

Jimmy exchanged a relieved glance with Kid. For now, they were safe, but Leroy soon tired of the Rambo game. He then stared at Jimmy.

'You're that Jimmy Wayne.' Jimmy smiled weakly. Leroy turned to Kid and asked, 'Why's he here?' He looked and sounded suspicious.

'Because I asked him to come,' Kid replied, thinking on his

feet. 'He's trying to write a song about motorcycle gangs, bit like *Easy Rider*. You're his research!'

'I ain't never been used for research before.' Leroy looked dubious.

Kid grinned at Leroy. 'Best stay away from laboratories, then!'

Jimmy stifled a laugh and glanced out of Kid's window. Rat Face was still staring at him.

'I like your music, Jimmy Wayne.'

Jimmy smiled weakly. He wasn't really in the mood for praise from a fan, especially one he was about to kill! 'Thank you, Leroy.' He decided to change the subject. 'What do you guys think of the guns?'

The three bikers looked as though all their Christmases had come at once. They were now picking up the guns and handling them as if they were beautiful women, which was surprising given their looks. They were all unlikely to have been anywhere near a woman who hadn't been tied up first!

Kid turned onto the side road and looked over at Jimmy. He mouthed the words, 'gas mask.'

Jimmy nodded and grabbed the face masks from the glove-box. He glanced behind him to see the dogs of war firing imaginary shots at each other.

Kid sighed. 'Boys will be boys!' It was hard to hear him through his gas mask. He turned to Jimmy. 'Hit the button, maestro.'

Hoffa looked up and saw the two of them wearing gas masks. 'Hey! What the fuck–?' His words trailed off as he began choking when the laughing gas filled the back of the van. Rat Face tried to get to Kid, but Kid just hit the accelerator, causing Rat Face to fall backwards into the rear of the van.

Jimmy was amazed at how quickly they went down. Within twenty seconds they were all unconscious. He kept his fingers on the button for another twenty until Kid told him to stop. He had to let down the window on the driver's side as the gas had formed a mist and he was driving in a cloud.

Kid neared a track and turned smoothly into it. 'Let's stop here and tie their hands before they come round.'

Zip ties are useful things. Within thirty seconds the three bikers were all bound hand and foot and deeply unconscious. Jimmy and Kid stood back and admired their handiwork.

Kid smiled. 'Well, I think that went well. Now all we gotta do is drive them to the canyon and you can do your stuff and get us three new songs.'

Jimmy heard what Kid said and it all made perfect sense, but when he broke it down, 'do your stuff' meant kill three men. Admittedly they were scumbags, but murder was not an easy word to digest.

Kid locked the back doors and looked at Jimmy. 'How you gonna kill them?' It sounded such an innocent question. He could have been asking, 'how you gonna put that shelf up?' but it was far from that.

'Not really thought about that yet. I kinda assumed we were gonna die before I got the chance!' Just as he spoke, multiple gunshots filled the air less than a mile away. It was coming from the Deltas' clubhouse.

As they scrambled into the van, Kid leaned out of the window and looked up the hill in the direction of the gunfire. 'And the wrath of Jack Lantern will reign down upon you and vengeance will be his.'

'We need to kill that fucker one day,' said Jimmy.

'Agreed, but that bastard deserves a record all to himself. Let's make it a concept prog album with one long track. We only need to kill Jack.'

Jimmy nodded; this was a good idea. 'D'ya think if we kill him slow, you know, tortured him a bit, we could get several movements to the song like a classical prog rock piece?'

Kid was thoughtful as he sped down the road away from the slaughter being enacted at the Deltas' clubhouse. After a long silence, interrupted only by distant gunshots and the sound of the Dodge's engine, he said, 'There's every reason to believe that if we killed him in stages, we could get a master work with several movements. I'm guessing these songs come from the energy released by the actual death, so if it was long and drawn out maybe the song would be long and drawn out.' Kid turned to Jimmy and beamed. 'We could have that rarest of musical commodities on our hands.'

'What's that, then?' Jimmy asked, looking at him.

Kid seemed triumphant. 'A prog rock record that people actually wanna listen to!'

As strange conversations went, this was probably the strangest ever for Jimmy in his life. As for Kid, it probably only just got into his top ten.

Jimmy looked into the back of the van and studied the sleeping bikers. They were all somebody's son. It was hard to justify what he and Kid were doing just to get some songs, but it wasn't just to get some songs. These scumbags had raped Wendy. They had killed and robbed. They had pushed drugs to teenagers.

The world would be a much better place without them. All this was true, but it still didn't make it any easier.

———◆———

Back at the Deltas' clubhouse, the bikers didn't know what had hit them. The police were out front telling them to come out with their hands up. Decca, their leader, was just about to do so when automatic fire came raking across the back of the clubhouse. It was a timber building, so the bullets penetrated it like a hot knife through butter. All around him Decca could see his captains falling. He ran to the front of the clubhouse, but Sheriff Pence's men were now firing at will inside. Decca didn't understand. Why were the police killing them? What had they done?

It may have looked like that to Decca, but Sheriff Pence knew exactly what was going on. He didn't bother informing his men. They had already unloaded a volley of fire into the clubhouse before ducking down behind their squad cars. The gunfire coming from the building was not aimed at them. It was Jack Lantern's assassination squad coming in from the rear of the building on a shoot-to-kill mission. He didn't want any of his men injured by trying to be heroic.

'Stay down behind your cars,' ordered Pence.

Officer Feemster, a young gung-ho hero in the making, called to Pence, 'Sheriff, what if I get in behind them and draw their fire?'

Pence definitely didn't want that. Jack's boys would kill him in an instant. 'Stay where you are, Feemster. They're not hitting jack shit. Sit tight and let's wait for our moment.'

Reluctantly, Officer Feemster crouched back down behind his squad car. To be fair, Sheriff Pence was right. For the amount of gunfire that was going off, very little seemed to be coming in their direction. 'Sheriff, are they having a fight among themselves?'

Pence nodded. 'Wouldn't be the first time. On the count of three, let's give them a four-second volley – see if we can take the wind outta their sales.' Pence flipped a new clip into his handgun. 'All loaded, boys.' He looked along the line of cars at the frightened faces of his men who were more used to arresting drunks and issuing speeding tickets. Except Feemster. He was smiling and obviously enjoying the adrenalin. He needed to keep that young man on a tight leash. 'On the count of three: One, two, three, FIRE!' Pence stood up, pointed his gun into the Deltas' clubhouse and unloaded the clip. As his officers filled the morning air with hot lead and splinters, he knew he was also filling bikers and timbers with police bullets which would show there had been a shoot-out. He was cleaning house as he went!

It was carnage inside the clubhouse, bullets rained in from both sides, and Decca realised he would not talk his way out of this one. He grabbed his trusted Uzi machine gun and charged down the steps firing down the side of the squad cars and hitting precisely no one. As he reached the bottom step, he saw every officer rise from behind their cars, all guns pointing in his direction. He then saw Sheriff Pence mouth something that looked suspiciously like 'FIRE!' He managed to say 'Oh' before the volley of bullets virtually cut him in half, but the 'shit!' part of the statement remained forever silent as he died before hitting the ground.

Terry Moist and his boys moved swiftly through the clubhouse mopping up the wounded. One came out of a cupboard with his hands up. They were still up as a bullet went through his head. Terry surveyed the carnage. No one moved, not even a moan. Every last member of the Deltas was dead – apart from three who were in the back of a Dodge heading for the song cemetery.

Once Terry was happy there were no survivors, he ushered his men out through the back of the clubhouse. Behind the bar he could smell bacon cooking in the kitchen. He slipped through the door, but the chef, actually a biker in an apron, was dead on the floor with bullet holes too numerous to mention. He resembled the sieve that lay on the counter with freshly washed mushrooms that would never be eaten.

Terry pulled out a rasher of bacon. Smoked and crispy, it tasted really good. He pulled out another rasher, and then unloaded his clip into the roof of the clubhouse as he left the building. He didn't want Pence's boys thinking it was all over just yet.

Officer Feemster looked across at the sheriff. 'You want me to take a look, boss?'

Sheriff Pence did not. 'Stay down, Feemster, this could be a trick.' He looked down the line of three squad cars to make sure all of his men were OK. They looked pale and scared, apart from Feemster, who looked as though he was itching to engage the Deltas. It was bad enough that Feemster was keen to enforce justice – if it turned out he wasn't corruptible, he could be a right pain in the ass. Pence listened hard and thought he could hear the engine of Jack's boys' vehicle as it slipped away from the scene of the crime. Now was his chance. 'Everyone stay down. I'm gonna take a look.'

Feemster jumped up. 'I'll come with you, Sheriff.'

God that boy is a pain in the ass, thought Pence. 'No, stay there and cover me. You see anyone move in there, you take them down.'

'Yes, sir!'

Pence slowly rose from behind his car and surveyed the scene. He felt the buzz of a message from his mobile. That would be the all-clear from Jack; now he felt confident to move. The Deltas' clubhouse was a timber-framed Swiss chalet construction, which now looked as though it had been visited by an army of armour-plated termites.

Holes littered the walls, windows were hanging out of their frames and a body hung out of a window. The front door was now just splintered wood and the leader of the Deltas lay dead at the bottom of the steps that led up to the front door of the veranda. Sam Black, also known as Decca, was clearly dead. The expression of surprise on his face made it clear that he'd not been expecting this, but then it's not usual for the local police to just turn up and massacre you – beat you up a bit, but not wipe you out in an ambush reminiscent of the St Valentine's Day Massacre.

As he stepped over Decca's body, Sheriff Pence couldn't help but think about the amount of paperwork that this was going to create. It was also going to take some explaining, if he ever had to explain it.

With his gun held out in front of him, he mounted the steps and slowly approached the front door. The door lay on the verandah where the volleys of gunfire had blown out the frame. Through the hole where the door had been, he could see the carnage that lay within.

Lantern's men had been very efficient. There would be no one left alive to shoot at him, but he maintained the pretence for the benefit of his men.

Once inside the door, he lowered his gun. The interior looked like a charnel house. It was a scene from hell, and he had helped to bring hell to this place. Somewhere he had taken the wrong turn and now here he was killing for Jack Lantern and tidying up the mess. Was it worth it for the money? He then thought about his fine house overlooking the golf club in Blackjack and his apartment and boat down in Florida Keys, and his mood lightened. Of course it was worth it!

CHAPTER 17
LAUGHING AND DYING

As the Dodge bumped down the ten-mile dirt road that led to the end of the canyon and the song graveyard, one of the bikers stirred in the back. It was Rat Face. His eyes opened and he looked around him confused by his surroundings. He was even more confused realising that his hands and feet were tied.

For a moment, Jimmy saw anger spark in his eyes but then he started giggling.

'They took in a lot of laughing gas,' said Kid, looking over at him. 'I reckon they're gonna be sniggering all the way into the next life.'

'Let's see if they're still laughing when you shoot them in the balls!' It was Wendy. She had materialised in the back of the van.

Jimmy turned to her and spoke without thinking. 'Hi, Wendy, we got them for you.' Then he remembered that Kid was sitting next to him.

Kid looked across at Jimmy, who seemed totally unfazed by the sudden turn in events. 'I take it the lovely Wendy has arrived.'

'Hi, Kid, good to see you,' replied Wendy, smiling.

Jimmy watched Kid carefully, but he had not heard Wendy or seen her in the mirror. 'Wendy says hi,' said Jimmy, becoming the interpreter between the dead and the living.

Wendy and Kid both looked disappointed. 'Guess it's only the person who kills you that can see you in the afterlife,' said Wendy, in a slightly more accusatory manner than Jimmy would have liked.

'Or the true love of your life,' he added quickly.

Wendy pulled a face. 'Yeah, that too. Maybe.'

'Ask her what she wants us to do with them,' said Kid, obviously enjoying the fact that they now had someone from another world sharing the van with them.

'No need to ask – I've already had my instructions.'

'And what would those be?' Kid seemed impressed.

'Shoot them in the balls!' cried Wendy.

'Shoot them in the balls,' translated Jimmy.

Kid burst out laughing. 'Most appropriate. That should curtail their rapeyness. Not sure it will kill them, though.'

'Chop off their hands so they can't rub them better.' Wendy was warming to her task. Only it wasn't her task – it was Jimmy's, and he didn't like the way this conversation was going.

'Look, Wendy, these guys are scum and I'm gonna kill them for what they did to you, but I can't torture them. I'm not Vinny or Carmine. I take no pleasure from killing. I do it because–'

'Because we need the songs.' Kid finished the sentence for him.

Jimmy didn't know what to say to that, mainly because it was true. Even Wendy, for a change, said nothing.

Kid continued, 'Jimmy, you're not a bad person. Fate has just pushed you into a corner, so you can either roll over and give up or kill a few scumbags and prosper. I vote we prosper!'

'Hear, hear,' called Wendy from the back of the van, where she was busy trying to stamp on Hoffa's head and disappointingly going right through. Sometimes being dead had its drawbacks.

After a few minutes they reached the end of the canyon. Kid looked up at the outcrop of rocks. He let out a slow low whistle. 'Wow, this is spectacular, talk about a natural amphitheatre, and that outcrop makes a perfect stage.' He turned to Jimmy. 'So is this where you come to play and write songs?'

Before Jimmy could answer, Wendy replied, 'this is where he comes to stifle them at birth, then he buries them here, along with the bodies.'

Kid watched Jimmy reacting to something that was being said but he couldn't hear. Clearly, Jimmy could see and hear Wendy; he wished he could.

It was obvious from the look on Jimmy's face that whatever was being said wasn't complimentary.

'Not a fan of your song writing then, Jimmy?' Kid couldn't disguise the amusement in his voice.

'Only the ones he writes after he's killed someone,' said Wendy.

Jimmy looked at Kid. 'She only likes the ones that are post-mortem, if you catch my drift.'

Kid did indeed catch Jimmy's drift and admired the eloquent way he described serial murder. 'Well, we have three more songs in the back once you've progressed them from pre- to post-mortem.'

All three of the bikers were now conscious and in various states of amusement; they were all trying to get free but were sniggering. Vincent managed to be both angry and amused.

'Untie me, you cocksuckers. Ha! Cocksucker!' They seemed to find the word endlessly amusing.

Wendy, still trying to stamp on their heads, was becoming extremely frustrated at her lack of a physical presence. 'Jimmy, get in here and flatten some heads for me, this is driving me crazy.'

Instead, Jimmy pressed the gas button to give the boys a happy state of mind, before he killed them.

'Don't overdo it. If you kill them here, we gotta carry them all way to the top.' Kid had a point.

He took his finger off the button. The bikers were now laughing like madmen. It hadn't affected Wendy; she was now trying to gouge out Hoffa's eyes and becoming very angry at her lack of success.

'I'm guessing Wendy is trying and failing to enact some serious injuries in the back,' said Kid, looking at Jimmy's appalled face.

'She sure is, and she's not liking the lack of results,' Jimmy replied with a smile.

Kid hopped out of the van. 'Let's get these boys up there and save her going out of her mind.'

Jimmy did likewise. When they opened the door, the three bikers rolled out and fell onto the sandy desert ground.

With difficulty, Rat Face staggered to his feet. He swayed for a moment, but his feet and hands were zip tied. As he tried to move forward, he fell like a mighty oak being felled and landed face first into the dirt. There was an audible *crack* as his nose broke on impact. Hoffa and Vincent looked at each other and then burst out laughing. Rat Face rolled over to face his taunts; his nose was flattened like a lump of bread dough thrown on a baker's table.

'Thnot fummy.' He listened to what he'd said. 'Ith's mott!' But it was; he started to laugh and so did the others. Wendy had had enough.

'Kill these clowns, will you? You'd be doing them a favour.'

It was almost as though Kid had heard her. He pulled out a penknife from his pocket and quickly cut the ties around the bikers' feet so they could walk. He then pulled out a pistol. 'OK, you lot, let's get moving.'

As the bikers swayed to their feet, Kid started to kick them up the steep path to the top of the song graveyard.

Hoffa turned back and looked at Kid. 'Are you gonna kill us?'

'Not me,' Kid replied, quite truthfully.

'Ha, ha, says he's not gonna kill us … ha! Good news!' spluttered Hoffa.

Kid prodded them again, and the three bikers swayed up the steep path like a bunch of hyenas.

As Jimmy watched them go, Wendy put her hand on his shoulder and he felt her lips gently kiss his cheek.

'Kill them slowly, Jimmy. Kill them for me and tell them who you're killing them for.'

Jimmy turned towards her to say he wouldn't, couldn't do that, but then he saw the look on her face and the tears in her eyes. He held her arms gently and gazed into her eyes. When he spoke his voice was gentle. 'What did they do to you?'

Wendy leaned forward and whispered in his ear. What she told him caused an anger to rise within him like a surge of molten rage – it was unspeakable.

He glanced up the path to the three laughing idiots and felt a pure hatred burn through him. He turned back to Wendy. 'Slow as you want, Wendy, slow as you want.'

When they reached the top, Kid was leaning on a shovel. The three bikers were still tied with their hands behind their backs sitting against the rocks where Kid had ushered them with his gun.

'Where would you like them buried?' he asked more jovially than was appropriate given the situation.

'Kid seems to be enjoying this a little too much,' said Wendy.

Jimmy turned to her and shrugged. 'Kid finds everything mildly amusing; he loves to observe new things. I think he's genuinely fascinated by all aspects of life.'

Kid heard what Jimmy had said. 'Ahh … the human condition – endlessly sad, infuriating, frustrating and joyous! What's not to love?'

'Well, when you put it like that.' Jimmy shrugged his most sarcastic shrug. 'Maybe you wouldn't be so cheerful if you had to top these scumbags.' Jimmy's words caught the attention of the bikers.

Rat Face turned to Hoffa and Vincent. 'Heth goming thoo mill uth!' It was hard to hear the fear in his voice because of the muffled delivery brought about by his mangled nose.

Hoffa looked at Vincent and in a perfect impression of Rat Face said, 'Yeth, he iths!' They both then dissolved in hysterical laughter.

Rat Face looked at them for a moment in disbelief and then slowly he, too, burst into laughter.

Jimmy walked over to where Kid was leaning on his shovel and pointed to an area just behind where he was standing. 'There, there and there.'

'Oakley doakley.' With an enthusiasm for physical exertion that Jimmy had never suspected Kid Oscarson possessed, he dug the graves like a diesel-powered digger. His mighty forearms and shoulders swung and heaved. Within fifteen minutes, he had dug all three to a depth of four feet. Deep enough to keep the coyotes from digging them up but a couple of feet short of the industry accepted six feet.

Wendy nudged Jimmy. 'You sure he hasn't done this before?'

'No, he's a pacifist.' Jimmy paused for a moment, and then called over to Kid, 'where did you learn to dig like that?'

Kid clambered from the third grave and caught the eye of Rat Face. 'This one's for you, Leroy.' He then winked at him.

Hoffa looked at Vincent. 'Leroy, fucking LEROY!'

Vincent turned on them. 'Thnot fummy!' But it was too late; they had already collapsed in laughter again. Within moments, Leroy had joined them, unable to sulk for more than a few seconds.

Kid brushed the red dust off his shirt and trousers before announcing, 'I used to be the gravedigger in Hell.' He seemed pretty pleased.

Jimmy looked at Wendy; Wendy just shrugged. 'You ask him.' Jimmy didn't have to because Kid was already expanding on the story.

'When I was a teenager back in Norway, I backpacked up to the north of the country.'

'I thought you were Swedish,' said Jimmy.

Kid stopped and gave him a look that could kill. 'SWEDISH! You want me to dig a hole for you, too?'

'No thanks, I wouldn't be able to perform the song, would I?'

Kid nodded thoughtfully. 'That's very true, Jimmy, but I'm a Viking from Norway. Don't ever call me Swedish … ever!'

'No problem, consider it not done.' This seemed to satisfy Kid. A broad smile spread across his face as he returned to the reminiscences of his backpacking youth.

'Near the top of Norway is a nice little town called Hell. It was summer and I needed a job and they needed a grave-digger. The winters are hard up there, and the graves need to be dug in the summer because you won't be able to in the winter. So, I pre-dug forty graves and became the Grave Digger in Hell.' A big smile broke out across Kid's face. 'Pretty cool story, eh?'

'Very cool,' agreed Jimmy.

'Talking about graves, isn't it about time we filled these?' Wendy, as ever, was straight to the point.

Jimmy nodded and checked the clip on his Glock.

Kid watched him do it and saw Jimmy's mood darken. He leaned the shovel against one of the rocks. 'Well, if you don't mind, Jimmy, I fancy a stroll. I like playing songs, but I have no interest in the song-writing process.' Which was a really nice way of saying I'll just leave the killing up to you.

As he strolled away down the steep path, Jimmy turned to the three bikers. He remembered what Wendy had whispered to him about who had done what. He stared at Rat Boy.

'You first.' He pointed the gun at him. 'Get up. Do it!' His anger was building now, and even through the fog of laughing gas, Rat Boy could see that he was in trouble. 'Stand over there.' Jimmy pointed at the first grave.

Rat Boy looked at the freshly dug grave and started to shake. 'No, don't do this.' He was begging now despite the occasional snigger. 'Why are you doing this?' He seemed bewildered by the anger in Jimmy's eyes and manner.

Jimmy scowled. 'Funny you should ask, Leroy.' Hoffa and Vincent began to snigger again. 'Do you remember the waitress from the Riviera that you three raped two years ago when she was leaving the Reservation?'

Clearly he did, because he glanced across at Hoffa and Vincent. They would have made terrible poker players because the guilt was written all over their faces.

'Don't bother lying. I know you did it.'

Leroy's mouth opened and closed like a fish on a riverbank as he tried to think of a way to lie himself out of the situation. Jimmy didn't give him the chance.

'Her name was Wendy and she was my girlfriend.'

Rat Boy picked up on what Jimmy had said. 'Was? We never killed her.'

'We know – he killed me,' said Wendy.

Jimmy turned to her. 'Accidentally.'

'Carelessly. Dead is dead,' Wendy replied with a shrug.

The bikers watched in amusement as Jimmy talked to someone who wasn't there.

Hoffa decided to ask the question that was on all their minds: 'Who you talking to?'

'None of your fucking business, but she told me exactly what you guys did to her. For three hours.'

Nobody was laughing now.

Jimmy raised the gun.

Wendy hovered at his shoulder; she was beginning to levitate with excitement. 'In the balls, Jimmy, in the balls!'

Jimmy loosened off two rounds. The first found its target; the second smashed Rat Boy's hip. He screamed a scream that no human should make.

Hoffa turned to Vincent. 'He shot Leroy in the balls!'

'Leroy for fuck's sake!' They both subsided in laughter again.

Jimmy moved towards the screaming, wriggling, agonised creature that Rat Boy had become. There was no need to shoot him again. On a scale of one to a hundred, his pain was at a thousand. He lifted his foot and shoved him headfirst into the grave. As his head hit the bottom, there was a crack as his neck broke and the howling fell silent.

Then turning to the other two bikers, Jimmy flashed them a demonic grin. 'Who's next?'

The sniggering stopped and they both tried to back away, but they were already up against the rocks.

Hoffa spoke first. 'Not the balls. Please not the balls.' Fear had finally worn away the last remnants of gas.

With crazed smile, Jimmy announced, 'Balls it is, then!' He let loose a volley of four shots into Hoffa's groin. He then turned to Vincent and shouted over Hoffa's agonised squeals, 'shall we make it a job lot?'

Vincent shook his head. 'No, please. I never did anything. I just held her down.'

Jimmy turned to Wendy. 'That true?' Wendy nodded. Jimmy turned back to Vincent. 'Hands it is, then.' He moved forward and roughly grabbed Vincent by the shoulder and flipped him onto his face, his hands still tied behind him. Jimmy proceeded to shoot both his thumbs off with the first bullet, and then several fingers with the next. He grabbed the screaming Vincent and dragged him to the second grave. He glanced over at Wendy, who seemed to have lost the stomach for torture.

'Finish it, Jimmy, this isn't us.'

Jimmy nodded and put a bullet in the back of Vincent's head, and then kicked him into the second grave before moving back to Hoffa and firing two bullets into the back of his head.

Suddenly, the canyon fell silent. Jimmy was breathing heavily, sweat poured from his brow and he surveyed the scene of his rage. He then felt Wendy's hand upon his shoulder.

'Thanks, I know that can't have been easy for you –' she paused for a moment, lost in the horror and enormity of what she had just witnessed. 'I shouldn't have asked you to do that. I just hated them so much – I wanted them to die in agony.' She stopped again struggling to put into words what she was feeling. 'I was wrong.'

Jimmy hugged her. 'It's over, Wendy. You can close the page on that book forever.'

Hugging him back, she said, 'Thanks, Jimmy, see you around.' She then just melted from his arms.

He looked up just in time to see her shooting up into the afternoon sky. He watched her until she was just a speck in the distance before disappearing among the wispy clouds.

This had become a very strange world in which he found himself. How would he be judged when his time came? Would killing scumbags be accepted as mitigating circumstances?

He took a deep breath; there was no point trying to rationalise or justify his actions. The past was a place you couldn't control – all he could do was try and make sure that he didn't get caught in the future.

The clock was ticking and he had a gig tonight. *Time to get these bodies buried!* He pulled Hoffa over to the last empty grave and pushed him in. He picked up the shovel and began filling.

Just as he was hiding the evidence of the freshly dug graves with a brush, Kid reappeared as if back from an afternoon stroll.

'Sounded messy.'

Jimmy just stared at him. 'It was meant to be. Special request!'

With a nod, Kid replied, 'what the lady wants, the lady gets!'

CHAPTER 18

GOOD DAY TO BE AN UNDERTAKER

David Parker stood on the front steps of the Riviera scarcely believing what he was seeing. Sheriff Pence and his three squad cars rolled slowly to a stop in front of the police station. All the vehicles were riddled with bullets and two had shattered side windows.

Pence climbed out first. He looked tired and there was blood on his shirt. One by one, his men climbed out of their vehicles. Most of them seemed stunned – only Officer Feemster, who David had got to know recently, seemed unaffected.

He hurried down the steps to where Officer Feemster was unloading guns from the boot. 'What the hell happened in Three Rivers?' asked David, unable to hide the shock in his voice.

Officer Feemster turned slowly. 'I don't know yet, Mr Parker, but I sure as hell am gonna work it out.'

David stood for a moment trying to work out what those cryptic words meant. 'A shoot-out, I'm guessing,' observed David as he looked down the line of bullet holes in Officer Feemster's car.

Feemster smiled. 'That will be that famous English irony I've heard so much about.' He stood up and moved closer to David. When he spoke, it was quietly so the other officers couldn't hear. 'We were sent to arrest the leaders of the Deltas, the biker gang at Three Rivers. We had an anonymous tip-off that they had a big stash of drugs and guns. When we got there, the sheriff called them to come out on the megaphone and then all hell broke loose.'

'That doesn't make sense. You wouldn't start firing on a group of armed police – they would have somebody getting the stuff away before you got in. Decca would've come out and tried to negotiate to buy time.'

'You knew Decca?'

'Yeah, he is a clever, if brutal man. He once tried to get me to pay protection money for the Rivera until some of my friends in Vegas pointed out the error of his ways to him. Did you say *knew*?'

Officer Feemster pulled off his hat and slowly rubbed his head. 'Oh yes, he's most certainly dead. There's a bullet in him from every member of the Blackjack police force.'

'Where are your prisoners?' David asked.

'No prisoners,' the officer replied with a smile.

David looked at him waiting for the explanation, but none came. 'There's twenty-odd members of the Deltas.'

'Were, Mr Parker ... *were*! Every last one of them is dead.'

'What kind of shoot-out did you have?' None of this made sense to David.

Officer Feemster moved really close to David and whispered, 'Not the kind that kills eighteen people. We fired a few volleys into that building, but when I got in there nobody was injured

– they were all dead. I've never seen a few volleys hit so many targets with such devastation.' He paused for a moment and looked over his shoulder to make sure his colleagues weren't listening. 'There were more bullets in those bodies than we fired, Mr Parker.'

David nodded slowly and said, 'Something is rotten in the state of Denmark.'

'*Hamlet*, act one, scene four. There is indeed corruption in this state.' David couldn't hide the surprise on his face. 'I was an English major in college; *Hamlet* was on the curriculum,' added Feemster.

While they were talking, Sheriff Pence had seen David in deep discussion with Officer Feemster and moved across to interrupt. He didn't trust Officer Feemster and he didn't like David Parker. 'I hope you're not discussing the events of this morning with a member of the public, Feemster.'

'No, Sheriff.'

David turned to Pence and smiled. 'Actually, we were discussing *Hamlet* in which, like Three Rivers, there appears to be an awful lot of death.'

The officer stifled a snigger while Sheriff Pence just looked at David with a total lack of understanding. 'You Brits are fucking weird.' He turned and walked away calling back to Officer Feemster as he did so, 'get those guns back into the arsenal, now!'

Feemster shrugged. 'Claudius calls.' He then gathered up the guns and headed after Pence.

David watched him go. He now knew that Pence was involved with Jack Lantern in some way. Feemster had told him. Claudius was the most corrupt character in *Hamlet*; he even murdered his brother to gain power!

As David walked back towards the entrance to the Riviera, he could see Jack Lantern standing at the top of the steps. He was smiling as he viewed the aftermath of the carnage he had created. As David approached, he pulled the fat cigar from his tobacco-slimed lips.

'Looks like Sheriff Pence has been annoying someone!'

'But who was the someone he did it for, Jack, that's the real question?' David tried to hide the dislike from his voice, but Lantern already knew David didn't like him – not many people did. The only problem with David Parker was that he didn't fear Jack like so many others, and that made him dangerous.

He took another puff on his cigar. 'I reckon it'd be a good day to be an undertaker in this town. Pity I never bought up old man Thead as well.'

'Old man Thead would never sell to the likes of you; he's got too much class!' With that, David left him standing there like a vertical walrus waiting for the fishing boats to return to harbour, sucking on his cigar and safe in the knowledge that he owned all the boats.

———◆———

The drive back from the song graveyard had been sombre. All the way down the ten miles of dirt road, Jimmy just kept staring at his hands – a killer's hands. As Kid turned onto the road, Jimmy looked across at him. He was a strange man but, he was sure, a good man.

'What's your take on all this, Kid, you must have some questions?'

Kid thought for a moment. 'My take for what it's worth is that you've made the best of a bad situation. Killing Wendy was –' he groped for the right word '– unfortunate. Not just for Wendy but also for you. To kill the woman you love because you drank too much is gonna fill you with self-loathing.'

Kid was giving his take a bit too literally for Jimmy's liking but he said nothing.

'Where you were lucky, Jimmy, is that it seemed to unlock an amazing gift for song writing. Must be something to do with energy release generated by a death. Whatever, you decided to use it for good.'

'Wendy persuaded me to do it,' Jimmy said.

Kid sat there just driving for nearly twenty seconds before replying, 'But did she? Is Wendy really a ghost or just a very real figment of your imagination? Nobody else has seen her or heard her, only you.' Jimmy went to interrupt, but Kid silenced him by raising his hand. 'Ask yourself do you really believe in ghosts? Do you?'

Jimmy thought for a moment. 'She actually set me free when I was tied up in Vinny and Carmine's truck. I was gonna die then, but Wendy appeared and cut me free and told me to run them down.'

'OK, I can see why you would think that, but are you sure you didn't manage to reach that knife and cut yourself free? You may have imagined that Wendy had appeared and helped you to get free, but could you have worked it out for your-self but attributed it to Wendy? You were, and still are, full of guilt, but it was an accident. The Wendy you see gives you the forgiveness you need but tempers it with some sharp humour.

I'm not saying I don't believe you, Jimmy, I'm just saying look at the facts.'

Jimmy hadn't really thought about it since that first morning all those weeks ago. Not since seeing Wendy's lifeless body hanging from the wardrobe with his belt around her neck, staring at the sculpture he had created, and then suddenly hearing her voice and turning and there she was, still alive. Was he trying to process it by imagining a world where she was dead but still sort of around?

'I don't know, it's not like I'm looking for her – sometimes she just appears out of nowhere and scares the crap out of me,' said Jimmy.

'The mind is a deep and complex thing, Jimmy, it can play tricks on you. I'm not saying that you don't see Wendy's ghost, I just want you to consider the possibility that you don't. Like The Temptations said, it could have been "just your imagination playing *tricks on you*".'

'I don't think so.'

Kid put his hand on Jimmy's leg and patted it. 'That's fine, just keep an open mind – helps you see the wood for the trees.'

Jimmy sighed. 'OK, Kid, consider my mind open.'

As they approached the town, they saw a fleet of four ambulances but they weren't in a hurry.

'Where do'ya think they're headed?' asked Jimmy.

'If I were a betting man, I would say to the mortuary or undertaker.'

Jimmy looked hard at Kid. 'You really think Sheriff Pence killed all those bikers?'

'Well, we know of at least three he didn't kill,' Kid replied with a chuckle.

'Yeah, but you don't think he killed all the others for Lantern, do you?' As Jimmy asked the question, he knew what the answer would be.

'Maybe not all of them. I think Jack Lantern's men did most of the killing. I don't believe there'll be any Deltas left when we find out the full facts, and this is good news for you, Jimmy,' said Kid cheerfully. 'Because Vincent, Hoffa and Leroy were gonna be dead tonight regardless of what you did or didn't do. This way we get three songs and your conscience can be relatively clear.'

'How's that work from a moral standpoint, then?' Jimmy wasn't convinced.

Kid rubbed his chin while he considered Jimmy's somewhat terse question. 'Maybe we could class your termination of the boys as a pre-emptive termination, a bit like putting an old pet to sleep. It's going to die, so you just hasten the process.'

'What, by shooting your pet in the balls!'

'Ooh, that had to smart!' Kid said, wincing. 'I think that would be frowned on in the veterinary world, but hey, who knows what goes on behind the closed doors of your local vet. Think of Doctor Donald in town – he would probably shoot you in the balls to cure a sore throat.' Kid laughed.

'Well, it would certainly take your mind off it!'

As they pulled up at the rear of the Riviera on the staff car park, they were still laughing as David Parker pulled open the passenger door. To his great relief he saw that his star attraction and the lead guitarist for tonight's show were both physically uninjured.

'Boys, I am so pleased you're OK.'

'We've just been looking at guitars, and then we went for a stroll in the mountains,' Jimmy said as innocently as he could, surprised by David's concern.

David looked at Kid and then back at Jimmy. They certainly didn't look like ramblers, and he had never known a musician take exercise voluntarily in all his years running hotels. 'Didn't buy any guitars in Three Rivers, then?' asked David, clearly showing that he didn't believe a word they were saying.

Kid decided to take David's scepticism and raise him. 'No actually, we did buy the guitars but we didn't want to leave them in the van while we were off walking. We asked the guy to ship them to us.'

Jimmy couldn't help but smile.

David turned his head to one side and gave Kid a quizzical look. 'Shipping a guitar from Three Rivers?'

'Two guitars,' interrupted Kid, now fully invested in the delusion he was creating. 'A really nice '68 Flying V and a Gibson ES-335.' David was about to comment, but Kid wasn't finished. 'Custom shop, but he had some Seymour Duncan pickups so it wasn't fully original.'

'This guy you bought them off, was he real?'

'As real as I'm standing here,' replied Kid with an affirmative nod.

David just stared at him sitting behind the steering wheel. 'You care to rephrase that statement.'

'No. I'm fine with it,' answered Kid.

David decided to give up his line of questioning because he sensed that Kid could go on all night building his fantasy world. 'When you two return to planet Earth, you might like to know that the whole of the Delta bike gang was killed in a shoot-out with Sheriff Pence's boys this morning in Three Rivers, the home of second-hand guitars.'

'What, all of them?' Jimmy looked intrigued.

'Let's go and have a coffee and I'll tell you everything I know,' David answered with a nod.

Jimmy and Kid didn't bother changing but went straight to the restaurant to meet David. He had already got the coffees and was sitting there waiting for them.

'Sit down, boys, we need to talk.'

They both sat down; it was clear that David Parker had something on his mind.

'Now look, guys, this shit is getting very real.'

Jimmy was a bit taken aback because he never heard David swear under normal circumstances.

'I don't know what you boys know, but I need you to listen and not give me any of your third-rate bullshit.'

Kid put down his coffee. 'I resent that, David, there was nothing third rate about the bullshit I gave you back there.'

Normally that would have made David smile, but not today. All he cared about was keeping his boys out of trouble. 'Jack Lantern had those bikers killed and Pence was in on the plan!'

Jimmy and Kid leaned in closer. Jimmy spoke first. 'We know, or at least we think we do.'

David looked both confused and frustrated. 'What the hell does that mean exactly? Either you know or you don't know.'

Jimmy glanced at Kid. 'Kid heard a whisper when he was down at the Reservation the other night that the Deltas were moving in on Jack Lantern's territory. They were selling drugs to his dealers. Undercutting him. Obviously, Jack wasn't gonna sit still for that, but I thought he would just break a few arms and legs until they toed the line.'

David shook his head. 'That's not how Jack Lantern works. He likes to send a message – the bigger the better.'

Kid cleared his throat just to make it clear that he had something to say. Jimmy and David turned to him and waited. 'Sheriff Pence has been corrupt and on Jack's payroll for years.'

'Can you prove it?' David asked.

'Not the kind of proof that would stand up in a court of law, but clear to anybody who knows how this works,' said Kid. 'Hanging around in the less salubrious bars of the neighbour-hood gives me access to a lot of gossip and rumour, but most of this stuff has a basis of truth. Pence was clearly turning a blind eye to Jackson Pollack's dealing in the Reservation and the Big Easy. A couple of members of the Deltas I got to know through playing at the Reservation told me that they were safe to deal in town because Pence was on the payroll. If Jack felt threatened, he would hit out. For what it's worth, when we were on the way up to Three Rivers this morning —'

'To buy guitars,' interrupted David sarcastically.

'Exactly,' replied Kid, choosing to ignore the barb, 'we over-took a truck full of Lantern's thugs. Terry Moist was in the passenger seat up front.' Kid looked at Jimmy and then David. 'Now, I would call that more than a coincidence. Where were they going with four police cars five minutes behind them?'

'To buy guitars?' David smiled.

Kid pulled a bored face. 'Really, David, they look like musi-cians to you? They were all wearing suits and looked like they'd shaved!' He had a fair point.

'Listen,' said Jimmy, 'we all know that Jack was behind this. We also know that Pence was in on it. But do we care? No harm done to us, and the Deltas were a bunch of scumbags. Jack cleaned house. Nobody's gonna miss them. As for Pence, just give him a wide berth. We're all gonna be in Vegas soon so he'll just be a footnote in history.'

David knew that Jimmy was right but it just didn't sit well with him. 'I don't like the idea of a corrupt sheriff in my town. I want him gone.'

'Well, unless he slips up on the paperwork, he's gonna get away with this one. Forget it, David, I know we will!' Jimmy said with a shrug.

David was resigned to agree, but surely there had to be a way to get Pence and Lantern.

'You understand odds don't you, David?' asked Kid.

'I'd better, seeing as I run a casino.'

'Then you'll know that Sheriff Pence and Jack Lantern will run out of luck if they keep rolling the dice. Just wait and let greed bring them down ... it usually does.' Kid was right, but David wanted results now.

'Officer Feemster told me that there were more bullets in the Deltas' clubhouse than they fired. He also hinted that the shots fired by the police couldn't possibly have had such a devastating effect. Sounds almost as if someone was inside the building taking the Deltas out under the cover of police fire with Pence out front trying to make it legitimate.'

Jimmy was nodding. 'There's a way round the back of their clubhouse where you can park up without being seen.'

David looked at Jimmy suspiciously. 'And how would you know that?'

'I played a gig there once a few years ago. Man, that was a lively crowd. We parked the van around the back. Terry Moist and his boys could definitely attack from there if Pence was in on it. Now I come to think of it, we overtook Pence and his men going up to Three Rivers and they were crawling along, not in any hurry at all.'

Kid nodded vigorously. 'Almost as if they were giving Lantern's boys a chance to get in position before they arrived.'

All three of them looked at each other, and knew they'd arrived at the correct conclusion.

'So, how do I prove it?' asked David.

'Know anyone in the FBI? Those ballistics won't stand up to scrutiny if there's a proper investigation,' asked Kid.

A big smile spread across David's face. 'It just so happens I do.'

———————◆———————

David Parker knew that he should just back away and let the whole situation die down, but he wanted to find anything he could use to bring down Jack Lantern. He walked through the rear door of the Riviera and looped around the back way and down onto the main road through town.

To call it a main road was stretching it as not many cars came down this way. All the attractions like the Riviera and the Reservation were at the top end of town; the bottom end of the high street was for the locals. Shops, barbers and a beauty salon with ladies hairdressers, a deli and a small supermarket. At the very end of the high street was a little side street. It was a dead end, which was quite appropriate as this was where Tom Thead's undertakers was located. Thead's had been there almost since the town had started, and Old Tom had run the business since he took over from his father in the seventies.

David peered through the window which bore the legend 'Call on Thead's For Your Undertaking Needs'. Whoever wrote that copy was clearly a frustrated poet.

The window display hadn't changed since David had been running the Riviera, but when you're the only undertaker in town you didn't need to be dynamic with your marketing. The coffin in the window may have been a bit direct, but Old Tom had cushioned the blow by a tasteful arrangement of dried flowers and a wreath that was clearly from a recent event as it was still fresh. Thankfully, he had remembered to remove the 'With Deepest Sympathy' card.

David pushed on the door and entered. The first thing that hit him was the quiet. Somewhere from a hidden speaker he could hear Faure's Requiem 'In Paradisum', if he wasn't mistaken. Blackjack could hardly be compared to 'Paradisum', but then Faure had meant Paradisum to be Jerusalem, and we all know what a calm and peaceful place that had turned out to be.

As David shut the door behind him, he heard the faint ringing of a bell and within a few moments came the patter of old Tom Thead's excited footsteps. When he saw David, his eyes lit up. Tom Thead loved everything about England; his grandfather had come from Worcester after the First World War to make his fortune, and he did. He'd opened a large carpentry shop and sold furniture all over the Midwest and Northern California, but Tom's dad didn't fancy the idea of employing a hundred people to make lots of types of furniture. He did, however, like carpentry, and he hit upon the idea of making coffins because people will always be dying, even during a depression. He cut the workforce down to thirty but still turned over the same as when they had been making furniture. The profits went through the roof, so he opened a string of undertakers to sell his coffins and that went crazy, so he franchised Thead's and they became the major undertakers for Nevada, Utah and Northern California. The Tom Thead that stood before David now was worth about $200 million but he just liked to run the Blackjack business and let his two sons and daughter run the empire.

'Hello, David, you've caught me in the quiet before the storm,' he said enthusiastically.

David pretended that he didn't know what he meant and glanced towards the shopfront window. 'There's a storm coming?'

Tom shook his head smiling widely. 'Not that type of storm. Haven't you heard about the big shoot-out at Three Rivers?'

'Yes, I did hear there had been a bit of a skirmish with that biker gang.'

Tom Thead waved his hands in the air. 'It wasn't a skirmish; it was a bloodbath and all the deceased are coming back here after the police morgue releases them.' Tom was obviously excited about this unexpected upturn in business. 'We haven't had a demand like this since that influenza outbreak in '84.'

David tried not to smile. Tom didn't need the money but he still delighted in a sudden burst of death.

'Seventeen Hell's Angels.'

David let out a low whistle. 'That's a lot of Angels headed for heaven at once.'

'Oh, these boys won't be going to heaven – they were bad boys,' Tom replied with a chuckle.

'I suppose from your point of view it doesn't matter where they're headed – you just have to set them on their way. How are you going to get paid? Most of these biker types are estranged from their families. How are you going to find the next of kin and get them to pay for the funeral?'

Now Tom seemed to be quivering with excitement. 'That's the thing, I won't have to. They all have insurance these days. I found that out a few years ago when four of them got wiped out by a trucker they annoyed. Thought I was gonna have to get the mayor's office to fund it, but it turned out they all had club insurance from their biker club.'

David was impressed. 'Wow, Hell's Angeling has come a long way since my day.'

Tom was shifting from foot to foot now. 'It gets better, David. They like to be buried with or sometimes on their bikes!'

David tried to visualise a Delta member sitting on his bike. The size of the grave would be at least double that of a normal plot, and there is no way they would fit in a coffin. Trying not to smile, David probed Tom for details.

'How does that work, then? Do you shrink-wrap them to the bike and then put them on a pallet and lower them in?'

Tom tried to look annoyed, but he knew David was teasing. 'No, we don't do that. What we actually do is build a pallet big enough for the bike to stand on and then once we've embalmed the deceased, we place them on the bike and then build a tasteful crate around them, which we then clad in some very nice ash boarding.'

David winced. 'That must be really tough on the pall-bearers. A Harley must weigh half a ton, and none of the Deltas were going to win "Slimmer of the Year".'

Tom smiled tolerantly. 'The pallbearer is a forklift truck. We have one in the yard, and we painted it black and put brass grab handles on it. We feel it helps to maintain the air of gravitas that such an undertaking, no pun intended, requires.'

Tom is a funny guy, thought David. Beneath that grey, seventy-something exterior beat the heart of a young man with a sense of humour. 'What if they want to be cremated? That could be tricky with a gas tank.'

'Oh my. I remember we had a man die in his sportscar a few years back. He wanted to be put in the crusher with it to make it small enough to bury. Well, naturally we didn't want to do this, but his girlfriend insisted and she was spending an awful lot of the money she was about to inherit from him.'

'This all sounds very tasteful,' said David, nodding.

'Oh, it got worse.' Tom grimaced at the memory. 'We built a little frame to keep him sitting upright in the car and superglued his hands to the steering wheel. Luckily, he had long hair, so we ran a little rod up his back and just inside his shirt. Around his neck, we used a spring-loaded zip tie to keep his head up. By the time we'd dressed him, he looked like he was just in the middle of a lovely afternoon drive.'

David couldn't conceal the broad grin on his face. 'I take it this was a convertible?' Tom nodded. 'Top up or down?' asked David as innocently as he could.

Tom grimaced again. 'Good taste dictated up. Sadly, his girlfriend had no taste.' Tom sighed. 'So, there we were on a raised platform around the car crusher. We'd put up some scaffolding and got a local scenery painter from the theatre in Marchant to paint a countryside backdrop. Like I said, no expense was spared.'

It was all David could do not to burst out laughing, so he just nodded and held his breath.

'We decked out the raised platform to look like a Route 66 gas station. So, we're all standing there, and he is sitting there, and she is crying but really loving the setting. Well, the reverend was from one of those churches that you've never heard of, but he is waxing lyrical about the deceased being on the highway to heaven and he's going to get there fast! That brought a few smiles, and then the moment came to push the button and start the crusher. We didn't want the sound of deforming metal to be his family's final memory, so we had a tape rigged with the sound of a V8 revving and Steppenwolf's "Born to Be Wild" blaring out.'

As Tom paused, David, who was struggling to breathe, could see that the old man was remembering the scene.

'So, up to that point it was unusual and a tad tasteless, but if that's what the girlfriend and the deceased wanted, so be it. Well, from "get your motor running" it was all going well, and then as we got to the "lookin' for adventure" part, things started to go horribly wrong. I don't know if you're familiar with the song?'

David nodded. By now he was incapable of speech.

Old Tom continued reliving his nightmare. 'Well, the next line, and I shall never forget it, is "and whatever comes our way". And something did come our way. As the car started to fold, the cloth roof tore down the middle and as the sides were crushed, the deceased rose upwards on a sea of folding metal like Neptune rising from the depths of the ocean. We were all now looking up at the deceased, who was still holding the wheel, mainly because his hands were superglued to it, but the front steering rack was being crushed and twisting. The deceased started to rotate with the steering wheel to the sound of the wooden frame supporting his floppy torso splintering. There was a terrible crack, and his head and shoulders disappeared from view as his legs and backside appeared. As they went up into the air, gravity took over and like a ventriloquist's dummy trying to do a headstand, his legs parted in different directions … it was most inelegant.'

David bit his lip hard and dug his fingernails deep into his palms as he listened.

'Well, this wasn't in the list of service at all.' Tom sighed. 'For a moment, we thought we were going to get lucky as the deceased completed his revolution and came to a halt upright once again. Maybe we should have pre-crushed a similar car beforehand, because what happened next will never leave me until the day I die. The wire around the deceased's neck attaching it to the rod down his back was spring-loaded to keep him in place like a bungee strap, as we figured he was going to look like a driver riding a bucking bronco when the car folded down. Well, the three sixty rotation must've wound the tension in the spring attached to his neck like an overwound clock. As the car sank down into the crusher, his head and shoulders were above the jaws; and as the line "explode into space" came in the song, that's exactly what his head did. It was still going up as "we can climb so high" sounded.'

David couldn't contain himself any longer; he collapsed in hysterical laughter.

Tom then started to snigger. 'My son caught the head and stood there with it while the girlfriend fainted.'

Between sobs of laughter, David managed to get out a few words. 'What … di-did he d-d-do with it?'

Tom breathed in deeply. 'He asked the deceased's son if he would like it wrapped!'

It took quite some time for the two men to recover from the hysterical laughter that Tom's reliving of the tale had elicited. It was just the tonic that David had needed, and Tom Thead seemed to enjoy himself, too. They were still smiling when they sat down in Tom's office for a cup of tea fifteen minutes later.

'So, Tom,' said David, 'when the bodies start arriving, I was wondering if you could do me a favour.'

Tom sipped his tea and tilted his head slightly to one side. 'And what would that be?'

David thought for a moment about what would be the best way to phrase his question without it looking as if he thought Sheriff Pence was complicit in seventeen murders and, by extension, corrupt, but there wasn't one so he just came out with it.

'Tom, I believe that Pence is corrupt and in the pay of a gangster from Vegas called Jack Lantern.'

Tom nodded and said, 'Oh, I know Mr Lantern.'

'You do?' said David, unable to hide his surprise.

Tom took another sip of tea. In Tom's world there was no need to rush. 'Yes, when my father started franchising the funeral parlours, Jack Lantern bought up six of them spread across Northern California, Nevada and Utah.'

While David took in this information, Tom Thead took another sip of tea and a bite of a shortbread biscuit.

'Yes, funeral parlours are great places to hide and get rid of dead bodies. In the smaller towns they sometimes have their own crematorium in-house. Not only that, but a coffin will hold an awful lot of drugs or used cash.' Tom nodded slowly. 'Yes. I know Jack Lantern, and a bigger piece of shit never walked this earth.'

For a second David was a little taken aback. He had never heard Tom Thead swear before. The information Tom had just provided made complete sense. Lantern always had his bases covered – that's why he was never caught.

'So you understand why I don't trust Sheriff Pence. He's very tight with Lantern. I have it on good authority that he turns a blind eye on Lantern's dealers in town,' said David.

Tom listened without raising an eyebrow. 'Pence is a punk. He only got the job because his uncle was mayor. I knew he was working for Lantern years ago. We had a body come in here from a hit and run. Pence was the officer in charge. Told me it was an accident and there was no next of kin. *Just get him cremated and his department will pay for it.* Pence just wanted me to put him in the oven there and then, but I said it needed to be serviced and that I would do it in the morning. I didn't care that the kid was a drifter who'd just got run over. He deserved to be treated with some dignity.' Tom took another sip of tea; his eyes were unfocused as he looked back into a distant memory. 'When I undressed him to clean him up, it was clear he'd been given a systematic beating. Broken ribs, there was also a stab wound and his hands had lots of cuts and bruises as if he'd been trying to defend himself. I knew there was no way Pence could've missed this. That wasn't the only suspect death that Pence has brought here. I guess what I'm saying, David, is that if you're telling me Pence is a corrupt scumbag, well, I already know.'

David breathed a sigh of relief. 'Glad you feel that way, Tom, because I think this shoot-out was a set-up by Lantern to wipe out the Deltas because they were dealing drugs on his territory. I believe that while Pence pretended to have a shoot-out from the front of the building, Lantern's assassination squad came in from the back and wiped out the lot of them. I think when they arrive you're going to find bullets in the back and shots obviously fired from close up. The police never got within thirty yards of anyone they shot, so it's not going to be hard to spot.'

'So, what do you want me to do with this information, send it to the FBI?'

David shook his head. 'No, Tom, don't do that. It would put you in danger. These guys are dead, we can't bring them back, and from what I've heard you wouldn't want to.' David paused for a second, and Tom finished his sentence for him.

'You would like me to take some photos for you to keep on file should the opportunity to use them against Lantern and Pence ever arise.'

David smiled; old Tom Thead caught on very quickly. 'That's what I would like, Tom. That is if you're prepared to do it?'

Tom smiled and gave a little chuckle. 'Oh, I'll do it all right. I already have a file full of dubious cases I've been building for such a day. All I ask is that you only ever use them if you have a good case to go with them. Nobody knows how far this corruption goes. Why isn't the coroner being called in? Why isn't he insisting on it? I know we live in the middle of nowhere, but that's not normal.' Tom took a last sip of his tea. 'By the pricking of my thumbs,' he added.

'Something wicked this way comes.' David finished the quote for him.

'Should've guessed an Englishman would know his Shake-speare.' Tom smiled.

David nodded. 'One of the three witches in the Scottish play I believe–'

CHAPTER 19

FAREWELL TO THE CANYON ROOM

Kid finished reading the three songs that Jimmy had thrust into his hand a few minutes earlier. 'These are damn good! When did you write them?'

'I'm not sure, when we got back from the song cemetery, I was exhausted. Must be the excitement of all that murdering.' He chuckled drily. 'Once we'd finished with David, I just went back to my room and passed out on the bed. I woke up three hours later and there they were, just like always.' He slowly shook his head. 'I wish I could do it without the killing, but I can't.'

Kid placed a sympathetic hand on his shoulder. 'Never mind, at least they died in a good cause – art!' He started to move away but turned back to Jimmy. 'And let's not forget, they were scumbags. Case of "justifiable homicide" if there ever was one.'

Jimmy thought Kid sounded convincing. 'So,' he said playfully, 'will you be my lawyer if this ever comes to court?'

Kid pursed his lips and shook his head. 'Doubtful, Jimmy. I'm more than likely to be in the dock with you as an accomplice.'

For some reason they both seemed to think this was funny. As they were laughing, No Relation, aka Joe, walked into the rehearsal room.

'What's so funny, guys?' asked Joe.

Kid turned to him with a serious look on his face. 'Well, compared to your drumming ... nothing.' Kid let that sink into Joe's brain before continuing. 'So, Jimmy has written three more songs, and I'm gonna take myself away and put an arrangement together. Be ready in about forty-five minutes, and when I come back let's all try and start the song together and then maybe finish together. What do'ya say?'

Joe shrugged. 'Very funny, Kid, but it ain't my problem if you're too fat to keep up.' This made Jimmy and Kid smile.

'A race it is, then.' Kid then went off to score the arrangements.

Jimmy loved the way they had always managed to spark off each other. There was no malice but just a band having fun.

'You heard about the shoot-out at Three Rivers?' asked Joe as he sat down on his stool.

'Yeah, me and Kid were up there looking at some guitars this guy had for sale and just missed it.'

Joe let out low breath. 'Pheew! That was too close for comfort. Don't want you getting killed when we're about to hit the big time!'

'Your concern is touching, Joe.' Jimmy chuckled. 'Rest assured your meal ticket to a better life is still alive and well – and writing songs.'

'More songs! You're turning into a regular Burt Bacharach. How many this time?' Joe looked impressed.

'Just the three,' said Jimmy modestly.

'That gives us ten, don't it?'

'One more and we have an album.'

Joe picked up his sticks and produced a low-rising drum roll. 'Ladies and gentlemen, I give you Jimmy Wayne and The Second Chance, live from the Golden Flamingo, Las Vegas. Fresh from his hit record now available from Small Print Records and produced by the great Michael Owens.' As Joe finished his mock announcement, a solitary pair of hands gave him a slow clap. They both turned around and there was Michael Owens.

Jimmy smiled and said, 'do you know who this is?'

Joe peered at the figure leaning on the doorframe at the back of the room. 'Nah, never seen him before.'

Jimmy walked towards the visitor with his hand outstretched. 'This, Joe, is the great Michael Owens you were just chuntering on about.'

'Oh, hello then, Mr Owens, hope you didn't mind the fanfare.'

'Not at all. It would be nice to get one every time I walked into a room, but I'm afraid I'm not that popular.'

Jimmy reached him and they shook hands. 'What brings you here, Mr Owens?'

'Jimmy, please call me Michael,' replied Owens, wincing at the formality of Jimmy's greeting.

'Sorry, old habits. My mom and dad always taught me to be polite.'

'Mine too. Good old English stiff upper lip, but that kind of formality won't work in the music industry these days, especially in LA.'

Jimmy had to agree. 'So, what brings you here, Michael?'

Owens wandered towards the front of the practice stage, grabbed a chair and sat down. 'Well, David has told me that you've written a lot more songs and more importantly they are really good!'

'Good?' chimed in Joe from behind the drums. 'They're bloody brilliant!'

Jimmy turned to Owens. 'They could be even better once we've developed them.'

'I like the sound of that. How many have you got?' Yesterday that question would have broken Jimmy out in a cold sweat, but not today.

'Ten.'

Owens did a double take. 'Ten? You have been busy! All originals?'

Jimmy nodded.

'Two to go, then. Looks like we're going to be recording in LA next week.'

Jimmy looked bemused. 'I thought we agreed eleven in total?'

'We did originally, but you seem to be writing a lot of songs around the three- to four-minute mark and I want about forty-five minutes, so I reckon two more should do it.'

Jimmy looked across at Kid, who shrugged. Owens saw the silent exchange.

'That's not going to be a problem is it, Jimmy? You seem to be in a rich vein of creativity at the moment.'

Jimmy looked hard into Owen's eyes. 'Whatever you want, Michael. Should be able to sort a couple more songs in eight days. It's been bloody hard work. I find the song writing process really heavy going. Don't know how some people just seem to bang out songs every day and make them good ones.'

Owens shrugged and said, 'Sometimes you have to leave a bit of blood on the floor.'

'Oh, I did that all right, Michael, lots of it!' replied Jimmy, stroking his beard thoughtfully.

———◆———

Jack Lantern was just enjoying a quiet gin and tonic with Lena when his phone began to buzz. Jack always carried two phones. One for mundane everyday stuff and the other he called the 'Bat Phone'. It was a number only given to a few people, and it was reserved for serious situations or emergencies. He glanced at the number and recognised Sheriff Pence's private number. Lena watched Jack check the screen, but she was getting up before he even said a word. She knew what that phone ringing meant: time to make herself scarce.

Jack looked up at her. 'Sorry babe, you know, work –.'

She waved his apology away. 'No problem, Jack, you take care of work and I'll go and listen to Jimmy and the band rehearse.'

'Yeah, good idea, baby. Just don't get too close – you know what musicians are like.'

Lena seemed to blush slightly as she scurried away.

Jack answered the call. 'What is it, Pence?' He was terse and to the point, but Sheriff Pence wasn't in the mood to be intimidated.

'You wanna tell me what Ted Baker was up to when he disappeared?'

Jack thought for a moment. 'Just collecting money and

keeping the dealers in line – usual stuff.' He heard a snort of derision down the line. Pence was not happy.

'Well, we found his pickup. It was burned out and he wasn't in it but we did find a body.'

Jack tried to understand this new information. The body couldn't be Jackson Pollack, or Ted would have come back, unless someone else had killed them both! The whole Delta thing was starting to make sense now.

'Do we know who it was?' asked Jack.

'Shit, I was hoping you were gonna tell me that. All we know is that the body was of a male, twenty-five to thirty.'

'That all you got?' It didn't seem much to go on.

'That's all we got,' said Pence impatiently. 'The guy was crisper than pork ribs on a barbecue.'

'You paint a lovely picture.' Jack smiled. 'So, what you gonna do about it?'

Sheriff Pence sighed. 'Not much I can do about it if you don't know who it is. The tailgate and lid were still locked when we found it, so what with the fire and a few weeks there wasn't much left to base an investigation on. You sure you don't know? Ted was working for you, after all?'

Jack took a swig of his drink. 'Listen, Sheriff, I employ guys who get the job done, sometimes.' He paused for a moment while considering his words. 'Sometimes they go "off piste" to get the job done. I can't be responsible for that, and I certainly don't wanna know about it because that would make me an accessory after the fact now, wouldn't it?' Jack Lantern could almost hear Sheriff Pence's brain whirring as he tried to bring some order to the events that had unfolded today in his usually quiet backwater.

'OK, Jack. Thanks for the help.'

Jack chuckled. 'Well, Sheriff, I wasn't really much help now, was I? Still, at least we know that Ted is really dead, don't we?'

Back in his office, Pence was shaking his head. 'No, Jack, we don't know that at all. Like I said, this body is not Ted's.'

'Sheriff, do you really think Ted's pickup would be left burned out with a dead body in the trunk if Ted was still alive? I reckon you killed the people who killed Ted today in Three Rivers.' Jack sounded pretty sure that he was right, but Pence had one more piece of information to share.

'We also found Jackson Pollack's vehicle burned out with Ted's.'

'Interesting, any sign of a body in that one?' asked Lantern.

'No. No sign at all.' There was something bothering Pence; Lantern could hear it in his voice.

'Get it off your chest, Sheriff. What's eating you?'

Pence took a deep breath. 'Well, whoever killed Ted and Pollack also set the cars on fire, so why didn't the other body get taken from the scene and buried elsewhere with the others.'

Jack shrugged. 'Does it matter? Dead is dead?'

'Well, yes, it kinda does matter, Jack.' There was now irritation in Pence's voice. 'We need to know who this body is. Why he was in there. Did the people who set fire to the vehicles even know he was there? Coroner reckons he was alive when the fire started.'

Jack winced. 'Oh, that's not a nice way to go. Flatbed barbecue, yuck!'

The band were finishing running through the three new songs when David Parker walked in just in time to hear Jimmy screaming the closing bars of 'Stairway to Hell'. He stood next to Michael. 'What the fuck is that?' he asked, a pained expression creasing his features.

Owens turned to him and smiled. 'Musical gold, David, is exactly what that is.'

'But he sounded in pain.' David was confused.

'Exactly, he is. You need to hear it from the start, and it will all become clear.'

No Relation put down his drumsticks. 'Jimmy, that is some fucked up shit, but I love it!'

Lewis was sitting at his keyboard with a big smile on his face. 'Yeah, that's some deep stuff right there, Jimmy. You ever thought about getting counselling?'

Everybody was laughing and smiling, even Doug the new bass player. This was his first rehearsal and he was playing some pretty different stuff.

'Is all your stuff like this?' he asked Jimmy.

Kid answered for him. 'No, some of it's really fucked up!' Everyone laughed and Michael Owens gave David a nudge.

'Look at the spirit in this band. These guys are ready to take off, David. I want you to manage them with me. Could you fit that in with running this place?'

'I've already sorted it out with Sam up at the Golden Flamingo.' Michael gave David a questioning look. 'Sam is my partner in this place. When he gave me the boot from the Golden Flamingo for my – boardroom manoeuvres – he offered me a share in this place if I run it and pick it up. I've made us both a lot of money over the last four years and when I told him about Jimmy and the boys really coming up with the goods, he came up to see them at the Canyon. He agrees with you, Michael, he thinks they're going to be huge.'

Owens raised his eyebrows. 'Boy, you really don't hang about, do you?'

'I try not to, that's why I asked him to give them a month-long residency, and he said yes provided he can wait until the record's out.'

Michael Owens just stood there silently mouthing the word 'wow'. 'You crafty old bastard, this is great news.'

'Yeah, it is, isn't it!'

'That was great, boys, really looking forward to hearing you play tonight.' Michael gave them all a wave as he left the room.

Kid turned to Jimmy; it was clear he was excited about what they had just done. 'That sounded good. Told you the screaming was a good idea.'

Jimmy wasn't sure when Kid had suggested it, but it had really worked. It was as though he said, 'when you're entering the gates of hell, you aint gonna hum now, are ya!'

Kid moved close to Jimmy and whispered in his ear, 'What do you think of Doug?'

'Pretty damn good. Lewis has come up with a real find there.'

'I agree,' said Kid, 'but his jazz chops are just showing a bit too much. Do you mind if I just have a quiet word in my musical director's role?'

Jimmy shrugged. 'Feel free, just don't scare him outta the band.'

Kid pulled what he thought was his reassuring face, but from where Jimmy was standing it looked more like the beginning of a stroke.

As Doug was putting his bass back into its case, Kid loomed above him. 'Hey, Doug, that was some mighty fine playing there, buddy.'

'Thanks, glad you liked it.'

Kid looked thoughtful for a moment. 'Now, I don't recall saying I *liked* it.'

Doug looked confused. 'But you–'

'Doug, you can play, we all know it, but this aint Art Blakey and The Jazz Messengers. It's Jimmy Wayne and The Second Chance. All these chord progressions and runs you're doing, it's like inviting a nun to an orgy. Let's just keep to the structure and let Jimmy tell the story. When the chance comes to "express yourself" I'll let you know. That OK with you, dude?'

Doug looked up at the six-foot-five towering Norwegian megalith. 'Whatever you say, Kid.'

Kid slapped him on the back, nearly breaking a rib in the process. 'That's excellent, and I really do dig your playing.'

On the other side of the stage, Jimmy was talking to Lewis. 'You sure I can't change your mind? This band is going places.'

Lewis smiled wistfully. 'If I was twenty years younger, I'd be driving the bus. I've been where you're going and it's fun, but it's a young man's game. I have all I need right here.'

'Damn. I knew you'd say that.'

Lewis nodded over at Doug. 'Got you a great bass player, though, didn't I? This stuff you're writing now, Jimmy, it doesn't need keyboards. That said, I wouldn't mind coming up to Vegas and doing the odd guest weekend.'

'Cheap weekend in Vegas for you and the wife?' Jimmy slapped him on the shoulder.

'Something like that,' Lewis replied with a shrug.

Jimmy knew that Lewis wouldn't be coming with him on this next leg of the journey, and it hurt. Lewis was like a father figure to him. More, because he had never respected his father, unlike Lewis. Lewis had made it to the 'big time' and unlike so many before him, he had kept his money and escaped unscathed. He viewed his days of fame as a bonus for years of hard work. When it was over, he just melted back into musical obscurity and plied his trade wherever the opportunity arose. For Lewis it was all about the music and the company of musicians. He saw something in Jimmy and even though Jimmy didn't believe in himself, Lewis always had. He never lectured or cajoled him; he just kept setting the right example in the hope that he would follow. And now, now the flower was beginning to bloom, he never suspected that Jimmy had the depth of introspection to write songs like these, but he knew he could sing them. In all the time he had known Jimmy, that voice had never let him down. It was only when he didn't believe in himself that he would fail to connect with his audience.

Lewis knew what Jimmy was thinking. 'You're gonna be fine, Jimmy. Just enjoy the ride and respect the music, oh, and save some money.'

Soon there was only Jimmy left in the room. He wanted to run through the chorus of 'Late Blossom,' a song about–. What was it about? Wendy probably. He thought he could work in a dual harmony with Kid. As he went through the intro, he became aware of a figure in the corner of the room – it was Wendy.

'Hi, you been there long?'

'Long enough,' she replied with a shrug.

Jimmy put his guitar down next to him. 'And what does that mean?'

'It means you'll be leaving here soon.' Wendy moved towards him; she looked a little sad. 'You and the boys sound great.'

Jimmy knew what she meant. 'If it wasn't for you, none of this would've happened.'

'Good to know I didn't die in vain.' Wendy smiled.

Jimmy looked pained. 'Not that, Wendy, you know what I mean … if you hadn't made me take you to the song cemetery, I would never have got the chance to sing "Vacant Stare".' Jimmy's words dried up; it was so hard to put into words. How do you thank someone whose death, for which you were responsible, actually saved your career? It's a tricky conversation, made even more so by the fact that he still loved her. 'Will you come to Vegas?' It was a sincere question. He liked having Wendy around – not so much when she just burst through a ceiling or a wall without warning, but just in general.

'I don't know, Jimmy. I like it round here. I know people; I've got friends. It's a proper country club for the newly deceased.' There was no trace of bitterness in her voice, but he could tell she wasn't the normal happy-go-lucky Wendy today.

'I'm not sure I can do this without you.' He wasn't. All the scumbags he had killed meant nothing to him, but Wendy, that was something he could never move on from. Having her around made it seem less final.

Wendy's eyes seemed to brighten. 'Shit, Jimmy, loosen up a little. You're gonna be a star soon.' Jimmy went to reply but Wendy kept talking. 'Anyway, I gotta tell you the reason I'm here, I have news, big news.' She paused for dramatic effect.

Jimmy sat there looking at her, waiting for the big reveal. Wendy dropped her hands to her hips and struck a sulky dramatic pose. 'Well, aint you gonna ask me what it is?'

'What is it?'

Wendy's face lit up. 'Glad you asked, Jimmy, there is news from Sheriff Pence's office that you need to know about.' He didn't like the sound of this. 'Cast your mind back to murders four and five.' Wendy shot Jimmy a questioning stare.

It all sounded a bit clinical when she put it like that. Jimmy tried to think. It wasn't easy, as he was thinking in song titles not victims. 'Was four "Scattered Bodies"?'

Wendy sighed. 'No, Jimmy, that was either Vinny Zito or Carmine Mallotides. No way of telling who because you ran them down together!'

Jimmy shuddered at the memory of those thugs flying through the air and the separation of arms, legs and heads and – well, it just wasn't a pretty sight.

Wendy tapped her fingers on one of the speakers. 'Well?'

He tried to think. '"Lonely Old Lady"? Was it Sammy? Because technically I didn't kill her. She died laughing.'

'Yeah, but who told her the joke? You told her one every time you went to see her, and you knew she had a bad heart. That's murder one, totally premeditated.'

'That's not fair – you know how much I loved her.' Jimmy guessed that Wendy had been watching reruns of *Murder, She Wrote* again.

Wendy winked at him. 'Course I do, Jimmy, but you have to admit it looks suspicious. A good prosecutor could make you look like OJ.'

'Innocent, then.' Jimmy shrugged.

Wendy rolled her eyes. 'Whatever. Now, come on, murders four and five. Let me give you a clue. Drug dealers.'

And suddenly there it was, clear as the moment it happened. Jackson Pollack and Ted Baker. Probably his most clinical killings.

Wendy could tell by his pained expression that the memories were flowing back.

'Jackson and Baker,' he said quietly under his breath as if he was ashamed of the memory.

'That's right, but you didn't know that Baker had someone tied up in the back of his flatbed truck. Someone who was still alive when you set it on fire!'

Jimmy was stunned. Could he have killed an innocent man? 'No way!' he shouted his denial at Wendy. 'I would've known.'

'How could you? Baker's flatbed had a locked top which you never opened.'

Jimmy let this information sink in, and sickeningly he remembered that he hadn't bothered to try opening the lid once he saw it was locked. He was in too much of a hurry to tidy up and leave the scene of his crimes.

'How'd you know this?' he asked.

'We have our spies everywhere. Ain't nothing you can do that the dead don't see. Maybe bear that in mind next time you feel like a bit of self-abuse.'

Jimmy shuddered at the thought of his grandma witnessing some of the stuff he had got up to over the years.

Wendy could see the distress in his eyes. 'Don't worry, Jimmy, it's not all dead people. Just those of us who aren't ready to go when we get called. We hang around and live vicariously through those that remain, but that means we get to find out about all the good shit.'

Jimmy didn't know what to say now faced with the news that he had barbecued an innocent person, and then something occurred to him. 'Where's the song? If I killed him, why don't I have a song?' He had a point.

Wendy thought for a moment. 'You're a man, aint you, Jimmy?'

'Last time I looked.'

'Well, you're staff, so you don't get any room service?'

'What's that gotta do with anything?'

Wendy gave him a pitying look. 'Like I said, Jimmy, you're a man. When was the last time you changed the sheets on your bed?'

Jimmy thought and soon realised that that particular domestic chore had probably never occurred to him unless something either sticky or very visible had managed to apply itself to the inner sheets. Wendy was tapping her fingers again. 'Less than two months,' he ventured.

Wendy pulled her most distasteful face. 'Ugh! You're disgusting, Jimmy Wayne – two months!'

Jimmy became defensive. 'Yeah, and I do it whether it needs it or not!' Wendy was, for a change, lost for words, but not for long.

'To think I had sex with you on it, in it, and come to think about it over it!' She smiled, and then Jimmy smiled.

For a moment there was silence between them as they remembered, but only for a moment, and then Wendy filled the empty void with judgemental criticism.

'Let's try and forget your primordial bedroom etiquette for a moment. Assuming –' she winced '– that's it's only two months since your last bed-sheet change.' Wendy shuddered. 'Ugh! Then there has to be a possibility that the song could be caught up in the sheets.'

'I would've seen it. Every song so far has been on the bed-side table.'

Wendy looked at him with an expression that if verbalised would have been a very Simpsonesque 'Doh!'

'What does that mean?'

'It means, Jimmy, that from there it could've fallen on the floor and gone under the bed, or it could've slipped off the bedside table and down the side of your unmolested mattress. Provided that none of the creatures, as yet undiscovered by science, has eaten it, that's where you're gonna find it.'

Jimmy didn't respond to the personal attack on what he regarded as his perfect hygiene. In his eyes, for a man, he was a domestic god; and Wendy, as a woman, and a deceased one at that, was not in a position to cast aspersions. Although, clearly, that's exactly what she was doing.

His mind was racing. Just suppose Wendy was right. That would be eleven songs. He was nearly there again. The morality of that thought hit him for a moment. If it was, then who was the person he had inadvertently barbequed. He needed to find out.

'I don't think you're right,' he said, getting to his feet. 'Especially about the two-month thing, but let's go and check.'

Wendy gave him the double thumbs up and disappeared backwards through the wall, taking one of the many post-mortem shortcuts she now used to get around the Riviera.

When Jimmy got to his room, Wendy was stood by the bed waiting for him. 'Have you found it?'

Wendy pulled a face. 'After your revelations I'm not going anywhere near that bed.'

Jimmy sucked his lips against his teeth in exasperation before falling to his knees to peer beneath his bed. As his eyes adjusted to the Stygian gloom, he began to see many things. Some that he vaguely remembered and some things he would want to forget, but the most disturbing things he saw were a couple of items, possibly food related, that were once something and were now on a journey to becoming something else. He shuddered and made a mental note not to look under there again. He would be leaving for LA next week, and whatever was in the process of evolution and decay would have to remain a mystery that he for one would never solve. What clearly wasn't down there was a piece of paper with his handwriting. He pulled back from the edge and stood up.

'Could you see anything?' she asked eagerly.

'Nah, clean as a whistle under there.'

Wendy stared at the back of his head, daring him to turn around and look her in the eye after a statement like that. He could feel them burning into him, so he studiously avoided her glare.

'Clean as a whistle you say, Jimmy?'

'Pretty much.' He ran his hand down the side of the mattress where it sat tight against the bedside table, trying to ignore the accusation in her voice, and then suddenly his hand felt paper. 'Got something!'

Wendy instantly forgot about male hygiene, or the lack of it, and started to elevate with excitement. 'Is it?' she asked, her anticipation palpable.

Slowly, Jimmy teased the notepaper out from its mattress crevasse. He held it up. It was in his handwriting and across the top in capitals were the words, 'TOO MUCH'.

Wendy punched the air and Jimmy was elated for a moment. One less song before LA, but then the thought of the unknown victim came back to haunt him. She looked at the expression on his face and knew that now was not the moment for triumphalism. Jimmy was hurting and wracked with guilt.

'Look, if he was in the back of Ted Baker's pickup, he was probably a scumbag anyway. Let me go and find out, and then I'll get back to you.'

'OK, thanks. I just hope you're right about him.'

'Me too,' she said, and then disappeared through the window – without opening it.

———◆———

Jimmy peaked through the door at the side of the Canyon Room stage. All three hundred seats were already taken and there was a keen pre-gig buzz of expectation. He smiled to himself and tried to take in the atmosphere of the room one last time. The Canyon was a great little venue, but it was a world away from playing in the Desert Bar. There, he was just the jukebox that nobody needed to put a nickel in. How he had hated those nights pouring his heart out with nobody listening. His words barely left the stage before they were consumed by the noise of gamblers pulling handles and glasses clinking at the bar. Even the strippers gyrating on their poles like auditioning firefighters played their music louder than his. Hard to believe all that was only eight or nine weeks ago. So much had changed. A career going nowhere was now on the launch pad to success: he had a recording contract, a residency at the Golden Flamingo in Vegas and ten great songs. On the downside, he had killed his girlfriend and become a serial killer. It was one hell of a trade-off, but you have to suffer for your art, and many people, mostly scumbags, had suffered for his.

He slipped back into the band's dressing room, closing the stage door behind him. He turned to look at the guys as they sat chatting and tuning guitars, No Relation was tapping out a beat on the back of the chair with his sticks, and there in the middle of the room was Lewis, the father of the band. This was the last time they would play together with Lewis as a regular member. Jimmy thought he should say something.

'Guys – could I have your attention for a couple of minutes.'

They all looked up and No Relation looked most disapproving. 'You ain't gonna pray are ya? You know I hate all that shit.'

'No need to worry on that front – no God-botherers in this band.'

Kid cleared his throat. 'Where do we stand on Buddhism?'

Jimmy thought for a moment before replying, 'For. If it does no harm, I'm for it.' There was a general nodding of consensus in the room. 'Good,' said Jimmy, 'now we got the religious semantics outta the way, maybe I can say what I was gonna say.' He paused to allow for the next interruption but none came; the band just sat there looking at him. Waiting for the words of wisdom to fall from their leader's mouth.

It had never happened before but they waited, more in hope than expectation, for Jimmy Wayne to say something inspiring. As Jimmy looked at them, he felt a surge of warmth and emotion rise through his body. It took a moment to realise what it was, but then it all became clear.

'You guys have been with me for the last few years. Not you, Doug, but if you stick around a few weeks it'll feel like years.' There were a few murmurings of agreement and a couple of muted laughs. 'You guys have become like a family to me. When you started with me, we were just a pickup band playing in a third-rate casino in the middle of butt-fuck nowhere. I let you down for so many years. I turned up to gigs drunk and I didn't respect the work, but you guys stuck with me. Almost as if you knew I had something better in me, and I won't forget it. All of you were good enough to go off and find a better band leader, but none of you did. For the life of me I can't think why, but I'm so grateful that you stuck with me.' Jimmy could feel a lump rising in his throat and his eyes were starting to burn as he fought to hold back the tears. 'We're on the verge of something special and we're all gonna take this ride together. Without The Second Chance, there is no Jimmy Wayne. Wherever I go you're coming with me. You may have heard a rumour, but I can now confirm that we have a four-week residency at the Golden Flamingo in Las Vegas, that's nearly eight hundred fans per night.'

No Relation gave a whoop of delight. 'Vegas baby!'

Jimmy smiled. 'The wages are going up and there'll be profit share on all album sales. *We* are a team and we are in this together!' The boys gave Jimmy a clap.

'Bravo, Jimmy,' said Kid, just before he slapped him on the back, nearly breaking a vertebra as he did so.

Jimmy smiled as he backed away to a safer distance. 'Lewis is the only one not coming with us.'

'Shame,' said Kid. Doug and No Relation just shook their heads.

'Apparently he wants to spend more time with his family. All I can say is they must be a damn sight nicer than mine.'

'Oh, they are.' Lewis grinned. 'Appreciably nicer than you lot, in fact.' They all booed him but not in a serious way. Jimmy held up his hand and the room fell silent.

'I just wanna say that this man believed in me when nobody else did ... not even me! He never stopped pointing me in the right direction and he was always on time and ready to play despite the fact his band leader was a hopeless drunk.' Jimmy looked at Lewis. 'I don't know what you saw, but I will never forget that you did and that you stuck with me when it would've been so much easier to walk away. I am cutting you ten percent of all the royalties on this record as a thank you.'

Lewis looked genuinely touched. 'Thanks, Jimmy, that's real nice of you.' The boys all began to clap. Lewis let them finish and added, 'God knows, I earned it!' They all laughed. When they had stopped, Jimmy had one more thing to say.

'This is our last gig in the Canyon, it's full, and tonight we're only gonna play our songs. We have nine rehearsed, which will give us just over an hour with a bit of live jamming. No covers – just Jimmy Wayne and The Second Chance doing their stuff. Let's knock 'em dead!' It wasn't the Gettysburg Address, but Jimmy had the boys all fired up and ready to play.

They exited the dressing room as if they were heading out to play in the Super Bowl. As they hit the stage, the dulcet tones of handyman Steve Cronkite announced them.

'Ladies and gentleman! Please welcome Jimmy Wayne and The Second Chance!'

The crowd went wild. Jimmy waved, picked up his guitar, nodded to No Relation and they were off.

They opened with 'Vacant Stare' and as its quiet intensity resonated around the hall, the crowd fell silent. The song sounded as if it was haunted, and the dissonant notes slowly drew everyone into the intensity of Jimmy's imagined world – only it wasn't really imagined.

At the end of each song there was a momentary pause before the applause erupted; it was almost as though the listener was in a state of shock because of the depth of emotion they were being exposed to. Jimmy and the band were pitch and note perfect.

Michael Owens exchanged a meaningful look with David Parker and mouthed the word, 'wow.' David nodded. This was something special. Jimmy had been building towards it for weeks, but now, unadulterated by other people's songs, Jimmy was singing his own material and creating a dark, sad but beautiful and enchanting soundscape. A world all of his own which he was drawing the listeners into. It wasn't a comfortable place to be, especially when he started screaming on 'Stairway to Hell', but now David could hear the full song, he understood. It all made sense, and this vision of a hell that the central character of the song had created left the listener in no doubt that this was a final destination. Jimmy sang the final chorus:

'I'm on a stairway to Hell
And I'm going down
Things are getting warmer
On the dark side of town.'

Michael leaned over to David and said in his ear, 'what the hell are you feeding him on?'

'You should've met him when he was depressed.' They both laughed because they, like Leonard Cohen, knew that there is money in misery. People do love a good wallow, and this record had deep waters in which to drown yourself.

When the band finished playing 'Cold Winds Blowing', the Canyon Room was silent for a full six seconds. It doesn't sound much, but it felt like an eternity; it was almost as if everyone was transfixed by the stories Jimmy was telling and enchanted by the musical patterns he and the band wove around those stories.

When the applause came, it was thunderous; and it went on ... and on. Just over two minutes. David timed it. Jimmy stepped up to the microphone and waited for the final applause to die down, and then he spoke.

'I want to thank you all for coming out tonight and sharing the evening with us. For me and the boys this has been a very special night. We've been playing here for over five years, not always in this room – sometimes it was in the car park!' Ripples of laughter ran through the crowd. 'As some of you will have heard, this is our last show at the Riviera.' There was an audible sigh of regret, which Jimmy let fall away before continuing. 'But it's not sad because we're off to make a record in LA, so if you like what you've heard here tonight, in a few months' time you will be able to buy it. I'm happy to announce that we're signed to Small Print Records in LA, and it's gonna be available at all major music stores and of course online from your retailer of choice.'

Another ripple of applause sounded throughout the auditorium; Jimmy held up his hand to silence it.

'If you can't wait that long and you've heard of a little town not far from here called Las Vegas, you'll be able to catch us at the world-famous Golden Flamingo. Check their website for details because, confession time, I don't know.' Jimmy paused for a moment while the room quietened down. 'I just have one last thing to say.' He gave a signal to the lighting engineer, and a spotlight illuminated Lewis who was sitting quietly at his piano listening to Jimmy. 'This right here is Lewis King. Some of you will know him from his days with the Texas Trucking Company – the band, not the haulier.'

There was laughter and applause from the hall. The Texans had been big in the eighties and nineties, and many people remembered them fondly. As the applause grew, Lewis was obliged to take a bow. Jimmy raised a hand to silence the crowd again.

'When I met Lewis, I wasn't doing so well, I was drinking and doing other stuff, and he took the time to show me the right path. Always there with a word of support when I needed it or a smack on the back of the head when I stepped out of line. I owe this man so much and I would just like to say, in front of all these people, thank you, Lewis, for everything.'

Lewis nodded to Jimmy and in the spotlight, Jimmy could see that there was a tear in his eye. The whole room was emotionally charged, but Jimmy decided to burst the balloon.

'Lewis won't be coming to Vegas because I had to sack him before the show. The last time he smacked me on the back of the head it was just a bit too hard!' Lewis laughed and the audience joined in.

Then, as the band gathered at the front of the stage and linked arms, the place went wild again. They bowed several times until the lighting engineer hit the auditorium lights and the fans realised that the show was over.

The boys jogged from the stage apart from Lewis, who paused to take it all in one last time. *Not a bad way to go out*, he thought.

CHAPTER 20

GOODBYE BLACKJACK, HELLO VEGAS

When Jimmy woke the following morning, the farewell gig was still warm in his memory. It had been a very special night, only slightly spoilt by the fact that it was his last with Lewis as a regular part of the band. He knew he would see Lewis again; he also knew that he would come up to Vegas and sit in occasionally. It was the ending of a chapter but not a final goodbye.

As he lay there playing back the images from last night, his reveries were interrupted by the discordant ringing of his room phone. He picked it up. 'Hello.' After only hearing light breathing on the other end of the phone, he repeated his answer, 'Hello, Jimmy speaking.' Silence on the other end again, and Jimmy was just about to put down the receiver when the familiar tones of Jack Lantern came leering from the speaker.

'I thought you would have some groupies sitting on your face.'

Jimmy groaned internally. 'No, Jack, I'm staff, we don't get room service.'

Jack seemed to find that hilarious. When he had stopped laughing, he said, 'You're a funny guy, let's hope you're still smiling when we work out what you owe me.'

Jimmy had been expecting this. Lantern knew he was about to strike it rich, so he wanted his piece of the action.

'Look, I will pay back that loan in the next few weeks – you know I will.'

Jack did not seem impressed. 'But I haven't told you what the interest is yet, Jimmy boy.'

'I don't give a flying fuck what you think you can milk out of me. We can sort it out at sensible rates or I'll see you in court and expose you for the money-lending scumbag you really are.' There was a snort from the other end of the phone.

'Fame ain't affected you yet then, Jimmy? Besides, we have to work out some damages.'

Now Jimmy laughed derisively. 'Damages, what the fuck for?'

'Well, for having an affair with my wife for starters.'

That took the wind out of Jimmy's sails. There was silence for a moment as he tried to think of a convincing denial. But before he could, Jack filled the void.

'Yeah, thought so, but thanks for confirming it. Then, of course, there's the killing of Carmine and Vinny.'

'Are you crazy?' spluttered Jimmy. 'They were trying to kill me. You saw me on the phone trussed up like a turkey on Thanksgiving.' Jack wasn't in the mood for listening.

'Yeah, yeah, Jimmy. You told me the story before, but there's just something that don't feel right. Your story was all very plausible, but, it just don't feel right.' Jimmy heard Jack slurp a mouthful of coffee. 'Tell you what, I'm a reasonable man–'

Jimmy snorted with derision. 'Who told you that, Al Capone?'

On the other end of the line, Jack smiled to himself; Jimmy was getting braver now he knew he was worth something. 'As

I was saying, I'm a reasonable man.' He paused for a moment as if daring Jimmy to interrupt, but Jimmy knew better. 'You gave me an explanation, and I think there's a possibility that the Deltas did it, I also think there's a possibility that you did it. So, in the interest of fairness, I'm only gonna charge you damages for the loss of Carmine. You can have Vinny on me.'

Jimmy wasn't overwhelmed by Jack's generosity. 'But I didn't kill either of them, so how is that fair – explain that to me?'

Jack didn't like Jimmy's tone. When he replied, it was clear that this was the end of the conversation. 'OK, Jimmy, I'm gonna say this real slow and I'm only gonna say it once, so listen very carefully. Carmine and Vinny were only there because you hadn't paid your debts. If they hadn't been there, they would still be alive, so it is your fault. Being a generous man, I am gonna cut you the benefit of the doubt and just charge you thirty thousand dollars for the loss of one of them.'

'How much!' Jimmy almost shouted. He checked himself instantly and then continued, 'How is that fair?'

'Do you have any idea how hard it is to find good thugs these days?' Jack sighed. 'They have to be able to multitask – negotiate, threaten, maim and kill – and that's before we get to concealing evidence and, of course, collecting the cash. You can't just place an ad or hire a recruitment agency.'

Jimmy had never thought about it like that. Why would he have? Jack did have a point; it was strange and terrifyingly obvious and it really didn't justify an argument.

Taking a deep breath, Jimmy replied, 'OK, Jack, let's negotiate when I actually have some money. Give me a couple of months in Vegas after the album is made, and we'll be in business.'

That had been the end of the conversation. Once Jimmy had conceded that this was indeed a negotiation, Jack was satisfied. He had presented Jimmy with an estimate and the invoice would follow – with added interest at a rate to be agreed by Jack.

Jimmy remembered his conversation with Kid about slowly killing Jack one day to try and produce a song with several movements. He guessed that Puccini may have been thinking along similar lines when he wrote the final aria from *Turandot*. 'Nessun Dorma' had always seemed so beautiful to Jimmy right up until the day his music teacher, Mr Price, explained it to him.

'Yes, you're right, Jimmy, it is a very beautiful piece of music, but do you know what it's actually about?'

Naturally, Jimmy did not. He was fourteen years old and living in the Pocono Mountains. That's about as far from culture as it's possible to get.

'Sit down and I will explain.' Mr Price sat down, too. This was going to take some time. '"Nessun Dorma" is the final aria from the opera *Turandot* by Puccini. Do you know who Turandot is?'

Once again, Jimmy didn't. He shook his head.

'Turandot is the princess and Calaf is one of her suitors in marriage. There were three of them.'

'She like a Mormon, then?'

'No, no, Jimmy, nothing like that. She was only going to marry one of them, but she had three fellas wanting to marry her.'

Jimmy understood that. His cousin Ruth had a lot of fellows keen to marry her, but that was mainly on account of the fact that she liked to sunbathe naked in the back field. There was a hill above the back field and sometimes, when Ruth was sunbathing, it was like the bleachers at a ball game up there.

Mr Price continued. 'Now, Calaf was looking for an edge, so he told Princess Turandot that if she guessed his name, she could execute him.'

'That's crazy, Mr Price,' Jimmy said, screwing up his face.

'I know, but you have to remember that Puccini was Italian.' Mr Price said it as though that was an explanation in itself. From all the Italians Jimmy had met up to that point in his life, Mr Price had a point.

'So, Princess Turandot is a bit tricky and she decrees that none of her subjects will sleep until they have guessed Calaf's name. Fortunate that he wasn't called Bill, eh, Jimmy?' Mr Price chuckled at his own joke.

'Wouldn't he have been called Luigi or something being Italian?' asked Jimmy.

Mr Price pulled a face; he was slightly disappointed that Jimmy had missed his joke. 'Now, this is where it gets nasty. "Nessun Dorma," she decrees, which means "let no one sleep", but here is where she shows herself to be a real psycho bitch.'

Jimmy was taken aback by the sudden vehemence in Mr Price's description – unaware as he was that Mr Price's wife had recently run off with Mr Toronzo, the music teacher.

'Now Princess "up herself" Turandot says that if they don't get his name by the morning, her subjects will all be executed. What a crazy bitch.' Mr Price was getting a little red in the face.

Jimmy was loving the story, but worried that Mr Price was approaching a stroke.

'So, she's going to spend the night torturing people, including the slave girl, called Liu, who loves Calaf, to get his name. She is a torturing, murdering bitch. Man-hater, I'm guessing.'

'So why does he want her then, Mr Price?'

Mr Price shook his head very sadly. 'We always want what we can't have, Jimmy, and even when we get it, that bloody Toronzo steals it from you.'

Now Jimmy was confused. 'So, was Toronzo one of the suitors, then?'

'Hell no!' Mr Price exclaimed with anger. 'If only he were the first suitor, he would've got his damn smooth-talking head chopped off.'

Jimmy laughed. 'That sounds like our Mr Toronzo.'

Mr Price fixed him with a look that could nail a liver to the door. When he spoke, his voice was dark and full of quiet rage. 'Never speak his name again.'

Jimmy had a lot of questions he wanted to ask but despite being only fourteen, he figured the look on Mr Price's face meant that it was best to move the conversation on. 'So why did the first suitor get his head chopped off?'

Mr Price breathed deeply and slowly, resuming control of his emotions. He flicked Jimmy a forced smile and said, 'well, you see, Jimmy, Princess Turandot was a bit of a man-hating bitch and she set three riddles to all three suitors, but if you got one wrong, well, it's off with your head. Now Calaf, crazy bastard, found this attractive and even gave up the slave girl who loved him, Liu. She wouldn't give up his name, so Turandot had her killed; and he just stood by and let it happen. Then Ping, Pong and Pang tried to persuade Calaf not to pursue Turandot.'

'Excuse me, Mr Price. Did you just say Ping, Pong and Pang? What kind of Italian name is that?'

Mr Price sighed. He was now bitterly regretting that he had decided to try and explain this crazy opera to his pupil. 'It was written by an Italian, but it's set in China. And yes, the names are rubbish, but Puccini had probably never been to China, yet he knew that ping-pong was a Chinese game so he threw in a "Pang" and bingo, he had three courtiers! You have to remember, Jimmy, opera is all about the arias, hence the saying "Some wonderful moments and some terrible half hours".'

While it was very funny, Jimmy was too young to appreciate it at the time.

Mr Price took one last deep breath as he prepared to plunge forward and finish the description of this stupid opera, which he was now beginning to hate. 'So, Turandot was a stuck-up bitch who didn't want a man in her life. She tortured innocent people to get her own way and made the lives of everyone around her a misery. Just like every bloody woman.' Mr Price rose from his chair. There were beads of sweat on his forehead and he had a reddish flush around his cheeks and neck. 'Well, Jimmy, now you understand *Turandot*, but more importantly you now understand that you just can't trust a woman – they will always break your heart.' Mr Price gave Jimmy a brief smile and then turned and walked away.

Jimmy watched his shoulders rising and falling and realised that Mr Price was crying. He decided from that day on never to listen to opera again.

As Jimmy lay on his bed, he realised that he hadn't thought about this conversation with Mr Price since it had happened over thirty years ago. Only now did he realise how very sad it had been, *poor Mr Price*. He also realised that he still didn't have a clue what *Turandot* was all about.

David Parker was sitting having a coffee with Michael Owens in his office at the Riviera. 'So, Michael, what's the next step with Jimmy and the boys?' As always, David didn't beat about the bush, which was good because Michael didn't either.

'We'll get them up to LA in the next couple of days, then we let them rehearse and develop two other songs, and then it's into the studio for two weeks.'

'As quick as that? Don't bands have to go somewhere exotic and take six months to a year over it?' asked David.

'Not anymore, thank God!' Michael leaned back in his chair. 'In the eighties when I got started, it was still tape. Everyone eulogises about how great analogue was but, man, you had to get everything right, took forever. Especially when half the bands were on their substance of choice. These days with digital, we can do four takes of each song and just splice the best bits together – word by word if we have to. Do it all digitally, decompress it and run it through assorted programmes to get the sound you want, and all for a fraction of the cost. We couldn't make it pay doing it the old way with all the downloads and streams that make the music virtually worthless, unless it's sold on CD or limited-edition vinyl. Most artists, apart from the huge acts, make the majority of their money from gigs and publishing. World's moved on, David. The music business is a tough place to be.'

This came as something of a shock to David, who had always assumed a record deal meant big bucks. 'So how do you make your money?'

Michael took a sip of coffee and gave a wry smile. 'That's a good question. I suppose I'm like one of those little fish that floats along next to a bigger one feeding on the leftovers. I'm known as a top producer, so people want me to make their records. They come to my studio and pay me well. Quite often I get to write a song or two for them, and I have built up a nice income on royalties from radio plays, etcetera. Those big budgets that used to get thrown around went a long time ago and they're not ever coming back.'

This was not the conversation David had been expecting. 'So why would you bother with Jimmy, then? He's barely a star anymore.'

Michael was nodding in agreement. 'You're right, he's not but he has a great story to tell. Playing a cabaret spot here and not even in a proper room like the Canyon, but on a stage shoved up the corner of the Desert Bar. No offence, David, but you can't get much lower on the musical pecking scale than that.'

David raised his eyebrows. 'I will take a bit of offence, but nothing that will lead to violence.'

'Pleased to hear it,' said Michael, before continuing. 'Jimmy has something. He's always had an interesting voice, but he never had any decent original material. Well, now he has. Some of it's a bit out of left field, weird even, but it has something. We don't know where he has suddenly found the ability to write but soon as I heard him, I knew there was something I could do with him. That's why I have a label. He won't cost a penny to sign, so the record will be cheap to make; and with the residency at the Golden Flamingo, he will sell enough CDs after the shows to put the record in profit before the end of the first month. If he does well, the Golden Flamingo will renew him and then he's on the launchpad.'

David could see that what Michael was saying made sense, so asked, 'So, is there a big market for–' he tried to find a word to describe Jimmy's new sound '–crazy music?'

Michael smiled. 'It's called dark blues Americana and yes, it's a growing genre – and, this is the important bit, it's across a lot of age ranges. Jimmy could catch fire, David, I really believe it.'

David was starting to believe it now. He had suspected as much when he saw how the audience had reacted to Jimmy's new songs, but having his friend, who knew the business, confirm it gave him the reassurance he was seeking. Before he could tell Michael his plans, his private line rang. He pointed at the phone and Michael nodded for him to take it.

'Hello, David Parker speaking.'

A quietly spoken voice came from the receiver: 'Morning, David. It's Tom Thead. You got a moment to talk?'

David sat upright and listened carefully. If Tom was calling, he must have news. 'Morning, Tom. Yes, I have plenty of time to talk. Have you found something?'

At the other end of the line, Tom drew breath and then began. 'Your suspicions were correct. I counted the bullet wounds. Unless they never miss, six police couldn't fire that many direct hits. It's obvious there were more gunmen involved.' He paused to let David absorb this information.

David already had and was moving on. 'And where do you think these additional shots came from?'

Michael looked up, but David held his finger up to his lips.

'From the back of the building I would say. Awful lot of shots on the backs of the bodies. If the police were attacking you from the front in a gunfight, I would expect you to turn toward them and return fire. This begs the question why are most of them sporting entry wounds in the back? It don't add up.'

It did to David. 'Were there any close-up shots?'

Tom looked at two of the bodies on slabs in his mortuary. 'Three of them have been shot close up – finished off would be a better way of putting it. Judging by the wounds, I would say the shooter was within six feet when he shot. I've seen this kind of thing before. There is no mistaking it.' This confirmed everything David had thought.

'Tom, you know this means that Sheriff Pence's statement of how it happened is a pack of lies.'

'Course I do, that's why I've taken loads of photos and put them in a file and emailed them to you.'

David was amazed. 'You know how to do that?' He heard Tom chuckle.

'I'm old, but I'm not dead – I just work with them. My son taught me how to do it so I could improve my filing in the business. I was getting buried, so to speak, under paperwork.'

This was what David needed: an insurance policy. 'Can we just keep this quiet for now?'

'Quiet as the grave,' said Tom.

'Thanks. If I ever get chance to use this, I'll discuss it with you first.'

At the other end of the phone, Tom glanced at the two bikers on the slabs. They weren't killed in an exchange with the police; they were assassinated. 'Let's hope you do, David, because I would like to see Pence getting what's coming to him. He's run this town like his own personal kingdom for too long.' He paused for a moment before adding, 'You have a good day, David.'

Michael was studying David with a confused expression on his face. Had he just heard what he thought he had?

David just smiled at him. 'Don't worry, Michael, just a bit of small-town gossip.'

'What, involving a corrupt sheriff and multiple murders?' Michael didn't look convinced.

'Like I said, just some small-town stuff. Don't worry, my friend, you're going back to LA in a couple of hours and nothing ever happens there now, does it?'

<hr />

Kid pushed his suitcase over the top of the speakers and squeezed the back door of the Dodge shut. 'That's it, Jimmy, all the luggage, guitars, mics and amps are loaded. We're done with this place. Tomorrow we're going to LA, baby.' Kid seemed more excited than Jimmy had ever seen him. 'You looking forward to it?'

Jimmy didn't know what to say. He had waited for a chance like this all his life, but now that the moment was upon him, he felt a strange affection for Blackjack and the Riviera.

When David had first hired him nearly six years ago, he was going nowhere and nobody much thought about him anymore. He wasn't even yesterday's man – more like the week before yesterday's man, and now … Funny how the world can change. The moon goes around the earth and the earth goes around the sun and time moves on, but he had been in limbo in this little corner of Nevada just marking time. Slowly going backwards from whatever low summit his career had once conquered. Yet now in just a few short weeks everything had changed. The old uncertainties which had actually become certainties had vanished. Lost in the graves of the recently deceased. Written in the blood he had washed from his hands and stained on his memory in a guilt that consumed him. No matter how much he'd tried to resolve it, in his mind there was no justification, only partial mitigation. This next stage of his career had been forged in death, and he'd been its creator.

He looked up at Kid. 'Think I'm gonna take a drive up to the song cemetery. I just need to say goodbye to – ' he trailed off, unwilling to finish the sentence.

Kid said it for him, 'Wendy. I think that's a good idea, Jimmy, say goodbye for me, too.' Kid chuckled. 'Although I'm pretty sure we haven't seen the back of Wendy Walmart yet.'

Jimmy smiled weakly. 'You know, Kid, I think you're right.'

———◆———

As Jimmy drove slowly down the track leading to the song cemetery, he was overwhelmed by a feeling of regret. He would give anything to turn back the clock and have Wendy with him again – alive! He wore his guilt like an overcoat on a hot summer's day. It enveloped him and made him feel so uncomfortable, but he just couldn't take it off.

'Time you got a grip of yourself, Jimmy.'

Jimmy jumped with the shock of Wendy suddenly appearing next to him in the passenger seat and her seeming to know exactly what he had been thinking. 'Are you in my head?'

'I don't know. Suppose I'm ubiquitous.'

'You-bic-what?' Jimmy asked, frowning.

Wendy looked at Jimmy as though he was an idiot child, again. 'Did you go to school at all when you were a kid?'

'When I had nothing better to do.'

For a few moments there was silence as they bumped down the track towards the end of the canyon, then Wendy said what they were both thinking. 'You coming to say goodbye?' Her words sounded like a door closing for the last time; a wave of hopelessness washed over Jimmy. It was huge and it was deep, and he knew he would drown if he gave into it.

He gripped the steering wheel tightly until his knuckles were white and the veins in his forearms bulged. Tears ran down his face. He had no words to say – nothing that could ever make this right. He was leaving the only woman he had ever loved to slowly decompose in an unmarked grave surrounded by killers and scumbags. Her family would never see her again, would never know what had happened to her. He had become the gate-keeper of so many secrets and too much sorrow.

At this moment, he wasn't sure if he could find the strength to carry on living the lie he had so carefully created. All these actions would one day lead back to his door and the dream he had created would crumble into dust. *Fame*, he thought, *I wanted it too much*. The lyrics of his own song had condemned him.

Wendy said nothing; she just sat there watching Jimmy slowly dissolving in his pool of guilt. She saw his tears flow and him biting hard on his lip to hold back the sobs that wanted to come. Eventually she could stand it no longer.

'For fuck's sake, Jimmy, grow a pair, will ya?'

'Sorry, but I'm upset.' Jimmy wiped his eyes and glanced at her reproachfully.

Wendy sucked her teeth dismissively. 'Jeez, I'm the one who's dead. It's me who's gonna spend the rest of eternity, or the end of the world, here. Not sure which will come first. Probably the end of the world because global warming is happening.' She paused again as another thought occurred to her. 'Do you think if global warming kills all the humans there will be an eternity? Is it only an eternity if it can be measured by humans? I suppose we're back to the old, "if a tree falls in a forest and there is no one there to hear it, does it make a sound?" question.' Wendy stared at Jimmy waiting for an answer. 'What do you think?'

'What kind of tree?'

Wendy let out a long sigh. 'A fuckin' semantic one, you bozo!'

Jimmy winced under Wendy's cutting remarks. 'You know, since you've been dead, your mouth has got even pottier than it was before.'

They drove along in silence for the next couple of minutes, and then Wendy started to giggle. 'What kind of tree? Boy, Jimmy, how'd you survive to be middle-aged?'

'Booze and women,' he replied without hesitation. 'And maybe a bit of food,' he added.

Wendy punched him on the arm. It was meant to be a playful blow, but for a dead person Wendy sure did pack a punch.

'Ow! What did you do that for?'

'Because I could.' She smiled, leaning her head against his shoulder.

'So, you did come to say goodbye, then?'

She closed her eyes and wrapped her right arm around his chest. 'What makes you think I won't be in LA and Vegas?'

'Can you do that?'

'Don't see why not. I've been to San Diego and Gary, Indiana.'

'Why did you go to Gary?'

Wendy shrugged. 'I figured that being dead I could live anywhere but, man, even the dead are leaving Gary. I'm dead and I've more life left in me than that place. It's kinda sad.' This was news to Jimmy.

'So, what you're saying is that there's no reason why you can't come to Vegas or LA.'

'Suppose I could.' Wendy didn't seem overexcited by the prospect. 'Would you want me to?'

'Yeah, if you promise not to keep scaring the crap outta me.' Jimmy stopped the pickup; they had reached the end of the track.

Around them, the walls of the canyon reared up like the biggest stadium Jimmy had ever seen and the rocky outcrop, where so many of the inspirations for his songs were buried, rose like the stage to end all stages. The song graveyard had produced eight songs; now it lay silent and peaceful holding its secrets like a pharaoh's tomb. Jimmy climbed from the pickup and grabbed his guitar from the back seat.

'Come on, I want to play you something.'

Wendy jumped out and followed Jimmy as he started to trudge up the steep slope. After about ten paces, she got bored and just hovered into the air and floated alongside Jimmy as he toiled in the morning sun. 'What song is it?'

'It's a new one. I wrote it for you.'

'Who did you kill?'

Jimmy didn't respond to this question and just carried on walking, but Wendy wasn't in the mood to let it go.

'Come on, Jimmy, you can't keep me in suspense. Who did you kill?'

After stopping to face her, he replied, 'Nobody. I wrote it from my heart to you.'

Wendy looked disappointed. 'Well, this is gonna be shit, then!' And then she just floated on up and away from Jimmy to the top of the outcrop totally uninspired by the prospect of having to listen to a Jimmy Wayne original.

Jimmy sighed and carried on walking. When he got there, Wendy was sitting on a rock with her fingers in her ears.

'OK, let's get this over with,' she said. Jimmy did his best to look hurt, but he remembered how many of his appalling songs he had made poor Wendy listen to.

He walked over to her and gently pulled her fingers from her ears. 'Give me one last chance with this one, Wendy. I really think I have absorbed something subconsciously from writing all those good songs in my sleep.'

Wendy pulled a face. 'OK, but only because I'm already dead. Normally listening to your songs makes me suicidal, but it's a bit late for that now!'

'Can you sing?'

'Like a bird,' she replied enthusiastically.

Jimmy had once heard her sing in the shower and if his memory served him correctly, the bird she was referring to was a vulture.

'Why you asking?'

'This song is a duet for you and me.' He thought Wendy would be touched by this, but she pulled a sceptical grimace.

'So how the hell do you propose that we perform this in Vegas?'

'It's not for sharing. This is just for you and me.'

Wendy looked disappointed. 'That bad, huh?'

'No, it's good, I think. Let me sing you the first verse.' Jimmy sat down on another rock facing out to the horseshoe canyon and imagined a stadium filled with tens of thousands of fans listening in hushed silence as he began to play the song.

'I hear that cold wind blowing
Through the canyons of my heart
I hear the voices carry
But I can't make me a new start
When I look into the mirror
I don't recognise myself
Just a love-struck loser
Who looks like someone else
There's a hole in my heart
Where my love escaped
Left me so empty
So desolate
But the wind keeps blowing
And there's no escape.'

Jimmy stopped at the end of the first chorus and looked up at Wendy. She was smiling.

'Did you really write that?' Jimmy nodded. 'Without killing anyone?' Jimmy nodded again.

'All my own work. You like it?'

'I love it. Where do I sing?'

'Second verse and second and third chorus, and last verse together.' Jimmy pulled out a sheet of paper with the lyrics scribbled on.

Wendy snatched it from him and found the second verse. 'OK, play me in.'

As Jimmy played the intro to the second verse, Wendy stared intently at the lyrics. He saw her foot begin to tap in rhythm to his playing, and then she sang:

'I told you that I loved you
But those words were wrote in sand
Gentle breezes took them
By the fates' harsh command.'

Her voice soared into the warm morning air like a lark ascending; it was the most beautiful thing Jimmy had ever heard.

'But if my words had reached you
Made you understand
Could you ever love me?
Build the life that we planned.'

Without hesitation, they flowed into the chorus together; their voices filled the air and rang out into the canyon. They sang in perfect harmony and the walls of the canyon gave a slight reverb to their voices, which sounded so beautiful that Jimmy found himself crying again.

They finished the song and Wendy turned to him. 'What do you think?'

'I think your voice has got a lot better since you died.'

'You're right, and your song writing has got a lot better since you started killing people.'

They both laughed. He went over to her and took her in his arms. 'I'm gonna miss you, Wendy Walmart.'

She leaned back and looked into his eyes. 'Wherever you are, Jimmy, I'll be there. Wherever there's a cop beatin' up a guy, I'll be there. I'll be in the way guys yell when they're mad. I'll be in the way kids laugh when they're hungry and know supper's ready, and when the people are eatin' the stuff, they raise and livin' in the houses they build, I'll be there, too.'

Jimmy nodded slowly in understanding. 'Steinbeck?'

'*Grapes of Wrath*.' she said, hugging him. 'Oh, Jimmy, you did read a book!'

He laughed, 'just the one, Wendy, just the one.'

They sang the song again several times, and then just sat holding hands and looking out as the sun rose across the canyon creating a palette of beautiful colours as it illuminated the rock face.

Eventually, Wendy turned to Jimmy. 'Time to go. You have a future out there waiting for you. LA and Vegas are just the beginning. Go and live that dream for both of us.'

He knew she was right, but it was hard to leave.

As if she could read his thoughts, she grabbed him tight. 'Wherever you are, Jimmy, just think of me and I'll be there – promise!' He knew this was true.

Slowly, he rose to his feet and picked up his guitar. 'See you around, Wendy Walmart.'

She winked at him. 'Count on it, Jimmy Wayne.' She slowly rose into the air and hovered above him for a moment. 'Bye, Jimmy!' And then she soared off up into the sky.

Jimmy lost sight of her in the rays of the rising sun.

Books to come in
The Comeback Trail trilogy:

BOOK 2

BLOOD ON THE TRACKS

BOOK 3

ALL THE WORLD'S A STAGE

Read an exclusive excerpt from Book 2:

BLOOD ON THE TRACKS

When Ma Lantern smiled the world became a frightening place. She used it as a mask to hide her true agenda. Slowly the rictus of her attempted smile faded to be replaced by her more natural scowl and the nature of the hidden agenda was revealed. 'So, you still going to kill Jimmy Wayne?'

Jack had been dreading this moment. When Ma had discovered that Jimmy Wayne had been screwing Jack's wife, she had wanted him dead. 'He's on the verge of making it big, we could –'

She didn't let him finish. 'Jack, you think you're tough and that everyone's frightened of you, that may be true.' She leaned across the desk; her eyes fixed on his like a cobra preparing to strike. 'But me, Jackie, they're terrified of me, even you are frightened of me. This business is tough, dog eat dog. I'm the Queen Bitch, this is my town and l want Jimmy Wayne's head on a pole!'

Jack shifted uncomfortably in his chair. 'Ma, Jimmy alive is good business, this could be a major score for us.'

'So you say Jackie but l aint convinced.' She slid smoothy off his desk with a litheness that denied her years. 'You got three months, if he hasn't covered his debt and put us in profit you bring him to me in the cellar!'

Jack shuddered. Just hearing his mother mention the cellar made him feel sick. Jack was a ruthless bastard but he always delegated his dirty work. He didn't want to be there when his orders were being carried out. His mother, on the other hand, did all the dirty work herself, she enjoyed it.